LOVES' COMMUNION

"Devondra!"

He wanted her. Dear God, how he wanted her. Right here, right now. More than he had ever wanted anything in his life he wanted to touch her everywhere. The danger they were now in only intensified that feeling. At any moment she might be whisked right out of his arms, away from his protection. And yet he didn't want to chance her hatred once again.

But if she could love me . . .

Oh, but she did. If she hadn't realized it before, she realized it now. If that silent declaration sent her hurtling over the edge of a precipice, then so be it. Life was all too short. In a world filled with hate, love was a precious thing. A rare treasure they might have little time to savor.

Quentin noted that she smiled, felt her press closer. "Have you ever ached for something, so much that it hurt?"

"Yes," she whispered, just as she was aching now.

Her answer emboldened him. "Devondra, I want you, but . . ."

Putting her hands to his lips, she silenced him. She lifted her head, searching his eyes in the gloom. What she read there made her heart reach out to his. "Then by all means . . ."

NOTORIOUS

KATHRYN KRAMER

ZEBRA BOOKS
KENSINGTON PUBLISHING CORP.

ZEBRA BOOKS are published by

Kensington Publishing Corp.
850 Third Avenue
New York, NY 10022

First Printing: February, 1996
10 9 8 7 6 5 4 3 2 1

Printed in the United States of America

To my father, Ervin Owen Kramer.
You are in my heart even though you are far away.
I treasure those moments we have shared.

Author's Note

The word *highwayman* holds a boldly romantic flair for those interested in the past. The first of the legendary highwaymen were Royalist officers who took to the road when they lost their property and were outlawed under the Commonwealth. That these men were familiar with the relatively new pistols gave them an advantage over their victims, who were usually armed with only swords. Organized bands of these robbers waited to plunder at such places as Hounslow Heath, Gadshill near Rochester, Shooter's Hill near Blackheath and Salisbury Plains in England.

"Gentlemen of the Road" or "knights of the road" are what highwaymen were sometimes called. Because they concentrated on the wealthy, they soon became popular heroes to the common man. No one of the poorer class was sorry when the Dukes of Northumberland or St. Albans were held up on the Heath. Indeed, to be robbed by a famous highwayman was sometimes regarded as something of an honor. The taverns and inns resounded with laughter when audacious villains pasted notices on the doors of rich Lon-

doners, instructing them that they should not venture forth
without at least a watch and ten guineas.

The heaths, forests and roads all provided rich pickings
for highwaymen lurking about with their cries of "Stand
and deliver" or "Your money or your life." It was no wonder
that journeys were taken in haste and certain tracts of the
countryside were crossed as quickly as possible. Where men
of wealth gathered, there were the highwaymen also, their
swords glittering in the moonlight and pistols primed and
cocked.

Many highwaymen lived a life of luxury and even enjoyed
being the object of legends and ballads. Even so, there was
a darker side. Gallows soon became as common along the
roads as inns. Public execution at such places as Tyburn
made examples of those who transgressed the law and were
unable to outwit their hunters. Betrayed for "blood money,"
many of England's bandit folk heroes ended their lives dangling from the rough wooden triangle of Tyburn Tree. So
plentiful became the gibbets on Hounslow Heath, that they
soon came to be regarded as landmarks and even were
included on eighteenth-century maps.

Executions soon took on the aspect of a fair, with orange
sellers, ballad sellers and pickpockets jostling their way
through the crowds. Often these morbid spectacles ended
in a riot, when a gallant hero was at last cut down from the
rope, leaving behind a widow, daughter, son or sweetheart
to mourn or plan revenge.

This is the setting for my story of a highwayman's daughter who finds herself at odds with the man responsible for
her father's hanging. Embarking on an adventurous path to
vengeance, she will find love where she least expects it.

Part One
A Dance At Tyburn

Middlesex and London, 1655

And naked to the hangman's noose
The morning clocks will ring,
A neck God made for other use
Than strangling in a string.
                    A.E. Houseman
                    A Shropshire Lad

Chapter One

Tension hung in the air like the quiet before a storm, a sense of danger all but barely perceptible to Devondra Stafford as she stood outside the Devil's Thumb Inn. Staring toward the road, she watched for her father, but the path was deserted. There were no shadows, no silhouettes, no signs of anyone at all.

"Oh, where is he? Where can he be?"

She was impatient, anxious to hear of the night's adventures and understandably on edge, for her father did not engage in just any profession. He was a highwayman. Indeed, every night that he went out on the road "Gentleman James" flirted with danger.

At a time when life for many English citizens under Cromwell's Commonwealth was colorless and boring, Devondra's life was vicariously exciting, although at times fraught with certain hazards. Her father was dashing. Daring. He was undeniably one of the most gallant of the Heath's highwaymen. Handsome. Noble. Charming. If he was a villain

to the rich, he was a man of heroic proportions to the poor
who lived in Hounslow Heath. Common people often bene-
fited from his plundering.

From his headquarters at the Devil's Thumb Inn, Gentleman James embarked on many an exploit that soon became
the talk of London. Though there were many highwaymen.
Gentleman James always brought a degree of glamour to
his roadway disruptions, perhaps because at heart he was a
true romantic. He could no more rob without a flourish or
gesture than he could help walking or riding with grace.

In truth, it was said that many a London miss secretly
fantasized about meeting him. And more so since the night
he had danced with a beautiful woman in lieu of robbing
her carriage. It had been the scintillating gossip of the city
that the dashing highwayman had promised to let the woman's wealthy companion off without paying a shilling if the
lady would but grant him a kiss.

Devondra smiled as the story once again flashed through
her mind, for she could well imagine her father being lenient
if fascinated by a pretty face. It was often said of him "If
male thou be, look to thy purse; if female to thy heart."
Times had been good for her and her father of late. His
nightly rides had not made of him a wealthy man, but they
had provided them with all the necessities of life, and a few
luxuries thrown in for good measure.

That had not always been the case, however. Once they
had been miserably poor. An impoverished Cavalier who
fought for the deposed King Charles I, James Stafford had
been stripped of all lands, titles and money when the Royalists lost. He had been in a sorry state, little better than a
pauper. Walking the streets of London, he had tried desperately to get any kind of employment available. Alas, the
answer had always been the same. The country was in a
state of turmoil. Massive taxation by Parliament to support

the war had caused hardship. Harsh impositions had been made on pockets as well as consciences. There were too few jobs to be had, and those jobs there were had been given out to followers of the winning side.

Her father had not given in to his fate. Taking to the road, the widowed nobleman had found a way to rise above his penury, albeit a way outside the law. Wearing a plumed hat, flowing cape, black leather boots, black shirt and trousers, riding a horse decorated with stirrups of silver he made his late-night ventures. Meanwhile the country swarmed with those eager to catch him.

"Have no fear. James is as elusive as the London fog. He can never be touched."

Without turning around, Devondra recognized the raspy voice of Tobias, her father's staunchest friend. "I'm not afraid."

"Then what are you waiting here for? It's chilly. You would be better off sitting by the fire."

"Like some tabby cat?" She shook her head. "No, I want to wait for him. I want to hear. . . ."

"About who tonight's illustrious 'guest' has been?" Tobias laughed. "All I know is that James planned to ruffle the feathers of one of Cromwell's roosters."

Devondra whirled around to face the short, red-bearded man. "Good!" She detested Cromwell and all who served him, the men who were responsible for the execution of an anointed king. Oliver Cromwell had stolen the rule of England away from the rightful authority. What was more, he was more of a thief than her father, for he robbed men of not only their money but their hearts and souls as well.

Law had been passed against swearing, dancing, card playing and football. Theaters and inns in London and well-populated areas had been closed. No one could work on Sundays. Last winter even Christmas dinner had been forbidden. Frivolity and gaiety were scorned. Devondra hated the Commonwealth and the strict laws that came with it. She longed for a return to things as they used to be. Perhaps then her father's lands and title would be restored, and he could give up his life on the road. In the meantime, oh, how she wished she could share in her father's adventures.

"I wish . . ." Though once he had let Devondra ride with him on some of his quests, the rules had changed and she had been left behind.

"That he would take you with him." Tobias's gap-toothed grin was sympathetic. "You know your father would not even consider it. Not now. Not with the reward upon his head at an all-time high."

She sighed. "I know. . . ."

Highwaymen were not worth catching until a reward was offered for their heads. In truth, Devondra supposed it to be a bit like betting on a horse race. If a highwayman was dashing and enterprising, he was likely to make much of a stir, thereby increasing his net worth. Thus, some reward "hounds" waited until a highwayman became decidedly notorious before they went in for the kill.

"But, Tobias, I want to feel the way he feels. I want to share in his dreams, his excitement. . . ."

"His peril." Tobias shook his balding head. "You know he will always tell you no."

"To protect me."

Tobias hurried to soothe her frustration. "James is a solitary man. He likes to go it alone." He shrugged. "Why, even I have been left behind of late, though to my own mind I am sorely need."

The sound of horses' hooves silenced the conversation.

"Father?"

Tobias raised his brows. "No." Putting his ear to the

ground, he came to the decision that there were several horsemen heading their way. "Who . . .?

Soon a dark blur, moving over the crest of the nearest hill, told the story. Coming toward the inn was a large party of riders. "Be they friend or foe?" Devondra questioned, peering through the dark. Alas, the round helmets and red sashes gave the men away. "Cromwell's men!"

"Bigod! But how . . .? Why . . .?" Tobias sputtered.

Devondra knew why they were coming. "Father!" she gasped in panic. She had to ride out and intercept him before he returned to the inn. Picking up her skirts, she ran toward the stables, far outdistancing Tobias, whose old war injury kept him lagging behind.

Devondra's chest heaved and her breathing became more labored as she moved to the stables. Slipping through the opening, she hesitated only a few minutes to catch her breath.

It was quiet. Only the nickerings and pawing hooves of the horses disturbed the stillness. Even so, she was nervous as she moved from stall to stall. She made her choice quickly: a black horse that would blend with the night. Her hands trembled as she lifted the bridle down from its peg on the wall. She had no time to light a lantern. Fumbling in the darkness, she sorted out and untangled the headstall and reins. With a curse she decided the process was taking too long; she would go bareback.

"Easy, boy!" Heaving herself up on the black horse's back, she leaned forward, her hands clinging to the animal's mane, her knees locked into his sides. Leaning low over the horse's neck, Devondra rode out into the night. Her last coherent thought was a frantically whispered prayer that she would not be too late.

* * *

Shifting uneasily on his saddle, Quentin Wakefield grumbled aloud as he guided his horse down the path. The roads between London and its surroundings were deplorable, little more than bridle paths linking one small village with another. Pitted and rocky, they were a hindrance to travelers. Moreover, in some areas enclosure made the path so narrow that coaches and wagons had to slow down considerably to pass safely through. It was no wonder that he, as magistrate, had heard so many complaints.

"And this stretch of land is the worst."

The Heath, or so it was called, was the most dangerous stretch of land in southeastern England. It was here that organized bands of robbers waited to plunder. Scowling at the reminder, Quentin clutched at his sword, then relaxed. After tonight there would be one less highwayman to worry about, one less irritation to get under his skin.

"Tonight Gentleman James has held up his last carriage." Betrayed by one of his own, that ill-fated highwayman's career would soon come to an end, Quentin thought with a sigh of relief. The soldiers who even now swarmed across the heath would corner the fox in his den. "And that audacious villain will swing!"

Suddenly, without warning, a satyrlike figure exploded into Quentin's view. Racing like the wind across the wide, marshy meadow toward the trees, the figure goaded him to give chase. If it was Gentleman James himself, Quentin would reap the glory of the capture. If not, nothing would be lost by the encounter. So thinking, he urged his horse into a gallop, avidly pursing the horse and rider.

Quentin's mount was more powerful in its strides, the horse more than a match for the other animal. With a feeling of smug satisfaction, he noted how swiftly his brown stallion closed the distance between the horses. "Stop, in the name of the Lord Protector!" he cried out.

Devondra heard the shout but had no intention of obeying. To the contrary, it only made her ride at a more frantic pace, for it could mean her father's death sentence if she failed. With the sound of horse's hooves echoing in her ears, she bolted down the road, all the while searching for any sign of her father.

At last she saw him far up ahead, moving without haste. Unaware of any danger lurking in his path, he was enjoying a leisurely summer night's ride.

Waving frantically, trying to alert him of the trouble that awaited him, Devondra cried out, "Danger! Watch out. Watch . . ."

Before she could utter another word a strong arm reached out from behind to grab her. "Warn him? I think not," she heard a man's voice exclaim.

Pulling away, Devondra tried to escape the man's grasp. Forgetting for a moment that there were no reins she reached out, but her hands caught nothing but empty air. She tumbled from the horse. "Uhhhhhhh . . ."

The hard earth rose up to greet her. The fall left her bruised and gasping for breath. And that was not the worst of it. As she lay on the ground she was covered by her pursuer's body. Held immobile by his great strength, she could not even lash out with words, for she was too winded.

Quentin did not suffer such an affliction. Angrily he rebuked the highwayman's obvious partner in crime. "You thieving rascal. No doubt you are no better than he. Well, fight all you want; you will not cheat the hangman! Not this time."

Hangman! The word pounded in Devondra's ears, giving her a resurgence of strength. Pummeling her captor's chest with tight fists, she fought to break free.

"Fie! Stop hitting me or I swear I will throttle you within an inch of your—"

A glimpse of the pretty face looking up at him stunned him. It was far too lovely to be that of a lad. Drawing back, Quentin gazed at the person he was handling so roughly. "A woman." The outline of breasts gave that away. That and the long dark hair that tumbled around the young woman's shoulders. This was no lad. She was wearing skirts.

Devondra found her voice. "Let me go!" she croaked, staring defiantly up at him.

"Let you go?" He laughed, relishing the moment most heartily. "Why, when it is not every night that a man comes up with such an unusual catch."

"Very funny!" she answered, then, temper getting the better of her, kicked him in the shin.

Quentin winced but did not cry out. He straddled her, holding her legs captive beneath his own. "Do that again and I will forget that I am a gentleman."

"Gentleman! I would take issue with that claim, sir. Bastard is more the word that I would use."

Her taunt took him by surprise, for bastard born he was. His mother had been a gentle dreamer, his father a roguish seaman who had never ceased roving the ocean. Glaring down at her, he was reminded of more turbulent times in his life. Cruel times. Times that had caused a bitterness to well up inside him like the poison of an ill-tended wound.

Reflected in the moonlight, his expression reminded her of the devil, quieting the tirade that was to come. Devondra tried another approach, pleading, "Please let me go!"

"So you can warn your highwayman?" Quentin shook his head emphatically. A man like Gentleman James did not deserve a chance at freedom. "No. Your lover will have to chance fate on his own."

She was frantic, knowing very well how precious the passing minutes were. "Not lover. Father," she gasped, trying to maintain at least some semblance of calm.

Quentin's face was dark and impassive, yet he set her wrists free and moved an arm's length away from her. "Gentleman James is your father?"

"He is!" she answered proudly. Recovering her strength, she sat up, scanning the horizon to see where her father had gone. Had he heard her warning?

"Well, fancy that." Damn; the man was a dangerous nuisance whose exploits had grown too notorious for him to be allowed to range at will on the roads any longer. Why then did the pleading tone in the daughter's voice stir him so? Why did the young woman's face so enchant him despite his efforts not to notice how she looked?

"Please, let him go."

She was asking the impossible of him, the haughty little witch. Why did she think he would give in? Because she knew she was beautiful?

"There is nothing anyone can do. Not now." Having a keen sense of military timing, Quentin knew that Gentleman James had no chance of escape. Even if he had heard his daughter's cry and turned back down the road, he would be hunted down. And more likely he had not heard. Returning to his quarters, he had probably already been surrounded. Nevertheless, Quentin loosened his hold.

"There must be!" Bolting to her feet, she brushed herself off. Without looking back, she ran toward her horse.

Quentin hurriedly rose to his feet, watching as she flung herself up on the animal's back without pausing to look back. And though he mounted his horse, strangely enough he did not pursue her.

Chapter Two

Hoofbeats. A steady pounding at first, they increased in volume as the riders moved over the crest of the hill. The Heath was disturbed by mounted men eager for the gold that had been promised to he who brought down Gentleman James. As the soldiers approached Hounslow Heath, the lieutenant divided them in two, sending half to the east and half to the west, as if this were some military maneuver. Then he divided each group yet again. As Gentleman James rode toward the inn, the command was issued and the highwayman was surrounded.

Watching from the hill, Quentin Wakefield could see the action reflected by the light of the moon. He thought it almost resembled some sort of board game. A game with deadly consequences. No matter how deadly, however, that didn't seem to daunt Gentleman James's daughter. Ignoring her own peril, she was riding straight toward the ensuing melee.

"Father! Follow me," he heard her say.

Weaving in and out of the foliage, father and daughter exhibited skillful horsemanship. A wild race began as Cromwell's armed men gave chase. Up the hill, down the dale, past thatched houses, through woods and across creeks, over bridges and up steep rises.

"Stubborn woman! That highwayman doesn't have a sporting chance of getting away," Quentin thought to himself. He had to admire her pluck and spirit. Most females would have been shaking in their shoes or seeking out a place of safety. The dark-haired young woman showed no fear for her own well-being; she was too busy trying to rescue her father. Obviously there was much more to her than just a pretty face.

As to her father, it seemed the stars were against him that night. A lucky shot from one of the soldier's pistols brought down his horse. The animal collapsed on the ground, nearly pinning the highwayman beneath the mountain of flesh. Just in the nick of time, however, he pulled himself out of the way. He had no choice but to take to his heels.

"The inn, Father. The inn." Devondra knew it was his only chance. If he could barricade himself inside, it would give him time to use the secret tunnel that led from the Devil's Thumb cellar to the cellar of the church. There he could hide until the tumult died down and the soldiers, cheated of their quarry, went away.

"The inn. A wise suggestion." The pursued highwayman ran toward the haven, slamming the door behind him. Devondra followed quickly. Bolting the door, then stacking benches, tables and barrels to block the portal, she worked beside her father despite his insistence to the contrary.

For a moment there was confusion. Then, as the soldiers realized James had retreated within the inn, there was an uproar. "Get him!" Striking, beating, tearing furiously, they

fought to break down the door. All too soon a loud thump
announced that they were using a battering ram.

"Leave me to my own fate, Devondra. This is not of your
making. You'll only get yourself killed."

"Or I will help you succeed in your escape," she countered.
"Come. Hurry." Lighting a candle, which she carefully
shaded, she moved toward the trapdoor. With one hand she
tugged it open.

The air rising up from the passageway was chilly and
damp, a reminder of the water of the nearby river, which
often flooded the hidden stairs. Wrapping her arms protectively around her body, Devondra led the way. She fumbled
through the darkness, bumping into obstacles and brushing
against spiderwebs. She was rewarded by the light that shone
like a pinhead at the end of the tunnel.

"Father! Father?"

The sound of breaking windowglass was her only answer.
Whirling around, she peered out and saw her father and one
of the soldiers engaged first in a swordfight and then in a
deadly wrestling match. More frightening still was the acrid
smell of smoke and the sight of the flames that licked at the
inn's walls. The soldiers had set the Devil's Thumb on fire.

"Run for your life, child!" James's coat and shirt were
ripped. His pistol and sword lay on the ground. The soldier's
fingers, twined about his windpipe, cause him to gasp and
choke.

"Run? No." It was out of the question. She was more
loyal than that. No matter what happened, she wouldn't let
her father be taken. Instead, she picked up a chair, wielding
it with deadly force upon the head of her father's attacker.
With a grunt he fell aside, freeing her father, at least for the
moment. All too soon, however, the first soldier was replaced
by another, then another and another.

"We're outnumbered!" It was no use. James Stafford knew it even if his daughter did not. "Bloody Hell. I'm done for."

"No, you are not." Ah, but he was. Devondra knew it. Still, she would not leave her father to face his fate alone. Like a carved statue she stood motionless as the band of soldiers descended upon them.

"Take them!" a voice shouted.

"Do what you will to me, but leave her alone!" Gentleman James moved toward his daughter, his hands outstretched in supplication. "She has naught to do with my sins." Despite Devondra's protestations and fearing for her safety, Gentleman James quickly surrendered to the soldiers.

In the street there was confusion as the townspeople realized the highwayman had been captured. Despite a backdrop of smoke from the steadily burning inn, they jammed close to the building to view the happenings.

"Stand back!" Quentin ordered, pushing them back. Hoots and catcalls were his answer. Openly the throng showed defiance to Cromwell's soldiers, at first in an attempt to rescue Gentleman James, and then in a selfish quest of their own. Ordinary townsmen soon became a dangerous mob, scuffling, fighting and shouting. Inside the inn there was looting.

Gentleman James's hoard was available for the taking. Money, gold, silver plate, jewels, watches, even embroidered silks, were thrown out of windows to be scrambled for by the crowd. That is until the building stood smoldering, a gutted black empty thing. Only then was any semblance of peace restored.

"Look at them! Greedy animals all," Quentin cried out in disgust. He cursed a string of violent oaths, then turned his attentions to other things. "The girl!"

He searched for her, but it was too late. She, like her father, had been swallowed up by the swarm of soldiers. A swarm that Quentin started to follow until he thought better of it.

What happened to the girl was none of his concern. At least that is what he told himself. Still, as he rode away from the town of Bedford, he couldn't get the highwayman's daughter out of his mind.

Chapter Three

A streak of lightning shot through the dark gray afternoon sky like a flame, illuminating the rough, wooden prison cart as it ambled up the cobblestone road. Devondra Stafford put her arms around her father, holding him as tightly as she could, trying to comfort him in this his moment of shame and peril.

"It will be all right, Father," she whispered against his chest. "It will be. You'll see." She was close to tears but forced herself to be brave, to calm her shaking voice for his sake. He'd get out of this. Somehow. Some way. Hadn't Gentleman James always said that he would be the one highwayman to cheat the hangman? Of course he had. If anyone could do it, her father could and would. She refused to believe that it was too late to save him. He was a hero to their small band of brigands. A fiercely loyal and brave man, he didn't deserve to die by dangling at the end of a rope.

Looking up, Devondra studied her father with worshipful

eyes, her gaze moving from the top of his gray-haired head to the toes of his high black leather boots. His manner of dress—the broad-brimmed hat with its jaunty feather, the hip-length black satin coat and high-waisted breeches, the cloak of matching color and fabric, even his shoulder-length hair and neatly trimmed beard and mustache, reflected his taste for luxury, his ties to the past and his nobility. Could any man be as tall, as proud, as handsome as her father? No. She doubted that any man could ever measure up to James Earlwood Stafford. Once he had been a nobleman, Sir James Stafford, the general of a king. Now circumstances had brought him to this sorry plight.

"It will be all right," she said again, more in an effort to soothe her own fears than to reassure her father. Dear God, they were taking him to Newgate Prison. Newgate! The very place brought stark terror to anyone who lived outside the law. Newgate—*Hell* was a far more appropriate name for it, and perhaps a far better destination. She could only hope that his stay there would not be long.

"No, daughter. It will ne'er be all right again for me." James Stafford's voice was a husky croak as he broke his long silence.

"But it will be. Tobias will think of a way to rescue you and—"

"No, I can't allow you to hold on to such a hopeless dream." His hazel eyes were shadowed and full of sadness. Cupping her chin in his hand, he forced her to meet his steady gaze. "You must prepare yourself for the fact that I am a doomed man."

"Doomed? No! I'll think of a way to get you free. You're not doomed." She shook her head violently, refusing to come to terms with what he said. There had to be a way.

"Devondra . . ." He was seized with heartache and fear for what the future held for *her*. She was young and beautiful, like a freshly blossomed flower. Her whole life was ahead of her. Even now she stood straight and proud, trying to hide her fears for his sake. "Lovely, lovely Devondra."

How like him she was, from the determined sparkle in those hazel eyes to the way she held her chin at a haughty angle. Even with the filth of the roads staining her clothing, the smudges of dirt on her nose and cheeks, she was the kind of young woman to make any father proud. No common lass this girl of his, but one as flawless as a pearl. A lady born and bred, though circumstances had forced her to keep company with rogues. Oh, how he wanted to be there to protect her against life's injustices, yet he knew this to be a foolish aspiration. Fate had forced him into a life of thievery, and now he had no choice but to pay the piper.

"Father . . . I . . .!" A boom of thunder made her shudder, and she thought of how much she hated storms. The rumble reminded her too much of the cannon that had belched fire during the all too recent civil war. Though she had been little more than a child, Devondra still remembered. It had been a fiercesome battle that had pitted those led by Oliver Cromwell against the King's forces and torn England asunder.

"It's going to rain." Tilting back his head, James Stafford looked up at the sky. "So many clouds. Like dark, angry ghosts. And soon I shall join them, all those poor souls who perished in—"

"No!" Devondra put her hands over her ears, but her father gently pulled them away.

"I'm not afraid to die, Devondra, though I fear the noose will be of a much coarser fabric than I am used to feeling against my skin." He tried to smile but couldn't quite get the corners of his mouth to turn up. "I have promised myself that I will be brave."

"It won't come to that. They won't hang you. They won't . . ."

He let out his sorrow in a long drawn-out sigh. "If you truly believe that, my darling poppet, then I fear for you."

James Stafford might have said more but for the sudden babble of the crowd that came into view as they reached the market square. Catching sight of the approaching wagon, the ghoulish spectators poured out onto the street, forming a circle around the slowly moving wagon and its guardsmen. "'At's 'im! Gentleman Jim 'imself. 'Eld up twenty-four carriages in just two months, 'e did!"

"A bold one 'e is!"

"Not so bold now, eh wot?" There was a snicker of laughter as the wagon jolted along. Fingers pointed. Eyes stared.

"Look at 'im in his finery. Well, the devil take him, I say!"

The parade weaved through the throng of onlookers. Devondra tried to keep from looking at the crowd, but it was difficult. The buzz of their excited chatter was nearly as loud as the toot of the trumpets that heralded the humiliating procession of the prisoners. Elbowing each other, pushing and shoving in their attempt to get a good look at the famous highwayman, they seemed more animal than human. Monkeys and apes, Devondra thought, remembering the animals she had seen at St. Margaret's Fair.

"They say he was a brave one . . ."

"Not so brave when the noose begins to choke him, I'd wager."

There were hoots and catcalls. Some threw stones, others sticks, and all jabbered as they looked at the two people in the cart. The wagon was surrounded by four burly mounted guards, but they didn't lift a finger to protect their prisoner. Devondra heard the men chuckling, as if the guards were enjoying the spectacle.

The throng followed the wagon as it proceeded down Tyburn Lane, then turned the corner and headed in the direction of the prison. Suddenly Devondra was angry. At the crowd, at the guards, at Cromwell, at fate, which had seemingly dealt her father a lethal hand. "You bloody fools!" Pushing against the sides of the wagon, she leaned over to give the hecklers a sharp tongue-lashing. "My father never harmed a one of you! He stole from the rich. The same men who in all their legality steal from *you*. Any of you who were in dire need were shone the warmth of his generosity. How can you be so cruel?"

"She's right!" One crone stepped forward. "One winter's night I was nigh on to freezing, I was. Gentleman James gave me his own cloak."

A small boy peeked from behind the old woman's skirts. "He filled my hand with coins once when I was in need."

"Once when I was stranded while traveling on the road he offered me a ride in his carriage," a young woman revealed.

" 'E's a gentleman's Robin Hood!"

"A good man, he is."

The mood of the crowd changed abruptly. Though they still followed after the wagon, it was in a more somber mood. Instead of taunts, they offered up prayers and sympathy, seemingly oblivious to the drops of rain that had started to fall, drops that soon turned into a torrent. As if someone had uncorked a waterbarrel, the clouds poured forth the sky's moisture. Rain from the heavens pelted the ground furiously. Angels' tears, Devondra thought, crying for her father, who they knew to be a good man at heart. A man who had shared his pilfered profits most generously with those who were in dire need.

"Bloody hell! We'll be soaked to the skin. Let's get out of 'ere!" An amply girthed guardsman hurried the proces-

sion, not wishing to suffer any discomfort. Slapping his hand
on the cart horse's rump, he hastened the wagon along.

"Merry-go-up!" The wagon lurched so violently that for
a moment Devondra was nearly thrown out.

"Devondra!" James Stafford's strong hands held on to his
daughter, keeping her from toppling to the rough cobblestones. He eyed the guardsman with disdain. "He's a fool!
Ah, that I had sword in hand; I would soon teach him a
lesson in manners."

"I doubt he is capable of learning," Devondra answered
scathingly. Brushing strands of her damp hair from her eyes,
she cautiously stole a glance at the men guarding her father's
every move. They were all four alike, and seemed by their
demeanor to be surly brutes, the kind of men Oliver Cromwell made use of. But soon the people would tire of the
Protector's iron hand. And when that time came, such men
as her father would rule again.

"Look at 'er. Ain't she somethin', Tom? I always 'ave
liked women wi' dark brown 'air. And those eyes. Brown
and green at the same time. She's a beauty, I'll give me
bloody oath on it." The man's stare in Devondra's direction
was bold. "And nice duckies! If she takes a loiking to me,
I'll 'ave a bit o' sport." Such talk made Devondra shudder.

"Takes a liking to you?" Throwing his comrade a bemused
smile, the other man shook his head. " 'Arold, look at the
way she's glarin' at you. As if yer were nothing but a bug
she'd like ter squash. Just because her father was one of the
king's traitors she thinks herself to be a lady." Pulling his
horse alongside the wagon, the largest of the guardsmen
looked threateningly into Devondra's eyes.

"I am a lady!" Her eyes sparked fire.

"Why, she's a real little wild cat, she is." The man reached
out to touch her, but she pulled away violently.

"Don't touch me!" Oh, how she loathed the man. He was

NOTORIOUS   31

enjoying her father's misery, wanting to take advantage of their predicament. Well, she would let it be known that he would have a real fight on his hands were he to take any liberties with her person.

"A cat, all right, 'Arold. Look at 'er put up 'er 'ands, as if she could fend me off." He barred his teeth. "If yer knows wot's good for yer sire, you'll sheath yer claws." Lurching forward, he caught Devondra by the wrists with an evil grin as his horse careened alongside the cart.

"You bastard!" Moving forward, James Stafford came to the defense of his daughter only to be struck down by a second guardsman's staff. He fell in a sprawl to the dirty, straw-covered floor.

"Father!" Devondra tried to go to him, but the guardsman held her much too tightly. A gust of wind blew her long, dark, tangled hair across her face, but she didn't think to brush it aside. "Please, don't hurt him!" The rain-soaked cloth of her dress clung to her curves like an icy second skin, the skin weighting her legs in sodden folds. "Please!" She shivered, her teeth chattering from a combination of the cold and her fear.

"Leave the girl alone!" The deep voice was authoritative, as if used to giving orders. In response, the guardsman let Devondra go. "See to your duties, Ridgewood!"

"Yes, sir." In the guardsman's confusion, the wagon was drawn to a halt.

Devondra looked up through her dark lashes at the imposing figure who had so quickly subdued the guardsman. His sapphire velvet coat was soaked. Tall and muscular, with a strength about him that was almost overpowering, he sat proud and straight upon his horse, despite the rain. A soldier, she thought, used to foul weather. Thick auburn hair brushed the back of his neck, just touching his shoulders. His jaw was strong and well defined, his nose chiseled to perfection.

Thick brows shadowed eyes of a pale, crystalline blue, eyes that seemed to look deep into her soul. He was handsome, with a bold look about him. What's more, he looked oddly familiar.

"Who are you?" she asked.

"You don't remember me, but I remember you—most vividly." His eyes swept over her, then focused on her face, remembering a few nights ago, when he had held her pinioned beneath him.

A quiver danced up and down her spine as she felt the heat of his gaze. In that moment she remembered who he was. "You!" If not for him, she might have saved her father.

"So, I see that you remember."

"I do!" she answered angrily. She met his gaze for a long moment, unable to look away. "Have you come to gloat?"

"Gloat?" He shook his head. "No." If the truth were told, he really didn't know why he had followed the prison cart. Perhaps because he wanted to see her again, wanted to make certain that she was all right.

Glaring at Quentin, Devondra knelt down beside her father. Though dazed by the blow dealt to him by the guardsman, he was seemingly uninjured. Taking his hand, she helped her father to his feet. "This will all be over soon." An ominous thought brought little peace of mind: Once they reached Newgate, then what?

Strange, Quentin thought, how innocent she appeared. Were looks really that deceiving? No matter. He hated to see such a lovely woman brought so low. "What are you doing riding in the prison cart? You are not a prisoner."

She looked over her shoulder to see that she was still the object of the handsome man's scrutiny. Oh, but she must look a sight, drenched as she was. If only the wretched rain would stop. Nevertheless, she kept her poise. "No, I'm not a prisoner, but someone in authority had compassion enough to let me accompany my father at this harrowing time."

"Indeed." He looked at Devondra, then at James Stafford, and then back at Devondra again.

Suspicious as to his questioning, fearful that he might cause a stir, she asked. "What is it to you?"

"To me?" He shrugged. "Nothing. I was just curious; that's all." And confused by the conflicting emotions that suddenly took hold of him.

"Curious?" Seeing that this man was at least interested in what was happening to her father, she thought perhaps this might be the chance she had been waiting for. "Well, then, I must say my father has been treated quite unjustly." She moved in the man's direction. "He is not some common thief to be bullied and pushed about. He is a man of distinction and pride."

Quentin cocked one brow. "Undoubtedly he is innocent . . ."

"Innocent. Yes! Yes!" Devondra felt uneasy in the lie, but quickly justified her father's actions in her heart. He had only done what he had to in order to survive. In truth, Cromwell was the real culprit.

"They all are," he answered with more than a hint of sarcasm. "Every one of them innocent. Not a man or woman in Newgate is guilty." His eyes were piercing. "Mistaken identity, I suppose."

Devondra nodded, knowing a moment of hope. "Mistaken identity. Yes!" The rain had stopped just as quickly as it had begun, and she viewed this as a positive sign. "My father is a good man! He has done nothing that should deserve such cruel treatment. Newgate should not be his fate!"

"God's blood, but you lie, madam!"

"What?" Devondra's hopes were shattered as she looked up. Gone was any trace of friendliness on the man's face. His features had hardened into a scowl.

"I said your words are false."

She winced at his accusation. "I do not lie. My father is a good man." He was at times the most noble man in all England, at least in her eyes.

"A highwayman!" His gaze burned into James Stafford's eyes with a glint of recognition. "One whom I have had the misfortune of meeting myself on the road." Wishing to put an end to the conversation, he nudged his heels into his horse's flanks. "Mistaken identity? I think not! Now that I look closely, I recognize the rogue just as surely as I recognized you." With a disdainful nod, he rode away.

"Wait! Please. Listen to what I have to say—" It was no use. He didn't pause or turn back once. In despair, Devondra hung her head. "I have made a mess of everything, Father. There was a chance, but I let it slip away."

Putting his arm around her, James Stafford hugged her close, bracing her against a bump as the wagon started to roll again. "No, 'twas I who ruined everything. I was a fool to be bold once too often. I should never have allowed myself to fall into such a trap. To be caught unawares. I should have been more cautious."

"It wasn't your fault. Father. How were you to know that Cromwell's soldiers would come to the village?" An obvious case of treachery. How else would Cromwell's soldiers have known that Gentleman James had a hideaway at the Devil's Thumb Inn?

"Aye, me thinks I was betrayed, but by whom or why I have not the foggiest notion." Shaking his head sadly, James Stafford remained quiet as the wagon approached its destination.

Though Devondra tried to keep up her optimism for his sake, her hopes had dwindled. Her father had never tried to hide his identity. There would be many who could give positive identification. Too many. No plea of innocence could be made. She had learned her lesson. But what then? She couldn't just give up and let her father hang. Her mind worked feverishly as the prison cart proceeded down the road, but to no avail. Then, when at last the ugly gray walls loomed before her eyes like a fiercesome monolith, her blood ran cold.

James Stafford was dragged from the wagon with as much deference as a sack of wheat. Nor was Devondra shown even a hint of gentleness. Pushed and shoved along, she and her father were led to that very place that brought stark terror to anyone who made thievery his way of life—Newgate.

"Well, well, well. 'Ere we are," the guardsman announced loudly, clucking his tongue. "Your new lodgings."

"Dear God!" Her mouth went dry. For a long moment she just stood there as her terror mounted. This nightmare was too real! She wanted to scream but held her silence because of her father. What if . . .? She forced the thought from her mind. She had to believe there was a way out of this predicament or go mad. Even so, the doors plaited with iron seemed to grin at Devondra, and she shivered as she was led toward the entrance. Then, all too suddenly, they were inside.

Chapter Four

The room was cold, despite the fire in the great stone fireplace. Or was it apprehension that chilled his bones? Quentin Wakefield wondered? Whatever it was, he had to admit that he was hardly looking forward to his meeting with Oliver Cromwell that evening.

What did he want? To gloat about the capture of James Stafford, no doubt. Stafford, who as one of the leaders of the Royalist Cavalry had been a constant thorn in Cromwell's side during the war. Undoubtedly the real reason he had been hunted down last night, or so Quentin suspected, recalling the events and the young woman who even now was still vivid on his mind.

Even soaking wet she was lovely. And vulnerable. He thought of the glitter of hope that had come into her eyes when she had thought that he might be able to help her father, the fierce way she had staunchly protected the highwayman, despite the danger posed to her own person.

She loves him. That foolhardy, vain, selfish man. A man

who had chosen to steal instead of work for a living, thereby risking his own daughter's future. *Despite all, he is a hero in her eyes.*

Her eyes. For just a moment they had been the window to her soul, revealing all the love she was capable of feeling. Love, something he had always envied. Something he had little hope of ever finding. Something he had always secretly feared.

I am more comfortable being alone. In truth, there were times when he had no fondness for people at all—at least those he was forced to keep company with of late. Once and only once he had felt love. She had been everything good. Beauty, kindness, generosity all wrapped up into one.

Trying to make himself comfortable in the hard-backed chair, he leaned back and stretched his legs. As he waited for Cromwell to make an appearance he thought about *her.*

Elizabeth Wakefield was a woman who always smiled, her thoughts soaring beyond her sordid surroundings. Quentin had sensed that she counted the days until the man she loved would return to claim her. Quentin had found himself sharing her dream, hoarding his fantasies as surely as a miser collected gold. But his father had never come back.

Quentin had spent many an early morning or late afternoon sparring with the other youths. And he had received more than a few lumps, scratches, bruises and black eyes defending his mother's name from those who taunted him. He had been called bastard more times than he could count, learning at an early age that strength was his only defender.

Nor had his mother had an easy time of it. Though she spoke not a melancholy word and always soothed his spirits, he knew she was lonely and overworked. She had conjured up a world of contentment where troubles could not bother her. Then, in an effort to find respectability, she had at last

married a thick-set, red-faced butcher who was beefy in
body and soul, and content to remain so.

Quentin had hoped at last to find a companion in the
portly Puritan but had instead received only scoldings and
the severest discipline. Telling the boy that a child conceived
in sin stood in mortal jeopardy of his soul, his stepfather
had made him work unmercifully hard, cuffing him if he
dared to complain. Quentin had toiled from early morning
until long into the night.

At last the abuse to his spirit and pride had become unbearable. Quentin had lost his temper, putting his fingers around
his stepfather's throat. It was a confrontation that nearly led
to murder, and though Quentin had loved his mother fiercely,
he had run.

In vexation, trying to put such memories out of his
thoughts, Quentin stood and paced up and down the long
corridor.

"Forsooth, Wakefield, I fear you will wear holes in my
carpet." The sharp voice crackled with an icy tone, and
Quentin felt the hairs rise on the nape of his neck. To be
blunt, he just didn't trust the man. Perhaps that was why he
whirled around, preferring to speak to Cromwell eye to eye.

"Or holes in my boots," he answered, assessing the man
who now ruled all England. Garbed in a plain-cloth suit,
dark of course, his hat worn without a hatband, the man
looked more Puritan clergyman than would-be king. Nevertheless Quentin affected a polite bow.

"You came quickly."

"Your message sounded urgent."

"Not so." Cromwell stood as expressionless and still as
a statue, then with a grim nod of his head motioned Quentin
into a small carpeted room. "But I will get right to the point."

"That being . . .?"

"The Parliament has offered me the Crown. What do you think?"

That it is the supreme paradox. Cromwell the king-killer, the so-called visionary, was being tempted to become King Oliver. A man who like Quentin, had come from humble origins. Born at Huntingdon, he was the son of a gentleman farmer. Arrogantly, his religious beliefs included a conviction that he was obliged to further God's will with all his powers. He also was convinced that he knew exactly what God's will really was.

"Well . . .?" Cromwell was impatient at the answer.

"Refuse it."

"What!" He was angered by the answer.

Quentin quickly explained. "To accept is to limit your power. You will be bound by precedents and by the rule of law. And, most importantly, it is a dangerous thing to restore the office that you have set aside."

"I see." Cromwell was silent for a long time. He tossed a log into the hearth of the room's small fireplace, watching the sparks swirl up. The crackle and slow hiss of the flames as they devoured the wood seemed to fascinate him. His eyes were fixed and staring.

King, Quentin thought. How ironic it would be were Cromwell to put the crown upon his own head—he who had fought Charles tooth and nail.

Cromwell had entered Parliament before England's Civil War, taking advantage of the conflict between the king and the Houses of Lords and Commons. The king thought he should have absolute power, but Parliament thought it should have more authority in government.

When the fighting broke out Cromwell had raised a troop of cavalry for Parliament and, with Quentin's help, led them with such success that in two years he was a lieutenant general and second in command of the Parliamentary army.

This New Model Army was largely responsible for the brilliant victories at Marston Moor and Naseby. He was a member of the court that had tried King Charles and sentenced him to death.

It was an act that had nearly been Cromwell's undoing, for Charles's dignity and forebearance had made his beheading a massive propaganda defeat for his opponents. His public execution at Whitehall had taken place before a stunned but sympathetic crowd. Alive he had been unpopular; dead the king had grasped a martyr's crown.

England was then declared a commonwealth, ruled without a king or House of Lords. The Commons became the ruling power, and the Council of State, of which Cromwell was a member, was appointed to carry on the government. As leader of the army, Cromwell was the principal leader of the new government.

But limited power had not been enough for him. Pressed by radical Puritans on one hand and by conservative elements on the other, he abolished Parliament, assuming the title "Lord Protector of the Commonwealth." As such he was an absolute ruler, a king in all but name, a man variously known as a saint, a demon, a military genius, a cold-blooded murderer, a defender of liberties and a bloody tyrant, depending where one's sympathies lay. And the man who held Quentin Wakefield's future in the palm of his hand. It was no wonder that he was wary as he watched the Lord Protector now. At least until he smiled.

"But of course, you are right. The way that I am, I am more powerful than Charles ever was." Slowly he walked to a wooden desk, shuffling and reshuffling the papers there. "I am more prophet than king, a Moses leading the Israelites to the Promised Land."

A strange thing to say, Quentin thought. "Moses?"

A gleam came into Cromwell's eyes. "The English people

have been in bondage in the Land of the Stuarts' Egypt,
struggling across the desert of misfortune, but I will lead
them." He paused, smiling. "I will need a right-hand man.
A man who shares my convictions."

Quentin Wakefield stiffened. He would be no man's
puppet. He would give England his loyalty, his life, but he
would not barter his soul for any price. "Your convictions
being . . ."

"That anyone who poses a danger must be removed."

Quentin knew what Cromwell was saying. "James
Stafford."

"Aye. Make certain he causes no more trouble." Having
spoken what was on his mind, Cromwell merely raised his
eyebrows in silent communication, then took his leave.

The air seemed to shiver. Shadows took on a harrowing
appearance. Had Quentin not known it before, he knew it
now. James Stafford's days were undoubtedly numbered.
But what of his daughter?

Chapter Five

The large room was a veritable sea of unfriendly, cold, merciless faces. These men had no sympathy for the thief who had humiliated them and their acquaintances at the point of a shiny silver gun. And yet the fate of Devondra's father was in their hands. She watched as the prison guard recorded her father's name in the tattered prison book. *James Earlwood Stafford*, he wrote laboriously with an ink-stained quill. *May 9, 1655*. Her father's incarceration was official, she thought, as she led him to a place at the front of the large room.

"I can only pray that God in his wisdom and mercy will reach out and touch those hard hearts," Devondra whispered. Sitting beside her father, she squeezed his hand as tightly as she could.

"I doubt that even He could soften them," James Stafford replied tonelessly.

"James Earlwood Stafford, rise to your feet!" The black-robed judge looked overly stern as he nodded to the prisoner from his seat on the high dais. To his side sat the body of men sworn to give a fair verdict. Fair? By the expressions on their faces, Devondra sincerely dreaded the outcome.

The trial, in fact, was a living nightmare, a mockery from start to finish. One by one all those whom the infamous highwayman had wronged were called forth to testify, every word that was uttered damning the man known as Gentleman James. The epitaphs hurled at her father's head were spewed out in anger and resentment, with little thankfulness that he had spared their lives. Others of his profession sometimes silenced their victims permanently, but James Stafford was a merciful man. Clearly, however, the highwayman would get no justice here. Her father was already tried and convicted in each and every heart. What made matters worse was that everyone in the room seemed to want to proceed as quickly as they could so that the next case could be heard. There was no time for any words of vindication.

It was a mimicry of all that was decent to have to experience this ghastly mummery of justice. James Stafford could say little in his own defense. It was written upon his face that he realized that his fate was sealed. His eyes sought out Devondra with a gentleness that touched her soul. Even with his world tumbling about him he was concerned for her welfare.

"Father . . .!"

"Hush!" The judge was quick to scold her. With a wave of his hand he signaled for silence.

Now the judge will offer up life or death with but the nod of his head, Devondra thought. Even so, she was stunned when the judge declared her father guilty. Perhaps she really had believed in miracles.

"You will be taken to Tyburn tree on the morrow and there before all you will be hanged." The words tolled like a funeral bell.

"No!" Devondra sprang to her feet, little caring what the consequences might be. She cared little at that moment for her own fate. "Please! I beg you for mercy. Prison perhaps, but not death! He has killed no one."

"All serious crimes are punished by the noose," the judge thundered in anger. "The law has given its judgment. The penalty for thievery is for a man to meet the hangman. And this he shall do, at the first crow of the cock."

She fell to her knees in supplication, fighting for time. A few days were all she needed, enough time to rouse Tobias and the others. "Not tomorrow. Give my father time to appeal his case."

"It is done." With an annoyed grunt the judge motioned the guards to take the prisoner away. Devondra was silent as her grief shattered her. All she could do was look at her father, and follow helplessly after him as he was tugged and pulled along.

"Go to Tobias, Devondra. There is no purpose in your being here. You are not a prisoner." James Stafford was adamant in his command. "Leave me. I do not want you to suffer here."

"Leave you?" It was unthinkable. Since her mother's death it had always been the two of them, Devondra and her father. They'd faced poverty together. Starvation. They'd braved the hard times because of their love for one another. They had shared the good as well as the bad. If there was nothing she could do to save him, then at least she would be there by his side to tell him that she loved him before he died. With that thought driving her, she numbly followed after her father.

"Devondra. Go back! I order you to obey me. It is not safe for you here. It is dangerous for you among these devils!" James Stafford was frantic in his attempts to dissuade her from such a devout show of loyalty. "Get out of here while you can. It is not you who is being punished. You are free. Go!"

"And leave you all alone? No." Brave talk, but in truth she fought against her cowardice with every step. Silently, she traversed the endless corridors and descended the steeply winding staircases that seemed to be taking her to the very depths of the earth.

The nauseating reek of Newgate enveloped her, assaulting her senses. The stench of unwashed bodies, human waste and mold swirled about like a thick fog, pressing upon her like a smothering blanket. Instinctively she put her hand to her nose.

"Newgate perfume," the odious, grinning guard informed her. "Mingled with the foul odor of death. From the bodies plucked from all the *trees.*"

Devondra shuddered at the reminder of her father's fate. She stared through the grates at the gaunt faces and the wild, hopeless eyes of those who gave visible proof of the suffering within the prison. Clutching hands reached out, begging for mercy, their misery tangible.

"For the love of God, get out of here," James Stafford growled in one last desperate attempt to make her see reason. "You are young. Your entire life is ahead of you." This place of death harbored ill for his sweet, sensitive daughter, she who had always enjoyed life to the fullest.

Devondra licked her lips and swallowed, trying to say something. No sound came, and then it was too late. Selecting a key from the large loop at his belt, the guard slid it into the lock.

"If you insist upon staying with him, get in there," he said. He opened a rusted iron door and pushed James Stafford and his daughter inside. "Hope you will be comfortable here." He slammed the door shut, his laughter resounding through the hall. "But then, your stay will be brief. . . ."

Devondra stared about her, examining the tiny cell. Dark
stone walls rose high about her, gleaming with moisture.
There were no windows, only the slits in the door to give
a view of what was going on beyond the grating. Clearly
there could be no escape; she would have to put an end to any
heroic thoughts. Her flesh crawled with a sense of danger;
something more was about to happen. She sensed it in every
nerve and sinew of her body.

"You should have listened." Stafford put his hand on her
shoulder. "But I am grateful that I have such a daughter."
Suddenly he seemed so tired. So old. As if today had aged
him tenfold. Certainly his eyes seemed sunken and filled
with immeasurable sadness.

"And I, to have you for my father." Taking her father's
arm, she led him toward the straw mattress in the corner.
It had been a long, tiring day. Even she, at her young age,
could feel the strain. "You need rest."

"Rest?" Sitting on the edge of the bed, he covered his
face with his hands. "Rest, you say? I'll be getting more
than my share of that where I am going. The grave shall be
my bed. No, I want nothing to do with sleep." Even so, he
seemed suddenly devoid of all strength. With a deep sigh
he sagged against the mattress and closed his eyes. Though
he fought slumber, the guttural sound of his snores soon
echoed in the room.

Devondra stood for a long time watching over her father
as if she could guard him from the danger that stalked him,
then settled herself on a small wooden stool. Only then did
the emotions of the past several hours catch up with her—
emotions and memories.

The early morning had started out pleasantly enough. She
and her father had enjoyed their breakfast at the Devil's
Thumb Inn, the quiet hideaway that had often sheltered them
between exploits. He had gone out on one of his many late-

night gallops, short journeys from which he had always returned safely, with little threat of pursuit. How were they to know that this particular night would shatter their lives? How could they have foreseen this vile betrayed.

Closing her eyes tightly, she relived that scene, heard the sound of horses' hoofs, saw the silhouettes of the soldiers. The troop of horsemen had come at a furious gallop. Even so, James Stafford would have had a chance of getting away if only she could have warned him in time.

Or had there been a chance? She would never know. What she did know, however, was that her father's love for her and his refusal to leave her behind had been the most noble thing she could imagine. When the soldiers had set fire to the inn and threatened to let it burn to the ground with Devondra inside if he did not surrender, he had given himself up into their hands. To protect her. To see to her safety. Was it any wonder, then, that she could not even think of deserting him now?

And now, tomorrow, my father is going to die, she thought mournfully.

A soft groan of despair tore from her throat. Her eyes stung with tears she could no longer suppress. Nor did she try to stop them. It was as if a dam had burst. Huddled against the wall, she cried until she was certain there could be no more tears left. Then, dashing the moisture from her eyes with the back of her hand, she made a vow that she would never cry again. Crying showed weakness and from this moment on she knew she had to be strong!

A rattle of keys jarred her from her thoughts. Looking up, she saw the face of the guard peering at her through the grill of the wooden door. Seeing him made her stomach turn over. Why was he back so soon? The interruption boded ill.

"I have a visitor for you," he growled, as if his coming was an inconvenience.

"A visitor?" Devondra turned toward her father, wondering if she really wanted to wake him.

"Not for him. For *you.*" There was a grating noise as he twisted the key in the lock.

"For me?" Tobias! He'd come with a plot to free her father. "Where is he?" Her eyes darted back and forth, searching for his jolly, rotund, gnomelike form.

"He wants to speak with you alone." Opening the door, he stepped inside.

"Alone . . ." It was an unusual request; Tobias never kept secrets from her father. But perhaps he was afraid of being overheard if they discussed the matter in the prison cell. "Well then, take me to him."

She started toward the door, then hesitated. Was this perchance some kind of game the guardsman was playing? Perhaps no one was waiting to see her at all. Perhaps all he wanted to do was to get her alone. All too vivid in her mind was her recent experience at another guardman's hands.

"Wait. I'm not at all certain I wish to go with you." She thrust back her shoulders and lifted up her chin. "How do I know there is someone waiting to talk with me? How do I know this is not a trick?" She had no reason to trust this man.

"Because I say so." With a grunt of disgust, he flung out his arms. "Argh! Stay here for all it matters to me. I don't care one whit what happens."

He started to leave, but Devondra reached out, grasping his coat. "Wait!" She had to take the risk. What other choice did she have? Her father's life might yet be saved. Patting the knife she had hidden in her stocking, she walked slowly toward the door.

Chapter Six

The reality of Newgate hit Quentin Wakefield like a physical blow. It was like being in the midst of a nightmare and wanting desperately to awaken. As magistrate of London, he thought himself prepared for what he'd find behind the filth-covered stone walls, but he was wrong. The noise, clamor and reek of the prison assaulted him as he traversed the endless corridors.

What a formidable place, he thought, eyeing the iron bars, the massive doors plaited with iron and mounted with spikes. It was starkly impressive in a sinister way. More like a series of cages than a place that housed human beings. Certainly a most horrifying place for a young woman, be she a highwayman's daughter or the devil's offspring.

"This way." The guard fit a key into the lock of a thick wooden door, hesitating, as if he expected Quentin to change his mind. With a brisk appraisal of Quentin's expensive garments, he muttered, "It ain't a sight for a gentleman wot might be squeamish."

"Squeamish?" Quentin laughed dryly, then quickly sobered. "During the war I witnessed every conceivable horror of man's inhumanity to man." As commander of Cromwell's leading regiment, he'd seen more than his share of the dead and the dying, men lying in pools of their own blood, and witnessed atrocities that still haunted him in his dreams. "There isn't anything on earth that could possibly shock me."

"Care to put a wager on that?" Cocking his head, he scrutinized Quentin. "Do you ever gamble, sir?"

Something in the guard's manner angered Quentin. He was much too smug for Quentin's liking, with a swagger that spoke of a man who was too sure of himself. Clearly he needed his comeuppance.

"I don't have time for any such foolishness. I have come here for a reason." Nodding toward the door, Quentin was stern. "Open it up at once. I have someone waiting."

"As you say."

Stony-faced, he followed the guard down the steeply winding staircases. The foul odor emanating from within deepened the farther he went, pressing upon him like an enveloping cloak. He flinched, anxious to be about his business and then be far away from this place.

Why in hell am I here? he wondered. Clearly it was none of his business. A thief had been caught and was now to pay his due. It happened every day to some poor dishonest soul or other. Even so, he had been driven to come to Newgate. Why? He was still confused as to what had possessed him. Why had that slip of a young woman made such a vibrant impression on him? Most certainly she was none of his concern. Why then had he been so irrevocably drawn here? What was it about her that had so deeply touched him? Her pride perhaps. And her steadfastness toward her father, though the rogue did not deserve it.

"Is she your doxy?" The guard's voice was an impertinent intrusion on Quentin's thoughts.

"What?"

"Well, there must be some reason you would journey into this hell to talk with a woman. I thought she must be your—"

"She's not!" Quentin's voice was harsher and much louder than it needed to be, perhaps because her beauty had stirred him to desires he didn't want to have. "I have come here because the girl has done no wrong and should not be held within these walls. Being a magistrate, I intend to see to it that she's freed."

"If you've come to take her away from here, you might as well turn right around and leave." The guard shrugged. "She wanted to be with her father. She's here of her own free will."

"Misguided loyalty," Quentin shot back. "The man is a scoundrel."

Gentleman James was a blackguard. During the war, as the king's general, he had been merciless. On the road as a highwayman he had taken particular joy in tormenting all those Cromwell had put in power. Even so, Quentin was sincerely sorry for the way he had roared at the young woman. He had ridden off in a huff because of her espousal of the highwayman's innocence when he knew it to be a falsehood. Yet he had to admit that his anger had been toward her father, and not at her.

Quentin would never forget his greatest moment of humiliation, when Gentleman James had forced him at gunpoint to strip off all his clothes and take to the woods quite naked. He could still hear the bold highwayman's laughter as he had informed his victim that he was but "settling an old war feud." Cromwell and his cronies had stripped him of all he held dear; he was merely returning the favor, he said.

"A scoundrel wot will soon be gibbet bait." Looking from

left to right to make certain he would not be overheard, the
guard added, "'course now, if there's enough coins exchang-
ing hands, anything can be done." His tiny eyes narrowed
to slits as he grinned. "Might make the young lady very,
very grateful. If you get my meaning . . ."

Quentin stared down into the fleshy, pockmarked face,
loathing the man all the more with each minute that passed.
"I do. Very clearly." He knew the type—a man who would
sell his own mother for the right price. "You speak of bribery . . ." A misdeed that carried its own punishment.

The guard was defensive. "Not bribery. Just cooperative
dealings, that's all." His stubby fingers fumbled with the
keys as he returned them to their resting place at his belt.
"Think on it." Snatching up a lighted torch, he ambled down
the corridor, saying over his shoulder, "Best follow me
closely. Men have been known to get lost down here." He
chuckled ominously.

Quentin's loping stride made it easy for him to keep up
with the bandy-legged guard as he led him to a large room.
Peering into the gloom, Quentin could see a slim young
figure approaching. Somehow he knew it was her even before
she came into focus, and he was surprised at the sudden
quickening of his heart.

"'Ere's yer visitor," the guardsman accompanying her
announced.

Flickering torchlight spilled into the room, momentarily
blinding Devondra with its intensity. She blinked several
times, then, shielding her eyes against the glare, stared at
Quentin in stunned surprise. "You!"

"I see that you remember me this time." He took a step
forward, bowing politely. His gaze took in the disheveled
mass of dark hair framing those unforgettable, expressive
wide eyes. Nao read a wariness in their depths.

"How could I forget?" He was just as arrogant as she

remembered, just as elegant and handsome. Devondra clung to her composure, regarding him coolly. She had been expecting Tobias. What was this man doing here? "Why did you come?" He had already made his feelings quite clear.

"I've come to take you away from this place!" There was a harshness in his tone as his eyes raked over her, as if he expected unquestioning compliance.

Devondra met him stare for stare. "As I have said a hundred times to all who are within earshot, no!"

"You can't mean that." She was even prettier than he remembered. Her features, in silhouette as she turned her head, were as delicate as a cameo. Her velvety soft skin stretched over bones of flawless symmetry. Though her emerald green dress was stained and wrinkled from the rain, she looked stunning nonetheless, convincing him again that Newgate was no place for her. Not for a day, not for another hour.

"I won't leave without my father." She could not seem to take her eyes away from his tall, muscular form. He had changed his garments and now wore a suit of deep plum, trimmed in gold braid. He seemed to favor bold colors, unlike the rest of the drab Puritans who now held the country securely in their hands. Clearly he was a man of importance. Hope surged within Devondra's heart that she might yet save her father. This man's visit seemed to offer her a last chance. She made another plea, her voice softer as she said, "Sir . . . my father is a good man."

On that matter he had his own opinion, but he kept it to himself, saying only, "I came for you, not to save your father." He wanted to make that perfectly clear.

"Then there is nothing more to say." Devondra turned her back and started to walk away, but he reached out and gently touched her arm.

"There is nothing to be gained in your staying here. All

you will get from your misguided loyalty is heartache. Surely your father must have said the same." Feeling the two guardsmen's eyes on his back, he whirled around, incensed by their stares. "Bigod, get out of here, the two of you. This matter should be dealt with in at least a measure of privacy." Like the rats that lurked within the crevices of the prison, they gave a squeak of indignation but scurried away, leaving Quentin alone with the young woman.

"My father has argued with me, but in this one area I have chosen to disobey. I will not go without him. I will not give up hope. Somehow there is a way. There has to be." Devondra faced her would-be rescuer squarely, knowing instinctively that the only way to win his respect was to be as strong-willed as he. "My father deserves a second chance. I will do anything within my power to see that he gets it."

It was dark in the room. Quentin grabbed hold of a torch and lighted it from one of the flickering wall sconces. He held it up so that the light spread throughout the room. His mind touched on what she had just said. She declared her intention to do *anything* within her power to save her father. That staunch vow intrigued him. Just how far would the young woman go?

"Would you really do *anything* to free him?" he asked, raising one brow as he stared boldly into her eyes.

"Anything!"

She needed to play for time. If her father was given as much as a week's reprieve, it was possible Tobias could gather together enough money to buy her father a bit of justice. Corruption was rampant at all levels of government; silver and gold, not ethics, ruled England these days.

"Indeed!"

He wondered just what kind of woman she was. There was an innocence in those huge hazel eyes of hers, yet he knew it might well be feigned. Living among thieves and murderers made her morals a matter for consideration.

Boldly, Quentin's eyes raked over her from head to toe in undisguised admiration. Oh, but she was tempting. Incredibly lovely. The highwayman's daughter. Gentleman James's only child. As rare a jewel as was ever stolen on the road.

Devondra flushed as she took not of the stranger's bold gaze. Undoubtedly her, like some of the others, could be bought were enough coins to cross his palm. Wasn't that where this conversation was leading?

She said quickly. "I . . . I'll make you a reasonable offer."

"Reasonable?" He smiled, doubly intrigued. This matter was becoming interesting. "And just what might you consider that to be?"

For just a moment she was flustered. The way his eyes were glittering made her nervous. Just how greedy was he? Though Devondra would have liked to keep her calm and barter with this man, she was desperate. What was money compared to her father's life?

"Fifty pounds!"

Her answer amused him, and he laughed. " 'Tis not at all what I had in mind."

Licking her lips, she braced herself for the bargaining she knew would follow. So this man was just as greedy as the other so-called men of justice. So be it then. If she had to spend the rest of her days toiling at the inn to recompense this man, she would gladly do it were it to mean freedom for James Stafford. "Sixty!"

Again he laughed. Was she really so naive as to be unaware of his desires, or was she merely being coy. "I want much more," he said huskily, his eyes devouring her again.

Devondra stiffened. "I'm prepared to offer you anything you wish," she said coldly, angered by his chuckling.

He looked at her for a long moment, his eyes expressionless, then he said bluntly, " 'Tis not money I want but *you*."

"Me?" An icy hand seemed to clamp around her throat.
Surely he couldn't mean that the way it sounded. Ah, but
he did, she realized as she heard his next words.

"I will see to it that your father is spared if you will spend
this night with me."

She sucked in her breath. At first her voice was only a
whisper in her own mind; then somehow she asked, "What
did you say?"

"You heard me." He took a step toward her. His voice
was deep. "What I propose, madam, is that I use my influence
to free your father if you would bed me."

He couldn't have made his meaning any clearer than that.
Devondra's mouth tightened in anger. What manner of man
would make such an immoral request? "You bastard!" The
arrogance of the man, to so casually suggest such a thing!
Trembling, she sank down on an old wooden bench.

"Call me what you will, that is the bargain I offer."

No! The word echoed inside her, a silent, fierce protest.
He must be one of the lunatics from Bedlam if he thought
she would agree. *Never!* Tobias would come, and he would
bring the others with him to free her father. It was only a
matter of time.

Time, she thought. Already the hourglass was running
low. She closed her eyes, trying to gain control of her emotions, but it did no good. All she could see was her father's
face when he was sentenced to hang. Tomorrow. So soon.
Too soon. With her father to hang the next day there was
little time to find a way to save James Stafford.

*Tobias will think of something. He will come. He and the
others will think of a way to rescue my father. They will!*

But she had to face the truth: Tobias wasn't coming. To
even attempt a rescue would be tantamount to idiocy. There

was no way that even the boldest renegade could get past
these walls. Nor could even the bravest fool have any hope
of stealing her father from the hangman. It was useless to
hold such a dream. Hopeless.

*I'll find someone else to help me. Surely I can find someone
with compassion. Someone who will understand.*

In London? She put her face in her hands. Hardly. It was
a city well known for its heartlessness. And what was more,
even if she did find someone willing to help her, it would
not be without a price—more than likely the same price
this man had put upon his intervention.

What can I do then? What hope is there?

Quentin watched the various expressions mold and shape
her face, watched her anger melt into confusion, and knew
he had won. "Your father has little time left. Unless . . ."
He inclined his head slightly toward her.

Her eyes were slits of fury. "You, sir, are no gentleman."
So many men had tried to seduce her, but she had always
prided herself in keeping her maidenhead. It was a woman's
treasure, her father had told her. Now this man was suggesting that he make claim to her for his own lustful delights.
It would be nothing to him; a moment of panting pleasure.
Unimportant and soon forgotten in another woman's arms.
Devondra, being the woman that she was, wanted to offer
her heart before consummating a union with her body.

"Ah, but I *am* a gentleman, a gentleman who treasures
beauty such as yours." He crossed his arms before his chest.
"But what I am not is a man who uses flowery words in
wooing. I saw you; I wanted you."

"And that makes what you just proposed all right?" She
shook her head. "No matter your supposed reasons, a woman
likes to be wooed, not bargained with!" she hissed.

He shrugged. "I haven't the time. I am a busy man. But
I came all the way to Newgate to help you. And help you

I will." He paused. "And if you accept, I get what I want and you get what you desire. What could be simpler than that?"

"Ohhhhhhh!" She bolted to her feet. Moving toward him, she was so enraged that she pummeled him with her fists. Alas, his chest was so hard, so firm, that it was she who suffered injury and not he. Tears stung her eyes as she looked down at her fingers.

"Enough!"

Suddenly Devondra found herself held tightly in an embrace, her breasts brushing against his hard chest. He whirled her around and she hung suspended in his arms, her toes dangling above the floor as if she weighed nothing at all. She met his glittering saphire eyes, and though she knew she should feel an aversion to him, another emotion swept over her. A quivering tension coiled in her stomach. A shiver rippled through her as she looked at the chiseled strength of his lips.

Slowly Quentin lowered his head, intending to take advantage of the moment and kiss her. Were her lips really as soft as they appeared?

Glaring at him, Devondra sensed his intent. "Put me down!" Quentin obeyed, though reluctantly, letting her slide down the hard length of his body. Hastily, Devondra pulled away. "You act as if you have already made your claim."

"I have," he answered. "It is only for you to make your decision."

She would have liked to throw her refusal in his face but knew such a reaction to be foolish. Frustration welled up inside her. "What choice do I have?"

"None." His voice was soft. Deep. Intimate, as he said, "But I promise you that it will be far from the sacrifice you envision." His fingers were surprisingly soft as he touched her cheek. "It will be a night you will remember all your life."

The touch of his hand made her shiver. It was an erotic caress that seemed to make every nerve in her body come alive. Nevertheless, she pulled away violently. "I'll never enjoy being pawed by such as you!" She shook her head, sending her dark brown hair swirling in a soft swish around her shoulders. "I'll remember that when I turned to a man for mercy he took advantage of my plight for his own lust," she answered haughtily.

"You are the one who said you would do anything to save your father," he chided. "I am merely accepting your offer. Now you must accept mine." Already he was formulating a plan in his mind. There were several men of law who owed him favors. He would collect the debts in the form of the highwayman's life. Odds were they would catch the rogue again anyhow, and send him to his proper justice.

"Why me?" she breathed. "You don't even know me."

"I know all there is to know. That you are beautiful and desirable." But perhaps there was more to it, Quentin thought. Perhaps it was a far different motive than lust that brought him here. Was it possible that this was his subtle means of revenge against the man who had wronged him? He didn't want to believe that about himself. "It will take quite a sum of money and the proper influences to free your father. Any man wants a return on such an investment."

"Indeed!" Devondra stiffened and turned away, carefully sorting out her thoughts. How could she do otherwise than agree? "All right then. In return for my father's life I will do what you will." The bargain had been made: her father's life for her virtue.

"Good." So she was to be his. Looking at her, Quentin felt the heavy thud of his heart against his throat. Oh, but he was impatient. This would be a night he would long remember.

Quentin removed his jacket and draped it around her shoulders; then, with a gentle pressure on her arm, he led her outside the room into the dingy corridor. One by the one the doors slammed behind her as they made the long trek through the maze. Then they were outside.

"My father. I must tell him . . ." Tell him what? That she was buying his freedom with her virtue? Her father would never allow her to make such a sacrifice. *'Tis not his choice to make. It is mine.*

The last door slammed behind her with great finality, resounding in her ears. There was no turning back. No chance to change her mind. Even so, for just a moment Devondra had the urge to flee, to run from this man who had made such an intimate claim on her.

"Shall we go?" Quentin asked softly.

Devondra paused to glance over her shoulder at the great fortress. A shudder racked through her body and she thought to herself that leaving this horrible place with such a man as this was almost as frightening an experience as entering it had been.

The air smelled so clean after the staleness of the cell. She breathed in the freshness deeply, then whispered, "Yes."

Quentin led her to where his horse was tethered. Taking the reins, he swung up easily into his saddle, then reached down for her, pulling her up in front of him. She felt the great strength of his arms as he clasped her around the waist. Then, before Devondra had time to reflect on what lay ahead, they were off. The great hoofs of the horse struck sparks as it traveled down the cobbled street, leaving Newgate far behind.

Chapter Seven

It was a chilling ride. All along the way Devondra viewed the dimly lit streets of London as if through a dream-inspired haze. This couldn't really be happening to her. Her father's capture, the awful journey to Newgate and now this trek through the city with a cold-hearted stranger was nothing more than a nightmare!

Hopeful that this was the case, she lifted her trembling left hand. Purposefully she pinched her right forearm, hoping to feel nothing, gasping as she felt pain. This was no dream!

Quentin heard her intake of breath and felt her tremble. Believing her to be chilled by the night air, he tightened his arms around her as he whispered, "The journey is not long. Wakefield Manor is past the city's gates, just beyond the forest."

"The forest . . ."

"A dangerous place; I agree." He raised one brow, smiling contemptuously. "It's said to be brimming with highwaymen; but then, you wouldn't know anything about that."

Devondra's face flushed as she remembered having once or twice accompanied her father on his late-night "business" ventures.

Quentin made no attempt to hide his disdain for those fellows who made their livings outside the law. "Thugs, robbers and blackguards!" They made traveling perilous. They abused, threatened and terrorized the law-abiding citizens of England.

Thinking of her father, Devondra hotly came to the defense of all highwaymen. "They are but men who have been forced to do what they must to survive. Cromwell, that common oaf who has set himself up as England's ruler, was unjust to outlaw these men for being loyal to their king. He forced them to penury and thus to a way of life that means taking what they must."

"*Stealing,* I believe, is what it is called! In truth, I would venture to say that not one thing is sacred to such as they. Not purse, nor coat, nor watch, nor—"

Again Devondra was quick to justify their actions. "Most are good men, gentlemen of the road whose only crime was to be defeated in their valiant effort to defend the Stuarts." An effort that had failed pitifully. King Charles had been beheaded and his son was a refugee in France, awaiting his chance to return to his rightful place.

"Gentlemen?" He shook his head violently. "Nay. Outlaws are what they are." For all he knew, she was dishonest as well.

"Outlaw?" No, not her father. The blood of crusaders, minstrels, jousting champions and nobility flowed in the veins of James Stafford. Indeed, in Devondra's eyes he was a hero, a man whose glowing hazel eyes melted women's hearts.

"Yes, outlaw!" Cautiously Quentin poised his hand near the hilt of his sword just in case any follower of Gentleman

James showed his masked face. Or any other highwayman, for that matter.

"I have no fear of *them*. Indeed, I would feel far safer with any of them than I would with you, sir," she said beneath her breath.

Quentin was angered by her barbs. "Then your trust is sorely misplaced." But what did he expect? Having lived among the rogues who haunted the forests and heaths, the girl could hardly be expected to exhibit good judgment.

"Misplaced?" Remembering the fellowship she had shared with her father's comrades, she vehemently disagreed. But what use was it to argue? Any words she might say would be wasted on such a man as this.

It was a dark night, with only a half moon to give light. The leaves and branches of the trees looked like black lace against the dark gray backdrop of the sky as they rode through the forest. Except for the hooting of an owl it was starkly quiet, as if the birds and animals were wary of any intruders, Quentin thought. No doubt if they could talk the creatures would have chilling tales to relate. Well, no masked man would dare take him unaware. So determined, he was conscious of every sound, of even the slightest movement.

Only when they were near the outer edge of the forest did he dare relax his guard. "We'll soon be there." He took in a deep breath of fresh air. "Ah, how good it is to get far away from the soot-poisoned air of London."

Devondra cast a quick glance over her shoulder at the seemingly continous line of roofs and chimneys far off in the distance. It was true; the increasing use of coal in the furnaces of London contaminated the air with smoke. And yet, despite the unpleasantness, she would have gladly returned. "How far . . .?

He pointed. "Look. You can see the lighted windows of Wakefield Manor through the trees."

"Wakefield Manor." Opening her eyes wide, she stared at the flickering squares that could be seen from the hillside and shuddered as she contemplated her arrival at the huge house. With sickening clarity she realized her predicament. She had rendered herself up to a man she didn't even know, had put herself at a stranger's mercy.

I don't know anything about him. Her heart hammered with fear as she remembered hearing about sadistic brutes whose pleasures of the flesh included beatings, violence and sometimes even another's death. How did she know that this lord of Wakefield Manor wasn't such a deviant? "Please . . ." She wanted desperately to go back. Even the horrors of Newgate were preferable to the unknown. Yet how could she be so selfish as to plead for herself when her father's life was at stake? Whether she liked it or not, this man's bargain was Gentleman James's only salvation.

Quentin urged his mount into a faster gallop. "You will soon be warmed by the heat of the hearthfire," he said, *and by my passion,* he thought but did not add. Bloody hell, but he was impatient. The fragrance of her hair, the closeness of her body and the memory that she was his, if only for this evening, were potent aphrodisiacs.

"Warmed?" Again she shivered, doubting that even the hottest fires could thaw the ice that now formed around her heart. Tensing her body from head to toe she fought a sudden hysterical impulse to pull free of his grasp, jump from the horse and run through the forest, back toward London.

Don't be such a coward, she scolded herself silently. Panic would do neither her father nor herself any good. Instead, she must force herself to remain calm. She had made a bargain that must be kept, no matter the consequences. So thinking, she tensed her body from head to toe, lifted her chin and mentally prepared herself as best she could for what was to come. She remained tight-lipped the rest of the way to the manor, ignoring the churning in her stomach and the weakness in her knees when she was at last helped down from the horse.

"Follow me." The words were spoken as his eyes moved slowly over her. For just a moment Devondra feared that her legs would give way, that she would collapse right then and there. She was terrified by what was to come. Would he fall upon her immediately, forcing her to give in to his lust? Or would he have at least some tact about his seduction. Deep in thought, she stood motionless for a long moment; then, taking a deep breath, she followed as he led her up the pathway to the manor's thick wooden door.

"So, into the wolf's den . . ." she whispered. A wolf's den that was furnished opulently, despite the somberness Cromwell's followers displayed in furnishings and clothing. As she entered the dim hallway, she noted at once that the lord of the manor had a penchant for colorful velvets, carved wood, Venetian glass, fine paintings and silver.

Quentin heard but chose to ignore her sarcastic comment about his home being a wolf's den. Slowly, insolently, his eyes moved over her as he shut the door behind them. Moving toward the fireplace, he hurried to start a fire. "There now you can feel free to make yourself comfortable." Removing his cloak and hat, he gestured for her to likewise divest herself of her outer garments.

Comfortable? "No!" she said quickly, tugging the folds of her woolen shawl more tightly around her. Devondra's eyes appraised the man of the house. The firelight emphasized the planes of his chiseled features, the mystifying depths of his blue eyes, and highlighted the red in his auburn hair. He made a dashing figure. There would be some women who would envy her being with him. Would actually welcome what was to come. But Devondra was not such a woman. And yet, she couldn't help but wonder what might

have happened had they met under different circumstances.
No doubt she would have been irresistibly drawn to him.

Quentin took note of the stubborn manner in which she
clung to her shawl. "So you wish to keep your wrap. As
you will." Walking toward her, he reached out and touched
the dark hair falling at her temples, then closed his fingers
in a fist. She was so very lovely. Looking at her now, it was
hard to believe she lived among rogues and thieves. How
true it was that looks could be deceiving.

Feeling the touch of his hand, Devondra cringed. Now that
the moment was at hand, she was assailed by nervousness,
wondering if she would have the fortitude to do what she
had so boldly promised. Again she feared a cruel assault.
The lord of Wakefield Manor, however, proved to have
more finesse than that, at least for the moment. Quickly
summoning his servants, he soon procured a table laden
with food. There was cold roast beef and mutton, plates of
warmed vegetables seasoned with herbs, a loaf of bread and
an assortment of fruit—apples, plums and pears. And wine.

Usually abstaining from strong drink, Devondra took three
long gulps from the glass offered to her, letting the golden
liquid warm her. Perhaps it would give her courage for the
ordeal to come.

"Easy . . . There is no hurry." Seeing that she had already
emptied her glass, he refilled it. The wine would relax her.
Perhaps then she would stop looking at him as if he were
some sort of ogre. "You may partake of as much as you
wish."

Crossing his arms, putting up one foot on a large stone
of the hearth, Quentin freely gazed at her, comparing her
in his mind to all the other women he knew, deciding at
once that she was much prettier. Her wide hazel eyes alone
threatened to enchant any man who gazed too long into their
depths. Moreover, there was an air of breeding about her,

or perhaps a haughtiness that was intriguing. Highwayman's daughter or not, she acted as if she were a princess.

Devondra was disturbed by his staring—as if she were part of the menu. Worse yet, there was a gleam in the depths of his eyes that was worrisome. Was it any wonder she quickly said, "Shall we eat, sir?" Walking across the room as gracefully as she could, she took a seat at the small round table.

"Eat?" Aspiring to more amorous activities, he nonetheless quickly remembered his manners. "As you wish." With a slight bow, he sat in the chair opposite her. "Your name ... Indeed, I don't remember if you have told me," he breathed.

"Devondra."

"Devondra . . ." An unusual name. He whispered it again. "Devondra."

"And you; how are you called?"

"Quentin Wesley Wakefield."

Devondra's eyes met Quentin's over the rim of her glass as she drank her wine. Strange; she had been determined to hate him because of the bargain he had made, and yet as they sat there together it was as if a cocoon of enchantment enclosed them. As if they moved in slow motion, she noted details about him. Gestures, expressions, his smile. There is much about him that is like my father, Devondra thought. The same strength, the same handsomeness, a similar charm. Why, for the moment, at least, she was almost enjoying herself. That is, until she remembered why she was there.

"Tell me about yourself," he commanded, picking up his knife and fork. He soon realized he was not hungry.

She eyed him quizzically, warily. "What is it that you would know?"

Usually a master at conversation, Quentin now floundered for something to say, all the while vitally aware of the

woman who sat across from him in the dimly lit room. "Tell
me about the men in your life. Is there an intended or a
lover?"

She shook her head. "No." As soon as the word was out
she wondered if she should have told a lie. Perhaps then he
would leave her alone.

Her answer pleased him. So he would not have to compete
with another man for her attentions and affections were
tonight to go as well as he hoped. "Just as well . . ." he said,
more to himself than to her.

For a long moment he said no more but just feasted his
eyes on her. He longed to caress the ripe firmness of her
body, to strip away those drab garments she was wearing
and feel her velvet flesh. Lord, did any woman have a right
to be so beautiful? She was like a rare jewel, exquisite. Did
any man have a right to possess such a woman, bargain or
not?

Rising, Quentin walked over to the fireplace to start a
fire, not because it was chilly but for something to do. He
watched as if flared up. "Devondra . . ." He shifted from
foot to foot, his eyes straying to the stairs, at the head of
which was a large feather bed. How odd that he was so torn
between lifting her up in his arms, carrying her up the steps,
making passionate love to her while at the same time feeling
conscience-bound to set her free of the damnable bargain
he had made. Was it any wonder that he scowled?

Devondra's reverie was shattered as she took note of the
expression on his face. "My father. You haven't changed
your mind. You will help him."

"Help him?" Quickly he nodded. "Yes. Yes." He had never
been a man to break his word, no matter the outcome.

She sighed with relief. "For a moment I . . . I feared . . ."

"That I would prove to be an unscrupulous bastard?"
Sitting down on the hearth stones, he stretched out his lean,

muscular legs, managing to look far more at ease than he felt. He regretted having put the log on the fire, for it was suddenly getting much too hot in the room. Reaching up, he tugged at his collar. "You need not worry. I always keep my bargains."

Devondra hung her head. "Then so will I."

Dragging his fingers through his thick auburn hair, he frowned. Why had he ever proposed such a thing? Surely not because he was without female companionship. Whatever the reason, he felt decidedly ill at ease now. He wanted her to come to his bed because she wanted him, not because she was being coerced.

"You will let me fall upon you to save your father's life." His tone was scathing.

His forthrightness stunned her, and she dropped her spoon. "If you want to put it so crudely."

"And had there been no such bargain, what then?" Another time, another place, might they have become lovers? His somber eyes stared at her so heatedly that she nearly felt their warmth.

Devondra fought against the sudden shameful tears that stung her eyes. "Then I would have had to find another way to save my father." She would willingly beg, borrow or steal the money to bribe her father's gaolers.

"I see." Another man, another bargain perhaps. But he had made his claim first.

"I love my father very much."

"Apparently." Which was too bad, because the devious, thieving bastard didn't deserve that kind of love. He was no better than the common pickpockets who haunted London's alleys, even if he did dress himself in finery and set himself apart as a so-called "knight of the road." Quentin shrugged. "Because of that and not because of any care I have for him, I will commute his sentence."

Hastily, Quentin summoned one of his servants, a tall young man he knew to be a skilled horseman. Taking paper and pen in hand, he scrawled a missive that would instruct the warden of Newgate to exchange Gentleman James's hanging for a prison sentence, which was nearly as bad as being hanged, in Quentin's opinion. Being condemned to Newgate was much the same as being sent straight to hell.

"Richard, take this to Newgate, posthaste! Hand it directly to Ebenezer."

"Aye, sir." The deference with which the messenger treated the master of Wakefield gave Devondra the opinion that they might well have fought beside each other in the war.

"There, 'tis done."

"For which I am most grateful." And thus it was time, as her father always said, to "pay the piper."

"Grateful." For some reason he loathed her use of the word. Perhaps It made him feel guilty. "Grateful, indeed."

"That you have saved my father's life." She clenched and unclenched her fists nervously. Until now her experience with men had been confined to kisses and gropings in the dark. She had vowed to save her virtue for the man she loved, but it was too late now. Or was it? She looked up at Quentin Wakefield.

"What now . . .?" Certainly she knew what was on *his* mind.

Her breath caught in her throat as she said, "That is up to you, sir." Would he let her go? Would he prove, after all, to be a gentleman? She could only hope.

Once again his eyes traveled over her body, drinking in her loveliness. It was obvious, now that her father's life had been spared, that she was anxious to be away from him. But what had he expected? Had he hoped she would freely offer herself to him? If so, he had been dreaming.

"How unfortunate that your being here with me tonight was naught but business."

She swallowed nervously, uncertain how to react. "Yes." And yet, if that were so, why was her heart suddenly beating so rapidly?

"Perhaps I should do something to change that." In a single fluid motion he rose and walked toward her.

In the fathomless depths of his eyes she saw the stirring of passion, and it made her tremble all over. "What do you mean?"

He answered in actions, not words. Reaching out, he stroked her arm, then knelt down, his face level with hers. Slowly one hand slid around her waist, bringing her up against him. The fingers of his other hand traced the line of her jaw, the contours of her face. His face came closer. "Shall we seal the bargain?"

Devondra could not answer. She could hardly breathe. It was as if all the air had emptied from her lungs the moment his lips touched hers. Gently at first, then with the arousal of desire, he explored her mouth.

Though at first she fought against it, Devondra's icy reserve began to melt. Her head whirled in a dizzying awareness of him.

The kiss was infinitely more pleasing than she could have imagined. His tongue touching hers tasted of the wine they had sipped. Returning his kiss with an unrestrained abandon, she felt desire spread languidly through her body, working its way from her knees to the top of her head. Time seemed to stand frozen. It was like an enchantment, a spell. She waited to see what would happen next.

Hesitantly at first, then with an increasing measure of boldness, she mimicked the gentle exploration of his lips and tongue, helpless against the powerful tide of desire that consumed her. A quivering sensation shot through her body as she felt his hand slide down to cup the soft fullness of her breast.

"So lovely . . ." His words came out in quick, panting breaths as his lips moved down her slim neck. Then he found her mouth again.

Quentin's kiss went far beyond a mere touching of lips. His tongue searched the moist cavern of her mouth in a gentle, exploring caress that intensified her newly found passion. How long he kissed her she did not know, she had lost all knowledge of time. Her world was in his arms, his nearness her only reality. Wraping her arms around him, she ardently embraced him, pushing away her modesty, her fear, as her senses clamored for him. His kisses, she hungered for his kisses.

"Devondra!" Lifting his mouth from hers, Quentin stared down into her flushed face. The heat of his body was steadily climbing. Standing up, he brought her with him, pulling her up against him, teaching her what male arousal felt like. Then he was sweeping her up in his arms and carrying her toward the stairs.

Gently he put her down upon the soft feather mattress, then positioned himself beside her. His hand closed over her breast to begin a slow, leisurely exploration. Tugging at her bodice, he bared first one breast and then the other, smiling at her sudden movement to cover her exposed flesh. He was surprised that she was such a modest young thing. Yet, instead of cooling his desire, she charmed him and fired him to a passion he had never felt before. Dropping his head, he kissed the valley between her breasts, then caressed each soft mound with his lips and tongue, teasing the peaks until she gasped.

Devondra had feared his lovemaking. Now, as his tongue and hands played on her body making it ring and quiver like a fine instrument, her mind whirled in confusion. Her defenses were devastatingly demolished by the cravings of her own body.

I am but fulfilling my part of the bargin, she thought to herself. And yet if that was so, why were her arms locked so tightly around his neck? Why was she filled with such longing? Why wasn't she protesting as he caressed the peaks of her breasts? She ached to be naked against him. Did that make her a wanton?

Quentin breathed deeply of her perfume. The enticing fragrance invaded his flaring nostrils, engulfing him. He didn't care who or what she was; he only knew that it seemed as if she had been made for him. Even now her gentle curves fit against the length of his hard, muscular body. "Devondra . . ." Removing his shirt, he pressed their naked chests together, shivering at the sensation. It was vibrantly arousing, sending a flash as rapid as quicksilver through his veins.

Slowly, leisurely, Quentin stripped away Devondra's garments. Then his fingers lingered as they wandered down her stomach to explore the texture of her skin. He sought the indention of her navel, then moved lower to tangle his fingers in the soft wisps of hair at the joining of her legs. Moving back, he let his eyes enjoy what his hands had set free.

"Do you have any idea how much I want you? Do you?" he breathed. Then he laughed. "Of course you do. That's the point in being so beautiful, isn't it? To tempt men beyond endurance." Taking her hand, he pressed it to the firm flesh of his arousal then bent to kiss her, his mouth keeping hers a willing prisoner for a long, long time.

The warmth and heat of his lips and the memory of her fingers touching that private part of him sent a sweet ache flaring through Devondra's whole body. Growing bold, she allowed her hands to explore him, delighting at the touch of the firm flesh that covered his ribs, the broad shoulders,

the muscles of his arms, the lean length of his back. He was
so perfectly formed, beautiful for a man. With a soft sigh
her fingers curled in the thick, springy hair that furred his
chest. Her fingers lightly circled in imitation of what he had
done to her.

"Blessed saints!" He had made a very good bargain, one
he knew he would never regret. Tugging impatiently at his
clothes, he flung them aside. She was his, he would never
let her go. Not now."

They lay together kissing, touching, rolling over and over
on the soft bed. His hands were doing wondrous things to
her, making her writhe and groan. Every inch of her body
caught fire as passion exploded between them. He moved
against her, sending waves of pleasure exploding along every
nerve in her body. The swollen length of him brushed against
her thighs. Then he was covering her, his manhood probing
at the entrance of her core.

Suddenly Devondra tensed, fearing the unknown. "I'm
not what you think," she whispered, "I'm—"

His kisses stopped any further words she might have
uttered. She felt his maleness at the fragile entryway to her
womanhood as he pierced that delicate membrane with a
sudden thrust. For one brief moment there was pain, but
then Devondra's passion rallied. Wanting to relish this new
feeling, she pushed upward.

"Bigod!" Only when he entered her did Quentin realize
the truth. It couldn't be. A virgin? This woman who kept
company with England's most devious lot was a virgin!
Even so, he could not pull away. She was so warm, so tight
around him that he closed his eyes with agonized pleasure
as he slid within her, moving with infinite care. He did not
want to hurt her, he wanted to initiate her fully into the
depths of passion. And love. Yes, love, for that was what

he felt at that moment. A tender feeling. Like the currents of the sea that surrounded England, his body drew hers.

Devondra's eyes showed first fright and then silent awe. It was as if she felt herself floating, soaring. Instinctively, she held Quentin tightly to her.

"Tighten your thighs around my waist," he instructed, moaning as she obeyed and moved in a rhythm that seemed to so perfectly match his. "Ah . . . yes . . ."

Devondra arched up to him with sensual urgency. She was melting inside, merging with him into one being. His lovemaking was like nothing she could ever have imagined, filling her, flooding her.

Quentin groaned as he felt the exquisite sensation of her warm flesh sheathing the length of him. He didn't want it to end. Highwayman's daughter she might be, but he wanted to keep her near him forever.

Richard spurred his horse along the road, determined in his mission. He had been told to get the piece of parchment to London as soon as it was humanly possible, and he intended to obey that command, even if it meant riding through the most dangerous stretch of countryside in the dead of night. He would arrive in time. He would!

Clutching his sword, he was resolved. Compelled. Driven.

Alas, the sound of horses' hooves disturbed his concentration. Alarm knifed through him as he saw the ominous shapes of three men riding on the road behind him. Were they following him, or was it just a coincidence? His question was answered as he continued on his journey.

Bending close to the horse, he sought a firm grip on the reins as he rode at breakneck speed, for he knew it could be disastrous if he were caught. Nevertheless, his valiant effort was all for naught. Not only was he overtaken, he was surrounded.

"Do not stir on peril of your life," called out the tallest of the three men. Brandishing a pistol, he looked to be the type of man who would not tolerate any defiance. Nevertheless, Richard's dedication goaded him into rebelling against being taken. His resistance was short-lived. Pursued, tackled and wrestled to the ground, he was soon rendered helpless.

"Search him!"

Mounted on a midnight black horse was a man powerful of shoulder and torso, a highwayman by the look of him. He was so arrogant that he did not even try to hide his scarred face. In his hand was a pistol, primed, cocked and pointed right at Richard's heart.

"I have little money on my person, but you may take it."

A half-filled purse and a gold ring was quickly taken, but the highwayman was not satisfied. Making good on his threat, the highwayman rudely thrust his hands into Richard's pockets.

"What's this?"

Despite a struggle, the missive soon changed hands. Carefully unfolding it, the scarred highwayman slowly read the words written there. Then he smiled.

"So, Jamie has found a friend and been given a second chance." Purposefully, accompanied by Richard's gasp, he cruelly tore the parchment in two. "Too bad it was intercepted." He clucked his tongue. "Poor, poor, Jamie."

"No!" Reaching out, Richard sought frantically to retrieve the two halves of the missive but to no avail. His only reward for loyalty and honor was a brutal blow to his head that rendered him senseless.

Chapter Eight

Moonlight flooded the room as Devondra and Quentin lay naked in the aftermath of their lovemaking. Gazing into her eyes, he gently brushed back the tangled dark hair from her face. "I can't let you go now." She was his from this moment on.

Snuggling against him, she whispered the truth. "Nor do I want to go." Far from being the humiliating experience she had feared, her initiation into lovemaking had been a deeply stirring and sensual awakening.

Clasping her arms around her body, she remembered every touch, every kiss and caress. Their being together had been the most beautiful moment of her life, a mindless delight of the senses and the heart. Nothing in the world could have prepared her for that moment. It was as if she had been starving all her life and had only now discovered food. But only Quentin Wakefield could whet her appetite. Now she wanted to be with him forever. To walk beside him, share in his dreams. But what were his intentions?

Kathryn Kramer

He cupped her face with his hand. "Tonight something happened. Something that has never happened to me before." His emotions were totally out of control, so much so that the thought of parting from her was deeply disturbing.

"Nor to me." So, he did feel it too, she thought.

He bent his head to kiss her soft, open lips. A kiss that seemed to last forever.

When Quentin finally lifted his mouth from hers Devondra could only stare. A deep yearning rose in her heart. Would he ask her to marry him? Or would he think her too far beneath him, she who was a highwayman's daughter? And If he did, could she be content with being his mistress? Could she relegate herself to such a relationship?

Lying there watching him, she was as still as stone. How did she feel about her? Did he care for her, or had it been only his body's cravings that he had assuaged? When he had entered her she had felt her heart move, had been full of him, full of love. But what of Quentin? What was he thinking now?

Quentin closed his eyes, remembering the passion they had shared. Never had he realized that making love could be like this, such shattering ecstasy. And yet what to do about it? Marriage?

No, that was out of the question. Cromwell would be unforgiving, marriage with the daughter of a former Royalist, a man who robbed carriages, would ruin him. And yet he didn't want to let her go. Emotionally, at least, he was tied to her. She had never known another man—How could he not feel responsible for her?

"Your father will be in Newgate for at least a year." A period of time in which she would be very vulnerable.

"Newgate!" She shuddered, though she had to admit imprisonment was better than hanging. At least he would be alive. And where there was life, there was always hope.

She had reason to be concerned, thus he hurried to reassure her. "I'll do all that I can to see that he is dealt with fairly." He reached out to stroke her cheek. "In the meantime, you will need someone to take care of you. Someone you can trust. Someone who cares." He paused, then declared, "As I do."

Her eyes searched his face. "I really believe that you do." She had judged him unfairly then, she thought, moving forward to brush his mouth with her lips. That simple gesture said all she wanted to say, that she cared too. For the moment the subject of his intentions were forgotten.

Slowly his hands closed around her shoulders, pulling her to him, answering her shy kiss with a passion that made her gasp. "Then it's all settled." His hands roamed over her body, lingering on the fullness of her ripe breasts, leaving no part of her free of his touch.

She gave herself up to the fierce emotions that raced through her, answering his touch with searching hands, returning his caresses. Closing her arms around his neck, she offered herself to him, writhing against him in a slow, delicate dance.

Sweet, hot desire fused their bodies together as he leaned against her. His strength mingled with her softness, his hands moving up her sides, warming her with his heat. Like a fire his lips burned a path from one breast to the other, bringing forth spirals of sensation that swept over her like a storm.

Quentin's mouth fused with hers, his kiss deepening as his touch grew bolder. Devondra luxuriated in the pleasure of his lovemaking, stroking and kissing him back. He slid his hands between their bodies, poised above her. The tip of his maleness pressed against her, then entered her softness in a slow but strong thrust, joining her in that most intimate of embraces. He kissed her as he fused their bodies together and her heart cried out from the depths of her soul.

Quentin filled her with his love, leaving her breathless. It was like falling over the banister. Falling and never quite hitting the ground. Her arms locked around him as she arched to meet his body in a sensuous dance, forgetting all her inhibitions as she expressed her love. A sensation burst through her, a warm explosion.

Even when the sensual magic was over they clung to each other, unwilling to have the moment end. Devondra was reluctant to have him leave her body, felt that surely the fire they had ignited tonight would meld them together for all eternity. Smiling, she lay curled in the crook of Quentin's arm, and he, his passion spent, lay close against her, his body pressing against hers.

"As soon as it is light we'll ride into London and gather your belongings," he whispered, still holding her close. "I'll do everything in my power to make certain you are comfortable here."

"Oh, I'll be comfortable." So comfortable that she felt a sharp tinge of guilt. While she was living in luxury her father would be suffering. No, she couldn't be that selfish, that disloyal. "My father . . ."

"Would want what is best for you."

"No!"

He put his finger to her lips. "Yes."

"No . . ." But even as she argued she knew he was right.

"I'll see to it that he is given special privileges during his stay in prison." There were several turnkeys who owed him favors, the others could surely be bribed.

"Then I am grateful once again." With a sigh, she snuggled up against him, burying her face in the warmth of his chest, breathing in the manly scent of him. She didn't want to sleep, not now. She wanted to savor this moment of being together but as he caressed her back, tracing his fingers along her spine, she drifted off.

When she awoke Devondra was disappointed to find that she was alone. "Quentin?" Wrapping a blanket around her naked body, she quickly rose from the bed, calling his name over and over. Then, from the window, she saw him riding in the direction of London. "Going without me." Yet she was not alarmed. No doubt he had been called into London on business. Well, she had business there as well.

I must see my father and tell him what has happened. How overjoyed he would be when he realized he was to be spared. But what would he think of Quentin Wakefield? Would he give her his blessing?

Devondra's hands trembled as she dressed, all the while mulling over the matter in her mind. She would tell her father everything. Tactfully, she would do what she could to make him understand why she had left so suddenly and where she had gone. Her father had to come to terms with what had happened.

"I'm not a child." No, not any more, and her father had to realize that. And he had to know that although he had never been beholden to any man before, things had changed. He needed friends were he to survive Newgate. Friends like Quentin Wakefield.

Running down the stairs and pushing through the front door, Devondra hurried to the stables, where she borrowed a horse. Then she was off, riding at a furious pace.

Following the winding pathways through the forest, past the city's gates, over the cobbled stones, she soon saw London Bridge looming up on the horizon. The early morning sun had risen in a cloudless blue sky, gilding the straw roofs of the buildings atop London Bridge. The wooden buildings leaned toward each other like gossiping neighbors.

"Violets. Gillyflowers. Lavender. How about a fresh bouquet?" A young girl held a bouquet toward Devondra hopefully.

"How much?" Her father so loved flowers; she thought he would appreciate a small bouquet. "How much for the lavender?"

"Tupence!" The girl's blue eyes sparkled as she looked up at her.

"Tupence?" Alas, she realized she had no money with her. Devondra shook her head, moving in the direction of Newgate.

The cobbled streets of London seethed with traffic; carts, carriages, and here and there a sedan chair, as well as pedestrians. Wheeled vehicles stirred up dust as they rattled by and soiled the garments of any who foolishly got in their way.

The walkways of London were a cacophony of sounds, animal as well as human. Horses neighed and dogs barked as they chased after wagons and cats. Men were shouting, women and children chattering. She was anxious to see her father, so anxious that she swore at the people who crowded the street and blocked her way.

"Merry-go-up, what is going on?" she called out.

"There was a hanging!" an old man shouted back, quickly handing a coin to a young woman selling oranges.

"Hanging?"

Devondra's blood ran cold as she looked in the direction of Tyburn Tree. There, dangling from the three-legged structure, she could see the silhouette of a poor unfortunate victim.

"Whose hanging?" The man was so interested in peeling his orange that he didn't answer until Devondra shouted again, "Whose hanging?"

He smiled, exposing his missing front teeth. "Why Gentleman James, 'at's whose."

Chapter Nine

The dreadful tolls of the great bell of St. Sepulchre's Church reverberated over and over again in Devondra's ears as she stared at the lifeless body swinging from the gallows. "Dead!" She was horrified. As she dismounted and slowly walked toward the gallows, she was filled with a soul-numbing grief that was nearly too much to bear. A grief that she gave vent to in an uncontrollable scream. The cry of a wounded animal.

"Miss . . . ?"

Several onlookers formed a circle around her, staring at her as if they feared she had lost her mind. And were the truth to be told, she had, at least for that moment.

"She's gone bloody mad!"

Ignoring them, Devondra closed her eyes and hugged her slender arms around her body. Sinking to her knees, she rocked back and forth, moaning over and over as she mourned the man she had so deeply loved. The man who had been more than a father. Friend, companion and hero,

James Stafford had been the very center of his daughter's world. Now he was dead.

"Father!" Closing her eyes, she sought to block out the gruesome sight of his swinging body, remembering instead what a handsome figure of a man he had been. A true gentleman, no matter his profession. A brave man.

As if the years had suddenly melted away, she remembered how dashing he had looked in his bright red Royalist uniform, wide-brimmed black hat and black leather boots. Mounted on a white horse, he had sadly waved good-bye to seven-year-old Devondra, hiding his tears as he had promised her that he would be back soon. It was the only promise he had ever broken, though that had not been his fault. How was he to know that the Civil War would last four bitter years?

"And now you have been taken from me again. . . ." But this time he would never be coming back. *I failed to save him. The bargain I made was meaningless.*

Guilt swept through her as she remembered the passionate hours she had spent at Wakefield Manor. She should have been at Newgate, should have been with her father in his last few precious hours. Instead she had been sharing Quentin Wakefield's bed. A man who had vilely betrayed not only her, but her father.

"I will commute his sentence," he had promised, scribbling with his pen. "Your father will be in Newgate for at least a year. I'll do all that I can to see that he is dealt with fairly. In the meantime you will need someone to take care of you. Someone you can trust. Someone who cares. I do."

"Liar!" He had whispered loving, tender words, had vowed to save her father's life, but the man in whose arms she had spent the night had failed to keep his word. "No! No!"

Though she was not a woman who was prone to tears,

she gave vent to them now. She had given him her trust. For a brief moment she had let him into her heart. Now her dreams were shattered in the most brutal way. She had been cruelly deceived by a man who had taken her virtue while never intending to save her father from the hangman.

But what of the message he had written, of the messenger he had sent? Had it all been little more than a mime? A ridiculous jest meant to earn her gratitude and trust? As she viewed the silhouette of her father from the corner of her eye, it appeared so.

"Such a cruel world . . ." But only now, as she struggled to her feet, did she realize how cruel it could actually be. "Oh, Father . . ."

It was a puppeteer's misfortune to come upon the scene at that moment. Manipulating two marionettes, one obviously a replica of Gentleman James and the other the hangman, the gnomelike man had the audacity to reinact the execution.

"Gather round all ye who traverse between here and Hounslow Heath and I'll show ye well that crime does not pay." He made one of the puppets bob up and down. "Isn't that right Jimmy me boy?"

"That's right. That's right." The voice he used was nothing at all like the fame highwayman's. It was much too high-pitched. "Oh woe is me. Woe is me. Just look where my villainy has led me."

"Ye will dance at the end of a string," the other puppet proclaimed. "Betrayed for blood money, ye will kick out yer life dangling from Tyburn Tree." The puppeteer moved his hand up and down, sending the marionette bedecked in hangman's garb into a lively dance.

"No. No. You will not make a puppet out of me. I, Gentleman James, will die at no man's hand. No common hangman will put an end to me." Thus said, the puppeteer acted out a scene in which the condemned highwayman leaped off the scaffold before the hangman could touch him.

"And thus the gallant rogue kept his vow. The curtain on the last act was his, twitched down by his own hand. Bold and defiant to the last, Gentleman James met his—"

The puppeteer did not have a chance to finish the scene. Grief and anger welled up inside Devondra with such intensity that for a moment she lost all self-control. Leaping upon the hapless man, she tore the puppets from his hands and threw the "hangman" to the ground, crushing him beneath her heel, and then cradled the replica of her father to her breast.

"She's crazed!"

"Mad as a hatter!"

"Fetch the guards."

Convinced that she was dangerous, the crowd quickly dispersed, fleeing in all directions. Devondra was left in solitude at last to express her heartache and grief.

Forcing herself to regain her composure, she let the puppet fall from her hands. Reaching out, she touched her father's lifeless body. There was a dirt stain on his velvet breeches that she unthinkingly brushed off. Her father was so fastidious about his person. So handsome and well-groomed.

And yet, what does that matter now? James Stafford was far beyond knowing or caring about the things of this world. *He is gone forever.*

"He was brave to the end."

Recognizing the husky voice of Tobias, she whirled around, grateful to see the familiar face of her father's faithful friend. "I know. It was not in my father's character to ever act the coward."

"You would have been proud." Standing with his wide-brimmed, plumed hat in his hand, the paunchy little man

with the bulbous nose, curly red beard and sparkling green
eyes wiped away a tear with the back of his hand.

Devondra's voice was choked with emotion as she whispered, "I want you to tell me all that happened, but first . . ."

Hastily taking the sword from Tobias's scabbard, she
angrily hacked at the rope that secured her father to Tyburn
Tree. Unlike the bodies of other condemned men, Gentleman
James's body would not be left hanging to rot as a lesson to
others. Nor would his body be stolen by those who dissected
human corpses to satisfy their morbid needs.

"Help me!" Together, she and Tobias cut down her father's
body and put it on Quentin Wakefield's horse. "I'll see to
it that my father rests in peace. They won't ever touch him
again." Her father would be given a decent burial. This much
at least Quentin Wakefield owed her. "Then I will bring
down vengeance on he who deceived me. This I vow!"

Before anyone could stop her, Devondra climbed up
behind the stiff corpse of Gentleman James and, putting her
arms around him as she clung to the reins, galloped off.
Gasping and panting, Tobias followed along behind, knowing full well where she was headed: Hounslow Health, the
place where the dashing highwayman had made himself at
home.

Chapter Ten

The rope swung back and forth from the Tyburn gallows like an ominous pendulum. An excited crowd fluttered about. A hanging day attracted huge, excited crowds who were anxious for entertainment.

"Look at them, mulling about like ghouls," Quentin said beneath his breath, troubled that men, women and children could be so enthralled by the killing of another human being.

Executions were necessary, it was true. Rogues, murderers and vagabonds were found in every corner of England, loitering on the streets and lurking in the shadows. Some were old soldiers, others laborers thrown out of work by the enclosures, some former serving men down on their luck. London had a menagerie of ragged, "rowsey" rabble. Priggers or Prancers lying in wait on the roadways, Swadders, Morts, Doxies and Dells levying a toll on the rich. Thievery was an art, and there were many talented in crime.

"And yet . . ." Quentin abhorred the gaiety with which the spectacle of punishment was greeted in the city. It was primitive, indecent. Nearly as revolting as the acts of crime that were rampant within the city's walls.

It was a point on which his philosophy differed from Cromwell's. The Lord Protector's intention was that executions draw spectators. He said that if a hanging did not draw a crowd, it didn't answer its purpose, that being a warning against crime. The truth was, however, that no matter how many executions there were, it didn't stop the evil being committed.

If the truth were told, some highwaymen were viewed as heroes by the common man. Some decent citizens secretly snickered whenever the wealthy were robbed of their riches at the point of a pistol by a cowardly masked rogue afraid to face his victim man to man.

"Yer too late for the 'anging, if that's what yer waiting for, sir."

"What?" Quentin's introspection was interrupted as a small boy tugged at his sleeve. "Hanging?" Another rogue, he supposed. "Whose hanging?"

The boy's eyebrows shot up in surprise. "Why, Gentleman James's, that's whose."

"Stafford's?" Quentin shook his head. "Oh, no. He was given a reprieve." He smiled knowingly. "By my hand."

"Reprieve?" The boy shook his dark-haired head. "Wouldn't be knowing about such a thing as that, whatever it is. All I know is that I saw the 'ighwayman dangling on that very gallows. Saw him with me own eyes. Gentleman James!"

A sick feeling churned inside Quentin's stomach. Something had gone wrong. He knew it, felt it. "Gentleman James was executed this morning? Is that what you are saying?"

The boy nodded. " 'E was."

Quentin swore violently. Though he had no fond feelings

for her father, Quentin had sworn to Devondra that the highwayman's life would be spared. He had promised!

"You are certain it was Gentleman James?" For just a moment he dared to hope.

The boy was offended. "If yer don't believe me, ask all those gentlemen ambling about."

That was precisely what Quentin did, only to find that the news was all over London. "Bloody hell!" Either Richard, his servant, had played him false or Ebenezer, the warden of Newgate, had betrayed him. Whichever had happened, he intended to find out. He had to know. If he was going to have to break the news to Devondra, he wanted to know the truth.

How am I going to tell her? What am I going to say? He had vowed to her that her father would be spared. "You need not worry. I always keep my bargains," he had boasted. In payment for that vow he had taken her virtue, a precious thing.

Mouthing a foul oath, Quentin practically flew to Newgate. Running up the steps, he swore like a madman, causing passerby to give him a wide berth. Once inside, he angrily demanded to see the warden.

He found Ebenezer sitting at a desk, stacks of documents piled in front of him. Hunched over the papers, he was scribbling something with his pen. Was it the same pen that he had used to send Gentleman James to his doom? Quentin wondered. He answered his own question: undoubtedly.

"So, since when do you ignore my dictates and administer your own authority?"

Looking up, the warden eyed Quentin with surprise. "What do you mean?"

"The highwayman. The Royalist rogue."

"Aye?"

"You executed him despite my instructions to the contrary." Outside he appeared to be calm, but inside he was seething. One thing he would not abide was anyone going against his orders. Obedience was something he had valued above all since his days in the military.

"Instructions? What instructions?" Ebenezer seemed genuinely surprised.

"I sent Richard with a missive giving James Stafford a reprieve. Didn't he deliver it to you?" Deliberately, Quentin stared the warden down. If he was lying, experience had proven it would be revealed in his eyes.

"I have seen nary a sign of Richard or of your missive!" the warden answered in a well-controlled voice. His eyes seemed devoid of any falsehood.

"I see." Quentin pounded the desk with his fist. "Bigod, if the lad has disobeyed me, he will be sorry."

"Perhaps 'twas no fault of his." Ebenezer folded his arms across his chest and leaned back in his chair. "Perhaps something happened to deter young Richard from his duty."

Quentin frowned as this possibility crossed his mind. After all, it was at a dangerous hour that he had sent the lad through the forest. "Pray God he did not come to any harm." Worried now for Richard's well-being, Quentin quickly moved to the door. He was about to walk through that portal when a cadaverously thin turnkey pushed him aside. "He's disappeared!"

Quentin and Ebenezer asked at the same time, "Who?"

"The highwayman!"

For just a moment Quentin felt a flash of hope. "He escaped?"

The turnkey shook his head violently. "But his corpse did."

"What?"

"The body was stolen. Cut down and spirited away."

"By whom?" Quentin demanded. It was bad enough to have to tell Devondra that her father had been executed without having to also tell her that his body had been the victim of thievery.

"Witnesses say it was a woman."

"A woman!" Ah, but of course. The highwayman was thought to be dashing and charming by those of the fairer sex. No doubt one of his paramours was responsible. Despite the seriousness of what had happened, Quentin laughed as he imagined the scene.

" 'Tis not a laughing matter," Ebenezer said. "We can't allow such a thing." He seemed to read Quentin's mind. "Even if the man was dead. He belonged to us to do with as we pleased." He was silent for a moment, then issued an order. "I want the guilty person found and the punishment meted out to be effectively harsh."

"Whipping? The pillory?"

"Either one." The warden rapped his fingers on the desk.

"Yes, sir!" With an awkward bow, the gaoler retraced his steps. Then, clearing his throat, he asked, "Even if the one who took Gentleman James down from the gallows was his daughter?"

"Daughter?" Quentin called upon every ounce of self-control he possessed.

"There were people who recognized her as the young woman who had ridden with Gentleman James in the cart going to Newgate."

Quentin stared at the turnkey, his eyes burning. "Dear merciful God!"

Poor Devondra. He could only wonder what she must have been thinking as she looked up and saw the body of her father swinging from Tyburn tree. How she must have hated him at that moment. She would think that he had betrayed her.

"I must find her." He had to hurry. There was no time to lose. He had to do everything in his power to make it up to her, if there was any earthly way.

Chapter Eleven

Eight tall wax tapers burned brightly, illuminating the room of the tavern with a gentle light. Voices merged in hushed tones as the solemn band said their last farewell to one of their own.

"Poor Jamie. Looks so peaceful, he does. Hard to believe he'll never wake up." Wisking out a white lace handkerchief, Tobias wiped at his eyes, then blew his nose.

No, he'll never open his eyes again, Devondra thought, staring down at the still form. Death. Oh, how she hated it. It was so grim. So final. It had robbed her of the people she loved most in all the world.

"I'm so sorry, little miss." Sensitive to her anguish, Tobias patted her on the shoulder.

She didn't respond for a moment. She hesitated to speak for fear of losing her carefully hoarded self-control. When at last she did, she asked only, "What do you suppose his last thoughts were, Tobias?"

He looked at her long and hard. "Hard to tell, but from

the peaceful look on his face I would say that he was thinking of you and remembering how much you loved him. And how much he loved you."

"Do you suppose?"

"I *know.*"

Oh, how she wished she could believe that. Wished she could erase the tortured pictures that flashed through her brain of her father slowly ascending the steps at Tyburn. She could envision the executioner slipping the rope around his neck, tugging tighter and tighter.

Quickly, she put her hands to her throat. "Tobias, do you think he suffered?" Though she knew the truth would be painful, she wanted to know.

"Hard to say. Some men's necks are thick and muscular, and it takes them longer to die than others, but your father was slim. God hope that his end came quickly."

"And mercifully." She closed her eyes, trying to shut out the images that danced before her eyes. It was no use. Despite her effort to block it out, she could see her father's body dangling from that rope. "Dear God, he died all alone." For just a moment her mind couldn't deal with anything beyond that fact.

"No, not alone." Sylvester wrinkled his nose in disgust. "He was surrounded by gawking ghouls."

"Hush!" Tobias poked his companion in the ribs, then hastened to sooth Devondra's mind. "Don't you be blaming yourself. Your father wouldn't have wanted you to witness that cruel spectacle. Besides, the last two days you never left his side."

A constant vigil had been kept over the body so that James Stafford's restless spirit would have companionship. Now, lying in state in the large smoke-blackened room at the Devil's Thumb, the tap room of which was being used as a funeral parlor, James Stafford looked strangely peaceful. As if somehow, even in death, he knew that now, at least, he was among friends.

"Oh, Tobias, it is so hard to believe he is gone, that he might have been left hanging—"

"If not for you."

Devondra shuddered as she contemplated what would have been done to her father's body had she not interceded. It would have been preserved with boiling pitch so that it would last a long time as it dangled from the gallows. "Gibbet fruit" was what execution victims were called when they were exhibited in such a manner to convey a warning to evildoers. Worse yet, her father might have been shamefully exposed like carrion for the ravens and the crows to feed upon.

Instead, he was dressed proudly in his Royalist uniform, his hair and beard carefully combed, his hands crossed across his chest, his sword resting by his side. Devondra would make certain that her father's body would be put to final rest with respect and honor.

"He looks fine enough to grace a memorial painting, aye, he does." Conan, a rotund middle-aged man of thirty-one years, stared down at the man he had always so greatly admired.

"A painting to bring Jamie immortality." Tobias was quick to pick up on the idea.

"Immortality, indeed." Jacob Jackson, the apothecary who had used his skills to act as mortician, grumbled. "I don't believe in such things as deathbed compositions. 'Tis vain and frivolous."

"Vain? Frivolous?" Conan smirked. "You sound like a Purtain, Jackson."

"Purtain?" the apothecary bristled. "Indeed."

Conan continued, "We should commission an artist." It was the fashion of the day to leave behind a loved one's likeness, done with colorful oils on canvas. "We could erect a memorial tomb and . . ."

Devondra shook her head. "I would rather remember my father as he was." Fighting her turbulent emotions, she stared down at him. He looked so stiff, so cold, like a big wax doll. "Oh, Father, you were so lively, so charming, so handsome. . . ." She damned Quentin Wakefield for the hundredth time. But he would pay for his cruelty and betrayal! An eye for an eye, it was written in the Bible. She would exact the penalty for his perfidy in full measure.

"If only we could have robbed the hangman." Tobias's tone seemed to say that he blamed himself for James Stafford's fate.

"But we could not. There were too many guarding him." Even so, how many times had Devondra shared that thought. If only . . .

"Had we e'en tried, we would have all ended up dancing in air ourselves," Sylvester insisted, wiggling his two fingers in the air as if they were dangling legs.

"Even so, we should have tried," Tobias countered. "James Stafford would not have stood by and watched any of us hang. He would have come to our aid even at the risk of his own freedom." He sighed. "Admit it or not, we let him down." He looked slowly from man to man.

"You talk rot. I agree with Sylvester," Conan insisted.

Devondra's eyes touched on the men who had been her father's companions these last few years, wondering why none of them had had the courage or cunning to enact a rescue. Were none of them capable? Had her father been the only daring and brave man in the bunch?

What about Conan? Surely he was a man of great cunning.

"No." Dark-haired, his face pockmarked, a sour expression as usual contorting his features, Conan seemed a most unlikely candidate to be a hero. What's more, he was not always honest, a legacy of his former profession, undoubt-edly. It was to everyone's amusement that Conan had once been a lawyer. Now he worked on the other side of the law.

Barnaby? Again, no. Tall and skinny, with a long nose that looked like a beak, he too appeared to be a poor choice to act the cavalier. He was too clumsy, too bumbling. Once a tailor, he was the one who often sewed the bands' gar-ments—including Devondra's colorful clothes.

Sylvester, perhaps? To him Devondra said a definite no. Sly, as he was nicknamed, was much too devious. Missing an ear, he was a butcher who used a meat cleaver instead of a pistol or a sword.

She turned her attention to Hyacinth, the only other female of the crew. A barmaid until Cromwell's reign closed the taverns, she had been out of work until she had come to the hideaway in the village of Teddington. A plump, bosomy, good-natured woman with bright red hair, she at least was honest and daring. Had she been a man, Hyacinth would have given Cromwell's henchmen a lively fight.

And lastly, but not of least importance, was Tobias. Loyal, steadfast, brave Tobias. Of all the men, he was the only one Devondra trusted completely. Had it not been for her father's orders, she suspected he would have at least tried to save his life, only to lose his own life in the process.

Noting her solemn expression, Tobias put his hand on her arm. "Are you thinking that I let your father down?" He seemed to be awaiting her scorn.

"No, Tobias. Sylvester is right; Father wouldn't have wanted any of us to swing." It was a bitter truth. "Once he was caught by Cromwell's henchmen, only God's angels could have rescued him." Or Quentin Wakefield—as magis-trate, he could have lessened her father's sentence. But he hadn't. Oh, how she despised him for that.

Solemnly, angrily, she knelt with the others, praying for her father's soul.

"Earth to earth, ashes to ashes, dust to dust: In sure and certain hope of the Resurrection unto eternal life," Hyacinth whispered, knowing the words by heart. The softness in her eyes betrayed the love she had felt for James Stafford, a love she had kept carefully hidden.

"Eternal life," Tobias repeated. "I pray Jamie enjoys the hereafter."

"And finds peace," Hyacinth declared.

There was silence as everyone showed proper respect. In a quivering voice Tobias read from the authorized version of the Bible, translated during the reign of King James.

The solemn service continued; not of the Puritan faith, for James Stafford would never have approved, but in the Anglican manner, and according to well-established customs. In James Stafford's coffin was placed a candle to give him light, food to sustain him and a hammer with which he could knock when he reached his destination. A shilling was placed in the dead man's hand, so that he might pay his way on the journey to the next world.

Paying his last respects, Barnaby, the tallest and thinnest of the highwaymen, took responsibility for the sins of Gentleman James. Taking the bite of bread and glass of wine handed to him over the dead man's body, he ate and drank, a process called sin-eating.

"In the midst of life we are in death," Devondra intoned. Hoping that her touch would protect him in the next world and as a last show of love, Devondra brushed her father's forehead with a kiss.

There were more readings from the Scriptures and prayers; then the gathering indulged in a farewell party that started out subdued but slowly turned lively. Story followed upon story, tale upon tale, with Gentleman James as the hero.

"A modern-day Robin Hood, he was," Barnaby exclaimed. "Always giving a goodly portion of his takings to the poor."

"He was polite," Hyacinth said softly.

"Kind," Devondra exclaimed.

"Dashing," Sylvester added.

"The epitome of a gentleman."

"Aye, he always said, 'Please' when he robbed the ladies."

"And 'Thank you' when they handed forth their jewels."

Tobias guffawed. "Oh, he had that flair. Why, I remember the time he was charmed by that young beauty. Asked her for a dance instead of asking for her money."

"And then there was the time when all he stole from a lady was a kiss."

"Oh, how we are going to miss him," Conan grumbled. "It will never be the same."

Conan held up an empty mug. "Jamie would have wanted a farewell party. Let's give him one, gents." In Conan's view it would be a gesture of affection and respect. Moreover, there was a feeling that a revel would in some way help to protect the departing soul from the dangers of its long journey. Thus, as time passed, the highwaymen eventually succumbed to their beer and wine.

"Alas, 'tis time to lay you to rest, Jamie." A sad truth, but one that could not be denied. The funeral procession carried their dear companion from the inn feet first through the front door. Before the procession set out sprigs of rosemary were given to the mourners to be thrown into the grave. It was a promise to the dead man that he would not be forgotten.

On the way to the churchyard, the coffin was carried in front of the mourners until the lychgate was reached. There the clergyman came to receive it. It was in that moment that all Devondra's self-control snapped. "No!" The thought of her father being put down in the hard, cold ground was more than she could bear. "He'll be all alone. You can't take him. You mustn't!"

"Little miss, it has to be. You have to let him go." Tenderly, Tobias enfolded her in his arms just as he had when she was a child. Soothing her, listening to her pitiful sobs, drying her tears. "Your father is in God's hands now."

Devondra's torrent of sorrow lasted but a short while. Just as quickly as her tears had appeared, her crying stopped. A cold fury took hold of her. It was said that love and hate were equally powerful emotions, and at that moment she knew that saying to be true. As passionately as she had loved Quentin Wakefield, now she hated him.

"Aye, he is in God's hands, but vengeance is in mine." She had to vent her angry passions, had to see that some kind of justice was done. If that meant taking matters into her own hands, then so be it. "Hear me well, Tobias," she said, her voice growing in volume to a shouted vow. "I will not rest nor seek my own happiness until Quentin Wakefield lies in his own grave." There would be a perverse pleasure in seeing justice meted out to the man who had betrayed her. Devondra gathered the others around her to formulate a plan.

Chapter Twelve

The forest was dark, eerie. The wind groaned. From the shadows, gnarled tree branches reached out like mammoth hands to grasp and grab.

Guiding his mount through the trees, Quentin Wakefield was tempted to turn back for a moment, but he didn't want to spend the night at his townhouse in London. Still, something just didn't seem right. He felt prickles up and down his neck. A premonition? No. It was just that his nerves were still on edge after James Stafford's hanging.

An unwelcome turn of events to be sure. Yet, something that couldn't really have been helped, considering the circumstances, he kept telling himself. Richard had been set upon by a small band of thieves. That was why the missive Quentin sent had never reached Ebenezer. What a strange turn of events. What an irony.

"Through no fault of mine my part of the bargain went unfulfilled," he said to himself, soothing his conscience. He had signed his name to a reprieve, had taken steps to have it delivered to the proper authority. Delivery of that piece of paper had not occurred because of a band of rogues. It was not his fault.

Clearly he held no sympathies for Gentleman James. Quentin still held the opinion that the fewer rogues in London, the better. It was just that when he remembered how fondly Devondra had talked about her father, he had felt sorry for her. A vagabond and thief her father might have been, but there could be no question that she had loved him.

"Now what is going to happen to her?"

His thoughts were distracted as he rode homeward. London's streets were filled with every kind of human vermin imaginable. A woman all alone would be vulnerable to trouble.

"Where is she?" He had searched every nook and cranny of London to try and find Devondra so that he could explain to her what had happened and offer her his protection now that her father was dead. But she had vanished. After hours of searching he had given up.

Suddenly a dark-clad figure, masked from eyes to chin, emerged menacingly from behind a clump of trees. A pistol primed and cocked was held in the right hand, a glittering sword held in the left. There was no mistaking his intent, but Quentin asked anyway.

"What do you want?" His eyes peered through the semi-darkness, scrutinizing the intruder.

"Get off your horse!" The command was made in a raspy whisper, as if the rogue sought to disguise his real voice.

Quentin wanted to refuse, to tell the bold rascal to go to the devil, but as his fingers brushed the cold metal of his sword he was plagued by another command.

"Touch that and you will regret it."

There was a tension in the highwayman that warned Quentin not to trifle here. For the moment, at least, he gave up any thought of heroics. He had to be cautious until he judged the measure of this man. Likewise, he had to find out if this was a random attack or if he himself had been targeted.

"I assure you, I have no wish to be pierced through or shot."

As the highwayman swatted Quentin's horse on the flank and then laughed as the animal trotted away, it was all he could do to maintain his self-control.

"I fear you will be sorely disappointed. I am not a man to foolishly flaunt my valuables so that they end up in a thief's pocket." Mockingly he tipped his hat. "Sorry. Another time perhaps."

The highwayman was not amused. "We'll soon see." Thus said, the dark-garbed vandal swept down from his horse. Rudely, he thrust his hand into Quentin's pockets, coming forth with only a few coins.

"I have only a few shillings." Quentin stared hard and long, taking note of the highwayman's features, which were outlined by the mask. He had a shrewd eye for details. Perhaps that was why something in the silhouette deeply troubled him. It seemed familiar.

Aware of Quentin's steady gaze, Devondra quickly turned her head. She thought of the plan she had formulated with the others. Knowing that this was the road that Quentin Wakefield would take back to his manor, they had watched and waited. Now, at last, she had him at her mercy. Still, she didn't want him to know who she was. Not yet. Not until she had finished toying with him.

Oh, but vengeance was sweet. He was in her power, just as her father had been in his. That had been the thought goading her on tonight as she braided her hair and fastened it with hairpins in a coil atop her head. Using a length of cloth, she wrapped it tightly around her breasts to hide the soft swell that gave away her femininity.

Garbed in her father's black-and-silver-striped velvet doublet trimmed with a thick white lace collar, black trousers,
knee-high black leather boots, black, broad-brimmed hat
decorated with a bright red plume and a cloak draped over
her narrow shoulders, she could have fooled anyone. A black
mask hid her face from forehead to mouth. Black gloves
covered her soft hands. At her side was a sword, and in her
belt a pistol with a wooden handle.

"Well, Tobias?" she asked.

"See for yourself." He held forth a small silver mirror—
confiscated goods, of course.

Checking her reflection, Devondra smiled. Even Gentleman James would not have recognized her. He would have
thought her to be a rival highwayman. "Now to deal with
Quentin Wakefield!" Thus said, she was off, hiding in the
shadows, to wait for the moment that had now come. "Take
off your coat!"

"My coat?" Quentin shook his head. He had been humiliated once by Gentleman James in such a way, and even
though the garment was not one of his favorites he vowed
never to be so again. "No!" Even when the highwayman
touched his sleeve with the edge of his sword Quentin stead-
fastly refused to cooperate. All the while he was assessing
the situation, trying to figure out a way to overpower his
adversary. Alas, that was a plan that was torn asunder upon
the arrival of two shadows.

"Stand and deliver," called out one of the men.

Quentin was quick to point out that he was standing.

"So you are." Sliding down from his horse, the tallest
of the newcomers tripped over his own feet as he moved
forward.

Quentin couldn't suppress a laugh. Certainly this one,
whoever he was, was not in the least bit graceful.

"Well then, your money or your life." The clumsy one held out a big gloved hand.

In a brisk and businesslike manner, Quentin answered, "I fear your companion has gotten to my ... eh ... finances first." As the man took a step forward, Quentin assured him, "Believe me, he searched me well." He winked mockingly, relieved somewhat by the presence of the bumbling rogue. At first he had feared that these men were companions of Gentleman James who imagined him to be in some way responsible for his death. Now he suspected them of being amateurs.

There was widespread underemployment in England. Agriculture was the major source of work, but the work in the fields was seasonal and hundreds of thousands found day laboring sufficient for only part of the year. Was it possible these were men down on their luck? No matter. Stealing was stealing.

"Look, why do we not let bygones be bygones," Quentin began, taking several steps backward. "If you will just be on your way, I'll forget tonight's transgression."

"Forget?" The first highwayman pulled the lock of his pistol. "Ah, but that is not what we want. We want you to *remember.*" Raising her pistol, she took dead aim. "Now do not stir, on peril of your life."

Hearing the click, Quentin quickly complied. Beginner or not, anyone armed with a pistol could take a man's life. "As you wish." He could not keep himself from saying, "But remember that although you have won this day, your victory will be short-lived." His tone was stern. "I intend to rid the road of such vagabonds as you."

"If you survive." The first highwayman nodded to the short, heavy-set fellow who joined him. This time Quentin lost a gold ring that was quickly twisted off his finger.

His father's ring—the only possession he had ever been

given by the man who sired him. The loss of it infuriated him. "That, you fool, will bring about your hanging," he threatened.

"To the contrary." Devondra's voice grew shrill with anger as she was reminded brutally of her father's execution. For just a moment she nearly gave herself away. Seeing Quentin Wakefield's quizzical look, however, she was alerted to lower her voice again. "That statement will bring about yours!"

"What?" Quentin stared coolly at the gun barrel trained upon him.

Defiantly the figure moved closer, his eyes staring malevolently at the man he held at gunpoint. Motioning with his sword toward a big overhanging branch, he made his intentions known.

"You can't mean it," Quentin raged.

"Ah, but we do." *He betrayed me, cold-heartedly allowed my father to hang. For that he must pay.* She was determined. Why then was her breathing so unsteady as she looked at him. "Get him ready."

Obeying, the bumbling highwayman held the steel point of his sword at Quentin's throat. Reaching inside his cloak, he brought forth a strong rope. Flinging one end over the branch, he formed a loop with the other end.

"You actually intend to hang me?" Quentin was more surprised than afraid. At the back of his mind he held the hope that they were only bluffing.

"A life for a life," one of the stocky highwaymen said, moving closer.

Quentin took note of this man's slight limp. An old war injury? he wondered. "Whose life?" he asked defiantly.

"Gentleman James," two of the highwaymen said in unison.

"Oh, so that *is* what this is all about." Quentin clenched

his hands, determined to proclaim his innocence, but when he opened his mouth to speak he was rudely silenced.

"Aye, this is what it is all about." That said, the shortest and stoutest of the highwaymen looped the rope around Quentin's neck, pulling it so tight that he nearly strangled.

Quentin's blood ran cold. This was no idle threat. Bigod, whoever this black-garbed highwayman was, he wasn't just threatening. "Wait! No matter what you think I have done, I deserve to be heard."

"You deserve nothing!" Again Devondra's voice was shrill.

Quentin looked into burning eyes, feeling the full impact of their anger. "Who are you?" His mind refused to believe.

"It doesn't matter." Boldly, she took a step forward, suddenly anxious to have done with it all before she changed her mind. All the while she was agonized by the turmoil of her emotions. Part of her wanted to see justice done, while another part of her ached at the thought of his death. "Hurry!"

Again Quentin felt the noose tighten around his throat, itching, chocking bruising. He reached up to loosen it but his attempts were thwarted. His hands were grabbed roughly and tied behind his back.

Devondra's heart thumped so loudly, she was certain it could be heard. She felt hot, she felt cold, remembering his kisses, his caresses, the way she had melted in his arms. For just a moment she was tempted to issue him a reprieve. Then her father's face floated before her eyes.

"Hoist him up!"

Strange, Quentin mused, the thoughts that flickered through a man's head as he faced his own mortality. It was as if the mind briefly touched on every important event, relishing the happy times, regretting all the mistakes, imagining things that were still left undone. And, strangely enough, he thought of Devondra Stafford, wondering what might have happened if . . .

"No!" He wouldn't let them kill him. He didn't want to die! He would fight these rascals as fiercely as he had the Royalists, he would—

Suddenly, Quentin felt the murderous pressure around his neck ease. Choking, coughing, he relished the fresh, wondrous breath of life.

"Someone's coming! Horsemen."

Thank God. Quentin knew in that moment that he might well have found himself hanging had it not been for the riders that came thundering up the road. Riders for whose timely entrance he would always thank God.

Despite the fact that the intruders thwarted her plan, Devondra was relieved by their intervention. It took Quentin Wakefield's fate out of her hands—at least this time.

"To horse!" she ordered. They had to flee. She didn't want to risk the capture of her companions. Still, she couldn't stop herself from issuing a challenge, flung over her shoulder as she enacted her retreat. "Be assured, Quentin Wakefield, that we will meet again." Then, as quickly as they had appeared, the three highwaymen disappeared, thundering down the road.

Part Two
A Highwayman's Life

The Heath 1656

The moon was a ghostly galleon tossed upon cloudy
  seas.
The road was a ribbon of moonlight over the purple
  moor,
And the highwayman came riding—
Riding—riding—
The highwayman came riding, up to the old inn-door.
The Highwayman I, Stanza 1

Chapter Thirteen

Soft wisps of sunshine pierced the grayness of the cloudy sky, touching on Teddington, a village safely nestled amid the dense forest adjoining Hounslow Heath. Isolated and quiet, it was a village much like any other. The houses were ordinary, half-timbered dwellings constructed of wood framing and masonry of the old Tudor style. The shops were small but filled with just enough goods to suffice the townspeople's needs. Each building was neatly surrounded by ragged hedges, tall trees and wooden fences. Dirt roads crisscrossed the tiny burg like a spiderweb, carrying wagons, carts and horses to and fro. A narrow river wound through the rolling hills and pastures like an amber ribbon supplying necessary water.

Indeed, Teddington could appear deceptively peaceful to an unknowing eye. To those aware of the truth, however, it was another matter entirely. They knew the silhouettes of the trees spreading wide arms over the thatched roofs ominously mimicked the infamous citizens who dwelled within. Teddington was the home of rogues who made their living outside the law. Numbered among those rogues was one of female gender quickly making a name for herself as "the Notorious Lady."

True to her word, Devondra Stafford had taken her father's place on the roads, competing with some of the Heath's most dangerous highwaymen. She was gaining a reputation for her daring by robbing all coaches, carriages and wealthy horsemen who crossed her path. It was proving to be a most profitable profession. More importantly, however, and what made it worth the risk, was the sense of freedom and power she had gained. A pistol gave its owner complete control and dominance over the person at whom the gun was aimed. "Your money or your life" was an ominous cry that made even the bravest men falter.

"We *will* meet again, Quentin Wakefield," she whispered now, gazing through the open window of the King's Head Inn, the place she called home. "And when we do I will say those words to you." Once he had held her in his power. Once he had stolen her virtue with the promise of her father's life. One day soon, however, it would be she who held the power over him. The power of life and death.

"You got away the last time but there will come another day." Oh, how she wanted to catch him in the forest again. He was the one particular "gentleman" for whom she was always on the alert. The one victim whose face she searched for each time she shouted out. "Stand and deliver!"

She breathed slowly, deeply, as if by so doing she could somehow rid herself of the dull, throbbing ache in her heart. A hurt that went far deeper than the death of her father. She had been bitterly wounded. Betrayed. Her naïveté, her proud dreams, her trust had all been shattered by her father's death. And because of one night in a man's arms. A man who had

cruelly deceived her. A man upon whom she would be
revenged.

"Soon, I swear I will have you within my grasp. And
when we meet, beware. . . . "

Clutching at the shutter, Devondra gazed upon the horizon
at the tract of wasteland known as Hounslow Heath. It was
level, open, uncultivated land with poor coarse soil, inferior
drainage and a surface rich in peat. Occupying perhaps
twenty-five square miles, it was thick with shrubbery, plants
and trees. Foliage that was a perfect cover behind which a
highwayman or two or even three could hide.

Part of the extensive Forest of Middlesex, Hounslow
Heath itself supported only a handful of tiny villages, including Brentford, Isleworth and Teddington. It was, however,
after London, the most important of coaching centers. Across
the Heath ran the Bath Road and the Exeter Road, upon
which there were many travelers, thereby making it
important to Devondra and to others of her profession.

No one was really certain where the boundaries of Hounslow Heath lay. Indeed, there were few who cared. It was
thought to be a tract of country to be crossed as quickly as
possible. A menacing place, to be sure. Dark. Eerie. A place
where a shadowy figure might suddenly appear from out of
the trees. Still, despite the dangers, fully aware of the risks
they ran, wealthy visitors to West Country resorts and court-
iers going to Windsor traveled by coach, horse or postchaise.
All provided rich pickings for highwaymen lurking in copses
bordering the lonely ways. Enough jewelry, coins, velvet
and lace to fill several pockets.

Nonetheless, there was a fierce contention developing
between the highwaymen living at the inn. Greed had reared
its ugly head, personified by a man named Richard "Scar"
Warrick. Devilishly clever, vain and purposeful, he was
determined to rule the Heath with as heavy a hand as did

Cromwell the rest of England. It had begun to appear that
Devondra had a deadly rival. And one who looked upon her
as fair game.

"Don't look now, but Scar is coming your way." Tobias's
soft, whispered warning sent shivers up Devondra's back.

Nonetheless she was defiant. "Oh fie, I have no fear of
him!"

"Well, if you don't, you should," Tobias scolded. "The
man is dangerous in more ways than one."

Scar, deemed himself the king of the Knights of the Road.
He had viewed Devondra and her companions as trespassers
and intruders from the first moment they set foot inside
the King's Head Inn. Brentford might have been ruled by
Gentleman James, he insisted, but Teddington and all within
miles and miles of its borders belonged to him.

It was an arguable truth. Devondra, Tobias and the others
were new to the village, having adopted it as their home, a
move made out of necessity. After her father's capture and
the burning of the Devil's Thumb Inn Brentford was too
risky a place to make their hideaway. If Cromwell's soldiers
had invaded it once, they might do so again. Teddington, a
village to the south of Brentford and west of the Thames,
on the other hand, was more isolated. More importantly, the
many highwaymen living in the village could fight against
the soldiers if need be. There was a better chance of survival
were Teddington to be attacked as Brentford had been.

"Scar *is* dangerous, Tobias," Devondra said. "But I won't
back down. I won't let him rule me by intimidation."

"That's not what I—"

The tramp of boots quieted Tobias. Though he tried to
hide it, the little man shivered as he looked up at the great
hulking figure of the highwayman.

"You. Leave. I want to speak with the woman alone."
There was a firm tone of command in his voice.

Slowly, Devondra turned around, determined to remain calm. "I want Tobias to stay. I want nothing to do with you, sir!"

"Oh, is that so?" The air crackled with tension. Hands folded across his chest, the highwayman boldly crossed the room, the heels of his knee-high leather boots clicking on the hard wooden floor. He seemed to be waiting for Devondra to back down. She did not.

"Yes, that's so! She wants naught to do with the likes of you." His green eyes flashing, Tobias moved forward on his stubby legs to block Scar's way. Alas, he was easily swept aside.

"Get out of my way!"

Now it was Devondra who acted as guardian, hovering over Tobias to ensure that he not be the victim of the Heath's biggest bully. "Fie, you overgrown oaf. Let him be. He thinks only of me and my well-being."

"God's teeth, he is like some overfed hound." Scar ran his index finger from temple to chin, tracing the pink, puckish scar that had given him his nickname. The scar was the only mark upon his cruelly handsome face. "Always nipping at one's heels."

"Hound?" Tobias was clearly insulted.

Scar took three steps toward him. "Aye. Or perhaps puppy is a more apt description." He smiled crookedly.

Tobias's face flushed. He stiffened. "Now see here!"

It looked as if a fight was in the making, a tussle Devondra wanted to forestall. Holding up her head, she boldly met Scar's eyes. "And you, sir, are a cur. A vicious mongrel who will snap and fight over any bone."

She had heard about Scar's encounters with Conan, Barnaby, Sylvester, Jacob and now Tobias. Encounters wherein he had tried to coerce them via threats into joining with his band of cutthroats and giving him a twenty percent share.

Well, she wasn't having any of that. Perhaps the males in her band always cowered before this tall, muscular braggart. She refused to do so.

Stepping directly in front of Tobias, she challenged Scar. "If you insist upon a fight, *I* will give you one."

"You?" Clearly he was stunned by her bravado. For a moment he simply stared, then he broke into raucous laughter.

Devondra didn't laugh. "I mean it, Scar. Leave me and my men alone!"

As quickly as he had given way to mirth, Scar sobered. "Indeed, I meant no offense." Taking off his red-plumed black hat, he affected a polite bow. "It is my intention to please you. Women as beautiful as you are rare. You are, or so I might say, the jewel of Hounslow Heath."

"Jewel?"

A gleam lit his heavy-lidded eyes. "Aye. Jewel."

Far from being flattered, Devondra found the compliment troublesome. She wanted nothing to do with this man. "Save your sweet words for the tavern wenches. I know your kind." She emphasized, "I repeat, leave me and my men alone."

"Alone?" A nerve in the highwayman's face ticked.

"Yes, alone!" Defiantly she swore. "None of my men would ever take up with the likes of you! Never!" She repeated the word, "Never!"

Scar Warrick was loathsome, a blood-sucking parasite whose brand of thievery was foul. Though there was a sort of honor among thieves, he was a man who was morally corrupt, a man with no soul, who seemed to enjoy killing. Like some monster with tentacles, he presided over his murderous band, urging them on, goading them into committing heinous crimes. Once Scar had been her father's fiercest rival. Now Devondra knew he was hers as well.

"Never is a long, long time." He shrugged. "But I'll wait."
Lazily he puckered his lips and blew her a kiss. "For you."

With undisguised loathing she breathed, "You'll wait in
vain." Her face was flushed with anger. "I will never bow
to you. My father roamed the Heath while you were still
creeping about the London gutters."

This was a truth that made him stiffen. As a boy, the
orphaned Scar had lived in the alleys, gutters and cellars of
London, keeping company with the rats. Perhaps that was
why he always seemed to remind her of one. "And now I
have rightfully taken his place."

"A fact that is most unfortunate," he hissed.

Looking into Scar's deep-set eyes and seeing the Devil's
soul reflected there, she intoned, "Nevertheless, it is true,
and I will do whatever I have to do to survive. Even if
means fighting you."

Scar's thick brows formed a *v*. "Fight?" Abruptly, his tone
softened. "Forsooth, I will do everything in my power to
change your mind on that score." The smile beneath the
dark mustache was anything but reassuring. "Besides, your
fight is not with me I would think, but with another."

Devondra winced at the reminder. It was true. Her real
quarrel was not with Scar but with Quentin Wakefield. One
day they would meet again. One day. Until then, she would
not even consider leaving the Heath. Like her father's ghost,
she would haunt the roadway that he frequented daily, traveling from Wakefield Manor to London and back again.

*Will you be riding through the woods tonight? Will you,
Quentin?* She sighed, anxious for the confrontation. He
couldn't escape her for long. One of these days he would
forget about his close call in the woods and grow careless
again. She would be ready.

"Perhaps tonight." With that thought in mind, she made

her way up the stairs. It was time for the Notorious Lady to make herself known once again.

Entering her room and bolting the door behind her, Devondra searched through her closet, smiling at the rainbow of garments that met her eye. Her reputation as a woman of cool daring and courage was not the only thing about her that was quickly making her well-known. The colorful costumes she wore were also responsible.

Devondra had outfits in nearly every hue imaginable. Red. Blue. Green. Gold. Black. White was for those moments when she decided to pretend to be angelic.

"The red!"

Slowly she began to undress, hanging her clothes in the closet haphazardly. Standing naked, she looked at her reflection in the mirror, wondering how long it would take before she could forget the touch of Quentin Wakefield's hands. How long?

She was lonely; there was no use denying it to herself. Though she was often in the company of those who lived at the King's Head Inn she felt isolated.

I want a man's arms around me. I don't want to be alone forever. I'm young. I want to be loved. More so now that she had experienced a tantalizing taste of what being joined with a man could mean. Liar or not, for one blessed moment Quentin Wakefield had given her a touch of Heaven.

"Even if he was a fraud he gave me that!"

Slipping on her undergarments, chemise, corset and numerous petticoats, Devondra tried to push the memory of that night out of her mind, but as usual it was impossible. Perhaps as long as Quentin Wakefield breathed the same air as she, looked upon the same stars, he would be in her thoughts. He had been the source of her greatest joy and her darkest grief.

Lover. Betrayer. The two would be forever entwined in her mind.

"I can not forget no matter how hard I try." Nor could she forgive.

Quentin Wakefield, you are as responsible for my father's death as if you had been the hangman. In truth, perhaps more so. Worse yet, he had allowed her to hope while all the while he had been planning to betray her. How then could she allow herself to have any fond memories of him?

"He is your enemy. Enemy!" She must always remember, particularly when gentler memories threatened to soften her heart.

Devondra's face grew cold and hard. Her soft mouth tightened. Picking up her mask, she held it in place, gazing for a long time at her reflection. She had put her trust in love only to suffer life's cruelest lesson. Now it was Quentin Wakefield's turn.

"Damn!" What was wrong with him? Quentin wondered as he stormed around the room. He was irritable. Time and time again he found himself retreating into an introspective shell.

"A house without a woman, a life without love . . . " he said. But then, wasn't that the future he had molded for himself? Wasn't that where his ambition had taken him?

Quentin tried to tell himself that it had been worth it. He had done the impossible. He had gone from being a lowly butcher's stepson to being a man of importance. A man who didn't have to answer to anyone save the Lord Protector of England. But once things had been very different.

Closing his eyes, Quentin remembered his troubled boyhood, days spent under the dominance of his foul-tempered stepfather, a thick-set, redfaced man prone to violence.

Resentful of his lithe, handsome stepson, he mistreated
Quentin, prophesying that the boy would come to no good.

"You young jackanapes. You are lazy. Afraid of hard work.
You will die without a farthing."

Quentin had proven his stepfather wrong, though not without suffering first. Gathering together his meager possessions, he had run off to London. There he had begged for
his bread, often suffering the pangs that came with hunger.
But he had survived and in so doing had become strong.

"And unmerciful . . ." The Civil War and his long months
with the Roundheads had particularly made him so, for it
had been a bloody and brutal revolution. Quentin had seen
so much suffering and death that it had desensitized him,
made him hard-hearted. But not so hard-hearted that he
wasn't troubled by his thoughts. Thoughts that were self-
condemning and remorseful.

I should never have made that bargain. It had been the
epitome of selfishness and conceit. A mockery of all things
that were decent. In short, it was the most despicable thing
Quentin had ever done. A young woman had desperately
wanted to save her father's life and he had taken advantage
of the moment to feed his own desires. Was it any wonder,
then, that his conscience bothered him?

Devondra Stafford has somehow softened me here, he
thought, touching his chest. She had warmed him, touched
a part of him that he guarded fiercely with iron walls. She
had given herself openly, completely, and in so doing had
touched his very soul. But oh, how cruelly she had been
repaid.

"If only I had foreseen . . ."

Yet how was he to have known that a promise made was
not within his control to keep? Or that paradise found could
so quickly be lost, leaving him feeling more alone than he
had ever felt in his life?

"Alone . . . " For a night he had glimpsed happiness. But 'twas only a dream. An illusion.

Pouring himself a glass of ale, he sat down on the bed, imagining for a moment that she was curled up beside him, only to blink his eyes and find himself once more all by himself.

"If only I could find her!" Devondra Stafford had disappeared, and Quentin had begun to doubt that he would ever find her.

Chapter Fourteen

Night ruled with a misty darkness, broken only by the moon's soft, glowing rays. Slanting down, the muted light touched the leaves and branches with a silvery haze. The ghostly hooting of an owl added to the eerie mood of the night as the two moved stealthfully through the forest in the darkness. Tobias and Devondra. Though there were times all of the band would ride, tonight only she and her most trusted companion stalked the roadway, for both had a personal score to settle.

"He should be coming any time now," Tobias whispered.

"At last!" Their spy in London had sent word to the inn that day that Quentin Wakefield had been seen on the road. Since hearing that message, Devondra had been unable to think of anything else. Anything at all.

How could she ever forget what he had promised that morning as he had stroked her cheek? That he would take care of her. That he would help her father.

"I'll do all that I can to see that he is dealt with fairly. In the meantime, you need someone you can trust. Someone who cares. "I do," he had said.

Oh, yes, he had cared. So much that he had let her father succumb to the steps and the string, the gallows.

Quentin Wakefield. Looking up at the sky, she could see his face as clearly as if he stood before her. His thick auburn hair, blue eyes and the stubborn set to his chin. Through a haze she saw etched on his profile the silhouette of her father, dangling from Tyburn's gallows.

Oh, but I will make him pay for what he has done. I will reap my vengeance! It was the only way to ease the anger curling deep inside her. A deep, dark resentment that was slowly eating away at her soul.

No matter what the price, I will have my revenge. So thinking, Devondra put her hand around the barrel of her pistol.

"Careful, Little miss." Gently, Tobias touched her arm, reminding her that she was pointing the barrel in his direction.

"I'm sorry." Loading and firing a gun was dangerous. It was not unusual for a pistol to misfire. No wonder Tobias was wary.

"I wouldn't want you to be blowing off my head, ugly though my face be." Cupping her face with his hand, he added, "Nor would I be wanting any mishap to mar your pretty face."

"I'll be careful," she assured him, quickly putting down the pistol, remembering that it was Tobias who had taught her how to shoot. He had shown her that the barrel was made in two parts and unscrewed to allow powder and ball to be inserted. Once the barrel was replaced, the pistol was fired, the ball hopefully expanding into the grooves in the barrel to hit its target without backfiring.

"Hopefully we won't have to fire a shot, for I do fear that were you put to the test . . . "

Devondra smiled. What Tobias was hinting at was that, despite his careful tutelage, she was really quite a wretched shot. Morning after morning, day after day, she had practiced loading, aiming and firing until her arms and shoulder ached and her ears rang with the thunder of the exploding gun. Still, she had yet to hit her target, unless it was at close range. Up to now, however, the bluff had been enough to frighten her victims.

"When the time comes I'll be ready." For just a moment Devondra was completely still as she prepared herself for what was to come.

"You never are afraid, are you?"

"No," she answered. Something deep inside was driving her, something much stronger than fear.

"And bigod, that scares *me* some times." He shivered.

Devondra turned her head, looking fondly on the man who had been so loyal to her father and now to her. "Don't be scared, dear, dear Tobias." Strange how once Tobias had looked after her. Now it was Devondra who saw the need to protect him. "I'm no longer Gentleman James's gentle little girl."

Little girl? Indeed not, Tobias thought. Devondra was a woman who made a fetching sight. Tonight she was dressed in a full-skirted gown of red velvet with full sleeves and a low, square neck. A wide-brimmed black hat with a red feather, a black mask and black gloves completed the picture. Her hair was plaited, positioned high on the back of her head.

"It's not your responsibility to look after me anymore," Devondra felt the need to say, noticing how avidly Tobias was staring. "I'm on my own."

"Merry-go-up! On your own you say." Tobias made no

secret of the fact that he disapproved of Devondra's new way of life. Still, there was no arguing with her. She was determined. "If only Jamie were here . . . " Perhaps he could talk some sense into his daughter.

"He is," Devondra answered with a toss of her head. For the first time she felt she was in control of her own fate. No matter what happened, she had made her choice. "He's looking down from heaven at this very moment."

"Shaking his head at the thought that you are tramping the Heath in his boots. Ah, Devon!" Suddenly Tobias put his finger to his lips. "I see someone!"

Devondra looked in the direction her companion's pudgy finger was pointing. Along the pathway, reflected by the light of the moon, a man rode, his head lifted haughtily. Backing their horses into a thicket of trees, Devondra and Tobias waited.

How will I begin? How exactly shall I punish him? The images that flitted through her mind were varied and confusing. One moment she visualized herself taunting him, bullying him; the next moment the image changed and she fantasized herself dancing naked in his embrace.

"Listen . . . " Tobias whispered.

Startled back to the present, Devondra attuned her ears to the sound of a horse's hoofs pounding out a rhythm on the dirt and rocks. Along the dark road the lone rider came. Closer. Closer. Still, Devondra and Tobias did not make a move. They didn't stir. Didn't even move a muscle. Until it was time.

"Now!" Devondra called out. Her order was punctuated by a pistol blast as she and Tobias made their presense known.

"Your money or your life," Tobias barked out.

"Get down; cast loose your horse." When the rider showed a defiant stubbornness Devondra said loudly, "Do as I say or I swear, Quentin Wakefield, I will part you from that animal most painfully."

There was a long moment of silence. And all the while Devondra's heart hammered so irratically that she was certain it would leap from her breast. Then a male voice cried out, "I am not Quentin Wakefield!"

Moonlight shone on the steel muzzle of Devondra's long pistol, the barrel pointed straight at the gentleman's heart. Grumbling, the man slid from his saddle, trembling with anger as he stared down the barrel of the shining muzzle so close to his nose.

Disappointment hit Devondra like a physical blow. Her voice was hoarse as she asked, "Who are you?"

"Who am I? Who am I?" The thick-set, red-faced man with dark-blond hair made little effort to hide his fear. His hands shook and his knees trembled. All the while he looked in stunned awe at the woman dressed all in red. "Who . . . who . . . are y-y-you?"

"Those who I encounter on the road call me the Notorious Lady."

He repeated slowly, "The Notorious Lady?" He continued to stare, his eyes moving appreciatively from the top of her head to the hem of her gown. "Lovely." He took a stop forward.

"And dangerous if you don't take her seriously," Tobias replied, nodding in Devondra's direction. "Like a red rose the 'lady' has thorns."

To remind the man that she was in control, Devondra held up her pistol. "There is a toll for using this road," she reminded him.

"A toll?"

"Aye. A fee we will take in silver or gold." There was the hint of a smile on her lips as she spoke, a gleam of mischief in the eyes that were visible behind the mask.

"A fee?" Taking off his tall-crowned, wide-brimmed hat trimmed with ostrich feathers, he made a plea. "I have little money. Believe me or not, I am not a wealthy man."

Devondra did not believe him. Thrusting her hand into a big leather pouch hanging from his saddle, she fumbled about for a long time. There was nothing but sheets of paper. Missives of some kind. Writings that were of little interest to her. Satisfied, she said at last, "He tells the truth. There is no gold within."

"Then he has hidden it elsewhere," Tobias said knowingly.

Fully aware of the risks they ran on all the great roads running out of London, gentlemen hid their valuables carefully in their boots and other places in which they imagined the highwaymen would not look. Little did they know that the men who held them at bay were well-informed of likely places for secreting property.

Devondra pulled the lock of her pistol so that the horseman could plainly hear the click. "Where is it then? Where have you hidden your gold and silver?"

"I . . . I have none!" He looked from Devondra to Tobias and back again, his eyes softening on her feminine form as if he fully expected her to be the most merciful. Little did he know.

"Undress!"

"What?" The man sounded calmer than he felt. "No."

"Yes."

It was no use for travelers to declare that they had nothing. It was all too easy to find out if what they said was true. While the muzzle of a pistol was pointed in their direction they were bidden to take off their boots and other articles of dress until their valuables were revealed. This disrobing was humorously known among highwaymen as "shelling the peas."

"Surely you don't expect . . . "

"Ah, but I do."

Something in her manner clearly troubled the opulently dressed, broad-shouldered man, for there was no more hesitation in him now. "Odd's body, you are cruel."

"Cruel and determined," Devondra exclaimed. She moved closer.

"Bigod. All right. All right!" Deciding to be cooperative, the gentleman revealed that he had hidden his gold in his boots. So many coins that it was surprising he could even take one step.

"A ha!" Tobias greedily rubbed his hands together as he slid from his horse and gathered up the coins. "Much better than the watches, fobs, rings and other valuables we would have to offer for sale to retrieve our profit."

"Much better!" Devondra agreed. Still, she was not completely satisfied. "Go on."

He did, stripping off his black hip-length coat, bright red sash, dark, high-waisted, long-legged breeches and stockings. "There. Are you satisfied? I have no jewels. Cromwell will not allow it."

Though Devondra realized that jewelry was frowned upon by the strict Puritans in any form, she had hoped. All that this gentleman had on was a gold chain that hung around his neck. Partially hidden by his undershirt, it twinkled in the moonlight.

"There is something we have overlooked," Tobias called out. He reached for the necklace.

"No!" Clutching at it frantically, the man seemed hellbent on retaining it.

"Hand it over or face the consequences," Tobias threatened.

Again the man refused. "This chain was given to me by my father. 'Tis all I have left of him."

"Don't be a fool! Take it off and throw it to me." Tobias responded, showing little concern for sentimentality.

Devondra, however, was more lenient. Thinking about her own father, remembering how precious were the few treasures he had left behind for her, she relented. "Let him keep it. We have taken enough."

"Let him keep it?" Tobias grimaced; then, seeing from the determined set of her jaw that she meant what she said, he shrugged. "As you will."

Quickly picking up his discarded trousers, the man stepped into them, then looked up. "Thank you. I will remember that about the chain, at least, you were kind."

"I had a father, too." Devondra whispered, grieving anew over her loss. Then, without another word, she touched her heels to the flank of the dark horse that she was riding and galloped off.

Chapter Fifteen

The windows of the King's Head Inn were dark, the lanterns extinguished. It was well after midnight and most of the patrons were abed. No wonder it was so quiet. Except, that is, for the noise the inn's sign made. Having come off its hinge, it was banging against the outer wall.

"Ah, what a night. I'm as hungry as the proverbial wolf at the door!" Remembering his manners, Tobias opened the door but stepped aside and let Devondra enter first.

It was smoky inside the King's Head. The smells from supper lingered, mixing with smoke from the kitchen stove, stale wine and ale. All these odors assailed Devondra's nostrils as she and Tobias entered the main room.

"What about you, Little miss?"

The aroma of rabbit stew left over from dinner teased her nostrils, reminding her that she hadn't eaten supper. "I'm famished."

"Well then. We'll feast and drink before we go to bed." Using his pistol handle as a club, Tobias banged on one of the tap-room tables. "Ahem. Ahem. Can we get some service here?" He banged louder. "Ahem. Ahem!"

"Hush!" Hurrying down the stairs, the innkeeper came towards them dressed in his nightcap and night gown. Growling, he gave warning to them not to awaken all of the other patrons. Catching a glimpse of the gold Tobias held in his hand, however, changed his attitude. "Ah, a profitable night." Doffing his night cap, he offered the hospitality of the house, insisting, "ye are my best customer, Toby, 'at's wot ye are."

Smiling at the compliment, Tobias greased his palm with two of the coins. Laughingly, he teased, "Don't bother to bite them. One thing you can say for Cromwell's cronies— they be not poor. I can assure you that they are real."

"Of course they are." Ringing a bell behind the bar, the innkeeper promptly summoned a sleepy young tavern maid. "Don't just stand there gawking. Our special wine for my friends. And light the hearth."

Muttering beneath her breath, the girl filled two glasses with the pungent-smelling red liquid and quicky set them down on a nearby table, ignoring Tobias' good-natured flirting. "There!"

Soon, despite the late hour, the tap room was glowing from the light of a blazing fire. The pewter-hung walls caught the glare, reflecting the orange and yellow glare and illuminating the scarred wooden tables, the uneven plaster on the walls and the bowed beams of the ceiling. The plank floor was sprinkled liberally with a mixture of rushes and sawdust and was badly in need of a sweep. The tap room of the Kings Head had seen better days, though fifty years ago it might have been grand, Devondra thought. Still, for want of a better place it was home.

"Time for a celebration!" Tobias called out, plopping his girth into the nearest chair.

Devondra, though triumphant about the night's pickings,

was in a less jovial mood. She couldn't help feeling disappointed that Quentin Wakefield had not been within range of her pistol. Still, she didn't want to dampen Tobias's mood. There would be another time. "A celebration!"

"Drinks for all our boon companions," Tobias insisted, sending the tavern maid on an errand to fetch the other members of the band. One by one she knocked on their doors, awakening them. Soon the tap room was filled with a low-buzzing chatter as Conan, Barnaby, Sylvester and Hyacinth joined their two comrades in arms. They were anxious to learn of the evening's happenings.

"Was it a rich one?" Hyacinth said and winked.

"Moderately so," Devondra answered with a sigh. In actuality she remembered very little about the man, her thoughts had been elsewhere at the time.

So fate was kind to you tonight, Quentin Wakefield. Well, little matter. Tonight it was the tawny-haired gentleman. One of these nights she would have Quentin Wakefield focused in the sight of her gun. And when she did . . .

"What about you, Devondra?" Tobias picked up a pewter plate. "Do you want a slice of cold mutton or a bowl of stew?"

"The rabbit stew." She was given a much too hefty portion, which she picked at with one of the new forks that were coming into use. A fruit tart was more to her liking—that is, until Tobias dabbled into it with his greasy fingers.

"Ahhh. Good!" With a roguish grin he stuffed his mouth full, then wiped his lips with his hand. "Hard work gives a man a healthy appetite."

"Hard work?" Hyacinth giggled. Sitting beside Tobias, she listened avidly as he spoke about the night's quest. If he exaggerated his own bravery and prowess, Devondra didn't mind.

"So, what about this man from London? Was he moderately rich?" Conan turned the conversation to his favorite topic: Money.

"See for yourself," Tobias grinned, his eyes gleaming with merriment as he plopped his leather, coin-filled pouch down on the table. The impact sloshed Devondra's wine all over the table.

"Allow me." Exhibiting rare gentlemanly grace, Barnaby mopped up the liquid with his handkerchief. "After all, I wouldn't want you to soil that beautiful red velvet gown that you are wearing." A dress that he, his scissors and needle had created.

"Rich enough." Reaching out his big hand, Sylvester hefted the pouch in his hand. "If you don't be minding, I'll go ahead and take my share." By mutal agreement all members of the band were given a small cut of the spoils even if they had not been present. Spilling the coins onto the table, Sylvester counted out the money. "Three, six, nine . . . " There were twenty-one silver coins and thirteen gold.

All eyes watched as the former butcher set aside three silver and two gold coins, a division that was not permissible by the band's agreement. It was obvious he was being too greedy.

"Ahem!" Reaching out, Tobias grabbed Sylvester by the wrist. "Put them back. 'Tis Devondra who will dole them out, as we agreed. She and I divide up half the money because we were the participants in the robbery. You and the others allot that which is left."

When Sylvester balked at Tobias's request Devondra said sternly, "Do it! 'Tis by your own word that you agree to those terms, Sylvester."

A grunt was her answer, but Sylvester soon obeyed. Then, as the tavern maid brought back full tankards, he raised his glass in a toast. "To the future. May all nights be as profitable as this one has been."

"To the future . . . " Devondra echoed. Raising her glass, she sipped the wine, nearly choking as she glimpsed Scar's reflection in the mirror. Bigod, *he* was coming.

Scar's menacing voice boomed out a mocking greeting. "So, the Notorious Lady has returned."

The west wall was stacked with large barrels that wobbled and swayed precariously as he passed. Devondra found herself hoping one would fall and crack Scar on the head, for it seemed the only way to avoid his unwelcome presence.

"I have returned."

Suddenly it seemed too quiet, with an oppressive silence that unnerved her, as if everyone had stopped talking all at once. But it was not silent for long. "Not empty-handed I would hope," Scar said.

"No, not empty-handed. Not that it is any of your business," Devondra declared.

"Ah, but it is!" Watching her intently, he held out his hand. "You see, I have set some new rules."

"Rules?" Conan moved forward, then quickly changed his mind. "What do you mean?"

Stealing the wineglass from Devondra's hand, Scar took a sip. "Just that from tonight onward I demand a tax of ten percent for the use of my roads."

"*Your* roads!" The very idea was preposterous.

Scar grinned. "And why not? There are lords who lease their lands. Why should it not be possible to demand rent for use of a road as well?"

Devondra glared at him through half-closed eyes. "Because you are far from a lord, Scar Warrick!" She clenched her fingers into fists, wishing violently that she were a man, if only for a little while. Long enough to pummel the arrogant bastard who had the effrontery to make such a suggestion. A tax, indeed.

Scar's eyes were hooded, but a muscle ticking in his

cheek, betraying his annoyance. "Not a lord, perhaps. But one who has the power to force you to my will nonetheless." He waited for Devondra's answer. "Though I would by far prefer to offer you my protection instead."

"Protection?" Devondra stiffened, intent on proving that she could take care of herself.

"And companionship." His piercing brown eyes swept over her with a familiarity that left no doubt as to his meaning.

Devondra's face burned as she again fought her anger. "I have no need of either," she exclaimed.

"Indeed." He had the effrontery to laugh. "Well, just remember my invitation if you find yourself with a *longing,* if you know that I mean."

She knew exactly what he meant. Quickly she turned her back on him, in the manner she always used with overbold men. Why was it that a man's thoughts were so often in his breeches? Magistrate or thief, they seemed much the same. "It will be a cold day in Hades before I would ever feel such a longing for the likes of you."

The surprise on Scar's face was obvious. He had not expected such an angry retort. "Perhaps that cold day in hell is closer than you think." Reaching out, he took her by the shoulder, his fingers melting through her flesh, as if to grasp her very bones. It was a punishing hold.

"Let go!"

It was a warning the highwayman did not abide. Instead, he pulled her to her feet, then brought her roughly against him. "Perhaps I'll collect my tax in another way." Slowly lowering his mouth, he made no secret of the fact that he intended to kiss her.

"No!" Devondra shouted, turning her head. Even her kisses she held sacred. She would not be touched by the likes of him.

Scar did not heed her wishes. Even now he was smiling, so smug in his self-assurance. Taking her face in his hand, he exhibited no gentleness as he forced her to look at him. "Yes," he said.

Well, so be it. Devondra thought. He left her only one course of action. She aimed her knee at his groin and placed a well-aimed blow that soon had the dark-souled highwayman doubled over in agony and humiliation.

"Devondra!" The others in her robbers' band gasped. There was a profound sense of shock and alarm.

"I told him no. He wouldn't listen." To her it had been as simple as that. Now, as she thought about her actions, she realized the consequences.

"Scar will never forgive what you have done." Sylvester said. "We're doomed. Far better to have sold your soul to the Devil than to anger him."

Shivering, Devondra gazed down at Scar's writhing form and agreed with Sylvester. Scar had forced her hand and she had reacted instinctively to his advances. Now, there was nothing else that they could be but enemies.

There was a chill in the tap room that could not be warmed by any fire. Scowling as he glanced down the length of the room. Scar sat with his feet propped up on the table, his glower daring anyone to interrupt his solitude.

"Oh, how I hate them! Jamie *and* that saucy little brat of his."

Even now he smarted under his humiliation. His growling stomach only added to his foul mood. Having one's lust cooled so abruptly did that to a man, he reflected bitterly. And yet his reasons for treating Devondra Stafford so brutally had little to do with any kind of attraction to her. Oh, no. There was another purpose in his trying to seduce her into his power.

"An eye for an eye . . . " A daughter for a daughter.

Closing his eyes, he was haunted by the image that danced before his eyes. "Annie." So young. Much too young to die. And all because of *him*. A sin for which Jamie had paid and yet, a tragedy that required another sacrifice.

"Oh. yes . . . "

The more he thought about it, the more determined he was. First the father and then the daughter, though he would revenge himself on the girl in a far different way than he had her sire. He would find a way to humble her, control her, bend her to his will.

"Jamie!" He grumbled, still feeling jealousy despite the fact that the man was dead.

James Stafford had been born with a silver spoon in his mouth, a spoon that had not tarnished even after the war and his disgrace. Like a cat he had somehow landed on his feet. Though he had lost everything of value, his life was filled with adventure as he rode the highways and byways as Gentleman James. Women were at his beck and call as he lived a life of varied pleasures, vices and dangers. An adventurer was what he had become, though often called both rogue and scoundrel.

Scar's life, on the other hand, had been fraught with misfortune and pain. He had struggled for every shred of power he possessed, slowly building up his gang of thieves and rogues. And yet for sixteen years there had been a ray of sunshine in his life. In truth, the only thing he had ever loved.

"Anne."

As she lay on the bed, slowly fading away, he had done something very unusual for him, he had prayed. Those earnest pleas, however, had gone unanswered. She now lay in

her grave, having taken with her a part of him that had died.
His heart.

The Tower Green rang with the clank of sword upon sword
and reverberated with the muffled oaths of the combatants.
Flickering torches illuminated the stones of the curtain wall
that encircled the White Tower. Competing with the moon's
glow, the blazing scounces cast bright light on the two men
absorbed in their mock battle.

A gleam of perspiration shone on Quentin Wakefield's
bare chest and arms, emphasizing the rippling muscles that
he usually hid beneath a white linen shirt and elegantly
tailored velvet coat. In his hand the stout-bladed, slashing
sword—the kind with which he had been so expert during
the war—seemed almost magical. As if somehow it had a
life of its own. After his close call with death in the Heath.
Quentin was determined to keep his fighting skills in shape.

"Take that," he said aloud, striking out with the sword with
such violence that it took his sparring partner by surprise.
Outmanuevering his friendly rival in a furious wielding of
sword upon sword, he left him winded and thoroughly
shamed.

"Easy, easy. God's teeth, you'll break my arm." Edwin
Trevor, rubbed anxiously at his wrist, then bent down to
retrieve the sword, which had been knocked out of his hand
by the impact of Quentin's thrust.

"Sorry!" Running his fingers through his tousled auburn
hair. Quentin raised his hand apologetically to the man who
had fought at his side at the battles of Marston and Naseby.

"But for a moment you imagined that I was someone
else." Sticking the point of his sword into the hard ground
of Tower Green, Edwin used it like a cane, balancing his
hefty weight. "Who?"

"It doesn't matter." Quentin had kept his humiliating experience to himself. Not even Edwin Trevor, his trusted friend, had been told about the night he had been threatened with a noose at Hounslow Heath.

"Some overzealous husband, angered that you dallied with his wife?"

Quentin shook his head.

"Some bold swain who was so foolish as to try and cuckold you with one of your paramours?"

Again Quentin shook his head.

"Cromwell?"

This time Quentin laughed. "Oliver can be irritating, but I assure you, 'twas not he who piqued my ire."

Edwin was curious. "Who then?" Tapping his foot impatiently, he threw out a few more guesses, letting Quentin know in no uncertain terms that he would not give up his questioning.

"All right, if you must know, I was accosted on the road, bigod!" That was all Quentin was going to reveal.

"By a highwayman?" Edwin was incredulous. "You?"

"Not one but three," he explained, hoping to soothe his injured pride.

"Well, that explains it." Edwin's voice lowered conspiratorily. "No doubt 'twas the same blackguards who stole my money."

"Money?" For a long moment Quentin was as still as a statue, then he laughed. "You were set upon too?"

A grimace flickered over Edwin's unshaven face. "Indeed. I would wager to say that there is hardly a man in all of London who hasn't been held up at gunpoint at least one time or another." He paused. "Damn it all, those rascals are becoming as bold as brass and as elusive as a whisper on the wind. Particularly that . . . that woman."

"Woman?"

"You haven't heard?" Edwin expelled his breath. "Well then, let me tell you all about her. From my . . . uh . . . personal experience."

"You were robbed." Quentin was interested in hearing about a woman who dared intrude on a man's devious profession.

"Aye, last night. While riding through the Heath." Edwin related the tale of the woman dressed all in red who had held him up at gunpoint.

"Were you afraid?"

"Yes and . . . and no." Suddenly Edwin, a man usually self-possessed and at ease, was flustered. "She . . . she . . . "

"Threatened you, humiliated you, robbed you and—" The look on Edwin's face seemed to tell another story. For a long moment Quentin studied his stupified expression, at last coming to a conclusion. "She charmed you, bigod. She did, didn't she?"

"She had the voice of a seductive angel. Soft. Low." As if in a trance, Edwin plopped down on a tree stump.

"And most assuredly she was pretty." Quentin scoffed, irritated by it all. The woman was a thief, not the sensual inspiration for a fantasy, as Edwin seemed to be inferring.

"Pretty? I wouldn't know. Her face was covered by a mask." Putting the fingers of both hands up to his eyes, he gave a demonstration. "Like this." He smiled broadly. "But if I were a betting man, I'd wager that she was."

"And I'd wager that her soul was black as hell! If she has a soul, that is."

Puzzled by the bitterness in his friend's tone, Edwin eyed him up and down, deciding at last to change the subject. "Have you noted that Cromwell is getting a bit ornery these days?"

"Cromwell? What has he to do with this?" Quentin

shrugged. "Unless you're trying in your way to tell me that he has been set upon by your mysterious lady."

"I daresay not."

"Too bad, for if he had, perhaps then and only then, would he realize the need to intensify the search for these wrongdoers." Since the capture of James Stafford, his old enemy, Cromwell's pursuit of the Heath's criminals had become lax. Slowly, Quentin raised his hand to his neck, remembering the awesome pressure of the rope. He wondered if he would ever be able to forget.

"I'm afraid Cromwell has more pressing problems—such as the fear of a mutiny among his own." Edwin stood up. Taking a step forward, he tapped playfully at his friend's shoulder. "I doubt that he will want to spare any soldiers at the moment, so if you are determined to rid the country of rogues and their fellows," he taunted, "you might well have to do it yourself."

"Do it myself." Quentin laughed at the very thought.

A few days later he was not laughing. The Notorious Lady had been so bold as to paste notices on several of the doors of rich Londoners, telling them they should not venture forth without at least a watch and twenty guineas in their possession.

It was daring. Audacious. Goading. As Quentin paced the corridors of Whitehall, he was incensed. The infernal woman was terrorizing the roads east and west of London. Worse yet, she was as Edwin said, "as elusive as a whisper on the wind."

Descriptions of the masked woman varied. Some said she was of medium height, some insisted she was tall. She was said to be clothed all in black, in blue, in green, in yellow or red velvet, wearing a plumed hat, a wide-brimmed hat or no hat at all. Most often she was described to have dark hair, but it was not unusual to hear that she was a redhead or even a blonde. Every description included a cloak, though beneath it the costume varied from a full-skirted dress to trousers, puffed sleeves to straight.

"A most profitable calling." Quentin mumbled sarcastically, upon hearing that the woman's latest wardrobe had been embroidered with gold and seed pearls. At her side had been a dagger in a gilt-dressed leather case. Her horse's trappings were said to be leather decorated with silver and gold.

It infuriated him that the poverty-stricken of the city and surrounding areas looked upon the damnable woman as some kind of heroine, a modern-day Robin Hood who often left mysterious gifts on their doorsteps. A starving old couple found sacks of flour, sugar and other stores. A poor miller's wife had been presented with a bolt of warm wool. Others had found gifts of coins secured in leather pouches with a cheery note, signed "With love, the Notorious Lady."

"Notorious, most assuredly. Lady, I sincerely doubt," he mumbled beneath his breath. Well, whoever the woman was, her days of roaming the highway were soon to be put to an end. It was a vow Quentin did not make lightly.

Chapter Sixteen

The sky was an ebony velvet curtain upon which a multitude of stars glittered like precious jewels. Twinkling. Pulsating. Glowing. The moon was at its quarter, just a winking eye of light that touched upon the rolling hills and the horseman traveling the rocky, pitted road. A horseman who was doing little to hide his presence.

"Here I am. Why don't you come and get me?" Quentin whispered beneath his breath as he rode boldly and blatantly through the Heath. He was teasing the highwaymen, dangling himself under their noses like bait. His objective: to come face to face with the woman who was so quickly becoming the main topic of London's gossip. The Notorious Lady.

The woman was becoming so famous that rumors were posting her everywhere where highway robberies were reported. She was said to have been spotted at Gadshill near Rochester, Shooter's Hill near Blackheath, Salisbury Plain.

It was even being said that she could be in at least two places at one time.

The roads from Hounslow Heath to London had witnessed astounding doings of late. A rash of robberies had occurred. It seemed that not only was the Notorious Lady active, but copycat villains were likewise busy plying their trade on the roads that spiderwebbed in and out of London. It had to be stopped.

You think yourself to be so clever, so elusive. Well, I will not be as easily charmed by you, you treacherous little witch, as was Edwin Trevor. Indeed, Quentin was determined to bring about the Notorious Lady's downfall one way or another. If that meant setting himself up as a target, so be it. He had to get a close look at the female highwayman so that he could be instrumental in her capture. Better by far to have at least a passing acquaintance with the enemy.

"It's time you and I met," he said, gazing intently toward a copse of trees.

Quentin tensed at the thought of an encounter, then just as quickly relaxed. It would take all his self-control to allow himself to be robbed without fighting back, but it had to be done if he was going to find out the Notorious Lady's identity.

"Bigod, I know you must be watching me. I sense it. I feel it." As he rode along he listened, smiling as he heard the leaves rustle up ahead. Someone was there. Waiting. He knew it. "Come and get me."

It was a whispered challenge that went unanswered. Even so, he knew someone must be out there. Closing his eyes, he could nearly visualize the form waiting behind the trees, hiding until he could swoop down upon him. Why then was it so deathly silent all of a sudden?

"What are you waiting for?" Quentin wanted to get the meeting over with. Hot mulled wine would be waiting for him at Wakefield Manor. He was anxious to partake of it, and to enjoy his hearth fire. That reward, however, was not to be his until he had his meeting with the Notorious Lady. A meeting that had slowly become an all-encompassing obsession.

"I'll prove to you that—"

Quentin reined in his horse, listening intently to the sound he thought he perceived. Hoofbeats! He thought he heard the faint clopping sound carried on the breeze. He listened more closely. Yes, it could be heard distinctly now. Horses. One. Two. Or perhaps three. Smiling slightly, he prepared himself for the inevitable meeting.

From her hiding place Devondra was smiling too. There was something about the way the rider sat his horse that was familiar to her. That and the broadness of the shoulders. "Tobias, it's him. I know it this time!" She had Quentin Wakefield trapped. At last.

"Merry-go-up!" Craning his neck forward, Tobias tried to get a clearer look, then his head bobbed up and down. "Aye, I think it is him, all right."

"Then there is no reason to wait. None at all." Most women enjoyed the comforts of life, staying by the fire on a dark night. Devondra was different. Her late-night encounters had given her a zest for life and a sense of excitement that couldn't be equalled. Most especially tonight.

"Then we ride."

Putting her heels to her horse's flanks, urging the animal on, she vigorously shook her head. "We ride." Thus it was that Quentin saw the brightly plumed and dressed young woman explode into view, an apparition in blue, mounted on a steed of midnight darkness. "Halt," he heard her command.

"What do you want?" He played the game as if he didn't

know what she was after. Ah, but he knew well what was to follow, and the very thought of it infuriated him.

"Disarm yourself!"

Quentin did so reluctantly. All the while he wished he could really tell her what he thought about her escapades. She stole other people's property. If she gave some of that to the poor, it didn't matter. The woman was a thief. Now she was going to steal from him.

"There. Satisfied?" he asked, throwing his pistol and sword to the ground.

"For the moment," Devondra croacked disguising her voice in a hoarse whisper, watching him as Tobias dismounted and picked up his weapons. Only by the greatest effort did she keep her hands from trembling as she held her pistol pointed in Quentin's direction.

Quentin felt the heat of the woman's stare and looked up. Only her lustrous eyes were visible. The rest of her face was covered by a mask. Still, there was something about the eyes that convinced him she would be beautiful. "We should be introduced."

"Indeed." Devondra tensed from head to toe, replaying again in her mind that first moment they had met. Something had drawn her to him then, the same something that was drawing her now. But this time she would do everything in her power to fight against it. To fight against him.

"You are the Notorious Lady, I do believe," he said mockingly, affecting a slight bow. He tried to read something of the features outlined by the mask but her face was too well hidden. "And I . . . "

"I know who you are!" Defiantly, she stared down her adversary. He had not even recognized her. She knew in her heart that there wasn't any disguise he could have worn that would have kept her from guessing his identity. Still, he didn't know who *she* was. Strange how that could both relieve and at the same time upset her. Part of her wanted him to know.

"You do?" Oh, but she had an insolent way about her. As if she were royalty. Even so, she intrigued him. "Then I must be more infamous than I might have suspected," he said, trying to treat the moment lightly.

"In truth you are," Devondra rasped.

The low, seductive voice made Quentin shiver, though he didn't really know why. He took a look at the woman who held him within her pistol's sights. Staring at her he felt his senses prickle. Why was that? What was it about her that was so exciting?

He stared though the dim light. Even masked she was a magnificent sight. Garbed in a full-skirted dress of royal blue embroidered with pearls, a wide-brimmed blue hat with silver plume and a jeweled mask, she was dazzling. Not to mention the figure beneath the dress. The narrow waist was every man's dream. Her bosom had just the right swell and fullness. Her neck was slim and graceful as a swan's. But again, it was her eyes that held him spellbound. Dark and unfathomable, they watched him steadily, fearlessly, as her lips curved in a smile.

"Who are you?" Quentin wondered aloud. No street waif this one. She was so poised, so sure of herself. Moreover, despite her profession she had the demeanor and speech of someone born among the upper classes.

"That is *my* secret." Touching her tongue lightly to her lips, she tried to ease their dryness. Or was she trying to remember what it felt like to have his mouth on hers? The very possibility caused her to clutch all the more tightly to her pistol's handle. "Enough talk. Give me your money."

Quentin had handled pistols throughout the war. He knew how heavy the weapon must be in her slender gloved hands. Even so, she had held it aloft with as much confidence as if it weighed little. That alone drew his unwilling admiration. And curiosity. What had drawn a woman like this into a highwayman's way of life?

Again he asked, "Who are you?"

There was no answer, though he noticed her mouth tighten. And all the while the masked woman continued to stare with her smoldering eyes.

Quentin met her stare head on. He would never let her see how difficult it was for him to maintain his composure. Now he knew how Edwin had felt when he had encountered this woman, for in truth, he was equally fascinated.

What a pity were she to be hanged. What a tragedy. What a loss.

Quentin stiffened as he realized how quickly he had fallen under her spell. Oh yes, she was a temptress. A dangerous one who could make a man forget anything. Even his sworn duty.

Devondra's eyes touched upon Quentin's hair, remembering how it had felt beneath her fingers. And his mouth . . .

Quentin noticed her stare . . . and returned it full force.

The woman was silent, though Quentin could sense that she was struggling not to speak. She wanted to talk—why then didn't she?

"Are you as beautiful as I invision?" His gaze assessed her thoroughly, trying his damndest to imagine her face. Suddenly it became an obsession. He had to see her. "Take off your mask," he blurted. Would she be just as beautiful as he perceived?

Take off your mask, he had said. Take off her mask! Oh, how she wanted to do just that, and hurl it in his face. She wanted to tell him exactly what he was. A betrayer. A liar. "Take it off . . . ?

"Yes." He watched her and waited, all the while trying

to ward off the fascination that was enveloping him. She was graceful. Alluring. Challenging.

Her voice was little more than a whisper. "I will, if you will take off yours."

"What?" He thought surely he had misunderstood.

She repeated, slowly. "Take off your mask."

Quentin was stunned. "I'm not wearing one," he said.

Devondra smiled. She spoke without a trace of emotion, and her coldness startled him. "Ah, but you are, deceiver though you be."

"Deceiver?" What did she mean? Quentin was taken aback by the anger in her voice. Certainly the woman was acting most strange. Frighteningly so. "You talk in riddles." A knot twisted his insides. It was all very puzzling, this feeling he had inside. "I . . . "

"You are much too talkative." Tobias chided. Though he had set himself apart from this reunion, not wishing to intrude, he now made himself known. "Stop your chatter, sir, and do as the lady has bid. Your money."

"Or my life," Quentin mocked. He doubted that his life was really in peril. That is, he did until the pistol in the lady's hand discharged into the air, the bullet whisking by less than a fingernail's width from his ear. His skin stung with the hot impact.

"Or your life," she answered softly.

"Then by all means," Quentin answered, playing the game. A well-filled purse, a ring and a gold belt buckle changed owners. With little ceremony the female highwayman took them from him, then paused.

"What more do you want?" Quentin growled, angry at having been robbed despite the fact that it had been part of his plan. "What would you have of me?"

What did she want? Devondra had been so certain that she knew. She had wanted to hurt him, to cause him pain—

as much pain as his betrayal had given her. Now, as she faced him, her thirst for his physical harm left an unpleasant taste in her mouth. She didn't want to kill him. Not now. What then?

"I want to see you ruined!"

"Ruined?"

"Aye!" Against her will tears filled her eyes. Though she blinked them away furiously they rolled down her cheeks. Quickly, she brushed them away. "I want to see you brought so low that even the street beggars will scorn you."

"Bigod!" There was such icy fury in her voice that Quentin cringed inwardly. His head swam with a hundred urgent questions. But though he might have wanted at least one of them answered, he was doomed to disappointment, at least for the moment. All he could do was stare at the Notorious Lady and her companion as they mounted their horses and galloped off without another word.

Chapter Seventeen

It was warm in the room, yet Devondra shivered as she took the combs out of her hair and tossed them on the small round table. They clicked and clattered, a soft noise that made her jump.

"Bloody damn!" Her chest was tight with hurt and sadness, yet at the same time she couldn't suppress a laugh. Was she losing all self-control? Was she slowly sinking into madness?

Looking in the mirror, she took off her mask and contemplated the reflection staring back at her. Who was that young woman who seemed so lost, so young, so infinitely vulnerable? It was not she! It couldn't be she. And yet, as she reviewed the events that had just taken place, she was confused by the turmoil of her emotions. Did she hate Quentin Wakefield or . . .

"No!" She wouldn't even contemplate the idea of loving him. Loving him *would* be insanity, the most foolish and dangerous thing she could ever do. The very idea made her seem too pathetic, and she wanted to be strong. And yet, she was helpless to deny the effect he had on her.

Devondra blinked at her image. Her emotional turmoil had taken its toll. The price she had paid was evident in the slimmness of her waistline, the high cheekbones that were becoming more prominent in her face. Her cheeks were hollow, her lids heavy. Her face held an angelic pallor. Though she did not see herself so, she was beautiful, yet that beauty held a fragility that was startling.

She tried to focus her thoughts on the triumph of the night. Surely she was a worthy heir to her father's domain. She had ensnared her quarry just as she had planned. She had humbled him, forced him to descend from his lofty pedestal. And tonight had been only the beginning. Before she was through Quentin Wakefield would lose everything. Under a constant bombardment of thievery, she would soon see to his ruin. Only then could she put away her pistol and mask. Only then would her night rides end.

"Only then," she sighed, throwing herself full-length across the wide canopied bed without undressing. Her eyelids felt heavy. She was so exhausted that she didn't even bother to take off her boots.

"So, there you are. I was worried." Exhibiting a motherly concern, Hyacinth pushed into the room. "But then, I'm always concerned when you make your midnight rides."

Devondra sat up. "I can take care of myself!"

Hyacinth shrugged. "Under ordinary circumstances I know that you can. When you have thumbed your nose at the Lord Protector of England, when there is a price on your head then I begin to doubt it."

Glancing through her tangled hair, Devondra frowned. "Would I be better off to cower? I would say no. My father must be avenged."

"Over and over and over?" Hyacinth put her hands on

her hips. "Oh, Dev, I loved your father with every ounce of
my heart and soul, yet I know he wouldn't want this." She
picked up Devondra's discarded mask. "You take such risks,
more so even than did your father. Sometimes I fear you
have a desire to meet the same fate that he did. Why else
would you cart danger so?"

Devondra answered truthfully, "I don't know." She rose
from the bed and began to undress, hanging her garments
with care on a hook beside the door. Hastily, she pulled her
nightdress over her head.

"Are you trying to punish *him* or yourself?" Hyacinth
angrily threw the mask to the floor.

Devondra's eyes glittered as she picked it up and hung it
on the hook with her garments. "I seek to bring retribution
down on him." She padded on stockinged feet to the small
dresser. Pouring water into the basin, she splashed cold
water on her face, drying it with soft linen that Hyacinth
held out.

"Dev! What are you going to do when Cromwell's soldiers
discover your hideaway and come after you? What then?"

Devondra's tone was harsh. "Hush! I do not want to speak
any more about it. My mind is made up. I will do what
must be done."

"Then I will keep silent, at least for the moment." Hyacinth's expression clearly said that her opinions would not
be muffled for long.

Picking up a hairbrush, Devondra ran it through her luxuri-
ant waves with crackling strokes over and over again. "When
I was a little girl my mother taught me to always brush my
hair a hundred strokes."

"And you do."

"Yes." Devondra sighed, remembering the lovely, delicate
woman who had given her such love. Frail of body, she had
been zealous of soul.

"She taught you well, for surely you have the most beautiful hair." Hyacinth ran her fingers through her own. "'Tis not overly curly and unruly like my own." Taking the brush from Devondra's hand, she took over the task of brushing, her hands strangely gentle for a woman so strong and big-boned. "Was she pretty, your mother?"

Devondra nodded. "Fair of hair, not dark like me. Father always teased that she was of Viking stock but 'twas not so because . . . " Tilting her head to one side, she studied the other woman. "Did you love my father?"

"Everyone did."

Reaching out, Devondra touched Hyacinth's hand. "No. I mean, did you really love him?" When Hyacinth did not answer she made up her own mind. "You did! Else why would you have so quickly stepped in to care for me and for him after my mother's death?"

There was a sharp tug at Devondra's hair. "Aye, I loved him, though I knew that he did not truly love me." She swallowed, then blinked.

"He did, in his way. It's just that my father could never be true to just one woman. Not even to my mother. Perhaps that was what broke her heart and . . . "

"But he was a good man nonetheless." Hyacinth closed her eyes. "Oh, Jamie. Jamie!"

"You can't forget him, can you?" Devondra pulled away. Neither could she forget Quentin Wakefield, no matter how hard she tried.

Trembling, she glanced toward the bed but her mind was too active now, too troubled to permit sleep. Sitting down on the bed, she leaned her head back and tried to quench the flame in her blood but his memory tormented her.

"Men are such selfish creatures." Nevertheless she could not keep her thoughts from him, picturing every detail of the night they had spent together. Beams of moonlight danced through the windows, casting figured shadows on the roof overhead. Two entwined silhouettes conjured up memories of the embraces they had shared.

"Selfish, yet they can bring a woman much joy."

Even long after Hyacinth had gone, Devondra lay awake. Wrapping her arms around her knees, she curled up in a ball. Closing her eyes, she envisioned again the face of the man who haunted her now. "Quentin." Mists of fog danced before her eyes. A mist that took on another man's face. "Father!"

"How could you, my darling? How could you forget even for a moment what he has done? Because of him I got my neck stretched. The *steps and the string*. That's what he brought me." Grabbing his neck, he stuck out his tongue in a gruesome mockery of those who were hanged on the gibbet. "And he will do the same to you if you don't beware. The man has no compassion. He is Cromwell's creature. Always remember that."

"Cromwell's creature." She tossed her head from side to side as visions swirled through her mind.

"There she is! Catch her. She's a thief just like her sire!" Scar was pointing his fingers, leading a group of scowling men toward her. She had to find a place to hide.

"She's a thief!" a chorus of voices gave warning. "Hang her!"

"Not now! Please. You must understand . . . "

"Hang her!"

"No, you won't get your hands on me." Pushing through the crowd that sought to capture her, Devondra moved toward a small speck of light. "The tunnel. If we can but reach it, Father, we will be safe! We'll be . . . "

Bright daylight played across her face, teasing her eyelids awake. Rubbing her sleep-filled eyes, Devondra propped herself up shakily on one elbow and looked around her. "Dear God!" A dream. Just a silly dream after all. And yet . . .

Quentin Wakefield stood with his hands clasped behind his back as he stared out through the diamond-shaped panes of the mullioned windows on the second floor of Edwin Trevor's townhouse. Below he could see the cobbled street, empty at this early hour except for the bellman, calling out the hour. Streets were not lit, nor were they patrolled. Thus in affluent parts of London citizens hired men with bells to act as nightwatchmen.

"Perhaps we should hire him to patrol the Heath, eh, Quentin, old boy." Coming up behind Quentin, Edwin Trevor pressed his large nose against the glass.

"Very funny!" Quentin was not in a joking mood. Not after what had been happening the last few days.

It was obvious that whoever the masked woman was she had a personal vendetta against Quentin. Not content in just robbing *him,* the woman was now stopping any carriage or rider traveling in the direction of Wakefield Manor. Was it any wonder that Quentin had soon found his list of visitors dwindling?

"I want to see you ruined," he said aloud, quoting her last words. It appeared that she meant to do just that.

"What?"

Quentin whirled around, clenching his fists. "She threatened to ruin me, Edwin. She said she wanted to bring me so low that even the beggars would scorn me."

"Whew!" Patting his friend on the back, Edwin seemed relieved that it was Quentin's misfortune to have angered the woman and not his own. "Perhaps whatever it was you have done you should have said you were sorry."

"Sorry?"

"Aye." Edwin rolled his eyes suggestively.

Quentin knew at once just what his friend was insinuating. "Oh, no. It isn't what you think. She is not one of my discarded lovers."

"No?" Edwin wasn't convinced. Perhaps because Quentin seemed never to be at a loss for beautiful and willing young women who were only ready to warm his bed. Women who Quentin seemed to tire of in a very short time.

"No!" His voice was so loud, it made the windows rattle.

"Then what caused her ire?" Fumbling with the red velvet draperies, Edwin, who had been an actor before Cromwell closed all the theaters, spoke in falsetto. "Believe me, you must have been a bad, bad boy."

"Or a much too law-abiding one." As magistrate he had undoubtedly made many enemies.

"H m m m m m. I wonder." Playfully, Edwin wrapped the red velvet around his body, used his finger as a make-believe pistol and reenacted the scene. "Stand and deliver!"

Quentin didn't laugh. Indeed, it was hardly a laughing matter. The Notorious Lady, whoever she was, was making him look like a fool. He had boasted to Cromwell that he would put a stop to the woman's midnight rides. Instead he had become her principal victim.

"Edwin, you should have seen the anger in her eyes." anger and pain. "And for the life of me I haven't an inkling why."

"You will," Edwin grimaced, "for I doubt you have seen the last of her." Picking up a bottle of brandy from a table near the window, he poured himself a drink. "One for you?"

Quentin declined the offer. He had to keep a level head if he was going to figure this out. "I'd prefer tea." The drink was imported from India and was so expensive that the dried leaves were kept locked up in a tea caddy.

"Tea it will be." Clapping his hands, Edwin summoned

a servant, who soon brought a steaming teapot and a china cup. "You know, despite what you tell me, I get the feeling you were just as intrigued by that woman as I." He looked over the rim of his glass. "Were you?"

Quentin saw no reason to lie. "Yes." Perhaps that made him a fool twice over. "I wonder . . . "

"If she is comely or as ugly as a pockmarked cow?" Edwin laughed. "It is impossible to know without removing her mask, but I would daresay she would be quite irritable were either of us to try."

Quentin poured himself a cup of tea, then plopped down on a padded chair, crossing one booted leg over the other. "Oh, but I asked her to, you know."

"You did?" He sloshed the amber liquor back and forth. "And what did she say?"

"That she would, if I would take off mine." A statement that still troubled him. What had she meant? And why had she called him a deceiver?

"How strange." Edwin thought for a moment. "Come to think of it, I do believe she had been expecting you the night I was robbed."

"Expecting me?"

Edwin shook his head. "Yes. Yes, I remember now. She called out, " 'Do as I say or I swear, Quentin Wakefield, that I will part you from that animal the painful way.' " He tugged at his collar. "Unfortunately it was I who suffered indignity at her hands."

"Indignity?"

Edwin Trevor flushed. "She . . . she forced me to . . . to strip."

"Indeed?" Despite his testy mood, Quentin laughed. "So, though you didn't get a chance to see her face, she saw a lot of you."

"I had no choice!" Edwin quickly related the whole story.

"Damnable shame that they found the money that I had hidden in my boots. Cunning lot, they were."

"Obviously she is experienced in what she does."

"Experienced." Reaching up, Edwin tugged at his collar again, this time entangling his fingers in the gold chain he wore around his neck. "And strangely compassionate."

Quentin cocked his head. "How so?" Certainly she hadn't shown any compassion toward *him*.

Edwin took a long quaff of brandy, then said, "She let me keep this chain, because I said that it was all I had left of my father." For just a moment he looked sad. "She seemed to understand. I do believe that she did." Watching Quentin intently, he went on. "I had a father too, she said."

"No doubt an upstanding fellow, judging from the kind of life she chose," Quentin quipped. Suddenly he frowned as a thought flitted through his mind, a thought he quickly dismissed. He didn't want to think even for a moment. . . .

Chapter Eighteen

The soft rumble of human voices stirred the air, competing with the drone of bagpipes, the strum of a harp and the muffled thud of a drum. The aroma of cooking meats—beef, mutton, wild boar, pigeon and partridge—blended with the smell of just baked bread, tarts and pies still warm from the oven.

Vendors of every sort imaginable were gathered, carrying sacks, pushing carts or balancing wooden trays. All were crying out their wares. Louder and louder, their voices competed with each other's as they sought to call attention to their specialties.

"Muffins. Freshly baked."

"Cakes. Cinnamon cakes! Melt in your mouth."

"Spices from the Indies."

"Minced pies. Tarts."

"Cider. Hot cider."

"Oranges. Throw me a penny and I'll gi' ye one."

The sun was bright. Devondra shaded her eyes with her

hand as she walked beside Tobias, enjoying the sights, sounds and smells of Bartholomew's Fair. A lively affair, it was the great London event attended by anyone and everyone who considered themselves important.

"Forsooth, you must be mad, little miss, to chance walking the streets in broad daylight." Squinting his eyes, Tobias gazed at her assessingly, deciding at once that her appearance today would most certainly attract attention.

Dressed in an emerald green velvet gown trimmed with gold braiding and lace, her hair softly brushed back over a crescent pad and coiled into a bun, a rope of stolen pearls at her throat, she looked to be the complete antithesis of a proper Puritan lady, who always wore black.

"What if you are recognized as . . . as . . . ?"

"I won't be." Devondra tossed her head defiantly. "No one has ever seen my face." She was always masked, always shrouded in a dark cloud of mystery. Like a phantom who made her appearance, then disappeared into the mists of the heath.

"But . . . "

Putting her index finger to his lips, she silenced Tobias's protestations. "Don't worry, I'll be careful. I just want to have a bit of fun, that's all. I feel couped up, having to stay at the inn like some night creature that only dares to make an appearance when the sun goes down."

Bartholomew's Fair was something by no means to be missed. It was a time for laughter and excitement, when those rich and poor, high born or low rubbed elbows. A place where even members of Cromwell's court felt free to frolic.

He has to be here. Somewhere, in this throng, Quentin Wakefield strolls about. Devondra was determined to see him again, this time in the daylight. This time she wanted him to recognize her, wanted to make him come face to

162 *Kathryn Kramer*

face with his conscience. That was why she searched the
face of each man she passed, be he watchman, soldier or
lord.

"Perhaps *he* didn't come," Tobias suggested, as if reading
her mind. Taking her gently by the arm, he led her in the
direction of a performing bear.

"Perhaps . . . " For just a moment Devondra was distracted
as the shaggy brown animal successfully juggled a large
yellow ball. "But I intend to search anyway."

"Why?" Tobias's tone was fatherly. "Why torture yourself
so? You can't bring your father back, no matter how much
you taunt this bold fellow."

"No I can't . . . " Devondra quieted. There was so much
that Tobias didn't know, wouldn't understand, that there was
no use talking about it. Something deep inside her wouldn't
be satisfied until she truly understood the workings of Quentin Wakefield's mind.

She wanted to know why he had done her the most grievous wrong. Ambition? Cruelty? Some false sense of justice?
Only he could answer: thus she had to talk with him. Meanwhile, she careened her way through the gawking crowd,
experiencing the moment.

"Ah. Look!" Tobias was enthralled with the booth where
an Irish giant was being exhibited. Short himself, he was
amazed as the man's height was marked off against the wall
in comparison with several others.

"Mmmm. He is tall, but . . . " Devondra smiled as she
realized the muscular red-haired man's height was being
exaggerated by the fact that the attendants had chosen only
those of low stature in order that the greatness of the giant
might appear to the best advantage. She didn't spoil Tobias's
gasp of pride when he was one of those picked to stand
beside the giant.

"Oh, but could we only get him to join with us," he

breathed, raising his brows at Devondra. "Just think how frightened Scar would be." He sighed. "Ah, but 'tis only a dream."

"Or were it possible to convince yon lad to come to the heath to be on our side," Devondra said, nodding her head in the direction of the strong man of Topham. His specialty was bending nails with his teeth and rolling pewter plates with his fingers.

Other things, too, were diverting, taking her thoughts elsewhere for just a while. There was the strange animal recently brought from Africa called a baboon, the pig-faced-lady, two jugglers, a gypsy fortune-teller and an Italian troubadour who strolled through the crowd favoring blushing young maidens with a song and a smile. Sweeping his hat from his head, he brazenly flirted with Devondra until she quite decidedly snubbed him.

"Ohhhhhhh." Tobias mockingly touched his chest. "The poor man's heart. No doubt you have bruised it beyond repair."

Devondra didn't smile. "A timely lesson, I would say. For he and for others of his ilk." Quentin Wakefield's face flashed before her eyes.

"Indeed."

Huffing and puffing, Tobias hurried after her as she flitted through the crowd and sighed with relief when at last she came to a stop in front of a small replica of a theatrical stage. It was true that Oliver Cromwell and the Puritans had closed down the theaters, but they did survive by way of puppet shows. This particular comic puppet play, imported from Italy, was always met with giggles and laughter.

"Ah, Punch and Judy." Tobias plopped down on an empty stool, settling in to see the show. Devondra stood beside him, her eyes focused on Punch, a rather ugly fellow with a large hooked nose and a hunched back. A great coward,

he was boasting about his courage and the marvelous things
he could do.

"I can do anything!"

"Like wot?" Judy, his wife, was doubtful. "Can yer cook?"
The puppet shook his head.

"Can yer sew?"

Again Punch shook his head.

"Can yer weave wool?"

"Welllllll . . . no!"

Judy put her tiny hand to her painted mouth as if to confide
to the audience. "And he most certainly isn't any Prince
Charlie in bed," she said in mock whisper, alluding to the
exiled Stuart. Picking up a stick, she banged him on the
head. "Ha, wot good are ye?"

"Good?" Trying his hand at such manly tasks as chopping
wood and wielding a plow, Punch was a failure. Even so,
he wouldn't admit it. Swaggering around the tiny stage, he
swore profusely, then paused as an idea took hold of him.
Fumbling to put on a mask, Punch declared, "I can rob
coaches." He disappeared under the stage for a moment and
when he reappeared held in his arms a wooden sword.

"Coaches?"

His head bobbed up and down. "Aye. Coaches. 'Tis a
highwayman I can be."

"A highwayman?" Judy collapsed in a heap of hysterical
laughter. "A highwayman!" She giggled outrageously again.

"Ha!" Losing his temper, Punch was quick to counter,
"Well, you're no Notorious Lady yerself. But oh, how I
would like you to be."

Tobias nudged Devondra in the ribs. She was more infamous than anyone had thought.

"Ha!"

"Ha!" Now it was Punch's turn to pummel Judy on top
of her head.

In a jarring tirade, Judy berated her husband, warning him soundly that were he not to change his ways he would be hanged. "Jack Ketch will get ye, this I vow!"

"Jack Ketch . . . " For a moment Devondra paled; then, without waiting to see any more, she hurried away, Tobias at her heels.

"You have to know. It is a possibility."

Devondra was chillingly silent. It wasn't fear for herself that had prodded her just now but sorrow. Jack Ketch had been the hangman who had put the noose around her father's neck. And all because of—

"Him . . . " Standing at the edge of a roped ring was the very object of all her angry thoughts. Tall and muscular, a white shirt hugging his wide shoulders, tight brown trousers outlining every inch of his masculinity, he was the kind of man who stood out in any crowd.

Devondra crept closer, her senses suddenly heightened, her emotions on edge as her eyes traveled over him. Look at the angle of his chin, jutting upward as if he and not Cromwell ruled the land. Oh, what vanity. What pride. And to think that the proper magistrate was setting himself up beside four other swordsmen as a champion, challenging any in the crowd to meet them in competition.

"Well, I'll be," Tobias exclaimed.

Devondra's tone was mocking. "Now, this should be entertaining."

A trumpeter beckoned the crowd. Devondra hurried to take a seat on a bench facing the candlelit platform, determined to cheer on anyone, any man at all, who challenged her adversary.

"Jonathan Hall." Whispering, the crowd instantly recognized the red-bearded man who came forward. He was a champion with the sword and in wrestling and was a familiar and welcome spectacle at these fairs. Employed to act as the guard in the jewel room of the famous Tower of London, Hall proved himself to be daring when he suddenly launched himself forward and leaped over the rope. Amid cheers and applause, he plucked up a sword.

"I challenge *you*, Wakefield." Jauntily, Hall threw off his cloak, casting it carelessly to whomsoever chanced to catch it.

A cheer arose and then, from others in the crowd who had aligned themselves with Wakefield, there came a boo.

"I challenge you to meet me with sword and in a wrestlers' fall."

"Swords first." Choosing a likely weapon, Quentin turned, startled as he recognized a face in the crowd. A face he had long been searching for. A figure from his dreams. "Devondra!" he said in a low voice, taking a step toward her.

She looks as beautiful as an angel, glowing, set apart from every other woman. He took another step forward. Beyond the first moment of recognition, however, Devondra gave him no notice. In fact, she purposely looked down.

I have to explain. She has to know that it was not my fault about her father. I have to tell her that my missive was never received. She must listen. But alas, there was no time. A fight had been promised, and until its completion Quentin could not preoccupy himself with personal matters.

"Let the combat begin." That said, the two swordsmen went at each other, their blades dulled, the points protected lest death win the contest.

Quentin struck out, only to have his blow parried. Hall lunged, likewise thwarted in his attempt.

The clang of sword on sword rent the air as the two fought a furious battle, a test of strength and skill. Though Devondra would never admit it aloud, she was impressed. The magistrate's skill had improved greatly. It was obvious he had been practicing. She and the others must remember not to engage him in a swordfight.

"He makes a good show for himself," Tobias whispered in her ear. "Me thinks your presence here will goad him on to an assured victory."

"Well, the fight is not over yet," Devondra declared, watching as both men were stripped to the waist and belted. For several minutes they circled about, each with his right hand cupping the right elbow of his opponent in English fashion. Then, as if by a single thought, both men grappled, battling rough and strong. Locked together they went down, rolling over and over, twisting and turning, smashing down the candles until Quentin pinned his opponent down.

The cheers were thunderous. Quentin, however, took little time to savor them. He had only one thought in mind as he slowly rose from the ground. Quickly crossing to where Devondra sat, he took her fingers in his strong grip.

"It's good to see you again."

"Is it?" Her voice was as cold as the north wind.

"Yes!" Remorse swept over him. If only things had turned out differently, perhaps they would be together. *If.* "Devondra . . . I . . . "

Yanking her hand from his grasp, she stared up at him, her eyes glittering. "I don't believe there is anything you can say to me to explain your treachery; however, there are many things I wish to say to you."

"Undoubtedly." He touched her lips with his fingers to silence her, "But first listen."

"Why? Words are meaningless. It is deeds that tell the story."

Ignoring her anger, Quentin hurried to explain. "The letter I wrote was never received." He repeated." It was never received!"

Silently she continued to stare at him, studying him keenly. If she hadn't known what kind of man he was, she might have mistaken the look in his eyes for one of true concern.

But she did know. "You, sir, are a liar!" And to think that she would have gone with him to the ends of the earth. "And I the biggest fool!"

"No!" How could he ever change her mind? How could he show her the truth? How could he reveal what was in his heart?

"Yes ... Quickly she turned her back to him, no longer able to meet his eyes without giving way to tears.

Fearing she might flee, Quentin reached out to grip her by the shoulders. "Richard, the man I sent with the missive, was set upon by highwaymen. He never reached London with ...

"Oh!" Anger rose up like poison, nearly choking her. Of all the excuses he might have invented, this was the most cruel. "To blame your perfidy on ... men like ... like ... my father! As if any of them would have had reason to see him hang."

"Nonetheless, 'tis true." Gently, he ran the fingers of one hand up and down her arm, trying to calm her. Oh, it felt so good to touch her again. Oh, how he wanted ...

Against her will her body was responding. A warm tingling swept over her, the first stirrings of desire at his nearness. "Don't!"

"It seems that I can't help myself," he admitted. Nor could he help what followed.

Devondra felt the power of his hands as he turned her around and pulled her toward him. He was close, so close that she could feel the warmth of his skin. His head was moving downward. She could feel the warmth of his breath on her lips.

"No!" She could feel her heart beating so loudly that her ears seemed to be ringing. She couldn't breath. Couldn't think. It was as if all her thoughts were melting away. Then his lips found hers, burning her heart, scalding her soul. For just a moment his mouth was the only reality as she gave in to the depth of her feelings.

Her head was swirling. Warmth shot through her body as

she felt his hand slide down to pull her tightly against him. Even through her skirt and petticoats she could feel the hardness of his arousal. She remembered the passion they had shared, the tenderness, the wonder.

Then, just as suddenly, reality hit her like a fist. His arms were holding her as tightly as if she were his prisoner. In truth, as long as she gave in to her emotions, she was. In his arms Devondra Stafford had ceased to exist. In her place was a spineless creature, one who could be so easily manipulated just by a caress, a kiss and soft words. A woman who could forget what had happened to her father.

Frantically she drew back. Reaching out, Devondra slapped the face of the man hovering over her. "Your kisses can not bring back my father!"

His eyes burned. His voice was husky, harsh. "Nor can your hatred."

That truth was gauling. "Nevertheless it is all I have," she answered. Oh, why couldn't she look away? Why was she rooted so firmly to the spot? Why was she searching his face, wanting so much to believe him?

"Ah, Quentin, here you are." Edwin Trevor's voice was an irritating intrusion. "To think you bested Jonathan Hall."

"Aye." Quentin's attention was diverted only for the space of a heartbeat. But it was long enough for Devondra Stafford to get away. "Damn!"

Looking over the heads of the crowd, he could see her pushing through, but though he tried to pursue her, his path was blocked by well-wishers, each patting him on the back, congratulating him on his victory. A victory that was hollow.

Oh, Devondra . . . " Her scent still clung to him, arousing him, reminding him. Alas, it was all that was left of her, at least for the moment.

Chapter Nineteen

The chamber was chilly and drafty, despite the fire in the great stone fireplace. Quentin tugged at his cloak, hanging from a wooden peg on the wall, and draped it over his shoulders, all the while reliving in his mind his meeting with Devondra Stafford.

She didn't believe a word I said. She accused me of being a liar. Even so, their meeting yesterday had reawakened a host of potent feelings. Longings and passion that he had nearly buried but which he knew could never be set aside again. Not now. Not after their kiss.

"This can not and will not be the end of it!" Somehow, some way, he had to find her again, had to make her listen. *Even if I have to hold her at swordpoint.*

"She was beautiful." Leaning against the wooden paneling, Edwin Trevor was studying Quentin with a quizzical expression. "Who was she?"

"Just a vision out of a dream." A vision he wanted to touch and hold and love.

Edwin was not content with such a glib response. "Perchance the vision had a name?"

"Devondra Stafford."

"Stafford? Stafford?" Edwin Trevor's mouth formed an *o* as he suddenly recognized the name. "Not the highwayman's daughter you told me about."

"The same."

"The one who almost tamed you. The one who got away." Edwin grinned as he toyed with the lace at his sleeve. "Well, from the look on your face when you were gazing into her eyes, 'tis on your mind to rectify that unfortunate turn of events. Am I right?"

"You are."

Closing his eyes, Quentin remembered how passionate she had been in his arms. She had melted into him like the ocean seeking the shore. She had wiped away all memory of the other women who had paraded in and out of his life.

"If only I can think of a way to get her to listen to the truth, that I *did* try to save her father's life."

Edwin toyed with a lock of his hair, a habit that was always annoying. "Dear boy, I daresay after what happened you are going to have the devil of a time convincing her of that." He paused for a moment. "That is, unless you abduct her."

"Abduct her!" It wasn't as though he hadn't thought about it, though he knew Edwin to be but jesting. "Indeed, I should and would, except for one thing."

"That being?"

Smiling faintly, Quentin whispered, "I can't seem to find her. Though God knows I've tried." There wasn't a nook or cranny in all of London that he hadn't had searched for the illusive Devondra Stafford. She was, however, nowhere to be found, a fact that piqued his suspicions.

"Maybe you have looked in the wrong places," Edwin

said quickly, trying to be helpful. "Perhaps you should search for her at night. On the Heath."

Quentin knew at once just what his friend was suggesting, that Devondra was living among thieves, rogues and others who had roamed at will with her father. Though Edwin was merely voicing Quentin's own thoughts aloud, he hurriedly exclaimed, "Don't jump to wild conclusions!" Such a slip of the tongue could put Devondra's life in danger.

"Don't blind yourself to probability." Plopping down on a chair, Edwin thumbed through a stack of papers on a nearby table. "I would venture to say the lady in question isn't spending her time knitting."

"No, I don't suppose." Walking to the window, Quentin looked out, watching as the sun slowly sank below the rooftops of London. The glory of the sky was like a fire, bold orange and gold and deep shades of lavender. Devondra was out there, somewhere, beyond the horizon, perhaps looking at the sunset just as he was now. If so, was she thinking of him at all? Was she remembering their all-too-brief meeting at the fair?

Devondra was remembering, all too vividly. "Liar!" Her face burned as she recalled every detail of the moment. Alas, it only made the aching in her heart worse. *I still love him.* It was a brutal confession to make to herself, yet one that had to be made as she stared stoically across the low rolling hills.

" 'Tis a lovely night, don't you think?" Tobias was totally absorbed in his admiration of the sunset. "A perfect night for lovers, or so I would say."

"Lovers!" Once a word that she had treasured, it now held a tawdry ring. "Lovers . . . " Her throat dry, she blinked against her tears. How could she have been so foolish? So naive? So trusting? "But never again!"

Putting her hands to her ears, she refused to even consider for a moment that he had been sincere in his attempt at reconciliation. She had believed him once, and it had cost her dearly—her father's life.

"His messenger was intercepted by highwaymen, indeed!" Even the lie he told was cold and calculating. Heartless, considering her father's profession and the way he had met his end. Did he really think her to be such a fool as to fall for such a story?

Undoubtedly. What greater fool could there have been than I? To have actually believed for a minute that he had loved her was the greatest stupidity. He had but used her body; that was all. As for her affections, she had fallen in love with a shadow, a dream, a man who didn't really exist.

"Tobias . . . " She paused at the sound of hoofbeats. A lone horseman was making his way up the long winding road.

The spot that Devondra had chosen was where the road to London topped a steep hill. She knew from having listened to her father relate his adventures what road the wealthiest men took from London. Tonight's pick was to be Godfrey Tarkington. A rich man. A proud man. A stingy man. One of the men who had sat in judgment upon her father.

"Is it he?" Thrusting out his chin, Tobias squinted.

Devondra didn't answer until she could be certain. At length, he came into sight. His tall, skinny, stoop-shouldered frame was highlighted by the colors in the darkening sky. "Yes. Fool that he is, he always travels alone." She was angered by the memory of the man's lack of empathy toward her father. "Tonight he will regret it."

"Aye, all is ripe for action." Leaning forward in his saddle,

Tobias rode into the road with a dash. Blocking the pathway, he halted the indignant rider.

"What's this?"

It was Devondra who answered as she gracefully guided her horse to the rider's other side, her pistol primed and ready. "You have the honor of being robbed by the Notorious Lady."

"Honor? Honor?" Godfrey Tarkington spat on the ground. His dark eyes were piercing as he stared brazenly first at Devondra, then at Tobias, and then at Devondra again. Frowning, he reached into his pocket, took out some silver and gold coins and tossed them on the ground. "Here, and have done with it!"

Tobias didn't bother to dismount. Clucking his tongue, he shook his head. "For shame! We had thought to be mindful of your rank, but such a pittance is insulting at best." He looked toward Devondra. "Shall we have him commence in shelling the peas?"

She smiled. "We shall."

Hearing that, the gray-haired man stiffened. "Doing what?"

This time Devondra's mouth was a straight line. "Take off your wig." When Tarkington faltered she commanded, "Now!"

Reaching up, he tugged at his long-haired, elaborately curled hair piece, revealing a bald head beneath. "There is nothing hidden underneath."

Disbelieving, Tobias snatched it from the old man's trembling hands. Holding it up, he examined it carefully. "Nothing aside from an onyx stickpin. Which will now decorate *my* cravat."

"Thieves! Robbers!"

Devondra's voice was cold. "Call us what you will. I care not what you think of me, for in truth the words apply just as easily to you. You who take from the poor to line your own coffers."

"I do not!"

"You do." She moved closer. "Let it be said that whatever we take from you tonight will find a better cause than decorating your cadaverish body."

Though what they took was not considerable—two rings, a pair of buckles and a small bag of coins—Devondra was satisfied. Just humiliating the man, the same way her father had been humbled, eased some of her anger.

"Here." She threw down his brown leather boots, after having made a thorough inspection of them. "Next time remember that the wig and the boots are much too obvious hiding places."

"Aye." Tobias was in a jovial mood, having found and enjoyed a long draught of some of the bottle of ale hidden among the man's possessions. "Think of what happened here tonight as a sort of blessing."

"Blessing?" Tarkington glowered.

"A lesson, as it were, in prudent traveling," Devondra said, joining in the banter.

"Bigod, you will learn a lesson as well." Lifting his hand, Tarkington pointed a bony finger in the highwaymen's direction. "A lesson in justice."

"Justice?" Devondra held her pistol aloft. "Justice? Indeed, sir, you have no conception of the meaning of the word." Without thinking, she blurted out, "Remember Gentleman James."

"Gentleman James . . . ?" Tarkington's beady eyes seemed to burn a hole right through Devondra's mask, and in that instant he realized who she was. "Bigod. His daughter. Of course!"

"Little miss!" Tobias knew at once the danger of having been recognized. His fear was short-lived, however. A dark-

cloaked figure crept out of the gathering darkness so stealthfully, so silently, that neither he nor Devondra were aware
until they heard a familiar voice.

"So this chicken lays golden eggs. I thought as much."

"Scar!" Beneath her mask, Devondra's face went pale.
Turning around, she stared at the dark silhouette with loathing. "You are intruding here."

"I've come to get my share." Urging his horse forward,
Scar held out his hand.

"Go to the devil!" Devondra refused to be intimidated.

"I am the devil," he replied. His laugh was evil personified
as he pulled at his black horse's reins. The animal reared
up on its hind legs just as a sudden crack of thunder pierced
the night. A jagged bolt of lightning followed, splitting the
darkness and illuminating the scowling, scarred face.

"Dear God!" With a terrified shriek, Godfrey Tarkington
took one look as the ominous dark-cloaked vision met his
eyes and panicked. Though barefoot, he thought of nothing
but his desperate need to get away from the scarred man he
believed to be some hideous demon risen from the bowels
of hell.

"Stop!" Devondra called out. Grabbing her horse's reins,
she started off in pursuit, only to stiffen as she heard the
explosion of a pistol. Looking toward Tarkington, she gasped
as she watched him slump. "No!"

"The fool! No one gets away from Scar!" Without a pause
or a blink of remorse, the highwayman blew at the smoke
coming from the barrel.

"You murderous beast!" A knot squeezed in the pit of her
stomach as she realized what had occurred. Without a flinch,
Scar had shot Godrey Tarkington down. Her roamings upon
the Heath had suddenly turned into a most deadly game.

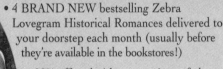

4 FREE BOOKS

These books worth almost $20, are yours without cost or obligation
when you fill out and mail this certificate.
*(If the certificate is missing below, write to: Zebra Home Subscription Service, Inc.,
120 Brighton Road, P.O. Box 5214, Clifton, New Jersey 07015-5214)*

Complete and mail this card to receive 4 Free books!

YES! Please send me 4 Zebra Lovegram Historical Romances without cost or obligation. I understand that each month thereafter I will be able to preview 4 new Zebra Lovegram Historical Romances FREE for 10 days. Then if I decide to keep them, I will pay the money-saving preferred publisher's price of just $4.00 each...a total of $16. That's almost $4 less than the regular publisher's price, and there is never any additional charge for shipping and handling. I may return any shipment within 10 days and owe nothing, and I may cancel this subscription at any time. The 4 FREE books will be mine to keep in any case.

Name _____

Address _____ Apt. _____

City _____ State _____ Zip _____

Telephone ( ) _____

Signature _____

(If under 18, parent or guardian must sign.)

LF0296

* * *

It was dark and dangerous, that time of night when thieves and other miscreants prowled. Was it any wonder that Devondra and Tobias tried to blend with the shadows as they made their way from the stables to the inn?

"Damn the man! He has put all our necks in a noose!" Tobias kicked at a stone, sending it flying. "Murder, bigod!"

A sudden brisk breeze chilled Devondra's body, or was it a sense of forboding? She tugged her cloak more firmly around her. "Scar is an overbold fool to kill one of Cromwell's men."

"A simpleton! Toy with him, yes. Shoot him in the back, no." Tobias shook his head. "Let us just hope that what occurred will in no way be traced to us."

It was smoky and musty inside the King's Head. The flames of lanterns flickered, casting eerie shadows against the walls. The smell of spilled wine, whiskey and ale mixed with the odor of sweat and leather. The clank of tankards, mugs and cups hung in the air. It was the last day of the week, and the patrons had lingered, ignoring the lateness of the hour. It was noisy, yet not any more so than usual. Why then did the laughter annoy her so? Because now she fully realized the danger she was in, from within as well as from without.

Devondra stared into the fire for a long, long while. A decision needed to be made as to what her next action would be, but her contemplation was shattered when the front door of the tavern was thrown open. The wind blew in gusts through the open portal, swirling about the cloaked figure that pushed inside the room.

"Scar!"

They stared at each other in silence, an angry challenge

in their eyes then, sweeping across the wooden floor, Scar reached out and took her by the shoulders. His fingers seemed to. melt through her flesh, to grip her very bones. "You should see your face, *wench!* You are as pale as a white mouse."

Devondra's breath hissed out in a low whisper. "You shot him in the back!"

Scar smirked, his eyes devouring her. "Why, so I did!"

"And it doesn't even bother you, does it?" The truth of his callousness curdled her blood. His violent nature sickened her.

"No!" His voice was toneless as he explained. "I have no qualms about killing anyone who gets in my way."

"Anyone?" She pulled away violently, feeling threatened.

He nodded. "Anyone." Reaching up, he loosened his collar, exposing the naked skin of his hairless chest, then tugged at a chair and sat down. "I killed Tarkington for you, you know."

"For me?" A likely story.

"Aye. I heard what he said. He recognized you." Turning his attentions briefly to the tavern maid, he snatched up a bottle of wine and drank directly from it without bothering to use a glass. The red liquid trickled down his chin, matching the scar that already marred his face.

"So . . . so he did. But . . . but I would have found a way to deal with that. A way other than murder!"

"A woman's way," he taunted. Like an animal, Scar made a growling sound in the back of his throat.

It was a sound that brought Tobias to Devondra's side. Having quickly drained a tankard of ale, however, he was becoming more optimistic about the night's events. "Perhaps no one will find Tarkington!"

Devondra was unnerved by a sudden roar of thunder. "And maybe they will," she said.

* * *

Dark gray clouds strangled the moon. Thunder rumbled overhead with the promise of a torrent. Already the road was muddy from the steadily falling rain. Gathering his cloak tightly about him, Quentin Wakefield uttered a curse beneath his breath. Tonight had seemed a perfect evening when they had set out, but the tranquility was now torn assunder by the threat of a sudden storm.

"I told you we should have stayed in London," Edwin threw over his shoulder.

"Even so, you were the first one out the door. Inspired, no doubt, by my invitation to enjoy freely of my wine cellar," Quentin called back.

"Bah! 'Twas you who couldn't wait to set out for your manor, despite the dangers. One would nearly think that you secretly hoped we would meet up with trouble."

Quentin swallowed his reply, fearing that anything he said might give away his true motives—that being his determination to locate Devondra Stafford. Edwin's remark about looking for her on the Heath had struck a nerve. It had to be true. Where else would she go?

"God's whiskers, she'll get herself hanged if she isn't cautious." Nowadays it was important what kind of company a person kept. Indeed, a man was known by his friends, judged by his peers and all too often betrayed by his enemies. That being the case, Quentin knew it to be imperative that he find her.

"Admit it!" Edwin cajoled, wiping his wet face with his hand. "You're searching for your lady love."

"God's teeth, I am not!" Quentin grumbled. He urged his horse into a much faster gallop. He was determined to ride through the rain, despite Edwin's complaining that they should seek shelter until the storm let up.

"I don't believe you, you know. I'm not such a fool that I don't realize just what inspired your sudden obsession to go home by way of the Heath."

"London bores me."

"So you risk being robbed on this road just to go in search of excitement?"

"Yes. These days traversing any roadway is a risk, but I refuse to cower." In truth, he thought bitterly, nowadays it would be difficult if not impossible to say which road out of London was the most infested with cursed highwaymen. Certainly all roads were exteremely dangerous for honest men. Even so, he wasn't going back to London. Not until he found her.

Edwin was philosophical on the matter. "Although I doubt there to be a saint in their ranks, even highwaymen are human. They are a fact of life that must be borne, I fear."

Quentin bristled. "By you perhaps, Edwin, but not by me."

"You would fight then?" Edwin was obviously uneasy with that thought.

"I would, and send any culprit straight to the gallows."

There was a long pause. "Gadfreys, Quen, you can't hang every perpetrator of wrongdoing in England. We wouldn't have anyone left." Edwin chuckled, but quickly grew silent as he sensed his companions' bad mood.

"I can. And will." He would see to it that law and order once more ruled the day. "The rogues need to be given warning." As for Devondra, that was a far different matter. He would hide her if need be.

"Give them a warning, is it? Well, you do that. *Alone!*"

"I'll understand if you insist on turning back."

"Turn back?" Looking over his shoulder Edwin seemed tempted. Then he shook his head. "Common sense tells me

I'm better off with you. Two, it seems, would be much safer company than one."

Not being of a mind to talk further about the matter, Quentin rode off, leaving Edwin behind. In the end, however, it was he who halted his mount, realizing the need to take shelter. He nodded in the direction of the roadway, which was quickly becoming a quagmire.

"Is something wrong?" Edwin shouted out, catching up at last.

"No. I just think it wiser to wait out the storm."

"Thank God!" Edwin shivered violently, following Quentin as he guided his mount to a grove of thickly leaved trees beside which stood a dilapidated woodsman's hut. "God allow that there be firewood inside."

There was not. Though Quentin was content with being out of the rain, Edwin was more particular. Stubbornly he insisted on searching the wooded area nearby for firewood.

"There won't be a dry piece of wood from here to London." Quentin called through the open door.

"Probably not, but if there is I'm the man to find it." Edwin retorted. Indeed, he did find something, but not what he had bargained for. "Quentin! Quentin! Come Quickly. Look here!"

Grabbing his tinderbox and a candle from inside the hut, Quentin harkened to the shout. Squinting, he could make out the outline of what he at first perceived to be a large sack. Then his eyes adjusted to the darkness and he realized it was something else: A human form.

"Bigod!"

Edwin turned over the body. Bending down, he stared into the ghostly pale face. "It's Tarkington."

"Dead?"

Listening for a heartbeat, Edwin nodded. "Dead." His hands explored, finding the wound. "Shot in the back."

"Murdered! But by whom?" Quentin had a suspicion, which was confirmed as he took note of Tarkington's bare feet. It was obvious the man had been robbed in a manner most cowardly. A manner that would most assuredly seal the malefactor's fate.

Chapter Twenty

All London rang with the tale of the highway robbery of the night before. Godfrey Tarkington had been anything but a popular man; thus it was little wonder that hardly anyone grieved at the news of his death. Even so, the murder had serious reprecussions. The constables, the headboroughs and the watch were taken to task for being ineffective in stopping the reprehensible wave of crime. Publically ridiculed, they were told that they would be dealt with severely if they allowed even one more criminal to escape.

As to those who *were* caught, it was announced that as of this day the time of sentimentality was at an end. Though gallows lined the roadways, there would be more gibbets set up. From now on all felonies were to be punishable by death.

"Let the bodies of those who profane England's lawful citizens be themselves profaned," Cromwell had decreed. Because he was known for his savage treatment of his enemies, particularly the Irish and the Scots, it was no wonder that this edict caused the common man to tremble. Cromwell governed arbitrarily, often imprisoning men without trial. He had created major generals and put them in charge of his "call to moral regeneration."

Sitting opposite Cromwell on the dais in the Star Chamber and beside Edwin Trevor, Quentin listened pensively to the discussion going on. They were talking of making the punishment for any crime more severe.

"Revive the tradition of torture in England, no matter that the law states otherwise," a corpulent councilor was saying.

"Aye, hang a few more on the gallows!" said another councilor.

"Let all evildoers see that Justice is still vigilant and ready to punish crime."

"Hang them in chains."

"Dangle them in iron cages until they rot."

"Strangle them. Make them choke until their tongues hang out."

"Put a few more heads atop London Bridge."

"Let them see first hand that harming one hair on a gentleman's head will make of them gibbet fruit."

The chamber rang with angry voices. All expressed their opinions, albeit in a different way. One thing that was agreed upon, however, was that up until now the law had been much too easy on transgressors. There were many prisons: The Tower, the Compter, the Clink, the Marshalsea, the White Lion, the King's Bench, Cripplegate, Ludgate, the Fleet and, most ominous of all, Newgate. It appeared that soon they would be bulging with prisoners, Jailed unfortunates who were awaiting the hangman.

"And what of the woman?" Edwin said behind his hand.

"Woman." Thinking that Edwin meant Devondra, Quentin was evasive. "What woman?"

"The Lady. The Notorious Lady." He grinned. "Most certainly you have not forgotten."

"Forgotten?" Quentin rasped angrily. "I doubt I will forget her for quite a while!" He clenched his fists at the reminder of his meeting with the sensuous female.

"If she were caught would you see her hanged too?"

"Hanged!"

"Shhhhh!" Putting his finger to his lips, Edwin reminded his friend to keep his voice down, then whispered, "Would you?"

Quentin started to say yes, then, as he recalled their encounter, he reluctantly shook his head. The idea of hanging a woman—any woman—left a sour taste in his mouth. "No . . . "

So many things about their meeting troubled him, particularly her strange statement that she would take off her mask if he would take off his.

"I'm not wearing one," he had said.

"Ah, but you are, deceiver though you be". . . .

"Deceiver . . . There had been such anger in her voice, as if he had in some way done her a grave wrong. She had acted as if they were already acquainted. As if. . . .

Like a fist to his stomach, an uneasy tension struck. *Could it be? Is it possible?*

"Jesus!" Forgetting himself, Quentin blurted the holy name and was embarrassed when all heads turned his way.

"Jesus?" Cromwell leaned forward.

"Will certainly be busy listening to a multitude of prayers," Edwin hurried to say. "Quentin thinks the condemned will be overeager to try and make amends. Poor devils."

"Devils, indeed." Cromwell sniffed indignantly. "There is no mercy for the guilty, even in heaven." Rising from his chair, he walked slowly across the room, coming to rest at Quentin's side. "What say you, about this matter?"

"I abhor all who have no respect for the law. They have brought themselves to a sorry end."

Smiling, Cromwell confided, "an end that you will hasten."

"I?"

Cromwell started to explain, then collapsed in a fit of coughing, lending credence to the claim by his enemies that he was not well. At last he recovered enough to say, "I want you to help me set a trap."

"A trap?"

Cromwell wrinkled his long nose. "To catch a thief, or several if all goes well."

"In the Heath?"

Cromwell's smile was crooked. "Aye, in the Heath." Taking Quentin aside he related his plan.

Chapter Twenty-One

It was a cloudless night. Thousands of stars blinked like watching eyes, peering down at the figures hidden in the trees. Sylvester, Tobias and Devondra waited, with Conan acting as a lookout a mile up the road.

"Forsooth, this matter of the highways is getting dangerous," Sylvester grumbled. "If we be ropedancers then we are treading on very thin rope."

"And does that make you afraid?" Tobias was interested.

"In truth yes. I have no liking for having my neck stretched." Reaching up, Sylvester nervously brushed at his throat.

Since the shooting of Godfrey Tarkington newfound hazards had come to those who made their living with a pistol. Travelers were going about the countryside more heavily armed and guarded of late. Moreover, the reward for the capture of any highwayman had been doubled and punishments made all the more harsh. That meant that Devondra and her companions had to be scrupulously careful lest they be caught.

"If you are afraid, Sylvester, Tobias and I will understand." Devondra pointed in the direction of the inn. "You may go back. As for me, I will not let Cromwell's ghouls intimidate me. Not until I have finished all that I have begun."

"Not until you are rich, you mean." Sylvester leaned forward. "Which could take longer than you first imagined, considering the penury of those we have robbed of late." He rubbed his hands together. "We need gold."

"And we will have it," Tobias called out, gesturing for silence. "Listen." A soft wind stirred the trees, carrying the sound of a rumbling coach to their ears.

"By my faith, a carriage. Well, 'tis about time!" Sylvester was impatient, having waited long over an hour, counting the shadows that passed in front of the moon.

"I know you are anxious, but be careful," Tobias cautioned. "Don't move too soon!" To make certain his order was obeyed, he reached out and grabbed the reins of Sylvester's horse. "Not until Devondra gives the word."

The wait was kept in stark silence, with no one uttering a word. At last, four white horses and their wheeled burden came into view, lumbering down the hillside. As the coach came closer, the three riders rode out from beneath the branches of the trees lining the road. Masked and cloaked, they drew their pistols.

It was all very simple, a plan that had been carried out many times. Sylvester would block the road and halt the driver, Tobias would cover the coach's rear. To Devondra was left the task of relieving the passengers of their valuables.

"Bigod, I've n'er seen a carriage move so slowly," Sylvester complained, shifting nervously in his saddle.

"Nor I," Devondra agreed, fighting the urge to touch her

heels to her horses' flank and go galloping up the road in
pursuit. She had to be patient, however, just in case there
was an armed guard sitting on the box beside the coachman.
To be imprudent could mean their lives.

"'Tis moving slowly because 'tis a heavy coach," Tobias
cut in.

Three pairs of eyes studied the vehicle as it was reflected in
the murky moonlight. "Unarmed, or so it appears," Sylvester
quickly noted.

"Unarmed? Good," Devondra breathed. Godfrey Tarkington's death had deeply troubled her. Robbing was one thing,
killing another.

"I wonder whose coach it is?" Tobias mumbled.

The mere possession of a coach meant distinction and
prestige. Moreover, the more distinguished a person was,
the more magnificent his coach had to be.

"It doesn't matter, so long as we will find ourselves face-
to-face with someone of means this time," Sylvester said
wistfully, still a bit perturbed that the first passersby tonight
had been naught but a tinker and a farmer.

Devondra's wish was more particular. As she looked
toward the road, she hoped against all odds that tonight
when the coach door was opened she would once more find
herself looking into a pair of crystalline blue eyes. She was
to be disappointed when the leather curtains were opened
at her raspy command of "Stand and deliver" and she found
herself looking into a woman's eyes. Green eyes that went
well with the long blond hair of the coach's occupant.

"Ooooooohhh!" The woman's shriek was full of terror as
she looked upon the dark forms that suddenly appeared out
of the darkness, silhouettes wielding shining pistols, riding
horses with silver-mounted trappings.

"Don't make a move if you value your life," Tobias
instructed. The driver sensibly threw up his hands.

Devondra was quick to promise, "We will not hurt you," adding, *"if* you do as we ask." She bid Sylvester to attend to the coachman, which he did, bidding the man to throw the reins across the backs of the ivory steeds. Devondra concentrated her attention on the female inside the carriage.

"I-I-I have no money with me," the woman pleaded, focusing her eyes in Tobias's direction. Perhaps because of his coat of brown velvet, the woman thought him to be somehow more civilized, and thereby her hope for clemency. Or perhaps she simply preferred to deal with a man so that she could manipulate the moment with the power of her charms. Whatever the reason. Devondra quickly made her authority known.

"No money? We soon shall see." Dismounting from her horse, Devondra reached for the door, yanking it open. "Get out!"

"Out?" The woman's pale skin grew even whiter. The long, slender fingers of her left hand tightened frantically around her throat, then moved to her mouth, stiffling a sob.

"Out." There was a keyed-up tension in Devondra that told the woman that she would not want to take any chances. She didn't have to say another word before the woman thrust her hand through the open coach door, holding out a well-filled purse.

"Your jewels, too," demanded Sylvester. Frightening with his missing ear and scowling mouth, he was promptly obeyed, though only a gold necklace, a broach and a ring were handed over. The Puritans disapproved of jewelery, most of London's citizens were sparsely adorned in public, though many had secret treasures.

Devondra took special interest in the ring, putting it on her thumb, as was the fashion of late. Holding her hand up toward the sky, she appraised her new possession. It proved to be a nearly fatal mistake, for suddenly the staccato pop of a pistol split the air, the shot missing Devondra's shoulder only by an inch.

"Little miss!"

Tobias was startled into action. Hurling himself at the door of the coach, he was soon wrestling with the lithe young man who had stealthfully hidden himself in the rear of the carriage beneath a blanket. Rolling over and over in the dust of the highway, they fought for each other's windpipe. At last Tobias got a stranglehold about the young man's throat. With one hand around the man's neck, Tobias secured the pistol and threw it out of reach.

"I'll be taking that, thank you." The young man soon found himself on all fours in the road as Tobias seized his collar with a strength that was surprising.

"Please . . ." Fearing for her life and that of her traveling companion, the woman gave vent to a flood of frightened tears.

"Blackguards. I'll see ye hanged, I will." The coachman, who had been silent up until then, voiced his anger, though he did nothing to come to the young man's defense.

"Hanged?" Sylvester's laugh was coarse. "I think not." He touched that place upon his head where once an ear had been. "They marked me once. I'll never let them lay hands upon me again."

"Nor I," Devondra echoed. She would never suffer her father's fate.

"Indeed." A deep flush stained the face of the lady. She seemed to have gathered up her courage, for she challenged, "I'll watch you hang at Tyburn. I swear I will. I'll know that voice of yours in hell. I'll remember. And when I do . . ."

For just a moment Devondra remembered the way her father had looked, swinging from Tyburn tree and she shivered. Nonetheless, she laughed softly. "I'm not afraid!"

"Well, perhaps you should be."

Devondra stiffened as she heard the voice that seemed to come out of nowhere. "Quentin Wakefield," she breathed. How had he appeared so quickly? Like a ghost suddenly coming from out of the mists.

"Drop your pistols. All of you!"

Climbing from his hiding place beneath the carriage's axel, Quentin gripped his wheellock pistol tightly, congratulating himself heartily on a well-set trap. He had ridden from London inside the well-padded coach, hiding himself in a hidden compartment beneath the carriage until the moment they reached the Heath. Now, he realized he had captured a more valuable prize than he could ever have hoped.

"A trap!" Oh, how infuriating! Once again, Devondra found herself at Quentin Wakefield's mercy.

Something in her voice caught his attention. Even when she was angry it was seductive, as was her appearance. Standing in a pool of moonlight, she was strikingly dramatic. Dressed all in black, she wore a silver mask and a hat with a silver plume. Oddly subdued, compared to the outfit she had worn at their first encounter.

"I prefer to say that I couldn't wait to see you again." Quentin said with a bow. He smiled as he heard the thud of the highwaymen's pistols, then repeated for the lady's benefit, "Drop *your* pistol."

Though Devondra was slow to obey, at last she did as he asked.

"I assume you have already met Jenny Bowen." He nodded in the blond woman's direction. "Bravo, Miss Bowen. A fine performance. Had the theaters not been closed in London by the Puritans you would be a natural for the stage."

"Bravo, indeed." Devondra angrily eyed her up and down, wondering if the woman was Quentin Wakefield's lover.

"How utterly clever and devious. Totally keeping to your character."

"My character?" Quentin stared at her, trying to discern her features, but all he could see were those lustrous eyes. Eyes that sparkled defiance despite the circumstances. "I asked you once who you are. I'm asking again."

There was no answer. She just watched him. So poised, so sure of herself. One might have thought he was her prisoner instead of the other way around.

"Bigod, I'll find out all when I take you before Cromwell." Reaching out, he grasped her by the wrist.

Devondra could feel the current of his anger. It burned her everywhere he touched, made her realize how deadly an enemy he could be. An enemy who would hand her over to the hangman just as he had her father.

"What you will find out is that I am your conscience," Devondra answered defiantly.

"My conscience." He took a step forward, all the while gazing into her eyes, eyes that most assuredly looked familiar to him now.

"If you look into your heart, you will know what I mean," Devondra answered.

Quentin moved forward, reaching for and tugging off her hat to satisfy his curiosity. Her hair was exactly the shade of dark brown that he had imagined. Curly, it tumbled over her shoulders like silken waves.

"Devondra!" He recognized that glorious hair, torn between anger and a strange uplifting of his heart. Unless he was seriously wrong, he had found her.

"I'm not that naive fool!" She denied the truth. Indeed, the innocent woman she had once been was dead.

"You are . . . " He lifted one hand, reaching for her mask.

"No!" Hastily, she pulled away, refusing to reveal her identity. "I won't become your prisoner! I won't let you take me." Stubbornness goaded her to ignore the pistol pointing in her direction and run.

"Stop!" Quentin didn't shoot, but someone did. In stunned horror, he heard the explosion that came from the bushes, heard the sound of scuffling boots as someone ran away. More horrifying, however, was watching her fall. "Devondra!"

Running towards her, he stared down, mesmerized by how vulnerable she appeared. Like a doll that had just been broken. An all-consuming sense of protectiveness surged through him as he knelt down. It was an emotion he had seldom felt for anyone.

"You shot me!" Her eyes were accusing as she stared at the pistol still in his hand.

"No," Anxious to vindicate himself, he exclaimed, "I didn't shoot you." That his pistol was still cool proved the truth of his words.

"Then who. . . . ?"

He shook his head. "It doesn't matter. Besides, whoever fired got away." His hands moved lightly over her, caressing as he probed. In that moment all else was forgotten.

Through a fog of throbbing pain, Devondra fought hard against the strong arms that held her immobile. She was afraid to trust him even for a moment. "Leave me alone!"

Chapter Twenty-Two

It was a ride Devondra knew she would never forget, a harrowing, frantic trek through the forest, over the hills and splashing across the river. It was a dangerous foxhunt in which they were the foxes.

"Do we have a chance?"

"Let us hope so." The consequences were harrowing. Most likely it would be a death sentence for Devondra Stafford and a charge of aiding and abetting a criminal for Quentin. *If* they were caught. Was it any wonder, then, that Quentin rode at a furious pace, holding on to her tightly all the while so that she wouldn't fall?

Pistols popped and cracked behind them. Men shouted epitaphs. Little by little, Cromwell's men were closing the distance between them, a frustrating fact that sent alarm knifing through Quentin as he took a look behind him.

"Bloody damn!" He cursed them, he cursed himself, wishing he had never been a part of this scheme. He should have heeded his gut feeling about the female highwayman, should

have known it was Devondra all the while. Perhaps, had he
known, he wouldn't have been galloping at breakneck speed
over rocks and stones now.

Uncomfortably stradling his saddle, stealing herself
against the pain stabbing at her arm, Devondra knew her
fate was in Quentin Wakefield's hands just as surely as her
father's had been.

"Quentin . . ." His name was a hoarse croak. Looking
over her shoulder, she sensed the peril they were in and
knew what he risked. "Why are you taking such a chance
for me? Why are you putting yourself in jeopardy?"

"Because—" Not one to spout flowery words, he said
merely, "Because you mean a great deal to me." No matter
what she might have done, he could not bear to see her
taken.

"But . . . but the soldiers will know what you have done
for me. They will say . . ."

"I'll take my chances." It was true the actress and the
others would undoubtedly reveal to Cromwell's men his part
in the escape. Though it was dark, they must have seen him
rush toward her, lift her up in his arms and ride away. He
could lose all when the puzzle pieces were put together.
Nonetheless, he didn't falter in his determination even for
a moment. The thought of Devondra Stafford hanging from
a gibbet was just too tragic, too horrid. Clenching his teeth
with determination, Quentin urged his horse on.

The sound of horses' hoofs, once a rumble in the distance,
were drumming louder. Closer. Or was it the sound of his
own heart beating in his chest that he heard? Determining
that it was both, Quentin moved toward the trees. Their
leafy branches and boughs might well be their only chance.
That and the darkness.

"Hang on for dear life!"

She did, staring wide-eyed as they plunged toward the

dense foliage, gasping as they narrowly escaped riding head-long into a tree. Never had she been in so much danger, and yet she couldn't keep from laughing softly at the thought of being rescued. And by Quentin Wakefield, no less.

Quentin was not laughing. He was drenched in perspiration from the strain and exertion of their ride. He was stiff. He was cold. Nevertheless, he was successful in his quest for refuge.

"Don't move. Don't make a sound. Don't even breathe."

"I—I won't."

From their hiding place Devondra could see the shadows of the men on horseback as they rode past, could hear their shouts and the plop of their horses' hoofs. She could nearly smell the sweat of man and beast as they passed within inches of the trees that sheltered the fugitives.

"Somehow they've vanished and why not? They must know this forest like the back of their hands," she heard one of the soldiers say.

"Aye, our plan went awry. Cromwell will be furious."

"Ha. If he thinks he could do better, then let him ride about this heath in the darkness."

"Aye, and the same goes for Quentin Wakefield."

"Wakefield!"

"He seems to have up and disappeared."

"Conveniently, if you ask me. But then, you know how it is."

"Aye, why be out rattling your bones when you can let us do it for you." The other men grumbled.

"What shall we do?"

"Move on. Somehow we'll find them. They can't have gone far."

Devondra breathed a sigh of relief as they thundered past. Three riders were not so hasty, however, and reined in their horses. Sitting astride the horse, completely motionless,

Devondra listened intently to the buzz of their voices, conversation that was threatening.

"I questioned Mistress Jennie Bowen. She said they were robbed by a female."

"The Notorious Lady!"

"Who else?"

"The overbold wench."

"Not overbold when we catch her. A stay at Newgate will make her see the error of her ways."

"Aye, she won't get far."

"We'll soon catch her and the devil she is riding with."

"They will both hang!"

Devondra stiffened at that bit of information and struggled to stay on the horse as a wave of dizziness engulfed her.

Quentin tightened his arms protectively around her. He leaned down and nuzzled his mouth against the soft flesh of her ear, sending every nerve in her body into erotic spasms.

"Hang? I doubt it. They have to find us first," she heard him whisper.

As the sound of hoofbeats pattered a rhythm upon the earth, moving farther and farther away, it appeared the soldiers wouldn't find them this time. The old battle tactic had worked, Quentin thought. For the moment at least they had escaped.

"What now?" Devondra asked.

"We'll double back, make a large circle and emerge from the trees to take a different pathway." He knew a shortcut to Wakefield Manor, one he had used out of necessity many times of late. "Come."

It was quiet. The darkness of the night enveloped Devondra just as surely as did the strength of Quentin's arms. She felt safe, at least for the moment. Contented. Turning her head, she looked at Quentin Wakefield through half-closed eyes, feeling something she hadn't felt in a long while. Safe.

"It's not much farther," he whispered in her ear, the sound of his voice deeply stirring.

"Good." Snuggling against him, she thought to herself how strangly right it felt to be in his arms, how natural to be traveling through the darkness with him. At least for the moment all her bitter resentment was put aside.

"A warm fire and tender care is all you need." He gripped her tighter, holding her against him, wrapping the voluminous folds of his cloak around her to give her warmth from the chilled night air.

"Devondra, whatever you might think, I didn't betray you. I did send that letter to London to see to your father's reprieve. You must believe me."

She turned her head, too weak and tired to argue. She didn't even want to think about it, though she answered, "I do."

Filled with a warm drowsiness that was intensified by the steady jogging rhythm of the horse and the pure enjoyment of being held by him, she closed her eyes.

Warmth. A deep voice whispering to her in the darkness. The gentle kiss of the wind on her face as they rode. The strong, steady up-and-down motion of the horse that rocked her to sleep. The deep, muffled heartbeat drummed in her ear. All these were comforting and soothing to Devondra, blocking out her pain as she snuggled against Quentin Wakefield's chest.

There is such magic when he touches me. It was like a fever, burning hot and cold at the same time. Indeed, he was the fever, consuming her, filling her, binding her to him with a most fragile thread. Something was happening, something she could not seem to control. She cared too much about him for her own comfort, yet she could not force herself to stop the emotions that enveloped her.

I've loved him all along. Even my anger wasn't strong enough to kill my feelings for him. Not really. And now . . . Now she realized how incomplete she had felt until this moment.

And therein lay the danger.

Opening her eyes with a start, she was suddenly more frightened than she had ever been facing the perils of the road. Love. It was the most blinding and dangerous of emotions. It made a person totally vulnerable and empty-headed, living in a world of stardust, longing for a smile, yearning for each and every scrap of affection.

Love. Moon dust and magic? For a time. But what happened when the magic ended? Or when a woman was again betrayed?

"Devondra, is something wrong? Is your arm bothering you?"

She turned her head to look at him, but his face was only a shadow. "No, it's just that I am cold," she said softly.

Immediately he harkened to her complaint, reining in his mount just long enough to take off his coat and drape it over her shoulders. Then, as if on impulse, he suddenly brushed her cheek lightly with his lips. "There, that will make you much warmer."

"Much . . ." She touched the place on her face where his lips had been and shivered. To her mortification and amazement she felt tears sting her eyes but couldn't begin to understand why.

"Devondra . . ." Slowly, as he pulled his cloak around her once again, Quentin traced the curve of her neck and shoulder, savoring the pleasure of having her skin beneath his hands.

Despite the fact that his hand felt comforting she recoiled, knowing very well where such caresses had led to once before. She had let down all her defenses only to be stung by the ultimate betrayal. She would not so easily give in to him this time.

"Don't!"

She heard him answer simply, "As you wish," and then they were riding again, traveling through the darkness. Only the moon pierced the blue-black sky, hovering up above like a big silver ball. As they rode along, Devondra stared up at it; then, giving in to fatigue, she closed her eyes, dreaming that she was riding a big black horse through a field of heather.

Chapter Twenty-Three

The mullioned windows acted as prisms, sending forth a rainbow of colors through the diamond-shaped panes. Colors that brought a warmth to Quentin's heart and soul as he stood by the bed.

"So, at last you are here where you belong Mistress Stafford." But oh, what a merry chase she had led him, and not only him but the citizens of London.

Staring at the face of the lovely young woman lying on the bed, he thought to himself how angelic she appeared in repose. Angelic and beautiful. Her dark hair fell across the pillows like threads of silk, framing the face that had been hidden by the mask he now held in his hand. A mask that was a chilling reminder of the life she had led the past few months.

"The Notorious Lady." A truth that was hard to believe looking at her. Her expression was so serene, so vulnerable, so strangely innocent for one who feathered her own nest by stealing from others. Looks certainly could be deceiving.

*Devondra is the Notorious Lady. The Notorious Lady is
Devondra Stafford.* How bizzare. And yet it should not have
been a surprise. *Like father, like daughter.* God hope that
did not mean she would come to the same grim end. Closing
his eyes, he was haunted by the image of the gibbet.

"No!" Her neck was so slim, much too delicate to be
violated by a rope. And, too, she was so young. Too young
to die before her time. "No, bigod!"

Reaching out, he smoothed the hair from her forehead,
renewing the vow he had made to himself earlier that night.
No matter what happened, no matter the personal price he
had to pay, he would not let her be taken. He could not live
without her, nor have any peace at all were she to be sent
to the gallows.

"I'll do whatever it takes to protect you."

Watching the motion of her gently rounded breasts rising
and falling beneath the covers, he succumbed to a deep
regret for the way things were. He was sorry for the angry
words that had passed between them in the past, particularly
words concerning her father, for he could never doubt that
she had loved the man most dearly.

"And undoubtedly he must have loved you too." A fact
that buffered his judgment of the man for the moment. At
least in sharing a deep feeling for her they had had *something*
in common.

From far away pealing bells sounded from an old Saxon
church, distracting him for just a heartbeat in time. Were
the bells calling people to Sunday services? he wondered.
Or was their tolling for an ominous reason? Putting his
hands behind his back, pacing up and down, he could only
wonder.

"Cromwell will not rest until you are captured. By escap-
ing right out from under his very nose you have wounded
his pride most sorely. But no matter what he does I promise

that he will not do you harm." He paused, looking down at the bed again, whispering to her sleeping form, "I promise, Devondra."

That promise called to his mind the promise he had *not* kept, the promise to save her father's life. James Stafford's death had undoubtedly been the catalyst that had sent his daughter down the road holding a gun and wearing a mask in her quest for revenge. Alas, she had so quickly tumbled into a profession that had put a price upon her head.

"How much, Devondra? How large is the reward for the Notorious Lady."

Too large. Large enough so that there would be few whom he could trust with the knowledge that she was here. That was why he had so quickly dismissed all his servants, sending them posthaste to his townhouse in London. All except for one, the kindly Mrs. Vickery, who had helped him tend to Devondra's wound and then tuck her in bed.

A fire burned in the hearth, its warmth spreading throughout the room, chasing away the chill of an early autumn morning. No one would know that what had fed that fire was the garments that would most assuredly have given Devondra away. One by one they had sizzled and sparked and then disappeared, leaving just one momento of her identity. A momento Quentin quickly threw into the fire.

"The cursed mask!" Oh, if only it was as easy to alleviate the tragic moments of the past and Devondra's hostile emotions as it was to dispose of that object of subterfuge.

While he watched the mask slowly disintegrate, memories swirled in his head. He pieced together the events of the night. He remembered how angry and defiant she had been while holding him at pistol point, and then how vulnerable she had suddenly appeared when she had been wounded. Even so, she had just as quickly turned from wounded kitten to as fierce a lion as had ever graced the Tower of London's zoo. She had raged at him, giving vent to all her pent-up anger. Yet, oh how light she had been when he had picked her up, how perfectly she had fit in his arms.

"And then, oh, our ride . . ." It had seemed that they had galloped through the darkness for an eternity before they arrived at last at Wakefield Manor. Lifting her from his horse, he had bundled her up in his cloak and carried her up the stairs. Placing her on his own bed, he had re-bandaged her arm, carefully tending her with little regard for his own need for sleep. Taking her hand in his, he promised not to leave her side.

I let you down when you needed me the most, but I will not let you down again. Never again, Devondra. And perhaps I can earn your trust even if you will not freely give me your heart. . . . At this moment he would settle for that.

"Ah, but I wish for much more. I want you to love me again, Devondra."

Love. Until this moment he had never really known exactly what it was. Now he did. It was caring for someone deeply and unselfishly. It was wanting to be with them forever. It was holding hands and still feeling like young lovers when you both grew old. It was total forgetfulness of yourself and thought of the other person's happiness and well-being. It was stardust, magic and moonbeams all rolled into one.

"Love is risking one's very soul for the sake of one smile," he whispered, gently touching her lips.

Devondra seemed to feel the pressure of his fingers for she opened her eyes. "Where . . .?" At first she didn't know where she was. She blinked, trying to remember why she was in a strange room and how she had gotten here, then one look at Quentin Wakefield's face brought it all back to her. She recalled the trap that had been set, remembered the agonizing pain when she had been shot, thought about how desperately she had wanted to get away from him.

"How is your arm?"

"It hurts," she answered, tentatively probing the bandage covering her wound. He sounded so caring, so concerned. She wanted to believe that he really did care about her, yet she feared being deceived a second time. What if his rescue of her was nothing but pretense, a game to be played on a late autumn night? What if even now Cromwell's soldiers were lying in wait, prepared to take her after their colleague had had his pleasure? What if . . .?

"It will pain you for awhile. I regret to say that I have no laudanum to help ease your torment. But perhaps my housekeeper knows of some herbs that will be of help." He stared at her intently, wondering what she was thinking. Her eyes looked so cold, so unrelenting.

"The pain I feel is nothing." Remembering the horrible sight of her father hanging from the gibbet, she said, "There is a much deeper agony, a pain that never goes away."

"For which I am deeply sorry." In an effort to comfort her he sat down on the bed and put his arm around her shoulder, but she pulled away violently.

She met his gaze with bitter eyes. "Sorry? Sorry, will not bring my father back to me."

"How well I know. I regret his death, Devondra, but 'twas not my doing. I fulfilled my promise by writing his reprieve. It was others who interfered in your father's fate."

"Others?" Pulling up the covers, she suddenly realized that she had been undressed. She tugged at the collar of the white cotton nightshirt, flushing a deep red as she realized that he had viewed her unclothed body. "Who?"

"My housekeeper and I tried to make you more comfortable."

She felt quarrelsome. "Indeed." She started to get up, but

a wave of dizziness interfered with her attempt to flee. "Where are my clothes?" If she could only get dressed, she would manage to get away from him.

"Your garments are gone."

"Gone?" She looked at him suspiciously, thinking the worst. "What do you mean?"

He had to answer truthfully, had to explain. "I burned them," he said, pointing at the crackling fire. "In there."

"You what?" She clenched her fists, her temper rising just as hot as the flames that had consumed her clothing.

A frown creased his brow. "'Twas the prudent thing to do, as you would realize were you thinking clearly. Were anyone to find even a scrap of your costume, it would target you for the hangman."

She swallowed the lump that rose in her throat. He had been wisely cautious. Even so, she didn't want to admit it out loud. "And thus you would hold me here. How clever of you."

He was caught off balance as she accused him of just what he had planned: to hold her at Wakefield Manor for safekeeping. "Surely you have to realize—"

A loud banging at the front door urged both Quentin and Devondra to silence. Quentin lived too far away from other houses for him to be having a casual visitor. Who then?

"Open up!" shouted a voice. "In the name of the Lord Protector."

"Cromwell!" Giving in to her fear, Devondra sat up, struggling to get out of bed. So, he had betrayed her after all, and now they had come to claim her. Well, they would never take her. She would get away before she was discovered.

"No!" Quentin's strong arms held her down. "There is no way you can leave without being captured. Cromwell will have his men everywhere."

She was understandably angry. "What shall I do then?

What do you suggest? Shall I just wait until they pour through the door and let them put me in irons?" She scoffed. "Never!"

His gaze held hers. "I'm asking you to trust me."

"Trust?"

"Aye, trust, for I have not given you over to your enemies so far. Nor will I."

Devondra looked toward the door with apprehension, then back at Quentin again. In that brief moment their dashing ride across the heath flashed before through her mind. He had helped her once, would he do so again? She wanted to believe that he would. Wanted that with all her heart. And yet . . .

"I won't betray you." The truth of that promise glittered in his eyes.

"Then do what you must." She watched him walk through the door. Then, gathering up every bit of strength she had, Devondra rose from the bed and followed, hiding in the shadows.

"Yes, what is it?" she heard him say.

"Sorry to bother you, sir but we are looking for a woman."

There was loud laughter from Quentin. "Ah, my good man, so am I. A pretty one, preferably."

"That . . . that's not what I mean!"

"We're looking for a fugitive," a deeper voice explained. "A woman wanted for robbery and other crimes."

"A fugitive?"

"Aye, the Notorious Lady."

There was a pause. "And you expected to find her here?"

"Welllllllllll . . ."

The deep voice proclaimed, "And why not? We saw her traveling the road that leads here."

"You saw her riding toward Wakefield Manor?" He sounded amazed. "Really?"

The silence was deafening. Then one of the men said, "Not exactly riding toward Wakefield Manor, but in this general direction."

The other man spoke up. "We lost her and her companion near the forest, but we thought . . ."

"That I had captured her." Quentin pounded on the open door with his fist. "Well, I have not, though I would give anything to have her within my grasp."

"So would I! I could well make use of the reward." There was another pause, then, "Are you certain she isn't . . ."

Quentin's tone was authoritative. "Quite!"

"Well then . . ." There was uncertainty in the voice.

Quentin's voice boomed loudly, "Thus, I would suggest that you look elsewhere. In the woods, for instance."

"The forest?"

"The forest. It would appear a wise decision to search that place where last the thieving rogue was seen, would it not?"

Both men spoke at once, anxious to please. "It would."

"Then by all means . . ." Quentin's words were punctuated by the slamming of the door. His boots made a clicking sound as he climbed back up the stairs. Seeing her standing by the banister, he said only one word. "Well?"

"I was afraid."

"That I would give you away. I didn't."

"I know. I heard."

He laid his hand on her shoulder. "But you are not quite sure that you believe. 'Tis far more comfortable to think ill of me, I fear."

It was. There was safety in maintaining her anger. But facts were facts and they proclaimed that Quentin Wakefield had come to her aid not once but twice.

"Devondra, I . . ." Before he could finish, she did a most

surprising thing. Rising up on tiptoe, she put her arms around his neck, and whispered a heartfelt "Thank you."

He smiled, then before she could say another word, his head came down, his mouth claiming hers in a gentle kiss.

"Mmmmmmmm...." She started to protest but how could she when she could hardly breathe. Her senses were full of him. The way he felt, so hard, warm and strong. The way he tasted, of ale. The sound of his beating heart, crazily pounding as fiercely as her own.

The pungent smell of leather and horses was still upon him, mingling with the scent of his skin. A strangely stimulating smell that spoke of his masculinity and made her vibrantly remember once more their late night ride. And the danger.

She hasn't pulled away. Because of that he moved his hand down her spine to press her towards him. The fingers of his other hand threaded through her hair, glorying in the silky softness as his kiss deepened. Then just as suddenly he pulled away.

Stunned, she found herself searching his face. Why would he kiss her and then step away?

"I made a promise to myself that you would be safe and that I would protect you. Even from myself," he whispered. He made a sweeping gesture with his hand. "So, make yourself at home."

She tensed. "At home?" What was he saying? She wanted to go back to the Heath. Her arm bothered her, but she wasn't some invalid.

"Aye, for you are my guest."

"Guest?" Her anger returned full force as she realized what he really meant. "I would say otherwise. I think that, in truth, I am your prisoner."

"No!" He sought to placate her. "I merely want to keep

you here so that you will be safe. Cromwell's men will be swarming all over the countryside like bees."

Devondra knew a moment of panic. "The inn! Tobias!" What if he had been captured?

He knew just what she was thinking. "If your red-haired friend has been taken, the last thing you must do is seek him out. To do so would bring about your own ruin." She had to see reason. "Here you will be protected."

"Protected?" The very idea that she would want to be harbored beneath his roof while her companions were endangered was ludicrous, and she told him so. After he left the room and closed the door behind him, as she heard the key turning in the lock, Devondra fully realized the final say was his and not her own.

Devondra looked through the small diamond-shaped windows of the bedroom, her mouth tightened in anger. She was a prisoner. There was no other word for it. *A prisoner.* Oh, she wasn't in a dungeon or inhabiting a cell at Newgate, yet the locked wooden door was nonetheless a reminder of the barrier between herself and her freedom. So much for Quentin Wakefield's hospitality.

"I am trapped like a bird in a cage," she exclaimed, "with no way to get out." Having examined nearly every inch of the chamber, she could attest to that.

Whirling about, she moved slowly again, standing up on tiptoe, getting down on her knees, examining every nook and cranny just in case she might have missed something. She came to the same conclusion. It was a luxurious room with an ornate fireplace, tapestried walls, tables decorated with silver, velvet drapes and a canopied bed, yet it was still a prison.

"Ohhhhhh!" She pulled at the heavy iron doorhandle until

the door rattled. Then, at last tiring of her tantrum, she returned to her place by the window.

If only I had my pistol, I would soon be out of here but undoubtedly he has disposed of it, just as he has done with my clothes.

Reminded of her sorry state, she touched her nightdress, which she discovered was, in truth, one of Quentin Wakefield's nightshirts. Resentment surged through her that he had taken everything. Protection, he had called it. Well, she had another word for what he was doing and for the lord of the manor, as well. How dare he keep her when she had no desire to be kept. And she would tell him so again if only he would appear.

As if she had willed it, the door opened, but it was not Quentin Wakefield who stood there. As Devondra turned around she saw a woman with a face full of wrinkles and the kindest brown eyes she had ever seen. The woman's hair, once red, had faded to a gray tinged with just enough of its original color to make it a strawberry blond. In her hands she held a tray with a silver teapot, cup, saucer and a plate piled high with fruit tarts.

"Who are you?" Devondra's resentment was written upon her face.

The woman smiled cheerfully, ignoring the frown. "I am Margaret. Margaret Vickery."

Devondra could not share the woman's cordial tone. "And I am Devondra." She waved her hand. "Now please go away!"

"Go away?" Laughter that could only be described as musical floated through the room. "My, such a mood, but then I daresay I can't blame you." Closing the door with her foot, she stepped farther into the room. "But I suspect that what I have brought you will soon change that frown into a smile."

"I'm not hungry!" The moment that she spoke Devondra knew that to be a lie. She was famished. Even so, she felt rebellious, wondering just what Quentin Wakefield would do if she refused to eat.

"Not hungry?" Setting the tray down on a small round table, she clucked her tongue. "Well, I'll leave this here just in case you change your mind."

"I won't." Slowly, Devondra's gaze moved toward the door, formulating a plan of escape. The door would be unlocked. All she needed to do was push past this frail-looking woman and the way would be clear.

"Oh, but I think you might once you get a sniff of what's in here." Margaret tapped the silver pot. "Hot chocolate, all the way from the Colonies."

"Chocolate?" For a moment she was tempted, then she shook her head. "You could bring me something to wear."

The woman smiled, clapping her hands together apologetically. "Of course. You can't float about the house looking like an impoverished angel."

Ever so slowly Devondra moved toward the door. "Any garments will do. Something of Quentin's, perhaps. A shirt. Britches and mayhap a hat." Though if she could just slip out the door she would be perfectly content to ride about the countryside with the tails of the nightshirt flapping in the breeze. If she could just slip out . . .

"Britches?" The woman shook her head empatically. "No. No, we must find something far more suitable for a young woman." She thought for a moment. "Ah-ah!" Walking to an old wooden chest by the foot of the bed, she rummaged through it.

For just a moment a flash of jealousy took hold of Devondra as she imagined being outfitted in one of Quentin Wakefield's mistresses' discarded garments. Perhaps that was what goaded her to make her dart toward the door.

"Oh no you don't!" For a woman her age, Margaret Vickery was astonishingly quick and agile. Hurrying to the door, she blocked Devondra's way.

"Please!"

There was a scuffle, one that Devondra would no doubt have won had it not been for her arm. As it was she was easily subdued. To her dismay, she watched as Margaret turned the key in the lock.

"Tut, tut, tut, my dear. The master says 'tis for your own good." Walking back to the chest, she returned to her exploring as if there had been no interruption. "Here it is."

Her chance at escape having been thwarted, Devondra turned her attention to the woman's "offering." The plain gray dress hardly looked to be fashionable, thus dispelling Devondra's suspicions as to its origins. She was surprised that the dress resembled Puritan attire.

"This belonged to Quentin's mother." The woman held it up. "And it seems to be nearly the right size."

"Quentin's mother?" Strange how she had never really thought about him as someone with a family. Devondra stared at the dress, trying to imagine what that woman must be like. Did she have the same piercing blue eyes? Was she stern? Or did she always smile? She put her questions into one sentence. "What is she like?"

Folding the dress over her arm, Margaret searched deep into the wooden chest once again, coming up with a small oval object that, upon closer inspection, proved to be a miniature. "See for yourself."

Taking the miniature from Margaret, Devondra peered down in fascination at the woman, who held little resemblance to her son. Her features were more delicate, the hair a tawny blond. Her eyes were gray and not blue. Full, pouty lips and a cleft in her chin gave her an earthy beauty that seemed at odds with her drab Puritan dress.

"Such an angel she was, or so I have been told." Margaret was wistful. "I fear 'tis a loss that the master has never quite gotten over."

"She's dead . . ." Devondra looked at the tiny painting again and wondered if Quentin Wakefield had held the same bond with his mother she had shared with her father. If so, she knew exactly how he must have felt when she died. For a moment all her resentment was thrust aside and she hurt for him.

"Poor soul. The doctor said her four humors were out of balance, though I can not remember if 'twas blood, phlegm, choler or melancholy that was pitifully low." She was so busy talking, she didn't see Quentin come in. "Whichever humor it was, the doctor's bloodletting did her little good. It was done too late, it seems."

"It should not have been done at all!" His voice was husky. Pain showed clearly in his blue eyes. "The man was a quack. He knew nothing of how delicate she was." Raw emotion was revealed as he spoke; then it was as if a mask dropped over his face, blocking out his feelings. Once again he was a man whose emotions were held tightly in check.

Devondra extended her arm toward him. "I'm sorry!" She looked back down at the miniature, running her finger across the image there.

"So am I. More than you can ever fathom . . ." He too touched the painting, his thumb gently brushing her hand as he did so.

Though it was but a brief contact, Devondra felt a shiver ripple up her arm. She looked up, searching his face as intently as she would have if she had never seen it before. Watching the flicker of his eyes, the movement of his mouth, she wished she could as easily see into his heart, his soul.

"You must have loved her very much."

"I did." He swallowed hard. Oh yes, he had loved her

fiercely. "Even more than I hated him." Closing his eyes he was haunted by an image from his past. He envisioned his mother, standing by his stepfather's side as he wielded his knive. She was working unmercifully hard, wiping at her brow, her flawless complexion as white as a sheet. "The bastard!"

Quentin had vowed that one day he would make a reputation for himself, earn his fortune. He had promised his mother that he would take her away from London and the stifling city air that seemed to torture her lungs. Those words came back to haunt him now, for he had been too late. This house and all the treasures within it would never belong to her.

The guilt he felt was overwhelming. He should never have run away. He should have stayed by her side, no matter the tortures his stepfather had inflicted on him. For a long time he fell silent, staring into his past.

Devondra didn't interrupt his thoughts right away. When she did she said only, "Tell me."

He wanted to confide in someone, yet as he raked his hands through his hair the words wouldn't come. He had bottled it up inside for too long. "I can't," he answered. "At least not now." Quickly he changed the subject. Turning to Margaret, he said, "I had Mrs. Vickery bring you breakfast, but it seems to be going to waste." Picking up an apple tart, he broke it in two, but she declined to take a piece.

"I want to go home," she insisted, her irritation returning.

"Home?" He wondered just where upon the Heath that might be.

"You know what I mean." She folded her arms across her chest, mimicking his stance.

In answer he reached inside his jacket, pulling forth a London newsletter, which he handed to her. It told about the recent capture of the highwayman Christopher Jackson and Cromwell's determination to rid the country of "like nuisances." "The Lord Protector has vowed to put a rope around the neck of anyone caught stealing on the roads," he said. "Anyone."

Realizing how useless it was to argue, at least for the moment, Devondra sat down on the bed, watching as Quentin Wakefield and Margaret helped themselves to the tarts and the hot chocolate. The delicious aroma floated upwards, tempting her beyond self-control.

So be it. *I will go on a hunger strike another day,* she thought. Pouring a cup of the dark liquid, she took a tentative sip, smiling to find that it was warm, sweet and sinfully delicious. Strangely enough, it made her feel better. Relaxed. At peace.

It was a peace that was shattered by Quentin Wakefield's curse. "Horsemen!" The men had come back. It appeared that his explanations earlier in the day were once more to be questioned.

"Oh, sir, what shall we do?" Margaret looked toward the door.

"The cellar! It is the only place we can hide her where she will not be found out."

Once more he was her rescuer as he took Devondra's hand. Then they were out of the room and running, as if the very devil was on their heels. Indeed, perhaps he was.

Chapter Twenty-Four

Holding Devondra firmly by the hand, Quentin moved to the drawing room of the manor. Walking over to the fireplace, he triggered a mechanism that revealed a secret passage to the cellars.

"The original owner of this house was a royalist. The cellars were used to hide their wounded during the war," he explained. He led her through the narrow entranceway, closing it behind him.

"Watch your step. The stairs are slippery."

In total darkness they plunged down, down, down, veering around sharp corners, moving to the left and then the right. The air was chilly and damp, and though Devondra affected an air of bravado, she was apprehensive.

"I hate spiders!" Not to mention the rodents that dwelled in such dark places. "And rats . . ." She shuddered.

"So do I. Particularly the two-legged variety." He squeezed her hand. "I am sorry to put you through this but it is a necessity."

She wanted to rage at him, quarrel, but she gave in to the truth of the situation. "I know." The odor of mildew wafted to her nostrils as they moved downward and she cringed. "But please, don't keep me down here for long."

"Only as long as is necessary." He felt a shiver convulse her slim frame and wrapped his arms protectively around her. An unpremediated act but one that felt strangely right. Pulling her closer, he nuzzled her ear. "Ah, but it seems as if you belong in my arms."

A yearning surged through her. If only things could be different between them. If only there would be no more arguments and she could forget the past, could freely give him the love that even now was curling through her.

"Quentin . . ." She buried her face against his shoulder. "Be—be careful . . ." He took his finger and wrapped a strand of her hair around it. The tone of his voice was jovial. "Ah, my stubborn, Notorious Lady, am I to believe then that you care?"

She answered truthfully. "You know that I do." Which made it all the more unnerving once he had left her. Huddled against the hard stone wall, her legs drawn up to her chest, Devondra listened to the sounds around her, wondering what was going on above.

Was Quentin in any danger for having saved her from capture? There was a very good chance that he was. Though they had been caught up in a world of their own, there were witnesses to their sudden flight. That actress and the carriage driver would most assuredly speak up. Their stories might very well be condemning.

"Merry-go-up!" A chilling thought flashed through her brain. *What if Quentin is arrested? What if he is taken away?* "What if I am left all alone down here?"

Frantically, she looked around her, trying to accustom herself to the enveloping blackness, but she could just barely

see the outlines of forms and shapes. Things that she suddenly identified by the sound of their scurrying—rats!

Dear God, she was barefooted and weaponless, without
anything to fight them off were they to attack. Nudging at
a stone in the wall, she hoped to find it loose so she would
have something to combat them but the strength of the cellar
spoke all too well for the builder, whoever he had been.

"Keep away!" She heard them rustling behind her and
turned her head, imagining the sight of their beady eyes.
Moving her hands, she searched for something, anything,
with which to fight them away. With relief she felt her fingers
touch something hard and cold. "A bottle!" Wielding it in
her hand, she dared the treacherous rodents to come near
her.

Something tickled her ear and she stiffled a scream, hastily
brushing it away. A spider? She clenched her teeth. Oh,
how she hated this darkness. It was nearly enough to drive
someone mad. That and the foul-smelling atmosphere made
this waiting game twice as long.

Was it possible for time to move so tediously slow? She
could hear the faint sound of water: drip, drip, drip, as if
tolling the time. No wonder it was damp. And cold. And
she was dressed only in a nightshirt!

"Brrrr."

Worse yet, her stomach rumbled its hunger and she regretted now that she had not partaken of the fruit tarts so artfully
stacked on that tray. She sighed, wishing that for once she
hadn't been so stubborn. More than that, however, she
wished that she could view the scene taking place above.
She could just barely hear the murmur of voices and the
creaking of the floor right above her.

That creaking was caused by Cromwell's boots as he
strode back and forth. "Damn it, man, I want to know what

is going on! A fugitive just disappeared into the mists and I have to ask myself how. And why?"

Quentin averted the Lord Protector's questioning gaze. "I wish I knew."

Stripping off his leather gauntlet, Cromwell slapped it against his wrist in obvious agitation. "You wish you knew!" His voice came out in a shriek. "It was your duty to keep atop things and to see to that infuriating woman's capture. Instead I hear stories that make me wonder just what really happened that night." His tirade erupted into a fit of coughing.

Quentin took a deep breath, determined to maintain his calm. He wasn't afraid of Cromwell, but he was wary of him; certainly he wasn't dealing with a fool. "It was dark."

"As nights usually are," cut in one of the men who had paid the manor a prior visit.

Quentin ignored the barb. "The plan worked to perfection. The Notorious Lady, as she is called, and a companion did just as you had suspected. They held up the coach at pistol point. Jennie Bowen . . ."

The tempo of the gauntlet's tapping increased twofold. "I know, I know. I spoke with her myself." His voice affected a falsetto as he mimicked her interview." " 'We were robbed by that terrible woman. I was nearly frightened to death.' "

"Aye, and then in the midst of the doings I sprang out of hiding," Quentin went on. "I forced the woman and her companion to throw away their pistols. They complied."

"So I have heard. The woman was caught."

"Aye."

"Excellent!" Cromwell strode forward, pausing but a foot away from the master of Wakefield Manor. "Then where is she? Please show her to me."

Quentin stiffened, remembering very vividly what had

happened next, seeing her fall, holding her in his arms. "She tried to get away. There was a shot."

"She was hit?

He nodded. "I followed her into the trees."

Cromwell seemed satisfied so far, no doubt because he had heard the same testimony from the witnesses. "And then what?"

Quentin shrugged. "I don't know. Everything went dark before my eyes. I only remember that her companion followed after me, to see to her welfare, or so I thought." He paused, trying to think up a plausible story. "It must have been he who hit me over the head."

Squinting his eyes, Cromwell looked doubtful. "So you are saying that you wounded our feminine culprit, that she ran off into the bushes, her roguish companion followed you when you went off to find her and then knocked you on the head."

Though Quentin wished he had been able to come up with a better excuse, he hastily agreed. "Exactly!"

"And it was he who rode off with the overbold wench?"

Quentin answered quickly, "It had to be he."

Cromwell paced up and down before the fire like an agitated hound. "She's dangerous! She's an outrage to all things decent."

"Aye. An outrage that must be stopped," echoed one of the men, anxious to please.

Stopped. Quentin's pulse quickened at the word. "What are you going to do?"

"Find her!" Cromwell walked to the door.

"Of course we must catch the chit. I will do all that I can."

Cromwell's eyes were cold. "I assumed that you would." Instead of leaving, he motioned to the two men who had accompanied him. "Search the house from top to bottom."

"Now see here!" Quentin's cheek twitched with irritation. Slowly Cromwell put his glove back on. "A mere formality, I assure you."

"A formality!" Inwardly Quentin seethed. Hadn't he ever heard that a man's home was his castle? Ah, but perhaps it was for the best, after all. Once he came up empty-handed he would have no more reason to be suspicious, and perhaps he would leave the manor alone.

"Your obedience is appreciated!" Cromwell looked back at Quentin, the animation he had shown melting away once again into icy reserve.

Such a cold man, Quentin thought. Cold, calculating and cruel. God help Devondra were she to fall into this man's clutches. That observation only made the situation more trying as he waited and waited for Cromwell's cronies to finish their exploration of the premises. Would they never be gone?

"Sir! Come quickly." The soldier's voice seemed to be coming from the master bedroom.

Quentin raised his eyebrows. "So . . ." Displaying an agility he had not shown since his days commanding the Roundhead soldiers, Cromwell took the stairs two at a time, Quentin following. They both pushed through the door. "What is it?"

"Someone was here. Drinking tea, it looks like."

"Hot chocolate," Quentin cut in. "And that someone was me." He picked up the cup, draining it dry. " 'Tis no matter of intrigue to have breakfast in one's bedroom." He laughed, offering his guests some of the tarts.

Cromwell, having overly excited himself, was angry. "You fools!" Much to Quentin's mortification, however, it was the Lord Protector who made another discovery—one that could not be as easily explained. "Why, look upon these sheets. Blood!" Worse yet, there were the remains of the shredded-up linen that had been used for bandages. "Have you been injured, Wakefield?"

Bending over, Quentin retrieved the damaging evidence. "I suffer from nosebleeds. An irritating nuisance at times."

"Nosebleeds?" Once again the Lord Protector was wary.

"I have been bothered with them since I was a child, to my humiliation."

"Mmmmmmm." Cromwell looked at the blood spot, then up at Quentin. "Could it be that you need to be bled from time to time?"

The reminder of his mother's treatment and therein the possible cause of her death caused Quentin to pale. "It could be."

"The next time you are in London I will have my personal physician take a look at you." Like twin coals of fire, the Lord Protector's eyes burned into Quentin's.

"How generous of you," he said in a tone he hoped did not reveal his annoyance. "Thank you, sir." Then, thankfully, the ordeal was over. The shuffling of footsteps going down the stairs announced that the men were leaving. Still, as he looked toward the bed, Quentin had the feeling that far from being over, the danger had just begun.

She was going to go mad if Quentin didn't come back soon, Devondra thought, grimacing as something scurried across her foot. Fearful that it was a rat, she lashed out with the bottle, giving warning. "Rats!"

Oh, how she loathed the vile creatures. A prejudice that increased more and more as she listened to the rats wander about the cellar, searching the floor for anything in the least bit edible. Including the taste of human flesh, she thought worriedly. Tales of rats eating babies, or chewing on fingers and toes, were prevalent.

"But you will not have a taste of me!"

The only cure for them was cats, animals that were dangerous to own these days. Superstition ran rampant. There were those who insisted there were witches roaming about. People with cats were instantly suspected because witches were thought to keep their own evil spirit in animals they called familiars.

A ridiculous notion, she truly believed, wishing with all her heart that the cellar was filled with a tabby or two right now. A good mouser would soon rid the manor of the nightmarish little beasts.

Keeping her eye on the rodents, she listened. Was she imagining it, or did she hear footsteps? Slowly the door creaked open, announcing someone's arrival, "Quentin!"

Suddenly the murky cellar was flooded with candlelight, making her squint. For a moment, as he set the candle down, she could see only his outline. Then, as she strained her eyes, she could recognize a face that to her eyes at that moment was the most welcome face of all.

"Thank God!" Rising to her feet, she collapsed into his arms, her exultation rising like a tide that surged within as turbulently as the sea.

"They are gone. At least for the moment." His arms were so warm, so comforting.

"At last." She felt herself sway with relief.

Tightening his arms around her, he held on to her as if to never let her go. She felt his breath ruffle her hair, felt the sensation down the entire length of her spine. She couldn't think, couldn't breathe.

In the silence of the room their heartbeats were audible, beating in unison. Taking her hand, Quentin put it on his chest, allowing her to feel his racing heart. Then his lips found hers, caressing her mouth in a kiss that went on and on.

God, she tasted so sweet! Why was it that whenever he was around her he lost all control? Her nearness was the only thing that could ease the demons that sometimes raged within him. Demons that had possessed him during the horrors of the war. It was then that he lived in a world where people lied, cheated, maimed and killed, turning on each other like the rats that roamed around in the cellar. He had learned to distrust, to hate, to fear. But with her, his feelings were gentler. The feelings in his heart gave him hope.

"Devondra!"

He wanted her. Dear God, how he wanted her. Right here, right now. More than he had ever wanted anything in his life, he wanted to touch her everywhere. The danger they were in only intensified that feeling. At any moment she might be whisked right out of his arms, away from his protection. And yet, he didn't want to chance her hatred once again, didn't want to coerce her.

But if she could love me . . .

Oh, but she did. If she hadn't realized it before, she realized it now. If that silent declaration sent her hurling over the edge of a precipice, then so be it. Life was all too short. In a world filled with hate, love was a precious thing, a rare treasure they might have little time to savor.

Quentin noted that she smiled, and felt her press closer. "Have you ever ached for something, so much that it hurt?"

"Yes," she whispered, just as she was aching now.

He answer emboldened him. "Devondra, I want you but . . ."

Putting her hands to his lips, she silenced him. She lifted her head, searching his eyes in the gloom. What she read there made her heart reach out to his. "Then by all means . . ."

* * *

The bedroom was bright with light, but not for long. Closing the drapes and lighting two candles, he had soon affected a romantic atmosphere. "You sent me on quite a chase searching for you. I wanted to explain, wanted you to know—"

"In my heart I do, now." A knot squeezed the pit of her stomach. Her eyes misted as she took a step closer.

For a long moment he merely looked at her, at the way the nightshirt clung to the tantalizing curves and planes of her body. His blood surged wildly through his veins as he slowly and sensuously reached out and took her by the shoulders. His fingers seemed to burn through the thin cloth, melting her flesh, stripping her very soul bare.

"So beautiful! How was I to know that one woman could get under my skin and become such an obsession?"

As if to familiarize himself with her again, Quentin slid his hands down her back to cup the firm roundness of her buttocks, lifting her closer to him. None of his expectations had readied him for this moment.

"Nowhere on the face of this earth will I ever find another woman to compare to the lovely, daringly bold Devondra."

She held out her hand to him. He waited, holding her gaze.

"There is no other woman but you, Devondra. Since first I met you I haven't even thought of being with anyone else."

"Nor could I."

She closed her eyes, parting her mouth to meet his gentle, searching kiss. Their lips touched and clung, enjoying the sweetness of newly rekindled love. She arched her back, responding eagerly as his hands stroked her. The heat of his body warmed her, aroused her, turning her thoughts into chaos.

His hands cupped her breasts, his expertise making them harden with desire. Slowly he pulled the nightshirt from her shoulders, being careful not to jostle her injured arm. His lips followed his fingers downward, kissing the soft smoothness of her breasts.

"You have flawless skin, like honey." He could feel the soft swell of her curves beneath his wandering hands. His breath came faster and faster. Devondra wondered if she was breathing at all. Wordlessly, she returned his kisses, trembling with pleasure as his tongue entered her mouth to probe the inner softness.

She moved closer, leaning against him as her fingers unfastened the buttons of his coat, then parted his shirt. Mimicking what he had done to her, she moved her lips to his chest. Her tongue explored his nipples, setting him afire. "My God, where did you learn that?" Jealousy surged through him as he imagined there had been someone else. He had wanted to be her only lover.

Her wide hazel eyes were soft. "I learned it from you, just now."

Together in the candlelight they moved their hands over each other, touching, exploring. Quentin was lost to the sensations she created. He loved the softness of her, the taste of her lips, the scent of her hair. Her body, with its curving slenderness, fully ignited his desires.

He kissed her hard and long, but soon kissing alone couldn't satisfy him. A blazing hunger raged through him. "My love, are you certain?" he said again. Compulsively, his hand onced again closed over her breast, his thumb moving rhythmically over the taut nipple.

"Yes . . ." She was so very certain. She knew beyond a doubt that she belonged with this man, no matter that their diverse lives made them an odd couple to mate. Love made the difference.

Quentin was like a starving man, driven on by his hunger. She was much too tempting, too warm, too loving, too responsive for him to resist. Even so, he knew he had to be gentle. He didn't want to injure her arm and cause it to bleed again.

"Your arm ... and ..." Though she had come to him, asked him to make love to her, he knew it had been a long time since they had been together. He wanted everything that passed between them to be beautiful for her.

"I'm sure we can find a way," she said with a smile, leading him toward the bed.

In truth, she was so caught up in the mindless delight of the moment, she wondered if she would even be capable of feeling pain. Never had she felt anything as stimulating, as stirring as her lover's hands upon her. A hot ache of desire coiled within her, and the thought occurred to her that she wished they were entirely naked beneath his touch. Reaching up, she tugged at the nightshirt.

"Yes ..." Quentin touched her hand. "I want to see you."

Shyly at first, then with more boldness, she slipped the fabric down over her hips, letting it fall to the ground. She stood naked and lovely in the candlelight.

"Do I please you?" She watched the expressions that chased across his face.

Quentin touched her with his eyes before his hands reached out to her. "Yes! Oh God, yes. Very much." His voice was thick, the words choking in his throat. He worshipped the sleek lines of her neck and let his gaze drop to her softly sculptured, full breasts. She was even more beautiful than he had remembered, her slender waist, flaring into rounded, womanly hips. Breathing hard with his arousal, he swept her body with his hands—from shoulders and breasts to hipbones and thighs.

Devondra tingled with an arousing awareness of her body, which was intensely sensitive. The lightest touch of Quentin's hands or mouth sent a shudder of pure sensation rippling deep within her. Reaching up, she tangled her fingers in the thickness of his hair. No matter what happened, she would have this moment to remember. This special moment. She would never forget the passion of his mouth, the sweetness of his kisses, the all-consuming joy of being with him.

Like a fire his lips branded her, savoring the peaks of her breasts with his mouth and tongue. "Your skin is so soft," he whispered.

"And yours so rough." She laughed softly and felt her heart move with love.

Without another word he took off his shirt, kicked off his boots and shrugged out of his trousers. Hovering over Devondra, he was strength personified. She caught her breath at the sight of his manhood, erect and proud. He took her hand, bringing it to his hardness. Shyly, Devondra encased the stiff, hard flesh, stroking it gently. She wanted to tell him how she felt, but she couldn't find the right words. Instead she tried to show him, mimicking his caresses as she slid her hands over his body. His intake of breath, the way he gathered her deeper into his embrace, told her that he liked her questing touch.

He came to her, enfolding her, kissing her mouth, her chin, her brow, her hair. Closing his eyes, he was driven beyond endurance by the touch of her hands, her naked body.

"Relax . . ."

Devondra lay back, her eyes bright and glittering in the candlelight. Quentin kissed her stomach, moved up to caress her breasts with his lips, then moved on top of her. His fingers trailed downward, tracing her spine. Then, with a sudden, powerful grip, he clutched the mounds of her bottom, pressing her closer. He was gripped by the deepest, most powerful desire he had ever felt in his life.

"Sweetheart, oh, sweetheart . . ." This was the woman he loved. Bold, passionate, responsive, and exciting.

She fit her body to his. Moving in a sensuous, dancelike motion, she drove him mad with wanting.

His mouth kept to its caressing, heated course, moving up her neck to devour her full, sweet mouth. Then he knelt, kissing the soft skin of her inner thighs. He felt her quiver as his fingers found her core and searched the soft inner petals. With wild abandon she opened herself up to new discoveries, sighing deeply as he savored the flesh of her secret place.

Quentin spread her thighs, holding them wide for his entry. Slowly he guided himself into her softness. Their bodies met in the most intimate embrace imaginable. He lay motionless until he felt her relax.

"Lock your legs around my waist." He felt the firm softness of her thighs as she tightened her legs around him and cried out.

He was infinitely gentle, knowing that it had been a long time since they had made love. His kiss muffled her cry of surprise. For a long moment he stayed fully within her, allowing her body to adjust to his sudden invasion, then Quentin began to sway in rhythm, a slow, deeply thrusting motion that caused his own body to tremble.

Devondra was consumed by his warmth, his hardness. She arched up to him, astounded by the pulsating explosions of her body, the pleasure she felt as they moved together. How could she have ever dreamed it would be like this? They were together in the final nearness, the ultimate discovery.

Lovemaking was the ultimate gift that brought two people together and made them whole.

Sensing her feelings, still breathless from the jolt of his own emotions, Quentin held Devondra close in his arms, fondling her gently as they lay together. He couldn't get enough of her. Far from quenching his desire, what passed between them had made him all the more aware of how much he cared for her. From this moment on she was his, for all their tomorrows.

Chapter Twenty-Five

Warmth surrounded Devondra, sensations of soft stroking hands that were glorious. Every part of her body absorbed the long, tantalizing caress and came alive beneath the questing fingers. With a soft sigh she gave herself up to the wondrous feelings. Slowly opening her eyes, she found Quentin lying next to her, his strong body entangled with hers. She smiled dreamily.

"Is this the way you treat all your prisoners?"

"No, just you," he answered. His fingers moved slowly up her arm, pausing just an inch from her bandaged wound. Satisfying himself that their vigorous activities had not started it bleeding again, he concentrated on his favorite part of her body, her breasts.

"Quentin . . ."

His arm curved possessively across her waist as he touched her. One of his legs was slightly bent, resting between hers with a familiarity that gave proof of the intimacy of this new phase of their relationship.

"Perhaps I should have allowed myself to be caught long before this," she breathed. Playfully, she laced her fingers together and covered her face, mimicking the mask she had worn on the roads.

He was strangely solemn. "Then you have no regrets?" Above all, he didn't want to have to deal with her hatred ever again.

She blew seductively on his ear. "Only that it took so long for us to find each other again." For what had passed between them was beautiful, incredibly so.

"Forsooth, my daring lady, it was not for want of my looking." Cupping her face in his hand, he was silent for a long time, just looking at her. At last he said. "I wanted to explain what had happened. I wanted you to know that it was not my fault that your father . . ."

"Shhh."

She didn't want to spoil the moment by thinking about her father's unfortunate fate. Reality was an intrusion, at least for the moment. She wanted to forget about Cromwell and the woes he had created, wanted to feel healed of the heartache of the past few months.

"Quentin . . ." Instinctively, she reached out to him and he responded, taking her into the warmth of his arms. The bodily contact sparked a warm glow deep inside her. "We were meant to be together. I sense it, I feel it."

"We *are* together." Compulsively, his fingers closed around hers. Lifting her hand to his mouth, he pressed his lips against the palm of her hand. He rested his chin on the top of her head, his arms holding her close against his heart. Her body was warm, soft and magical in its power to excite him, yet his passion was tempered with tenderness.

Devondra took a deep breath and let it out in a sigh. "Together. But for how long?" She couldn't stay here forever. Though they were able to exist in a dream world for an hour, a day, perhaps even a week or more, reality had a way of intruding. The world would catch up with them.

"I wish I could promise you eternity, but . . ."

The soft glow of sunlight cast a muted glow over the lovers. Devondra could read the worried furrow of Quentin's forehead. A curl had fallen across his brow. She reached up to brush it away.

"Something is troubling you. Tell me."

"I think Cromwell is suspicious of me. I know the man well. He will not rest until he has satisfied all his curiosities." He clenched one hand into a fist, then relaxed it. He wanted to be her protector, wanted to take care of her, wanted to be able to make promises, yet how could he when his own future was an unknown?

"What if he finds me here?" A wave of anxiety shot through her, not for herself but for him.

"He won't!" No matter what he had to do, he wouldn't give her up to the Lord Protector. "You are safe."

Devondra brought his hand to her cheek and rested it there. "My being here could mean your ruin. It would be far better if I just disappeared." The words fell heavy on her heart even as she spoke them.

"Disappear?" She had given him the first love and peace he'd known for a long while. How could he ever force himself to say good-bye to her? "I won't let you." There was a glow in his eyes as he gazed down at her. He caught her lips, gently nibbling with his teeth, then his mouth, hard and commanding, fastened on hers, stealing her breath away.

It was a long kiss, a caress of mouths that met with equal fervor. Hot. Searching. A kiss that made Devondra feel alive.

His eyes moved over her, the powerful spell of her beauty setting him ablaze. He wanted to touch her, know every intimate part of her, wanted to make love to her in such a manner that no matter what happened she would never forget him. With that thought in mind, he began the slow, caressing motions that had so deeply stirred her the night before. He touched her from the curve of her neck to the soft flesh behind her knees and up again, caressing the flat plain of her belly. Moving to her breast, he cupped the soft flesh, squeezing gently. Her breast filled his palm as his fingers stroked and fondled.

"You have the most beautiful breasts."

His touch penetrated her skin with a sensuous warmth. Devondra caught her breath. Arching up, she lifted toward him, her skin aching to be fully explored. He knew just how to touch her, how long to linger so that her whole world became centered on the homage he was offering with his hands and mouth.

She reached for him, trembling in eagerness as she slid her arms around his neck. "You saved me from Cromwell, but who is going to save me from you?" she teased.

Quentin smiled. "Believe me, dear lady, I have seen proof that you can take care of yourself." Whispering her name, he moved over her, feverish with desire yet at the same time determined to make love to her slowly, with loving consideration.

Devondra was not content to be only the recipient of pleasure but felt a need to give pleasure as well. With that desire in mind, she moved her palms over the muscles and tight flesh of his body, reacquainting herself with the expanse of his shoulders and chest. His skin was just as she remembered, smooth and firm, roughened by a thatch of hair on his chest that she toyed with dreamily.

"Devondra!" A long, shuddering sigh wracked through him. "If ever you have had me in your power it is now," he admitted, consumed by his arousal.

It was an interesting revelation that Devondra savored. She was instilled with a newfound confidence, knowing she could stir him so deeply. She continued her exploration, as if to learn every inch of him. In response she felt his hard body tremble against hers.

"Ahhhh." The sound came from deep in his throat.

Stretching her arms up, she entwined them around his neck, pulling his head down. Their lips met in a long kiss that sealed the promise of their newfound love. His mouth played seductively on hers, his tongue thrusting into her mouth at the same moment his maleness entered the softness nestled between her thighs. She felt his hardness entering her, inch by inch, moving slowly inside her until she gasped with the pleasure. Cradling the curves of her buttocks in his palms, he lifted her up to his thrust, sheathing himself completely in the velvet of her flesh.

"Heaven. Pure heaven," he sighed, feeling himself surrounded by her warmth. She was ecstasy personified, branding his heart, his soul.

This time their lovemaking was slow and leisurely as he blended his flesh with hers. She arched up to him, joining him in the ultimate expression of love, breathing hard as he moved up and down, fulfilling her most passionate dreams. Her heart moved and she cried out his name. As he surged inside her, she felt as if for just that moment in time their souls touched, caressed and merged into one.

In the silent aftermath of passion they lay, content just to be together. Devondra's head rested against his chest, her legs entwined with his. "What are you thinking?"

"I wish—" Foremost of all, that he could change the way things were.

"If wishes were horses, beggers would ride," Devondra breathed, remembering her father's favorite phrase. And yet she wished, too, so many things.

"And all things in life would be fair."

"But they are not," she said sadly. "There are some things

that must be accepted and risks that must be taken." She paused. "All I ask of you is that you love me."

Touching her face, he kissed her. "I do. Oh, Devondra, I do so very much." As if to give her proof, he held her tightly against him as if he would never let her go.

The room was dark. Clad in the white nightshirt, her dark hair loose about her shoulders, she sat huddled in bed, her eyes focused on the sky as she reflected on the way she had spent the day. Love, Devondra thought, had a way of bringing gentleness to the heart even in the midst of the greatest anger. It brought peace. It soothed loneliness and swept away bitterness. It brought a sense of completeness she had never felt until this very moment.

"Oh, what a blessed emotion . . ."

Fascinated by it all, she turned over on her side, watching Quentin Wakefield as he slept. Her eyes touched on his forehead, the angle of his jaw, his nose, his neck his hands, his shoulders, remembering.

Aye, she loved him, desired him. There could never be any doubt of that henceforth. Even now she could feel the world whirling and spinning around her as she remembered his hands upon her. But what now? Where did they go from here?

For the first time Devondra regretted the way she had spent the last several months. She wished . . .

"But the die has been cast. I am what I am. It is too late."

Or was it? Closing her eyes, she dared to hope.

Thump!

Opening her eyes, she turned her head in the direction of the sound.

Thump! It sounded again and again and again.

Slowly, carefully, she disengaged herself from Quentin's

embrace and went to investigate. Pushing aside the curtains, she looked at the moon, which hovered in front of the window like a big silver ball. A tempting prize. If only Devondra could have reached out and plucked it out of the sky, she would have at that moment.

"Just to see if it is as beautiful up close as it is far away," she whispered, distracted for a moment, until she caught sight of a form silhouetted by the moon. A limping figure. "Tobias!"

A staunch friend to the end, he had come, no doubt, to rescue her. The question was, did she want to be rescued? A part of her said yes. A part of her said no. Still, she had to go out and talk with him, had to caution him that Cromwell's men might be lurking in the dark somewhere. With that determination in mind, she slipped Quentin's blue velvet coat over her shoulders.

Slowly, cautiously, she moved to the door, trying the handle. It was unlocked. No doubt Quentin assumed that she would not want to risk an encounter with the soldiers. Dare she chance it? Should she even try? Or should she tell Tobias a fond, tearful good-bye and stay behind?

There was no one there to confide in, no one but herself to make the most difficult decision of her life. She moved past the silent form on the bed, thinking all the while. The strong muscles of his body beckoned her, tempted her, made her heart ache as reason invaded her mind. She had set her fate in motion the very first time she had worn a mask, cocked her pistol and engaged on her life on the roads. Despite all her dreams, it was too late to turn back now.

"Thus, it must be good-bye." She couldn't think only of herself. There was Quentin, first and foremost. If she allowed him to harbor her, there would come a time when her presence would send his world crashing down upon his head.

She would bring about his ruin. How then could his love not turn to resentment and later to hate?

And Tobias—how could she desert him after all he had done? He needed her, even though he thought it was she who needed him. Then there were Hyacinth, Conan, Sylvester and the others. Without her strength they would fall victim to Scar, or worse they might try to mastermind a robbery on the roads and be caught in the bargain.

She had to leave! Even so, it was no easy matter. Standing over Quentin, she felt rooted to the floor. She wanted to touch him, wanted to wake him to say good-bye. Wanted . . .

"Foolish girl!" He was a magistrate and she the most wanted woman in all of England. No matter how much she wanted to believe, there was no future for them. Not as long as Cromwell held England.

With agonizing clarity she knew her place was on the Heath. And yet, even as she slipped out of the door, she felt her heart break. The worst was still to come. Tomorrow she would feel the loneliness, the sorrow.

The evening was only a little cool but she shivered as she clutched the coat around her body and moved out into the darkness. Moving barefooted across the hard ground, she made her way to the spot where she had last seen her portly companion.

"Little miss!" His voice was filled with relief and cheerfulness as he hailed her. "Over here." Hiding in the shadows, he proudly displayed the horse he had "borrowed" for the rescue.

"Tobias . . .—" For just a moment she was tempted to send him away, at least until he related the dangers he had risked to come to her aid.

"We have to hurry! Sylvester is guarding the road up

ahead, but we don't have long until the patrol of soldiers rides by again."

"Tobias—" Devondra looked back toward the manor, hesitating as wondrous memories took hold of her.

"Little miss!" Gently, Tobias touched her wounded arm. "He took care of you but then, I had little doubt but that he would."

"Yes, he took care of me." Infinite care.

"Then perhaps in the future we will spare him, eh?" The little man laughed.

"Perhaps." Devondra swallowed her tears. As she climbed on the horse's back, she felt the most terrible emptiness she had ever known.

Was it the stark quiet or some inner voice that awakened him? Whatever it was, Quentin opened his eyes, shifting his body as he reached out. The bed was empty.

"Devondra!" Somehow he knew that although he searched every nook and cranny of the room she would not be found. Even so, he was not content until he had tried to find her.

Hurriedly pulling on his trousers, he ran down the stairs. "Mrs. Vickery! Mrs. Vickery!"

The housekeeper, startled by the harsh note in his voice, nearly dropped the tray of cups and saucers she held aloft as he collided with her in the kitchen.

"Where is she? Where has she gone?" In his foolishness he actually hoped that somehow Devondra Stafford would materialize from out of thin air like a ghost.

"Gone?" The surprised look on the housekeeper's face clearly gave proof that she had not been responsible for spiriting her away.

"In my nightshirt, bigod!"

"I fear so, sir. The poor little thing."

Quentin fought against his temper, but it reared its head nonetheless. Damn! He felt betrayed, angry. He had been so certain that the love he had exhibited would be enough to hold her that he had left the door unlocked. Alas, his beloved guest had taken advantage of that fact and escaped. The more fool he.

"How could she? How could she be so unwise?" Balling his hands into fists, he strode back up the stairs. Dressing as quickly as he could, he made his way to the stables, determined to find her before someone more threatening did.

Chapter Twenty-Six

Their horseback ride was fraught with danger. Tobias and Devondra rode for what seemed an eternity, looking behind them from time to time to make certain there was no sign of pursuit. With relief Devondra saw that, although a few miles back several soldiers had been following them, the horizon was now empty of any horsemen.

"We lost them."

"At least for the moment."

Aware that they couldn't allow themselves the time to gloat, they kept riding. This was their territory, country that they knew like the back of their hands. Let the patrolling soldiers try and catch them. Devondra knew they could lead anyone a merry chase.

Past fertile fields and through the forest they journeyed, intent on reaching the inn. Taking the lead, Tobias swiveled in his saddle, looking over his shoulders at Devondra as she bravely and daringly kept up the pace despite the fact that she was barefoot and only half-clothed. He decided at once that her father would be proud. With her long dark hair flying wildly behind her, she was a sight to behold.

"You look like some ancient Celtic or Viking goddess," he called out. "Can you make us fly?"

"I wish I could," she answered, cheerful despite the fact that the jouncing horse and her tight grip on the reins was reawakening the pain in her arms. Moreover, her long, bare legs were unused to such constant friction. Her tender flesh was chaffed and the nightshirt, twisted tightly around her hips, rendered little protection at all. Nevertheless, she wasn't one to whimper. Once they reached familiar ground, she urged her horse on to an even faster pace, soon passing Tobias.

"Wait!" he called out, urging his horse to catch up, then reaching alongside her. Together they exploded out of the trees, galloping over the meadow. "It seems that I rescued you none too soon, for I have never seen you to anxious to get back to the King's Head," Tobias called out when at last they had slowed down.

"Anxious?" Sadly, Devondra looked over her shoulder, wondering if Quentin Wakefield had noticed her untimely departure. What was he thinking? What was he feeling?

"Ah, such a frown. Am I then to believe that you weren't really in such a hurry to make your escape?"

Devondra's silence answered for her.

"Well, I am not surprised," His tone was fatherly, "You care for him. Why not admit to your feelings?"

Devondra was not in the mood to talk about matters of the heart. She feared that she might give away the depth of her emotions, thus she stubbornly insisted, "The only 'feelings' I have right now are those of pain." She clutched at her arm.

"Bah! I don't believe it." Emphatically, Tobias tugged on

the reins. "Just as I do not believe that he has no feelings for you."

"Forsooth, I have little doubt that he wishes to wring my neck," she whispered, looking back once again. Would he follow her, or would he be too angry?

Galloping into the night for what seemed like hours, Quentin was indeed in pursuit, stubborn in his effort to catch even a glimpse of Devondra Stafford. Straining his eyes as he scanned the horizon, however, he felt only frustration. She had covered her tracks all too well.

"But if I am right, she will be headed in the direction of the Heath."

Sending his horse splashing through one of the murmuring streams that lead eventually to the Thames, Quentin guided his horse in that direction. It was a decision that at last paid off several miles down the road.

"Devondra!" Though she was little more than a speck in the distance, he knew it to be her. The white nightshirt was like a flag, catching his eye. With a soft laugh he continued his wild ride, which swiftly closed the distance between them. They seemed to be heading toward Teddington.

Following at a careful distance, Quentin discreetly rode after the white-clad figure. She and Tobias passed through the woods and orchards and through the peaceful village of straw-thatched houses.

Devondra moved gracefully and confidently through the darkness, her bare feet making no sound. Likewise, Quentin went too, careful to make certain that Devondra and Tobias did not see him. Tying his horse to a small cedar tree, he moved into the shadows, watching as she ducked inside. He followed.

His war years had given Quentin the ability to move with

cunning stillness and to hear things that most men would have ignored. These two skills he put into play now, suspecting it was possible that his life depended just as much on caution tonight as it ever had. Moving swiftly through the door, he froze against the wall, hunkered down and waited.

Devondra lit a lantern and hung it on a peg to illuminate the stall as she slipped the saddle off the horse. "When the danger is over I want to get Quentin Wakefield's horse back to him, Tobias." She didn't want him to think she was a horse thief on top of everything else.

"Return it?" Untangling the reins of his own horse, Tobias was thoughtful. "Hmmmm, never thought about giving anything back."

"We must. I didn't want to steal from Quentin Wakefield, Tobias." Sadly, she tugged at the sleeve of the blue velvet coat. She wasn't certain she wanted to steal from anyone. Not anymore. Strange, how just a few hours could change someone's whole way of thinking.

"Then why did you?" Stepping out of the shadows, Quentin moved toward her.

Startled, Devondra stepped back. She recognized him. All of her carefully constructed emotional walls crumbled. "How . . .?"

For a long moment he merely looked at her, at the way the nightshirt clung to the tantalizing curves and planes of her body. Then he explained, pointing to her white garment, "It was like a banner, leading me along the way."

"So that you could spy on me." She felt vulnerable to his scrutiny. Her heart drummed in her ears. Strange how she could be angry and elated at the same time.

"Devondra—"

They stared at each other for a long while, two silhouettes in the semidarkness, each assessing this meeting and wondering about the consequences. At last Quentin reached out and took her by the shoulder, his fingers so warm they seemed to be melting through her flesh.

"Come back. Staying here will only bring about a tragic fate."

She bristled. "I can take care of myself!"

"Can you?" The scolding tone of his voice was tempered by gentleness as his hand moved up to caress her cheek.

"I have to." And yet she trembled with the desire to lean toward him, to seek safety and love in the warmth of his arms. Instead, she pulled away from him, heading toward the door. "Go back to your own world, Quentin, for I refuse to stray from mine."

"Go back!" Folding his arms across his chest, he was determined to be just as stubborn as she. "No, now that I know this to be your lair I intend to play a waiting game if I must until such time that you, dear lady, come to your senses."

He was so cocksure, so arrogant, that she was incensed. "Waiting game, is it? Well, prepare yourself for a long stay, for I will not desert my companions."

"And I will not desert *you.*" This said, Quentin sat down on a pile of straw, doing his best to make himself comfortable.

Quentin lay awake in the darkness of the stable, shivering against the chill as he swaddled himself in his cloak. "Stubborn woman!" *She will get herself hanged.* What on earth had possessed her to flee from the safety he could offer and ride straight into this hellhole? And what had possessed him to follow?

Quentin listened to the noises of the horses in the stalls and the wind rattling the loose boards of the stable walls and cursed himself for being the world's biggest fool.

"So much for being a knight in shining armor." His gallantry and concern had most obviously gone unappreciated. The haughty little chit had dismissed him without even a care, acting as if he and not she were in the wrong.

Well, the devil take her, and all her beloved companions as well. If she would not listen to reason, he would let her be the sacrificial lamb. He would leave her at the first light of dawn, he would . . .

No. He made a vow to wait and that was exactly what he would do, even if it meant sleeping on the straw without so much as a pillow. Oh, but he longed to have Devondra in his arms, her body pressed into his own, warming him. The very thought of her brought forth achingly sweet memories, wishes and dreams.

Chapter Twenty-Seven

Sitting before the fire clad in a flannel nightgown, a blanket pulled close around her to ward off the night's chill, Devondra sat in a chair near the bed watching the leaping fire tickle the stones in the hearth. She had made a fine mess of things. Nothing had turned out the way she had intended.

She had left Wakefield Manor to try to keep Quentin from danger through his association with her, yet here he was in Teddington. Refusing to listen to his own common sense, he had set up a makeshift shelter in the stables where he insisted he was going to remain to keep an eye on her.

"Protect me?" Sadly she shook her head. Having put himself right in the midst of rogues and thieves, it would be he who needed protecting. And yet, she couldn't deny that a part of her was glad that he was here. Hadn't she looked over her shoulder from time to time on the road tonight, hoping for just such a thing?

I didn't want our parting to be the end. And yet, how could she really believe that love between them had any real chance of surviving? She didn't fit into Quentin's world. Her very presense there created danger for herself and for him as well. The same could be said for his intrusion tonight. Just his being on the Heath imperiled his very existence and put both their fates in question. Yet, she hadn't been able to get him to leave.

"Unless I go with him."

Leaning back in the chair, wrapping her arms around her knees, Devondra curled up in a ball and closed her eyes, trying to envision what living at Wakefield Manor would be like. Tranquil. Serene. Comfortable. That is, until the question of her past was eventually put into view.

"He could not hide me away forever."

There would be acquaintances, associates and friends who would intrude upon the manor, as people were wont to do. My Lord This and My Lady That would insist upon meeting the young woman whom gossip said Quentin Wakefield kept hidden. He would be forced to make some kind of introduction.

"May I present the woman I love, Devondra Stafford," he would say, hoping to himself that they would not recognize her without her mask and pistol.

Devondra could nearly imagine the excitement and the craning of necks as all within the drawing room tried to catch sight of her. And all the while, she would fear hearing the inevitable.

"Bigod, something about that young woman looks strangely familiar."

"What did you say her name was? Stafford? Stafford?"

She would wait nervously for that moment when recognition dawned in their eyes and they remembered her father, each silently making a list of the valuables they had given up to his hand. *And perhaps to mine.*

She could change her name. Create a new identity. *And*

live a grievous lie. A lie that might someday bring the whole world crashing down around their heads. Cromwell was known to be an intrusive man, a man who would soon make her his business. What then? What would be the price to be paid? Quentin's fortune? His future? His very life?

She shivered, trying to push away her pessimistic musings, trying to replace them with thoughts of hope instead. Perhaps things wouldn't be so bleak. Perhaps love, as the poets said, could triumph after all. Perhaps . . .

She remembered the passion of their lovemaking, his diligence in finding and pursuing her. A diligence that certainly had not been rewarded.

Devondra rose to her feet. Padding on bare feet to the window, she looked toward the stables. It was so chilly out tonight. Autumn was here, with winter fast approaching. Quentin Wakefield would be cold. And lonely. Wasn't she?

The memory of his hot, soft, exploring mouth and husky voice tormented her with yearning. She imagined his strong arms holding her, caressing her. She remembered how he had molded her body to his, how he had woven a web of enchantment around them with his love.

"I want—"

Snuffing the candle on the table by the bed, she slowly removed her sleeping garment, hanging it up on the horizontal pole above the head of her bed. Standing beside the soft feather mattress, she let her hair swirl about her shoulders, the long tresses tickling her back as she swayed from side to side. It was a sensuous, enticing feeling that sparked a yearning within her to have Quentin beside her, loving her.

He was so close. So close. Why must she be alone tonight when he was so near?

Quickly, her decision was made. Just as quickly, she pulled the nightgown back over her head. Plucking up a robe and a heavy quilt, she headed for the door and then the stairs, feeling light of heart as she made her way to him.

The dark, silent night was broken only by a soft shaft of moonlight that guided Devondra's steps as she made her way to the inn's stables. Nearly tripping once or twice over her long nightgown, she was nonetheless in a lighthearted mood as the stable's heavy wooden door loomed into sight.

"Oh what would you give to be my love and live with me forever? Would you dance with me and steal my heart and love me upon the heather?" she sang softly as she walked. "Would you be my fondness and delight and . . ."

The heavy door creaked as she pushed it open with her knee.

"And be true to me forever?

She stopped singing. Inside the stables it was dark, with eerily shifting shadows. And quiet. The animals had ceased their moving about and now were placidly at rest in their stalls. Devondra hesitated for a moment in the wide open doorway then, resolutely, she stepped over the threshold.

Her footfall was light, nevertheless, the sound was easily discernible in the silence. Having been fearful of closing his eyes lest he somehow fall asleep, Quentin had been concentrating his attention on a crack in the stable roof, watching the faint glimmer of moonlight that floated through the opening. Now, he concentrated on the intruder who moved through the door. Like a cat to a mouse, he pounced.

"Ohhhhhhh!" she gasped as a hand clamped onto her shoulder.

"Devondra!" His touch softened. "I didn't know at first who you were and I feared . . ." Remembering her recently injured arm, he said, "I didn't hurt you, did I?"

"No." Strange, but now that she was here she felt uncomfortably shy. "I . . . I . . . came . . ."

"To argue with me again. Well, let me emphasize, I will not—" He paused as he spied the blanket, stopping his tirade as he realized that she had thought of his comfort. "For me."

"And for me," she whispered, setting the bundles down on the ground.

Quentin reached out, cupping his hand against her cheek. Oh, how lovely she looked tonight, with her hair hanging loose and her mouth smiling. "I hope I may take that as an invitation."

Devondra played coy. "You may take it as a sign of my concern and compassion. It grows cool on the Heath this time of year."

"Indeed it does." He drew her to him. "And no doubt lonely." His lips brushed hers lightly. When she did not pull away, but responded by leaning closer, he captured her lips in a long, passionate kiss.

Closing her eyes, Devondra enjoyed the spark that always kindled between them. Time seemed to be frozen as they explored each other's lips. They were caught up in the spell of an all-encompassing, glorious need . . .

The sharp snap of a twig broke the spell all too suddenly. Pulling away from Quentin and turning around, Devondra saw the personification of her worst fears standing in the doorway.

"Scar!" Her voice was shrill.

"I didn't frighten you, did I?" His manner said clearly that if he hadn't, he meant to do just that now.

"No." How long had he been watching them? "What are you doing here?"

The twitch of his cheek sent the scar emblazoned on his face into a macabre dance. "The innkeeper complained to

me that the stables were infested with rats. I came to elimi-
nate them."

"You?" Her stance was defiant, although she controlled
her panic only by force of will. Scar posed a serious danger
to Quentin—more of a danger than her lover would ever
guess. "I would be more apt to think that you came to join
them."

Though obviously angered by her comment, the ominous
highwayman purposefully ignored it, turning his attention
to Quentin. "Ah, who have we here? A newcomer to your
beggarly little band?"

Quentin started to introduce himself, but Devondra
wouldn't give him the chance. "Yes, a new addition to the
Notorious Lady's retinue."

"So!"

Seeing the cold, unrelenting expression on the man's face,
Quentin thought that he looked like a messenger of Satan
himself. Far from making him want to flee, however, it only
made him more determined. If this was the type of man
who roamed the Heath, he would never leave it until he
took Devondra with him.

"I welcome you to the Heath." Scar's icy stare measured
Quentin man to man as well, deciding that he might have
met his match here. Still he could not seem to resist saying,
"But I warn you, there must be honor even among thieves.
What is due to me I expect to be given freely."

"What is due you, Richard Warrick," Devondra snapped,
losing her temper, "is a much deserved date with the
hangman!"

Instantly his hand was on her arm, squeezing, either purposefully or accidentally, that part of her flesh that had been
seared by the lead ball. Devondra paled, then gasped as pain
knifed through her.

"Let her go!" With an outraged growl, his blue eyes dark with anger, Quentin lunged savagely for the highwayman.

The sound of flesh against flesh rent the air as each man landed blow after blow. They fell to the ground, rolling over and over as they struggled with deadly determination. Devondra was powerless to do anything but watch as each man suffered punishing punches and kicks. Quentin soon had a cut over his eyes, Scar a lacerated lip as their breathing came in ugly, rasping sounds. Still they did not stop.

The fight went on until Quentin's head throbbed and flecks of black danced before his eyes. Even so, he had no intention of quitting. A man like this would only take advantage of any show of weakness or retreat. Instinctively, he knew he had to make a stand and make it now or fall victim to a bully.

When at last his opponent tired and the dust had settled, it proved to be true. Though the highwayman's piggish eyes were filled with anger and hatred, there was another gleam that showed within as well: Respect.

"You have not seen the last of me!" Scar hissed between clenched teeth, slowly getting to his feet. "I swear that someday I will cause you such pain that you will wish that you had never been born!" Thus said, Scar waved his hand airily, threw his cloak over his shoulder with a flourish, then left the stables as quietly as he had entered.

Chapter Twenty-Eight

The yard was silvered with the moon's muted radiance as Quentin and Devondra made their way to the inn. Disturbed by the confrontation with Scar, they decided that it would be much safer amidst the patrons there.

"A congenial man," Quentin grumbled, dabbing at his sore eye. "I hope that the others are not like him."

"They aren't." Reaching up, she gently brushed away the blood. "Despite our profession you will find that even highwaymen are human." She shuddered. "Except perhaps for Scar."

"Scar." He said the name with loathing. "I have heard a great deal about the murderous highwayman. Now I know that the rumors were being kind to the devious bastard!" It seemed perfectly natural to drape his arm protectively across her shoulders as he remembered his bloody confrontation with the fellow. She was his. From this moment on she always would be. "I don't want to ever let you go!"

Remembering how he had charged to her defense, Devon-

dra leaned against him, smiling as his lips moved along her
forehead, brushing gently along the heavy brush of her dark
lashes, teasing the line of her jaw, then caressing her neck.

"And I don't want you to."

His emotions caused his throat to tighten, making his
voice very husky. "I want to make love to you again and
again."

"And I would have you love me again, sir, now that I
know to what delights you can take me!" Devondra arched
against him in sensual pleasure, her hands sliding over the
muscles of his arms down to the taunt flesh of his stomach.

"Oh, how you tempt me." Quentin's eyes moved toward
the stables. His strong fingers stroked and fondled her breast
as he struggled with his longing. "But I think we should
move on to somewhere safer."

He held her hand as they opened the thick wooden door
and tiptoed out. Inside they found the inn to be in total
darkness. Not even one candle was lit. "Deserted! Everyone
must be abed."

Devondra paused to listen before following Quentin
inside. As she moved, she tried to tread lightly so as not to
set the floorboards creaking, but each step seemed to explode
in the silence.

Quentin led her to the stairs. Their fingers moved over
each other's faces. "Quentin . . ." She lifted her arms to
encircle his neck and clung to him, her breasts pressed
against his chest. "Thank you."

Quentin buried his face in the dark cloud of her hair,
inhaling the spicy scent she always used. "For what? For
caring?"

"Yes." And for so much more. "And for making my heart
come alive again." Her body arched against his as he
caressed her. His fingers seemed to be everywhere, touching
her, setting her body ablaze with desire.

Mutely Devondra nodded, a mischievous smile trembling on her lips. She leaned against him, outlining the shape of his mouth with her fingertips. " 'Twould seem to me that a featherbed would be much more accommodating to lovers than the hard ground."

" 'Twould seem."

Laughing, she gently prodded him up the stairs, leading him to the third room on the left. Pushing open the door, she lit just one small candle, then made a sweeping gesture with her hand. "My castle."

Quentin looked around, the room. There was a colorful quilt on the bed, lace on the pillows, and a peg hanging from the door, covered with petticoats and a chemise. A red-wigged doll, clothed in a faded green satin dress puffed out by a farthingale, drew his eye. It held a place of prominence at the head of the bed.

"My father gave that to me. Of all the things I own, I treasure Elizabeth the most." Picking her up, she stared at the doll for a long time, then placed her on a chair beside the bed. "We were wealthy then." A time long past.

"The only toy I ever had was a miniature sailing ship." It was brought back from one of his philandering father's trips across the sea as a gift for his mother. He shook his head sadly, remembering the day it had been crushed beneath his stepfather's heel. "We were very poor."

"The war changed a great many things for all of us, or so it seems."

"So it seems." He wondered if she, like so many others, had suffered. Had she gone hungry? Been left out in the cold?

"My father dreamed of someday going back to our old house." Alas, a dream he would never fulfill.

"Devondra—" His breath was a warm tickle, stroking her ear.

Standing before her, so close that there was barely an inch between them, he slowly undressed her, slipping her robe down around her hips to fall in a heap at her feet. He tugged at her nightgown, watching as it slid down her body. "You are so beautiful," he whispered, bending down to kiss her breasts, first one and then the other. Slowly, he peeled off his own clothes, letting them fall where they might.

Devondra moved her body against him, feeling the burning flesh touching hers. If she had been cold before, now she was not.

"Your hair is tangled." He seemed to take great delight in running his fingers through the soft strands. Devondra could feel the rhythmic movement of his fingers as he stroked. The touch of his hands in her hair caused a fluttery feeling in her stomach. A shiver danced up and down her spine. She leaned against his hand, giving in to the stirring sensations.

Quentin's fingers left the softness of her hair. He clasped her shoulders, contenting himself in looking at her for a long moment. The hunger to be near her, to touch her, to make love to her had been with him all evening. Now that dream was a reality.

"Are you warm?"

"Mmm!" she answered, burying her face against his chest as he swept her up in his arms. He carried her to the bed, gently lowering her to the soft feather mattress.

Staring up into the mesmerizing depths of his eyes, Devondra felt an aching tenderness for him. Reaching up, she clung to him, drawing on his strength and giving hers to him in return. She could feel his heart pounding and knew that hers beat in matching rhythm.

Caressing her, kissing her, he left no part of her free from his touch, and she responded with a passion that was kindled by his love. Her entire body quivered with the intoxicating sensations he always aroused in her. Tonight she wanted only one thing—to feel his hard warmth filling her, to join with him in that most tender of emotions.

Always before when they had made love, Devondra had been a bit shy, holding a small bit of herself back from her pleasure. Now, she held nothing back. Reaching out, she boldly explored Quentin's body as he had done hers—his hard-muscled chest and arms, his stomach. His flesh was warm to her touch, pulsating with the strength of his maleness. As her fingers closed around him, Quentin groaned.

"Devondra!" Desire raged like an inferno, pounding in his veins. His whole body throbbed with the fierce compulsion to plunge himself into her sweet softness and yet, he held himself back, caressing her once more, teasing the petals of her womanhood until he could tell she was fully prepared for his entry. Her skin felt hot against his as he entwined his legs with hers.

"Love me. Love me now," she whispered. Her frantic desire for him was nearly unbearable. Parting her thighs, she guided him to her with an ardor she had never shown before. Writhing in pleasure, she was silken fire beneath him, rising and falling with him as he moved with the relentless rhythm of their love. Hot desire fused their bodies together, yet there was an aching sweetness mingling with the fury. They spoke with their hearts and hands and bodies words they had never uttered before in the final outpouring of their love.

In the aftermath of the storm, when their passion had ebbed and they lay entwined, they sealed their vows of love with whispered words. Sighing with happiness, Devondra snuggled within the cradle of Quentin's arms, content.

"I love you." Quentin placed soft kisses on her forehead. She mumbled sleepily and stretched lazily, her soft thighs brushing against his hair-roughened ones in a motion that stirred him again. He touched her mouth in a kiss with the intention of making love to her again but saw that she was asleep.

Lying there, her dark hair billowing out around her, she looked so fragile, so small, but he knew what strength and determination she possessed. Tomorrow might bring hardship, perhaps even danger, but he knew Devondra would find a way to survive. She was keen of mind, brave, loyal and filled with a resolve to make the best of any situation. Perhaps, in truth, they had a lot to learn from each other in the days ahead.

Muted rays of sunlight fluttered through an opening in the inn's shutters. From beneath the window the sound of the first cock's crow reminded Devondra all too jarringly that morning had come. Stretching her arms, she opened her eyes as her hand made contact with solid flesh. Quentin. He had come, making good on his promise of "tomorrow." Now his arm lay heavy across her stomach, the heat of his body warming hers as they lay entangled.

The sound of his steady breathing made her heart begin to pound wildly. A flush of color stained her cheeks as she remembered the words she had said, the things she had done. Undeniably she had been bold, but caring about him so deeply had made her brazen. It seemed a wanton lived inside her body, an ardent woman who responded unashamedly to Quentin.

"Lover," she whispered. Once Devondra might have thought the word to have a tawdry ring to it, but feeling as she did about him, she couldn't believe that the passion and joy they found together was wrong. He knew just how to touch her, how long to caress her, knew all her sensitive

spots. In a tender assault of kissing, stroking and teasing
her with his tongue, he knew how to bring her again and
again to a heart-stopping crest of pleasure.

Rising up on one elbow, she looked at him now with
aching tenderness, for he looked so much younger when
asleep, not at all like England's magistrate. He snuggled up
against her, his powerful body sprawled across the bed as
if he didn't have a worry in the world. Reaching out to touch
a lock of dark hair that had fallen across his brow, she felt
just as protective of him as he felt of her. She wanted to
make him happy. Could she?

It certainly seemed so. His face had the calm peace of a
contented man. Breathing a sigh, she remembered his kisses,
his caresses, the awe-inspiring moment when he had made
her a woman. And last night had been just as magical;
perhaps even more so. She remembered his eyes bright with
desire, his lips trembling in a smile as he kissed her.

Once, she might have blushed at the thought of a man
learning every inch of her body, yet with Quentin it seemed
as natural as breathing. That thought made her smile as she
again stretched languorously. She felt happy and blissfully
carefree.

It was all so very simple. He was her man and she was
his woman. Though she longed for a firmer commitment
from him, wanted with all her heart to be his wife, what
they had was enough for now. Whatever happened, she
would never be sorry for what had passed between them.
Far more unsettling was the fact that she might never have
experienced the ultimate joy of his love.

Leaning forward, she touched his mouth lightly in a kiss,
laughing softly as his lips began to twitch.

"Devondra?" Quentin cherished the blessing of finding
her cradled in his arms, her mane of dark hair spread like

a cloak over her shoulders. He smiled. "Good morrow, fair lady. What a welcome surprise."

"For me as well as for you." She snuggled into his arms, resting her head on his shoulder, curling into his hard, strong body. "I trust you slept well, without the feathers tickling your nose," she said with a laugh.

"Aye, I slept very well. Such enjoyable activity as we partook of last night always makes me sleep like a babe."

His hand moved lightly over her hip and down her leg as he spoke. Weeks of frustration and worry seemed to have melted away. She was his! At last he had come to know the glorious sweetness of her body. Heaven, her body had been pure heaven. She had made him the happiest man alive.

"I'd like to wake up every morning and find you next to me." But he was not sure just what the future had in store for them thus, despite his smile, there was a hint of a furrow to his brow. "Devondra—"

"Hush!" She didn't want to spoil the morning by letting reality intrude upon her dreams. She knew just what he was going to say, he was going to talk again about the danger she was in. "We must content ourselves with the moment we have together, no matter how short they might be."

He started to speak, but again she silenced him. There was something she had to say.

"If . . . if the worst happens, Quentin, if by some ill fortune I am sent to . . . to the gallows, I want you to know that you have given me something wonderful and beautiful to remember."

"No!" The very thought was much too painful.

"Yes." By virtue of the life she had chosen, her capture was a possibility and one she had to accept.

"Oh, Devondra!" Cupping her chin in his hand, he kissed her hard. Moving his hands over her body, he stroked lightly—her throat, her breasts, her belly, her thighs.

Devondra closed her eyes to the feelings she was becoming familiar with now. Wanting to bring him the same sensations, she touched him, one hand sliding down over the muscles of his chest, sensuously stroking his flesh. Then they were rolling over and over in the bed, sinking into the warmth and softness. Devondra sighed in delight at the feel of his hard, lithe body atop hers.

A loud pounding at the door interrupted their pleasure. Rising up from the bed, Devondra cast a worried look in the direction of the sound. "Devondra?" It was Tobias.

"What is it?" Devondra did her best to sound sleepy.

"Sylvester has been arrested." Tobias's shout was like hearing a tabby cat roar.

"Arrested!" Leaping out of bed, she covered her nakedness with a sheet and padded to the door. "How? When?"

Standing in the doorway, Tobias hung his head. "The fool. He went out on the road alone. It appears he rode right into a trap."

"A trap!" Remembering her father, Devondra clenched her jaw as she looked over her shoulder at Quentin. The expression of surprise upon his face completely exonerated him, however.

"Aye. A trap." Tobias started to enter the room but, looking toward the bed and seeing Quentin, he blushed and took a step backward. "Just like what happened to your father." The little man balled his hand into a fist. "Methinks perhaps there be a traitor in our midst."

"A traitor?"

"Aye, and I think I have an idea just who that might be." There was a pause, then he blurted in unison with Devondra. "Scar!"

Chapter Twenty-Nine

In the inn's small taproom, the smell of spilled wine, whiskey and ale mixed with the odor of sweat and leather. The clank of tankards, mugs and cups rang in the air, accompanying raucous laughter and boisterous chatter. The smoke of the cooking fires was thick. The hearth fires danced and sparked, illuminating the faces of the inn's patrons as if through a fog. Faces that Quentin tried to decipher as he sat at a table in the corner.

"Ha! Friends she calls them," he mumbled, taking particular interest in the personages Devondra had pointed out. "If you ask me, they are as unGodly a lot as was ever gathered together."

Quentin scowled as he caught sight of the stocky, ill-tempered Conan lounging about near the door. His small, piggish eyes and the manner in which he would not meet one's eye hinted at a less than sterling character. And then there was Barnaby, the tall, skinny, clumsy rogue who Quentin had seen spying through keyholes. Likewise an unsavory character, if ever there was one. That was not to mention the other assortment of rogues, thieves and God-only-knew who that were assembled beneath the inn's roof. Men, whom Quentin had sought to put behind bars or string up from the gibbet. Even the innkeeper, a swarthy, bearded, gap-toothed man who wore a patch over his eye, looked like an escapee from Newgate.

"This is no place for Devondra!" Indeed, among this throng she was like a swan amid swine. Somehow he had to get her away from here, even if it meant carrying her away forcibly.

"Ah, here you are." Tobias grinned in greeting, his eyes gleaming with merriment as he plopped his girth down in a chair next to Quentin's.

"Aye, here I am," Quentin replied curtly.

"Sitting here empty-handed," Tobias good-naturedly chided. "Well, leave it to me to bring you some cheer." Pounding on the table, the little highwayman summoned the tavern maid. "Ale here."

"Ale." Boldly eyeing Quentin up and down, she made it a point to linger.

"Aye, ale!"

"Anything else?" Though she spoke to Tobias, she bent over Quentin, offering him a view of well-rounded breasts.

His smile faltering, Tobias barked out, "A plate of bread and cheese."

"Bread and cheese." She said the words seductively.

"Two ales and a plate of bread and cheese and *nothing else,*" he grumbled, giving her a swat on her behind to move her on her way. "Brazen doxy!" he mumbled beneath his breath. "Clearly she should learn a lesson in manners from Hyacinth."

"Hyacinth?"

Tobias pointed across the room where a voluptuous, red-haired woman dressed in a white cotton shift covered with a russet-colored bodice and skirt was engaged in conversation with two men garbed in doublets and breeches that were sadly out of fashion.

"Devondra's most steadfast friend, she is. Took her under her wing when her mother died." There was a soft glow in Tobias's eyes. "A good woman she is."

Quentin was not so easily convinced. Still he was amused as he watched Hyacinth skillfully dodge the amorous gropings of one or her companions. It was obvious she could take care of herself, as was exhibited when she at last resorted to spilling the contents of a full mug of ale in her pursuer's lap.

Tobias reached out and touched Quentin's hand. "Do not judge Hyacinth, or any of us, too harshly until you have walked a mile or two in our shoes. Despite our outward trappings and appearance, there are some of us whose hearts are made of gold."

"Or solid stone," Quentin exclaimed, nodding in Scar's direction.

"Ah, yes. Scar," Tobias whispered. "The would-be king of the roads and, I fear, Devondra's greatest enemy."

"Why?" Quentin had a need to know.

Tobias heaved a sigh. "Several reasons, really. First and foremost I suppose because 'twas Jamie who gave him the frightful facial wound that gave him his name."

"Devondra's father?"

Tobias shook his head. " 'Tis a long story, the gist of it being that Richard 'Scar' Warrick and Jamie Stafford didn't quite see things eye to eye. Jamie always held to a code of honor. In truth, in all his years as a highwayman he never robbed a man who could not well afford it, nor ever even thought of killing a man in cold blood. Scar, on the other hand, seems to enjoy inflicting misery."

Remembering his scuffle in the stables, Quentin said, "So it would seem."

"He is at times, I fear, a man without a soul."

"There are some who have said that of Cromwell," Quentin replied, recalling their last conversation.

"But at the same time he is a man of pure genius whose network of spies could soon rival that set up by Walsingham in Queen Elizabeth's time." Tobias pointed toward the floor. "Down in the cellars are work benches where Scar's men can change the appearance of a watch or chain or brooch so skillfully that the rightful owner would never even recognize it." Taking his ale from the tray of the tavern girl, Tobias drained his mug dry and nodded for another.

He continued, "Not only that, he is a masterful counterfeiter who has the skill to forge documents. A talent he often put to use during the war for both sides, I fear."

"He was not a royalist?"

Tobias was scornful. "Richard Warrick has no loyalty to God, king or country. He goes where it is the most profitable."

"I see." Quentin eyed the aged cheese and stale bread dubiously, deciding to partake only of the ale. "Is that what put him at odds with Devondra's father?"

"Aye. Jamie and Scar were like cat and dog. Sooner or later conflict was bound to break out." Tobias stuffed his mouth full of cheese, talking as he chewed. "Think of Jamie what you will, he was at heart a decent man. Moreover, he would not abide willful killing, which is why he tangled with Scar in the first place." Taking an ample bite of bread, he continued. "Seems he came upon Scar just as he was going to slay a hapless merchant whom Scar had bound and gagged and drug into the thicket."

"They fought." Quentin took a long draft of his ale.

"Aye, and Jamie suffered for it, though not such an obvious

or lingering injury as his adversary did." Impatient for a drink, Tobias motioned to the tavern maid and was rewarded with a full mug. "The merchant was saved, but, alas, Jamie's act of mercy was what done him in in the end."

"Done him in?" He took another drink.

Tobias hung his head. "Methinks it was Scar who sold out on James Stafford that woeful day."

"For the reward?"

"That and for pure vengeance." Tobias leaned back in his chair, his expression pained as he thought about that time. Suddenly he seemed determined to change the subject. "Ah, but I am hopeful that there will be better days."

"Better days?" Quentin frowned.

"Aye." Tobias propped up his feet on the table, letting his gaze roam over the room. For a moment he looked like a tabby cat reclining before the fire, then he said, "Ah, how I love the warmth of a good fire. And good companionship. And, of course, a good drink of ale. That in the end is what contentment is all about, is it not?" He made a wide sweep with his hand. "Cozy, isn't it?"

"Cozy might be one word I would use," Quentin answered dryly.

Tobias closed his eyes. "And the other words?"

Quentin came right to the point. "This inn, and all within it, pose a danger to all that I hold dear."

Boistrous laughter and mumbled voices filled the air, drowning out Tobias's reply, but all such rowdiness stilled as the crowd caught sight of her. As if on cue, Devondra made her entrance, slowly walking the length of the vast room, her head held high. Dressed in a full-skirted gown of pearl-colored satin, with a mauve fitted bodice, she was a fetching sight.

"That being Devondra." Tobias looked at Quentin intently

as he went on. "You think she is going to come to harm if she stays among us."

"I know it! Don't *you?*" As if to emphasize his argument, he pointed in the direction of Scar.

Tobias looked at Devondra, then at Scar, then at Devondra again. "I . . . I don't know."

"Well, I *do.* You have said yourself that Scar is Devondra's enemy."

"Yes . . . yes, he is." Tobias would not meet Quentin's eye. "But—"

"There can be no 'buts' about it. Maybe not today, maybe not tomorrow, but sometime in the future Gentleman James's daughter will follow the same pathway to the gibbet that her father rode down if she does not make a change in her life and remove herself from Scar's path."

Tobias did not reply. He merely stared at Quentin, his face a puzzled mask, as if he was sorting things out in his mind.

Quentin pushed on. Somehow he had to get Tobias on his side, had to make him see. "Can you live with yourself if the worst happens, Tobias? Can you?"

"I . . . I . . ." Like a frog catching flies, Tobias opened his mouth again and again, but no words came out.

Quentin hurried on. "How long before your 'friend' Scar betrays Devondra? A day, a month, a year?"

It was food for thought. Tobias clenched his hands in his lap, looking so bewildered that Quentin couldn't help but take pity on him. In his way Tobias was a caring man, different from the others.

"Ah, my two favorite men." Though she tried to sound casual, Devondra's eyes sparkled with a look of curiosity as she moved toward the table. "Tell me, Tobias, are you keeping Quentin amused?"

"Definitely."

She smiled. "Good, for with all my heart I want him to like it here so that he might stay, at least for awhile." She took a seat beside Quentin, leaning her head upon his shoulder. The familiarity did not go unnoticed by Tobias.

"Devondra, I . . . I have been thinking," he began, nervously twiddling his thumbs. "I'm . . . I'm getting more than a bit gray in the beard. Too old, it seems, for the foolishness I've been involved in of late."

She was stunned. "Foolishness?"

"Aye. Riding about in the chilled dark of night on that tiresome horse, jiggling my bones. I . . . I . . ." He shrugged.

"Tobias, what are you saying?"

He banged the table with his fist, exhibiting a rare defiance. "That I am tired of riding the roads, tired of putting my life in danger for a handful of gold." He looked down at his boots. "And so should you be. Why, I . . ."

The sound of broken wood shattered Devondra's reply. A tumult arose from all sides of the inn at once. Three men posted as lookouts burst into the room to give the alarm— too late, or so it seemed.

"Soldiers!"

Hard on their heels, Cromwell's men poured into the room through doors and windows, with swords drawn and pistols ready.

"No!" Devondra's first impulse was to flee, until she realized that all routes of escape were blocked. Worse yet, there were three soldiers for every one of theirs.

"Don't move, Devondra." Quentin's stern advice hissed in her ear. "There is no crime in being in a tavern. Keep still. They won't know you."

Ah, but she feared that they did. Somehow. Some way.

"Stand back and you will come to no harm. We seek one particular woman, and she only," called out one of the soldiers, a tall, overbearing man who strutted about like a rooster in the barnyard.

"A woman?" At first there was chatter; then, just as suddenly, the tap room quieted. As if enchanted, turned into stone, the patrons didn't talk, didn't run, didn't move a muscle.

"The Notorious Lady by name."

"The Notorious Lady?" The crowd played innocent.

"Aye." Working his way through the crowd, the tall soldier examined first one woman's face and then another, moving toward Devondra.

"She's not here!" called out a young man.

"We do not even know her," cried out another.

"Go out on the roads if ye dare and mayhap ye will have more luck," chortled an old man. "That is, if ye are brave enough to face her man to man." There was laughter. Joviality that quickly ceased as it was soon proven that the soldiers meant business.

"Torch the damnable place!"

The barked command was met with hostile silence, a quiet that was broken by one whispered voice. "No!" Devondra couldn't let the others suffer because of her.

"Who said that?" The soldier strutted back and forth, eager to corner his female quarry.

It was then that Hyacinth took a step forward. "I did. I am the woman you seek. I am your highwayman," she smiled, "or should I say woman?"

Devondra gasped, but before she could speak the tavern maid stepped forward, to take credit for Devondra's identity. "I am the Notorious Lady," she said.

"No, 'tis I," called out a gray-haired old woman whose

duty it was to clean up the tavern after all the patrons had
retired for the night.

Though there were only nine women in the room, each
and every one of them made claim to Devondra's alias,
staunchly protecting her. Even a few of the men, calling out
in falsetto, claimed to be the Notorious Lady. It was, however, a ploy that didn't work.

"Fools and liars that they be, arrest them all!"

It was then that Devondra pushed her way forward. She
had transgressed, and it would be she who would pay the
price, and she alone. "*I* am the one you seek."

"Devondra, no!" Quentin tried to restrain her, tried to
keep her from being foolishly brave, but she ignored his
plea. Taking several of the soldiers upstairs, she proved her
identity as the Notorious Lady by showing them not only
her garments but her masks as well.

"Seize her!" Roughly, she was set upon, her hands tied
behind her back. Then she was pushed down the stairs.
Missing a step, she tumbled.

"Take your hands off her, you bastards!" Lashing out with
flaying fists, Quentin fought to come to her side. Standing
with feet apart, he held up his head defiantly. "I am the
Magistrate of London. By the authority vested in me, I tell
you, let her go."

"Magistrate, is it?" The cocky soldier grinned. "And are
you then Quentin Wakefield?"

Quentin boomed out his answer. "I am!" He looked toward
Devondra to give her reassurance. Somehow all would be
well, or so his eyes promised.

"Then you are under arrest as well for conspiring with
an enemy of Cromwell's justice!"

"Justice?" Quentin looked with surprise as two of the
soldiers ran toward him. It was such a sudden move that he
tried but was unable to make an effective defense. Though

he was able to wrench away one of the soldier's pistols, it was knocked out of his hand. Unarmed, he suffered the punishment of battering fists and kicking feet and the greatest injustice as the butt of a pistol was aimed at his head.

Part Three
Betrayed And Beloved

London 1655

Love seeketh not itself to please,
Nor for itself hath any care,
But for another gives its ease,
And builds a Heaven in Hell's despair.
William Blake
The Clod and the Pebble. Stanza 1

Chapter Thirty

Just as it had been when her father had been tried, the court room was filled with noisy, laughing, jeering people. Elbowing each other for a better view of the proceedings, they took great delight in viewing the sentencing of such an infamous miscreant as the Notorious Lady. Their voices echoed through the room.

"So that's her!"

"Aye. Look at 'er, will yer. She doesn't look so frightening without 'er pistol and 'er mask."

"Not frightening at all, but damnably beautiful."

"Aye. Such a pity to 'ave that pretty neck strained by the 'angman."

"Do you think she will hang?"

"How can yer even ask? She'll 'ang, all right."

"Early to trial, neck stretched a mile, as they say."

Listening to the morbid conversation, Devondra reached up and touched her neck. It was true that when a malefactor was caught he or she was quickly brought to trial. Though she might have wanted to be optimistic, she couldn't really believe that she would find mercy here. Cromwell had gone to great lengths to capture her. Why would he let her go free?

"But, oh, if only . . ."

Devondra recalled with dismay how she had found herself tied hand and foot and thrown aboard a jolting and bumping cart bound for Newgate. Worse yet, there had been enough of Cromwell's men in the cart and surrounding her on horseback to make rescue by her friends a hopeless matter. Now, just a day later, she stood at the prisoner's dock in a court of justice all alone. Alone, that is, except for the brawny guards to her left and to her right. It seemed that Cromwell was taking no chances.

A trial, they called it. A mockery was what it was. The verdict would be guilty before the jurors even sat upon their benches along the far wall. Resentfully, she looked in the judge's direction and found him staring at her with a scowl.

The trial, of course, would most likely be only a formality, as anyone who had stood on the prisoner's dock well knew. Unless a miracle was performed from Heaven she would be found guilty. Moreover, the criminal, be he robber, highwayman or popish priest, was expected to accept with courage his death by hanging before a huge, excited crowd.

Devondra shuddered at the thought. *I will be hanged just like my father was.* Hanged. She was haunted by the prospect. How could she die when she had only just begun to realize what life was really about?

"Oh, Quentin. Why didn't I listen to you? How could I have been so foolish?" She had made a fatal choice and now the time had come when she must pay most dearly.

So many regrets. So many . . .

Perhaps more than anything she regretted that their love had never really had a chance. Her fault. Hers! She should never have left Wakefield Manor. She should never have returned to the inn. But she had.

And what of Quentin? It deeply worried her that she had not heard one word from him. What had happened to her lover? Had her foolishness brought him down as well? She sincerely hoped not. Lifting her eyes, she scanned the crowd, hoping to see his face. He was not there. She felt a tremendous loss, more alone than she had ever felt in all her life.

Devondra's eyes swam with stinging tears. *I loved him,* she thought. *Whatever happens, I hope he knows that, hope he knows how much I will treasure the time we shared.* Indeed, they were moments she would have in her heart until she went to her death.

My death! As the proceedings were conducted with calm indifference, it soon became apparent that time might come sooner than Devondra could ever have imagined. There was a great deal of form to the trial, but no compassion; considerable interest, but no sympathy. She watched through her tears, assessing the judge, who sat pompously straight; the Lord Mayor mimicking an equal measure of dignity; the barrister, who seemed anxious for the morning to be over.

The other prisoners were dealt with quickly and efficiently. The first was impenitent and bitter at the thought of dying for taking a purse. In the end he was sentenced to a long term in Newgate. Three prisoners were condemned to the gallows, two to the pillory and one young lad was given the lesser penalty of the lash. Taking a deep breath, Devondra prepared herself for her own ordeal. She was determined to face whatever happened with dignity. She would not sulk or worse yet fling curses at the judge. What she had done was wrong—there could be no denying it—and yet . . .

Suddenly the judge was talking to her.

"What is your name?" He eyed her sternly, and Devondra wished she had a mirror and a comb. She hoped she did not look as unkempt as she felt. *Oh, what I would not give to be able to once again hide behind my mask,* she thought.

"Devondra Catherine Stafford," she answered.

"Stafford," several voices echoed, in tones that seemed to say that they remembered another who had borne that name.

The judge towered over her from the height of his bench, studying her critically. "Have you any witnesses to speak to your character, girl?"

Devondra hung her head. She could hardly call upon Tobias, Conan, Barnaby or Hyacinth to testify to her better qualities, considering their own profession. And Quentin? Once again her eyes scanned the room, hoping against hope. He had saved her once. Could he save her again?

"Have you any witnesses, girl?"

"Witnesses?" Sadly, she ascertained that *he* was not there. Thus she answered, "No!"

"No witnesses," the judge repeated, nodding to a clerk, who scratched down the information on a long roll of paper.

"No witnesses . . ." the crowd murmured.

"The charge is stealing on the roads. How do you plead?"

"I . . ." The penalty for stealing was clear. Even taking a purse from a traveler could bring about a sentence of death. How then could she freely admit it?

"How do you plead?" The judge raised his brows, obviously anxious to get the matter over and done with.

Ignoring the judge's impatience, Devondra tried to regain her composure. It was true that she had not witnesses as to her virtues, but it was equally true that there were no witnesses who could be called against her. No one had ever seen her face. No one could say for certain that she was the one who had terrorized the Heath. Perhaps she could recant her admission at the inn. Perhaps . . .

"How do you plead?"

A stir fluttered over the spectators like a brisk wind. Each and every eye turned her way, waiting for her reply. The answer, however, came not from Devondra, but from a man standing several feet behind her.

"She is the woman who plundered the roads from London to Hounslow," said a raspy voice. "She is the Notorious Lady; I so swear."

Whirling around, Devondra looked angrily at her accuser, stunned as she recognized the impressively garbed man. There, dressed all in red, and holding the silver staff of his office, sat none other than Richard "Scar" Warrick.

"You!"

Scar smiled. "Yes. Me. Thief-catcher to the Lord Protector and principal witness against *you.*"

"Thief-catcher!" Brutally, the truth hit her in the face. Scar wasn't a highwayman at all. He was one of *them.* Or was he? Just what ties of loyalty did a man like Scar Warrick ever obey?

Whatever loyalties he might have had, Scar Warrick soon proved that he had none at all to the occupants of the King's Head Inn. His words put the noose around all their necks, for although he included in his testimony his own dark deeds, he blamed them upon her companions'. She had never truly realized how utterly loathsome he was. Loathsome and deadly. Because of his testimony Devondra heard the judge read her sentence: "Guilty!"

There was little more that could be done.

"You will be taken to the gallows at Tyburn in two days' time and there you will be hanged." Was Devondra mistaken, or was there a flicker of remorse in the judge's eyes? "And may God rest your soul."

"Rest? My soul?" Devondra's eyes scorched Scar as she looked at him. "My soul will not rest. It will come back to haunt you, bastard that you are. Only when you have kept your date with the hangman will I call back my ghost."

"Ghost!" Scar Warrick's manner was mocking. Still, as Devondra was taken from the room, she was shocked to see that he crossed himself.

Justice. That was the word Quentin pondered as he sat on the small bed in his cell. Justice. As magistrate he knew it to mean "the administration of what was just by the impartial adjustment of conflicting claims," the meting out of merited rewards or punishments. To Cromwell, however, it meant something much more sinister. It meant seeking vengeance upon all those who did not see things his way. In truth, even an anointed king had been put to death because he had not given in to Oliver's whims.

Oh, Devondra! How heavy a price would she pay for tweeking the Lord Protector's and his cohorts' noses with her antics? Alas, he knew all too well. Hadn't he himself sent many an unfortunate on his way to either heaven or hell? Strange that now he found himself regretting it. Perhaps, when all was said and done, he had learned a lesson in humanity and mercy.

"I pray I have not learned too late."

He was being kept in a cell in the Tower of London, which at least was better than being condemned to incarceration in Newgate. At least Quentin had that. The illustrious Tower, where many noble prisoners had been confined before their death. To pass the time he counted them off. Catherine Howard, Sir Thomas More, Lady Jane Grey, Edmund Nevill, Anne Boleyn. Ah, yes, the Tower had an interesting array of ghosts, each with a sad tale to tell.

As for himself, he remembered being brought in through the river entrance, Traitors' Gate, looking around in sick despair as the full realization of what had happened hit him full force. He remembered the soldiers coming to the inn, remembered Devondra's confession. He had not been able to save her this time, and the failure tore at his heart.

Where was she now? What was happening? Was she lonely? Afraid? He could well imagine that she was, being incarcerated in the hellhole. Even *his* courage was shaken, though he had been here less than a night and a day. He had begun to fear that this was to be his prison for many years to come, day following day, month following month. Forgotten by the outside world. Was there sufficient evidence to convict him? He doubted it. Not unless false evidence or bribed witnesses were used against him. Still, he might be kept there until he was old and gray.

Dark walls rose high about Quentin, so high that the ceiling seemed to be shrouded in gloom. Bars on the window blocked his view of the sky. Ominous silence surrounded him, except for an occasional drip, drip drip. It was damp in the stone room because of a recent rain. The little bit of air that drifted through the window was musty and held the unwelcome stench of the Thames.

"A sorry end to your son, Mother." Yet, it was not his own fate that haunted him, but that of a bold, flashing-eyed girl. "Devondra." She was so young. Much too young to die, and yet there were those even younger dying every day, victims of Cromwell's reign.

Quentin stared around him with burning, angry eyes. "Justice. Ha!" He knew there would be little enough of it shown to Devondra. The die was cast. It had been the moment the soldiers had descended on the inn. Devondra would hang unless he found a way to save her.

Save her? How could he, when he wasn't even in a position to save himself? Already his manor, his title and all his possessions had been striped from him. He was powerless.

That was Cromwell's penalty for a man falling in love and trying his best to save the subject of his adoration from pompous prigs.

Worse yet, it was a fact of life that crime in England was big business. A good many men profited from misdeeds. Lawyers, of course, who pocketed large fees. The judges. The jailors. The aldermen. The hangmen. The lord mayor. Even the chaplains or ordinaries of Newgate were amply provided for. And himself?

In self-condemnation he hung his head. Aye, it was true. He had risen to power because of the ill-fortune of others. Now he was paying the price, and there was nothing to be done unless . . .

He had to escape. There was no other choice. *I'll leave this cage and find some way to save Devondra before it is too late.* On that he was determined. It was the only thought that kept depression at bay as he stared at his surroundings.

Chapter Thirty-One

"Let us eat, drink and be merry; for tomorrow we may die," Devondra whispered, applying the saying in the Bible to her own situation as she sat clasping her hands together tightly in the gloom. Newgate. In mortification she had watched as the guard had recorded her name in the large leatherbound prison book.

"Ye look familiar."

"I've been here before."

"Ummmmm?" He cocked his head, then looked sympathetic as he remembered. "Ye were here with yer father."

"Yes, I was." Then she had been a visitor; now she was a prisoner awaiting her execution.

Two days. That was all the time that had been allowed her. When that time had passed, when the light of the third day shone its early rays on the earth, she would be hanged. A gruesome, undignified death wherein the victim dangled from a rope, kicking and strangling.

"Ohhhhhhhhh!"

Better to have met her end on the road. Oh, yes, that would have been far less painful. As it was she would be merely the subject of some lively entertainment for a ghoulish crowd. She would be a curiosity, a diversion from their dreary lives.

And all because of Scar. A blackguard. A traitor. A spy.

No, because of what I have done. She couldn't blame anyone else. As she sat forlornly in the far corner, hugging her knees to her chest, her hair falling into her eyes, she repented.

Too late . . .

Closing her eyes, Devondra remembered being led along the dank, dimly lit stone passages, remembered the thick, iron-hinged door swinging open. She had been pushed into a foul-smelling cell with a small barred window. A place that she would leave only on the day of her trip down the road to Tyburn and—

The gibbet!

Her eyes were blank, disbelieving. Tears dampened her cheeks, but she didn't even try to brush them away. She was beyond fear; she was numb. Then, just as quickly, her courage returned. She would not go to the gallows a shaking, quaking, pitiful sight. She would be brave! Strong!

Don't let yourself give up, no matter what has happened. Lifting her head, she stared through the gloom, assessing the stark gray stone walls and the thick door. A door that could only be opened by the guard with a key. Was there any possibility of escape? It didn't seem so. As a matter of fact, she couldn't remember ever hearing that anyone had gotten out of here. Even so, there was a part of her that didn't want to accept reality.

"There has to be some way out!"

"Out?" A voice from the corner, a darkened shadow, rasped in disbelief. "Of here?"

Rising to her feet, Devondra nodded. There were five other women sharing her cell. If she could but rally them, perhaps there was a way. "Yes. Surely there is a loose stone or two. We could dig and—"

"Dig?" The eerie quiet was shattered by bitter laughter.

"And go where? This prison is naught but a maze. Even if we could get out of this cell, we would be trapped."

"Like rats," came another voice.

"Which is all that we are in the Lord Protector's plan."

"Aye, rats. To be disposed of as soon as possible."

"Rats, indeed." Devondra paced, frantic in her desperate need to think of something. At last she moved toward the door, clinging to the iron grill as she rattled it back and forth, testing its strength. The clanging sounded through the stillness of the early morning, but Devondra didn't care. She would not, could not, sit meekly in her cell and await her fate. She must find some way to free herself.

"Stop that! Ye'll get us all in trouble," warned the voice from the corner.

"Oh, let her be. At least she has some spirit left. Not like the rest of us. Helpless creatures all."

The woman from the corner inched her way toward Devondra. "Go ahead. Let your anger out. Yours and mine . . ."

Devondra rattled the door again, not in anger but in curiosity. It was an action that brought reward as she made a gratifying discovery. "The grill. It's loose." First measuring the grill's length and width, then her own slender proportions, she tried to calculate the possibility of climbing through the opening, were the grill to be forcibly removed.

"You there! What are you about?" A gaoler appeared at the door of the cell to thwart her planning.

"I demand to see the Lord Protector," Devondra blurted out, thinking of an excuse for her disruption.

"Demand?"

"Yes. I want to answer directly to him for any wrongs I may have done."

"Answer to Cromwell?" The guard was stunned. "And just why should he listen to anything you might have to say?" Suddenly interested, he pressed his large nose against the grill. "Unless, that is, you would like to tell him just where he might find others of your kind. A trade, we might say. Your life in exchange for theirs."

Devondra backed away. "Never!" Though she feared death, she abhorred the thought of being a turncoat more.

"Never?" The gaoler grinned. "Oh, I don't know. As the time draws nigh to your hanging, you might change your mind." With that said, he disappeared, leaving Devondra even more frustrated than before.

"He's right, dearie. When it comes to hanging day you'll change yer mind."

"Aye, there isn't a soul in all of England who wouldn't turn his own mother in to escape the gallows."

"There is someone." Haughtily, Devondra held up her head. "I wouldn't!"

Sitting back down, she fought to keep up her courage. As the day passed hunger, cold and thirst took an awesome toll on her spirit. She fought against her tears, her thoughts turning to Quentin. Was he all right? Was he free? Or was he suffering for the wrongs she had done?

"If only—"

A rattle of keys jarred her from her thoughts. Looking up, she saw the face of the guard peering at her through the grill. "I have a visitor for you."

"A visitor!" Immediately her heart was lightened. It was Quentin. Somehow he had found a way to see that she was granted a pardon. He had come to take her away!

Excitement buzzed in her head. Hastily combing her fin-

gers through her tangled hair, pinching her cheeks and brushing at her drab gray dress, she readied herself for the meeting.

But it was not Quentin. The man who stood staring at her
through the grill was a stranger, a ruddy-faced, white-haired
old man whose toothless grin was somehow as chilling as
ever Scar's countenance had been.

"Good day," he said, as the guard pushed him through
the opened door. With a grunt he pulled forth several sheets
of paper from under his coat and a pen.

Thinking him to be there to hear her make a list of her
companions', identities and misdeeds, she shrugged him
away. "I have nothing to say to you. Not now, not ever!"

"Ah, but I think you will when you realize what fame
you can bask in from my efforts," he said, then he made a
grab for her hand. He squeezed her fingers in his clammy
fist. "I'm Reverend Paul Pureney, anxious to jot down your
exploits for the eager public to read."

"Paul Pureney," scoffed the voice from the corner.

"Reverend Pureney!" Devondra had heard all about him.
He was a typical ordinaire. Blusterous, bloated and snuffy, he
was ready to take advantage of any infamous highwayman's
misdeeds to fill his own pockets. As if his job as chaplain
of Newgate and his annual salary weren't money enough.
In truth, Devondra had far more respect for the hangman;
at least his was an honest job.

"Tut, tut, tut. Imagine at last having the good fortune to
speak with the Notorious Lady." He bowed. "I am indeed
honored."

"I fear your good fortune would be at my expense," she
answered scathingly, knowing without asking what he
wanted. It was his intent to grant her ghostly counsel with
the pretense of unburdening her soul. In reality he wanted
an authentic account of her life and short career on the roads
to tantalize his readers.

More keen to nose a story for his broadsides and hypocritical pamphlets than to lead a sinner to repentance, he was not alone. Such pamphlets were exceedingly popular, particularly on execution day.

Reverend Pureney had the good sense to look sympathetic. "Ah, yes, of course. And might I say how sad I am to see such a lovely young woman in such a place."

"Sad enough to somehow get me out?" When he didn't answer she answered for him. "No. Were I to be freed you would lose your precious story." And if she did not grant him the story, the "facts" would be improvised. Men like Pureney had little care for accuracy and produced the most commonplace stories with the most threadbare last dying speeches garnished with haphazard texts.

"Ah, young woman, do not be too hard on me, for was not me who put you here." He hiccoughed, a sign of his intemperance.

"No, but 'tis you who will profit happily from my death." Worse yet, there wouldn't be a penny's worth of truth in anything that was written. Moreover, the nauseating pages would be certain to make Pureney some sort of hero whose benevolence and perseverance brought the Notorious Lady to tears of true penitence.

"As will you profit when your soul is freed from its dark cloud," he countered. "Oh, dear lady, renounce your wicked, wicked ways."

"I already have," Devondra answered, "without any help from you." She tried to keep her calm. "Nor will I offer you any help."

"Here, here!" A soft round of applause from the inmates proved that their opinion of the chaplain was the same as hers. Nevertheless, as Pureney left the cell, Devondra experienced a hollow victory. It was cold. Cold and penetratingly damp. What she would not give at that moment to have Quentin Wakefield's arms enfolding her, keeping her warm.

"Quentin . . ." With all her heart she wished she could see him again.

Quentin, always such a freedom-loving man, could not stand the thought of being imprisoned. It was too humiliating. It made him feel helpless. Worse yet, his confinement made it impossible for him to save Devondra from the hangman.

"Oh, my love!"

He could barely stand his wretched surroundings, the foul-smelling straw on the floor, the cold, the darkness and the loneliness. Even so, he knew that as bad as his surroundings were, Devondra's were far worse. God only knew what wretchedness she was enduring as her day of death rapidly approached. He had seen for himself the horrors of Newgate.

Last night he had imagined her standing before him, her satin-smooth skin dirt-stained, her lovely dark tresses matted, her clothing ragged and torn. Holding her arms out, she had pleaded with him in much the same way she had pleaded with him to save her father.

"Her father . . ." Burying his face in his hands, Quentin remembered all too well what had happened to him. But it must not happen to her! She was much too brave.

He thought about the last time he had seen her, knowing well that Cromwell's henchmen would never have identified her had she not stepped forward to protect her friends. If she, a woman, could be so loyal, could he ever face himself if he were to let her down and if not surpass, then at least match her bravery.

But how? How could he do anything when he was locked in?

Anxiously, he looked around, critically assessing his surroundings. The prison rooms were not cells at all, but were adapted guard chambers. Bars were not needed, for only arrow slits admitted light and air. What offered him some hope, however, was that some prisoners were granted the liberty of a walk over the leades above their lodgings, allowing them exercise. That is, if they were manageable or influential prisoners, or if they had friends of influence on the outside.

"Edwin!"

Edwin Trevor was the answer. He had sympathetic allies in high places. But now that Quentin had fallen from grace, would Edwin want to take a chance on helping him? All Quentin could do was to wait and see.

"Guard!"

The yeoman warder in charge of Quentin's confinement quickly answered the summons. Unlike the ghoulish gaolers who haunted the corridors of Newgate, they were respectable fellows who generally lived with their families in the top apartments of each tower.

"Yes?"

"I need to send a message to someone." Hastily scrawling on an old piece of parchment he found in his cell, Quentin handed it to the bearded warder, thus putting the first phase of his plan into action.

If Edwin proved to be a true friend, then perhaps he would find himself moved to the rooms above, where he would be allowed excerise in the grounds in the company of a gaoler. But even at that, partial freedom was not complete freedom. Somehow, some way, he had to plot his escape.

Meanwhile, what resources could he use? many facts had been filed away in his mind during his years in the military. Now Quentin brought them forth to use. He had a fine mind, great physical strength and a few friends on the prison staff, but he had to hurry. He did not have much time. Time was running out for Devondra. Spurned on by desperation and worry over Devondra's fate, Quentin formulated his plan.

Chapter Thirty-Two

It was cold and damp despite being midmorning. Devondra reached up to pull her threadbare blanket over her chilled form. She was tired. Last night she had spent the whole time prying at the screws and nails that held the grill to the cell door. Using an old spoon left over from dinner, she had worked diligently. All the while the shrieking voices of the prisoners had echoed and reechoed through the thick stone walls.

Trying her best to ignore the gruesome sounds, Devondra had continued her attempts to loosen the grill, only to make a disheartening discovery. There was a stout iron bar an inch thick that had been so placed that it would block the passage of anyone who tried to escape. Even so, she had steadily picked at it, determined to work it loose. Now she lay motionless, all too aware of the groans around her. Unlike her, the other inhabitants of the prison cell *had* given up hope.

"But not me!" She needed but a quarter hour of rest before

she could try again. Somehow that bar would be pried off and when it was she would climb through the opening and set off on her way to freedom.

Devondra knew that her hair was matted and her garments dirty. Perhaps the lack of a mirror was a blessing. In truth, far from worrying about her appearance she was of a mind to let herself go. Then the guards might stop eyeing her up and down, giving her the jitters with their bold stares.

"Look at 'er; ain't she a sight, Edward, me boy," She had heard one gaoler say.

"Aye, I like wenches wi' dark hair. But we had better be careful."

"Why? Where she is going, a woman doesn't need to worry about keeping her virtue."

Devondra had listened as the turnkeys talked, shivering convulsively. Touch her? Never. She would kick and bite and give them trouble if they even tried. Why, she would die before . . .

"Die!"

A sudden shrieking, snarling, shouting fight broke out in the cell that adjoined hers. Voices told of several women fighting over the ownership of a tattered blanket. Bolting from her bed, Devondra watched as the gaoler quickly came upon the scene and attempted to stop the violent quarreling. The women, however, professed no fear of the gaoler as they flew at each other. Misery, it seemed, dissipated fear.

"Aye, get back yer dogs!" the guard growled testily, wielding a heavy bar that Devondra's fingers itched to possess. With it her chances of escape would increase twofold.

"We be not dogs. We're human beings," a high-pitched voice wailed, yelping as the bar made contact with her arm.

"You are anything that I say. And that is the way it will be until you hike up the gallows steps!"

"Better the gibbet than this stinking hole!"

"Hell on earth," or so one prisoner had aptly named it. A place Devondra would not want to stay in too long. Violent attacks from fellow prisoners were commonplace, and even the slightest offense was punished by a whipping from the guards. A person always had to be wary, for there was no one who could be trusted. It was everyone for himself, with no thought of kindness. Whatever remained of innocence or honesty was certain to be lost in the depths of Newgate.

"Rats, filth and starvation," she whispered, softly wishing with all her heart that she was anywhere but here.

Oh, would she ever be free? Ever feel the rain on her face or see the sun, or look up at the stars or hear the birds' songs in spring?

Devondra fought against her anxiety as she lay back down upon her bed of moldy straw. Stretching out her arms and legs, she closed her eyes. *Be brave! Be strong! Don't let yourself give up no matter what happens.*

Though she didn't realize it, she must have fallen asleep. She didn't know how long she had been lying there. Then she heard the bells and counted the strokes. One, two, three. It was three o'clock. Only a few hours remained before night fell again, and she had not yet broken free.

The sounds of London—the rattle of wagon and coach wheels on the cobblestones, hammers pounding, men, women and children chattering, horses' hoofs clattering, dogs barking, traders yelling, and the general din of pedestrians as they wound their way past shops and stalls—filtered through the arrow holes in Quentin's cell.

And the bells. Always there were bells, announcing the hours of the day as they passed, reminding Quentin that time was all too quickly running out.

And still no word from Edwin.

He felt betrayed. He had put his trust in friendship, but it seemed that those held in disfavor had no friends. Edwin had seemingly turned his back upon him. Thus his last hopes of saving the woman he loved were perilously close to fading away.

Devondra. His mind was haunted by the memory of her sweet smile, the shadow-darkness of her hair, the way her cheeks dimpled when she smiled and her large flashing eyes. Stretching himself out upon his cot, he willed himself to conjure up memories of her. Only thus could he bear the torture of the passing hours.

He was too immersed in those memories to hear the door open; thus he did not realize that he had company until a man's shadow crossed his path. "Well, a fine bowl of pudding you've gotten yourself into, I must say."

Whirling around, Quentin was surprised and immensely gratified to see Edwin Trevor standing there.

"You've come to help me?"

"Yes, bigod, for it seems to me I couldn't do you any more ill than has been heaped upon you already!" Carefully tiptoeing through the straw on the floor, Edwin's grimaced showed his displeasure. "Disgusting. Cromwell should be ashamed that his magistrate has been put in a place such as this." He turned to the guard. "See here, I am not without some authority hereabouts and I abhor these surroundings."

Taking out his money pouch, he dropped coins into the warder's palm and smiled. "I think you know what I mean."

"I can't move him, sir. I've my orders."

"From whom?"

"Administrative headquarters."

Edwin Trevor waved his hand. "And I have mine, from sources much higher and more powerful." Never one to take no for an answer, he persisted. "Quentin Wakefield is no conspirator awaiting the rack, nor has he been condemned to a rope or the axe. He is a man of high rank and as such should be treated with greater deference."

"Deference?"

"Esteem. Honor, my good man."

The warder thought for a moment. "I seem to recall that there is a room available in one of the towers." He started to leave, then turned back. "A small one, I must say."

"Good." Edwin flung the whole money pouch at him. "Get it ready."

The door shut with a resounding bang.

"Ah, money. It works every time."

"Therefore pity all those who have none of it," Quentin answered. His mood was grim as he asked, "Have you come to help me escape or just to see to my comfort?"

"Both!" Spying a stool, Edwin picked it up, disgruntled when he saw that it was the home of a spider. "Bigod!" Mumbling beneath his breath, he brushed it off, then sat down. "Your ladylove doesn't have much time left. Tonight the bell will ring for her."

"Tonight?" As a solemn exhortation to the condemned criminals in Newgate, a hand bell was always rung beneath their window on the night before their execution. A chilling reminder. "So, time has passed much more quickly than I had supposed." Quentin's heart thundered in his chest.

"As it always does," Edwin answered with a sigh. He grabbed Quentin by the arm. "Tell me, Quentin, for I have to know; Was she worth it? Was she worth losing everything for?"

Quentin answered without hesitation. "She was. If I had it to do all over again I would, just for the warmth of her smile."

Edwin shrugged. "And they say there is no such thing as love. But then, I have always said that love is but another form of insanity." He lowered his voice. "I will have it all arranged."

His friend explained the details of the plan to him. Once Quentin was esconsed in his new quarters, Edwin would visit again. This time beneath Edwin's doublet would be a rope, wound around his body. And a grappling iron wrapped up in his cloak.

"You can swim, can't you?" Edwin asked.

"Aye, and could since I was a boy." Suddenly Quentin's eyes widened. "Oh, no. Not the filthy . . ."

"Ah, yes. A little dip in the moat. For love's sake."

"For love's sake." But then, if he could save his lady, it would be a small price to pay.

Edwin continued. "There is a narrow ledge beyond," he nodded with his head. "Of course, you will have to be careful lest the sentries see you." He kicked at Quentin's tall leather boots. "Best go without these, old friend."

"Barefoot." Quentin laughed. "Reminds me of the time that we were trying to sneak past the royalist army, old friend."

"And you had to sneeze." Both men smiled.

"We were nearly caught." Quentin shook his head. "I won't sneeze this time." Because there was much more at stake than just his life. This time Devondra's fate rested on him.

Chapter Thirty-Three

Quentin's new living quarters were much more comfortable. Instead of straw on the floor there was a rug. The bed, although it had a straw-filled mattress, was at least less lumpy than the cot had been. There was a chair and a table. What was the greatest blessing of all, however, was a window. If it did not afford him a view of anything other than another tower beyond it, at least it was far better than being enfolded by the gloom.

Despite his new lodgings, Quentin paced back and forth in his cell, wearing a path in the carpet with his boot soles. He had to get out of here! He had to in order to afford himself time enough for a rescue. Already it was growing dark. Each bong of the bell brought Devondra closer to the gallows.

"Oh, Edwin, hurry!" He was impatient to have the rope and grappling hook in his hands. He was anxious to be free.

Walking to the small barred window, Quentin stared out to the darkening sky. His eyes focused on the giant slabs of pale limestone looming to the east, walls at least eight feet thick, built to prove William the Conqueror's power. For a moment he knew a twinge of apprehension. The fortress looked awesome and unescapable from where he stood. Was it?

No. There had been a few who had escaped these walls. On the other hand, many had tried, including a Royalist whom Quentin himself had imprisoned within this very tower.

It had been about seven years earlier, as the Civil War was dragging on. Though Quentin greatly admired the Royalist defenders and particularly their commander, Arthur, Lord Capel, he nonetheless had had to bring him to this very tower. Just like Quentin, Capel had devised a scheme to escape via the moat, and just like Quentin he had friends who had brought him a rope. He had looped that rope around the bars and eased himself out on the narrow ledge beyond, lowering himself into the stagnent waters. He had broken free, only to be recaptured later.

Taken back to the Tower, Capel had been put on trial, with Quentin in attendance. It was trial that had created a great debate within Parliament itself. Cromwell himself had praised his loyalty to the throne, adding that because of such integrity Capel would have to die. And die he had, killed by the blow of an ax.

Stepping back from the window, Quentin flinched as he remembered. So much for Cromwell's mercy. And Quentin's own.

"Is your ghost haunting this tower now, Capel? Is it laughing at me? Taunting my hopes to succeed where you failed? Is it?"

"Not much of a view, is it?"

"What?" Slowly turning around, Quentin quickly realized that it was no ghost who spoke, but Nevin Bowen, the warder, a tall, gangling fellow whose doublet sleeves always fell well above his wrists. He was a man with a ready smile whom Quentin had found congenial. It seemed he might be tricked into sharing information about the Tower guard's comings and goings. It was worth a try.

"I said, 'tis not much of a view. You would have been far better off to have quarters on the other side, but I fear Sir Charles is firmly ensconced there." He held out a tray. "You must be famished, having had to eat the slop they give you down there." He looked down at the floor, as if his eyes could see through the stone toward the cells. "Much better food up here."

The tangy smell of freshly caught fish filled the room, but though Quentin was hungry, he couldn't swallow a bite. He was much too nervous and fidgety to have an appetite.

"Hmmm, our cook's specialty. But then, perhaps you are the kind who doesn't favor fish. I'll try to remember that." Nevin set down the tray on the small round table. "I'll keep it here, just in case." He thought for a moment. "Do you play chess?"

"Chess?" Quentin shook his head, for he found that game rather boring.

"Do you read?"

To this Quentin said yes. "Avidly."

Nevin smiled. "Good. Good, for there has to be something for you to do to wile away the time." He reached into a small pouch that hung from his belt. "Just in case you said yes, I brought you a book."

The leatherbound volume was thick, its pages dog-eared. Quentin was touched by the gift. "John Donne."

"Aye, one of the truly great metaphysical poets. He fuses thought and passion, maintaining the separate and warring identity of the conceit." He smiled. "Heady reading, but I thought that you, like I, might enjoy it."

"I do."

The warder jabbered on. "Oh, I know you don't want to be here and all, but if you think of it, 'tis not so bad. Impressive fortress, you know, the full title being the Ancient Palace and Fortress of His Majesty's Tower of London." Putting his hand to his mouth, he amended, "Or should I say the Lord Protector's Tower."

"You may call it anything you like," Quentin assured him.

"And do." Nevin laughed, then eagerly began to talk about his favorite subject. "It's a maze of portcullises, heavy wooden drop gates, hung-in arches to be lowered in times of alarm. Through the Bloody Tower archway looms walls and more high walls." He laughed. "Begun by William the Conqueror, it was, though it was not completed until ten years after his death. Supposed to be a palace fortress, so we have no dungeons to speak of, nor were there any modes of torture until the Duke of Exeter brought them here during the War of the Roses."

"It was then that it was first used as a prison, or so I recall," Quentin said dryly.

Nevin plopped down in the old wooden chair, as if settling in for a long visit. "Oh, no. In the year 1100 Ranulf Flambard, Bishop of Durham, was imprisoned by order of Henry the First." Nevin stiffened. "Escaped, he did, from an upper window. Down a rope that was smuggled to him."

"Indeed." Quentin averted his eyes, though he could feel the warder's stare.

"Don't you be getting such ideas, though, because a hundred and forty years or so later the Welsh prince Gruffydd ap Llewelyn, a prisoner of the third Henry, tried to do the same thing, improvising a rope of knotted bedsheets."

"You don't say." Impatiently, Quentin tapped his foot. This was not a subject about which he had intended to converse.

"The bedsheets came apart and he plunged to his death."
Nevin clapped his hands together. "Boom! Poor fellow."

"Poor fool!" Quentin replied, hoping that he, like Llewelyn, would not meet the same fate.

"The deeper one goes into the fortress, the more hopeless
the chance of escape. Alas, if you have any hope of leaving
here, it will have to be at Cromwell's grace." Neville raised
his brows. "Which well may happen. After all, the only
thing you were guilty of was being unwise in love, or so
I've heard." He leaned back, nearly tipping over the chair.
"You were the lover of the Notorious Lady. Now fancy that.
Certainly something to tell my wife."

Clenching his jaw in impotent fury, Quentin mumbled,
"Then tell her as well how it tears at a man's guts to know
that the woman he loves is to be hanged on the morrow,
while all the time he is boxed up in stone." He said again,
"Tell her!"

"I . . . I . . . I will!" Visibly shaken by the vehemence of
Quentin's reply, Neville bolted to his feet, his eyes looking
toward the door as he clutched at his ring of keys.

"Or better yet," Quentin whispered, his eyes making a
silent plea, "take pity on me. Let me out, let me go to her,
and then you can tell your wife about a happy ending."

"Let you out?" Squinting, Nevin stared at Quentin as if
he had lost his mind. "Oh, no! I could not! To do so would
assure my own trip to the gibbet."

Quentin returned to the window, staring at the stone tower
that blocked his view of London. "I know! It was just a
desperate notion."

Closing his eyes, he couldn't help but imagine how it
might be were he to arrive at Tyburn just in the nick of
time. Taking out his sword, he would sever the rope that
chapped Devondra's slim neck. He would gather her up in

his arms, put her upon his horse and ride off into the sunset. And never, never, would he let her out of his sight again.

"Nevin?" He turned, only to find that the room was empty.

Devondra was not alone, though, as she looked up and saw who her visitor was, she wished that she were. "Scar." *What the devil was he doing here?*

"You expected me?"

Just seeing him again made her stomach queasy, yet she greeted him haughtily. "This is Newgate. It's crawling with rats. What difference does it make if this cell has one more?"

Her insult, as usual, did not seem to phase him, for he merely sighed. "Oh, Devondra, Devondra, how it pains me to know that at dawn you are going to die, when your fate could have followed a far different path."

Angrily, she flipped her tangled long dark brown hair away from her face. "That path meaning that I could have aligned myself with you?"

Taking several steps toward her, he reached for her hand. "Yes. I would have protected you and—"

Devondra recoiled from his touch. "I would far rather hang!"

"And you will."

Her look of defiance wavered for just an instant, giving away her fear. "Thanks to you." He had betrayed both herself and her father, and all for what? It was a question she put into words. "Why?" she asked.

"Why?" He seemed startled that she would ask.

"Not because of lust, surely. There's never been even a spark between us. Nor have Tobias and I ever been serious rivals to your domain. Why then? Why did you give witness against me? What foul pleasure could you reap by bringing me so low?" When he didn't answer she asked again.

"Tomorrow I go to the gallows. Surely I have a right to know the reason for your hatred."

A myriad of emotions passed over Scar's face, all of them wretched. At last he answered. " 'Twas because of your father and . . . and Anne."

"My father?" She shook her head in confusion. "My father is dead. And as for Anne . . ." Devondra's eyes widened. Once she would have been innocent of what he meant; now she suddenly realized. "Oh!"

Scar's face contorted into an ugly mask. "He seduced her and by so doing brought about her death."

Her gasp pierced the small room. "What?"

"She died because of a child that grew inside her womb. The midwife couldn't save her."

She remembered Scar's daughter Anne, a lovely though frail young woman who had the appearance of a china doll. She had been Scar's fondest treasure. Pretty though she had been, however, Devondra found it hard to believe that her father had dallied there. Though her father's worst fault *had* been womanizing, Anne had been much too young.

"No. I don't believe it."

Scar snarled rather than replied. All the while his face was contorted with murderous anger.

An anger I do not deserve. It was chilling to realize that even Scar's attempt to debauch her had been fired by hate. Blaming her father for lying with his daughter and getting her with child, Scar had somehow wanted to even the score in the same way. When that had failed he had resorted to far different means.

"Even if what you tell me is true, *I* had nothing to do with Anne's tragic fate. Neither my death nor my father's can bring her back."

"But it can quench my thirst for revenge."

"And what then?" In truth, at that moment Devondra felt

far sorrier for Scar than she did for herself, for the hatred that was consuming him would bring about a torturous evil that would survive beyond the grave.

"Then . . .?" For a moment Scar looked dazed, as if he could not even think beyond his desire for vengeance.

"Aye, what then?" The tinkling of a handbell accompanied Devondra's lament, purposefully reminding her of her ensuing trip to the gibbet.

"You prisoners that are within, who for wickedness and sin, after many mercies are shown, are now appointed to die tomorrow in the forenoon," a voice cried out. "Give ear and understand that tomorrow morning the greatest bell of Saint Sepulchre shall toll for you so that all Godly people, hearing that bell and knowing it is for your going to your deaths, may be stirred up heartily and pray to God to bestow His grace and mercy upon you whilst you live."

The voice continued. "I beseech you, for Jesus Christ's sake, to keep this night in watching and prayer, to the salvation of your own souls, while there is yet time and place for mercy, as knowing tomorrow you must appear before the judgement-seat of your Creator, there to give an account of all things done in this life, and to suffer eternal torments for your sins committed against Him, unless upon your heart and unfeigned repentance you find mercy through the merits of the death and passion of your only . . ."

"Shut up!" Shouting at the top of his lungs, Scar lunged forward, tipping over a cot as he made his way to the door. Banging on the thick wood, he admonished again, "Shut up!"

"Look, will ye, 'e's gone berserk."

"A candidate for Bedlam, by me word."

Fearful lest he turn his outrageous behavior against them, the two guards carefully opened the door. Before Scar knew what was happening, they stationed themselves on either side of him, seizing and binding his arms behind his back as they pushed and shoved him from the cell. All Devondra could do was to watch as the perpetrator of her greatest defeat was marched down the hall. Still, as the cloak of night all too quickly descended, she felt a small ray of hope that Scar's temper tantrum was in some small way a sign of remorse.

It was late. Quentin stared out the window, wishing that somehow he had the power to push back the darkness and kidnap the moon. Anything to keep the night from steadily passing by. "Where the devil is Edwin?"

He worried. Perhaps his sounding off to the warder had brought about his own doom. Maybe Edwin had been denied a visit. Maybe something had happened to ruin all their plans. Maybe . . .

A rattle of keys announced that once again Quentin was not alone. Looking up, he fully expected to see the warder's face at the grate, coming to take away his plate. Instead it was Edwin.

"At last."

"Ah, old friend, I bring you a message from Cromwell," Edwin said aloud, stepping aside to reveal the warder behind him.

"And I in turn have a message for him," Quentin blurted out. "Tell him he can go straight to hell in thanks for the misery he is causing me." He looked toward Nevin instantly, regretting his anger, for the man had the look of an apprentice frightened by the growling of a dog. Thankfully, however, he scurried away.

"Shame, shame, shame, Quentin. I do believe you've spooked that poor man. Ah, but nevertheless, your grouchy manner has at least offered us a measure of privacy."

A privacy that Quentin wasn't quite sure he could trust. He had heard stories of warders listening at keyholes; thus, before he spoke his mind, he went to the door, examining it to make certain there were not any unfriendly ears hovering about. Satisfied he turned to Edwin.

"Has Cromwell really sent me a message?"

"No."

"I didn't think so."

"I have a present for you." Slowly, smiling all the while, Edwin stripped off his doublet, exposing the long length of rope wound round his waist.

"And such a fine present . . ." Quentin's hands trembled as he fumbled to unwrap it; then, fearful that it might be discovered, he hid it under the bed.

"And the hook." That was hidden beneath the folds of Edwin's cloak and likewise soon found a spot beneath the cot. "Listen and listen well for I have studied the pattern of the guards' comings and goings in the tower."

Edwin noted that there was at least a half hour's stretch between the guard's third and fourth shifts: More than enough time for Quentin to get far away from the Tower's walls.

"There are four checkpoints in all, each to be passed by without being seen." He ticked them off. Bulwark Gate and the Lion, Middle and Byward towers. "Better yet, if you escape by water, at the bottom of the Byward Tower where you now are housed, there is a moat. It obtains its water from the River Thames."

"And from the mud, sewage drains and slime," Quentin grumbled. "Even so, I understand what you are saying. If I can just get as far as that moat and swim to the wharf, I might go undetected."

"Except perhaps for the way you will smell after your journey by water." Edwin wrinkled his nose. "I know of a shallow route, formed where the dumped refuse has piled high and where sluice waters have deposited sand and rubbish. I think you might not have to swim at all, but only wade across the moat at that point."

"Wade?"

"Aye. Once you break free meet me at my townhouse. I'll have a change of garments for you, and a horse."

"And a sword and pistol, if you please." Giving in to his emotions. Quentin did a rare thing. He gave Edwin a hug. "Ah, my friend, I will always be grateful. If we never see each other again, I want you to know that."

Walking to the window, Quentin filled his lungs with air, ignoring the dank smell of the moat's water, feeling a new vigor, a renewed stirring of hope. With the help of God and Edwin he would escape. Thus began his plan.

Chapter Thirty-Four

"Stone walls do not a prison make, nor iron bars a cage," Quentin mumbled, quoting the poet Richard Lovelace. Using every measure of strength he possessed, he pulled at the bars, bending them just enough to allow his body through.

He looked out. The night was particularly dark, with only a quarter moon. Thus he hoped that with the aid of a dark cloak he would have at least a chance. That is if he could get out of his cell without being seen.

"I will!" Although the fortress seemed impenetrable he would soon be leaving here. That thought gave him a heady feeling of deep satisfaction. If he got free, Edwin had informed him that a young lad would be waiting by the wall to lead him toward a boat. It sounded so simple, so foolproof, that he really thought with proper timing his escape could be accomplished. With that optimistic thought in mind, he walked to the grill of the wooden door and looked out. The warder had finished his rounds; now it was time for the count down.

Taking another breath, Quentin counted to ten; then, loop-
ing the rope around the bars, he eased himself out on to the
narrow ledge beyond. The sound of footsteps and the
creaking of the door hastily sent him up the rope again, the
muscles of his arms cramping painfully from the strain.

"The warder!" With a mumbled oath he scrambled through
the window just as the door swung revealing the warder
bearing a tray of food.

"The cook made pigeon pie! I thought you might like
some." Keeping his eye on Quentin lest he lose his temper,
the warder set the tray down. "Might cheer you up a bit.
And here's a glass of ale to wash it down."

"Thank you."

"There's plum pudding too." The man's expression was
sympathetic, and Quentin wondered if the pudding was his
way of showing sympathy for his prisoner's situation. "I
remember you once told me that you liked it."

"I do."

"I . . . I was remembering what . . . what you said, about
your lady and all. You have my deepest sympathies."

Quentin nodded. "I can tell, and I thank you for it."

The door was ajar and the warder's back was toward
Quentin as he advanced toward the table: a perfect set-up
for escape. Yet it was a chance Quentin didn't feel he should
take, particularly since it meant he would in all likelihood
have to cause physical harm to the warder. That would do
his cause no good. Instead, he waited impatiently for the
warder to leave, which he did at last.

Quentin climbed back through the window, gazing down
at the murky waters below. The water looked deceptively
shimmery in the dim moonlight. And cold. He heard the
sounds of streetlife. It was all so near, his freedom. Between
him and it were no locks, doors or bars. There was only a

great height. How far? At that moment it might have been a thousand feet or more—or less.

Slowly, he took a deep breath. The invigorating air filled his lungs. In the distance he could hear the chimes of Saint Sepulchre's church, could see the faraway flicker of torches and lanterns.

He looked down again. The Tower's walls were smooth. There was not the slightest chance for fingers or toes to take hold were he to slip from the rope. Remembering the warder's warning about Llewelyn's deadly plunge, he imagined for just a moment what would happen if his hands couldn't hold on to the rope.

It didn't matter. Wrapping the other rope and grappling hook around his waist, he pushed through the window. Slowly, he climbed down hand over hand. Down. Down. Down, until his fingers were raw and bleeding.

High in the air he dangled. To his dismay, he found the rope was too short. His calculations had been wrong. There was nothing he could do but drop.

"Ouch!" The wind was knocked out of him as he hit the hard ground in the outer ward, the domestic area of the castle. Nevertheless, he managed to struggle to his feet, then listened cautiously for the sentries' measured tread. Then he was moving toward the outer wall.

I did it! But his feeling of euphoria was short-lived. The sentries paced nearby, guarding gateway and walls, preventing a quick dash for freedom. One cry and the whole tower would be swarming with guardsmen. He had to be careful.

Using the grappling hook, he pulled himself up, stealthfully working his way along the battlements until he judged himself to be poised above the "shallow" route Edwin mentioned. Deftly he secured the grappling iron to the stonework, throwing the rope over the side. Then, hand over hand, he lowered himself into the blackness down below.

"Ugh!" Loathing the thought of falling into the slimy and evil-smelling waters of the moat, he let go.

There was a loud splash. Too loud! Quentin feared for a moment that the noise would alert the sentries, but no pursuit ensued. Shivering against the water that immersed him, he dog-paddled desperately, all the while sinking deep into the foul-smelling ooze.

Stench filled his nostrils from the bubbles rising to the surface; it was no wonder he fought diligently to keep his nose and mouth above the water level. Even so, it was a nightmare of struggling and paddling.

At last, collapsing in a sprawled heap on the bank, he reached safety just as a pair of soldiers burst out of the Byward Tower. Crawling, huddling, Quentin was on the alert for any shout or sign that he had been spotted. Much to his relief, there was none.

He had made it! Still, he was ever aware of the need for haste. As quickly as he could, he dragged himself up just as a shadowy form approached.

No! Quentin could see the outline of the stern and bow. A boat rocked up and down in the water.

Too exhausted to escape, Quentin dreaded the probable and rejoiced in the slim chance.

"Sir, Edwin Trevor sent me. I had almost given you up for lost, having waited where you should have emerged over there." The lad pointed.

"Bless you, then, all the more for lingering." Quentin pulled himself aboard, smothering himself in a soft piece of canvas.

Together he and the lad rowed; then, upon reaching the other side, they deserted the boat. Quentin hurried through the dark alleys. Slipping on the cobbles, stumbling, rising to his feet again, he somehow reached Edwin's door. There he found himself embraced by his anxious friend.

"You made it!"

"I made it."

Within a half hour he was warm and safe and dry in Edwin's townhouse in the city, but there was no time to rest.

The cell resounded with the snores of the inhabitants. Even so, Devondra felt all alone. What hour was it? She didn't know. All she did know was that Scar's accusation troubled her deeply.

"My father would never have taken to his bed someone younger than I." And yet, if he had not, where had Scar gotten such an idea?

Closing her eyes, she tried to remember anything her father might have said or done to in any way hint at a liaison with Anne, yet to Devondra's best knowledge it was Hyacinth who always held his heart and thoughts, Hyacinth who shared his bed.

In truth, Devondra had barely even known Anne, except for having seen her now and again. While she and her father had been living in Brentford, Scar and his daughter had been hiding away in Teddington, far enough apart that it had been several days before they had heard word of Anne's illness and death.

"From a fever," Scar had said. Now was she to believe that explanation had been a lie? And what of her father? Though he had shown regret for the death of a young woman before her time, he had shown no sign of guilt.

I cannot believe they were lovers. Having experienced such wonder herself, she thought she would have sensed some of the signs in her father. But if he had been innocent of such an affair, why would Scar be so certain? Certain enough to wreck such a twisted revenge?

"Perhaps I will never know."

"Pssst!"

Hearing the sound, Devondra looked through the grill of the wooden door just in time to see a piece of paper floating down to the floor. Ignoring it, she turned her head, focusing her attention once again on her meeting with Scar, until the voice in the corner cried out.

"Bless my soul. A recantation! For the Notorious Lady!"

"Let me see." Instantly Devondra was on her feet, angered by the thought. But not so angry that she didn't read the account of her life by the light of a sputtering candle.

"A Lady's Recantation or, the life and death of the Notorious Lady Stafford now hanging in chains at Tyburn," It read. "Delivered to a friend, a little before execution; wherein is truly discovered the whole mystery of that wicked and fatal profession of padding on the road."

"The very idea!" Quickly, Devondra scanned it, thankful that she could read. She found that it said very little about her early life, when or where she was born, the position her parents had occupied. Nor did it give her Christian name. What it did have was a title page wherein she had supposedly repudiated her evil ways, including murders she had never even instigated, much less done, then begged to be forgiven.

"How vain," it read, "are the thoughts of those who while they enjoy youth and beauty never consider they are mere statues of dust, kneaded with tears and moved by the hidden lusts of restless passions; clods of earth which the shortest fever can burn to ashes or hanging dissolve into nothingness."

Pureney's recantation read that the Notorious Lady had once thought herself one of Heaven's favorites, and had persuaded herself that her misdeeds would never be discovered. But the Lord Protector, Cromwell, with the help of God, had found out about her evil doings and, having overpowered her, had taken her away.

"Freeing the roadways of a great menace and danger!"

Devondra read on, *"learning"* for the first time that she had been orphaned as a babe. There in the orphanage she had learned to scramble for every crust of bread, at last sinking into poverty. Walking the streets of London, she had found a purse lying in the gutter. It was the start of a life rent with sin and a profession that goaded her to steal again and again.

"Lovers she has had aplenty, including as it were, several members of Parliament themselves."

Her hands trembled; still, what horrified her the most was that the pamphlet spoke of her being gibbeted, her body swinging and gyrating in the wind. As if whoever wrote the account had been a witness.

It concluded, "Reader, let me assure thee this is no fiction, but a true relation of the Notorious Lady's life and conversation. Penned by her own hand and delivered into mine to be made public for her countrymen's own good, in compensation of the many injuries she hath done them."

"Injuries!" Surely for those she had already paid. Or if she had not, she was soon to suffer.

Crumpling up the pamphlet, Devondra threw it to the ground, infuriated that the piece of paper declared her dead. She wasn't, not yet. But what were her chances? As time marched on, as she sat huddled in the cell, she had to admit that her future looked bleak.

Chapter Thirty-Five

Devondra was awakened by the same bells that had at last lulled her to sleep. Lying lethargically on her cot, she had long ago passed over the dread of death. Instead she contemplated things she'd hoped not to have to think about until she was old. Life. Death. Heaven. Hell. It looked as if she was going to find out sooner than she had expected just what happened when a person's breath was stilled.

"Oh, dear God!"

Although she had spent the late-night hours preparing for what was to come. Devondra knew she wasn't ready. Not yet. She had only just tasted of life. There was so much more to enjoy. Yet each minute that passed brought the moment of reckoning closer and closer. Still, there was a part of Devondra that hoped beyond all hope of some last-minute reprieve. Quentin was her only hope now, and a part of her prayed deep down inside that he would be able in some way to use his influence to stop her from swinging. That last hope faded and died as she saw the gaoler's face staring at her through the grill of the thick wooden door.

She had hoped until the last for a miracle, but now, as the hours had dwindled, so had her faith. She suspected that her execution, just like her trial, would be a muddled nightmare.

"It's time!" announced a gruff voice. Moving through the door, he pushed a bundle into her hands, which she soon discovered to be a few of her own garments.

"I'm to dress in these?"

The guard nodded.

"I see."

To add insult to injury, she was to wear one of her own outfits, a red velvet full-skirted dress, mask, plumed hat and black leather boots. Indeed, the populace expected no less and was ready to applaud the highwayman who made his exit in gala costume.

"Then so be it!" She would give them a show. She would be poised, going to her death in a manner marked with distinction and flair. Surely her father had done the same. "Let them see that the Staffords knew how to live and how to die."

She could only hope that God in his mercy would make her death quick. Meanwhile, Devondra did her best to dress as slowly as she could, even taking a sponge bath with her meager ration of water. She knew she had to relish each minute of extra life as a thing to be treasured.

"Hurry!" The gaoler was obviously impatient.

Standing in her chemise and petticoat, she ran a comb through her hair, then bent to the task of putting on her stockings. The red velvet dress followed, to be laced up by the gaoler himself.

The gaoler, an old man with gray hair and beard, seemed to be moved as he touched her, for he whispered in her ear,

"You be too young to die, miss. Too young. Listen to me and listen well. Plead your belly. Tell them that you are with child, whether it be true or not. It will give you extra time."

"To languish here?" She sighed as she shook her head. It wasn't that she hadn't thought of that excuse herself, knowing that English law strictly pervented the death of the innocent babe within the mother's womb. The truth was, however, that such a lie wouldn't work. She had just had her monthly time, and such a thing could hardly have been kept a secret at Newgate.

"Then may God have mercy on your soul." The gaoler stepped away after handing Devondra her fancy hat.

"I would like to think that he will." Trying to keep up her spirits, she put the wide-brimmed creation upon her head with a flourish, then tied on her mask.

"Ooohhhh." Even her cellmates, steeped in their own misery, appreciated the sight she made.

"The crowd outside will not be cheated, even for a minute."

"Indeed, they will not." The gaoler took out his keys and opened the creaking door; then he led Devondra out to the corridor. Sandwiched in between several gaolers, she followed them in procession. It was a death march and it felt and looked like one, but Devondra walked with her head held high. She would, as she promised, give her audience a show.

The great bell of Saint Sepulchre tolled as Devondra was pushed through the gate. Putting her hand to her eyes, she cringed against the sudden bright light of the sun. For a moment she was blinded, but all too soon she saw them.

Sightseers, well-dressed men and women as well as girls and fellows in rags, stood before Newgate to watch as the condemned woman was sent on her way to the gallows.

"The Notorious Lady!" she heard them cry out, as if she

were some kind of celebrity. In truth, she was, at least for
the time being.

"She's beautiful!"

"Dressed just like I've heard!"

Hawkers and tradesmen had taken advantage of the event,
selling everything from small cakes to baubles. And dolls.
Small masked replicas of Devondra dressed in a gowns of
scarlet, tiny pistols in hand were virtually flying out of the
sellers' hands.

"Come, into the cart with ye," a growling voice commanded. From the west gateway of Newgate she was to
begin her journey down Hangman's Highway.

A jab to her ribs hastened Devondra along. "Ghouls!"
she retorted, wondering how these ordinary-looking people
could so calmly assemble around the death cart as if awaiting
an entertainment. There was no anger in her now, only a
strange feeling of calmness. What was done was done.

Lifting up her skirts, Devondra made a graceful entrance
into the cart, marred only as one of the guardsmen shoved
at her from behind. Then a drumroll sounded as the rope
was looped over her head and around her neck. In the two-
wheeled cart, the noose a symbol upon her person, seated
upon her coffin, she would ride to Tyburn. With her was a
minister of the church. Before and behind rode guards, and
a file of soldiers brought up the rear.

Riding backwards in the cart, the rope already around her
neck, she was solemn, wishing for just a brief glimpse of
Quentin before she died.

What had become of him? Not knowing was nearly as
bad as suffering her own fate. *Oh, Quentin, where are you?
Why haven't you at least come to bid me one final good-
bye?*

It was by tradition a point of honor to take the last journey

to Tyburn as gaily as though one were the central figure in
the city's merrymaking.

Still, Devondra could hardly force herself to smile as the
cart moved along. How could she even pretend to be jovial
when she knew what would happen upon her arrival at
Tyburn? The executioner would stop the cart under one of
the cross beams of the gibbet and fasten one end of the rope
to it. This done, he would give the horse a lash with his
whip. The cart would be pulled from beneath her feet and
she would end up swinging.

The descent of Holborn Hill was the first thing that lay
before the procession. Once down the hill they were halted
beside the porch of Saint Sepulchre. Here the criminal, so
soon to die, received a large nosegay from the clergyman.
The nosegay was tied with white silk ribbons.

Like the bouquet of a bride, Devondra thought, and it was
only then that tears stung her eyes. She would never be
married to Quentin, never bear his child, never share her
life with him, never hold his hand, feel the strength of his
arms or experience the magic of being loved. Nevermore!
But, oh, how she wished . . .

The procession passed the boundaries of the City at Holborn Bars, where the ancient timbered and gabled buildings
of Staple Inn could be seen across the road. Threading the
narrow passage of High Street and Bloomsbury, they passed
St. Giles Pound, heading for Tyburn Road.

Tyburn, or *Tye Bourne,* meant two streams and had
obtained its name from the two branches of water that flowed
down from the Hampstead Heights toward the Thames.

At the Crown Inn there was a brief halt, where, according
to custom, the landlord presented the prisoner with a mug
of ale. Her hands trembling, Devondra toasted the crowd.
Then the procession moved on, the rabble of the city following, some in wagons, most on foot. Children ran at the

heels of bedraggled women. Sometimes entire families were crowded together to see the sight. Some rode on horseback, some walked and a few enthusiastic sightseers ran all the way.

The cart rattled down Oxford Street, past Edgeware Road, the crowd behind it increasing. It was a fighting, blundering, tumultuous mob, a mass of half-savage human beings pressing on one another. The men-at-arms had their hands full clearing a path for the cart.

Devondra tried to keep from looking at the staring crowd, but it was difficult. The chattering, cheering and laughter was louder than the sound of the drums that accompanied the throng. Elbowing each other, pushing and shoving in their attempt to look at the red gowned woman, they hardly seemed real. Indeed, the entire scene appeared to be some dastardly farce.

Then, all too soon they arrived. The grandstand was a landmark, a permanent structure at Tyburn. There were those, it was said, who paid half a crown for seats in that structure, just to witness the final scene.

"I'm going to die!" Devondra whispered. She had not fully realized it until now. She was going to die.

The rope around her neck, which she had tolerated all along the roadway, now seemed as if it were torturing her. It scratched her skin. It was heavy. She felt as though she might choke.

She was going to die. Alone. Sometimes friends or relatives would help speed the death of a loved one. They would pull the dying person by the legs and beat his breast to dispatch him as soon as possible. Devondra, however, had no friends in the crowd. Not Hyacinth. Not Tobias. Nor Quentin.

This is how my father felt. Deserted. Closing her eyes,

both happy and unhappy events in her life flashed before her eyes.

From out of the crowd a dark-clothed man stepped forward, a scroll in his hand. "Devondra Stafford, the Notorious Lady, you have been tried and found guilty of robbery on the Lord Protector's highways. You are to be hanged by the neck until dead. May God have mercy on your soul!"

"No," she breathed. She wanted to fight against the hands that held her, wanted to scream, and yet somehow she managed to maintain a semblance of self-control until her hands were tied behind her back and the rope hung over one of the gibbet's beams. For the first time in her life courage failed her. She gave vent to her anguish. Her wail blended with a deep voice that cried out from the crowd.

"Wait!" Remove your hands from her or pay with your lives!"

"What?" The watchers gasped in unison. Every head turned at the same time. Who was this masked and black-garbed man sitting astride a midnight dark horse and holding a sword in one hand and a pistol in the other?

"Scar!" Devondra cried out. She imagined that in the last few hours his conscience had bothered him and that thus he had come to her rescue.

The horseman rode his mount through the crowd, nearly trampling the stubborn few who would not move back. In that moment it was as if time crawled in slow motion.

Devondra watched in silent amazement as the rope, which trailed behind her over the end of a cross beam, was severed. Then she felt herself lifted up in strong arms, found herself astride her rescuer's horse. Then they were riding down the very same road but in the opposite direction from which she had come as the crowd applauded and cheered. Usually the throng hissed and booed, angered to have been denied the spectacle if a prisoner was pardoned at the last minute, but clearly they did not feel cheated today.

"Hurray for the Notorious Lady and her lover," they called out.

Lover?

Looking into the blue eyes that twinkled from behind the black mask, Devondra knew it to be true. She knew those eyes. Not Scar at all, but Quentin.

Her heart swelled and she felt a happiness and a giddiness that was almost beyond enduring. He had come. He had rescued her!

"Quentin!"

His heart reached out to touch hers, singing with the words: She was alive. *She was alive!* He had come in time. Patience had paid off, at least this time.

As he had watched from the shadows, as he had seen them dangle the rope around the gibbet's beam he had known his greatest grief, fearing that he hadn't made his move in time. Now he could not take his eyes from her, even though his attention should have been on the road.

"Oh, Quentin I had given up hope. I . . ."

He tightened his arms around her quaking body. "Shhhhh. I did come. You're safe now."

She closed her eyes and snuggled against him. "Mmmmmm. Safe." Suddenly her eyelids flew open. "But where are we going? Where can we hide?" Cromwell would have lookouts posted everywhere once he heard what had happened at Tyburn.

"To the Heath. 'Tis the only place where we can hide until I can book passage for France."

"We can't go there, for we've a far greater enemy there than in all of London." Scar would undoubtedly betray her again if he had the chance.

"Then where?"

"I don't know." But they had to find someplace to hide, and soon. Though the gaolers and sentries had not given chase, the cry would go out. It was only a matter of time before they would be hunted down.

The rhythmic pounding of horses' hoofs matched the pulsating beat of their hearts as Devondra and Quentin sought a hideaway.

"Half of London must be in pursuit of us by now!"

"And there is nowhere for us to hide."

"There is much more to rescuing than just whisking a fair damsel away," Quentin lamented. "I fear much more." Tenderly, he smoothed back her hair. "I want to keep you safe."

Devondra reached up and brushed her fingers across his face, tracing the lines and hollows. "No matter what happens now you will always be my hero." She leaned back against him with a contented sigh. "If I live to be a hundred, I will never forget the way my heart soared when I realized that you had not let me down, that you had come. Despite all."

"I love you, Devondra. Never doubt it."

"You have proved it today, my love." Taking hold of his hands as he grasped the reins, she gave them an affectionate squeeze. "Ah, but now I fear that because of me you have been brought all too low."

"Not because of you." Quentin's jaw ticked angrily as he told her about his sojourn in the Tower. "It was because of my blindness. I thought Cromwell was the answer to all the injustices in England, but I was wrong. He merely replaced one tyranny with another."

Devondra knew that truth all too well. "He has been vindictive in his punishment of those who fought to save the Crown. If he had not been, then perhaps my father . . ."

"'Tis too true." It was a truth he could see plainly before his eyes as they rode through that part of the countryside that had been scarred by the war. Quentin's eyes took in the horrors—burned buildings and fields—that gave testament to the battles that had devastated the landscape.

"His cruelty has even invaded our nursery rhymes."

Cromwell's soldiers had marched in a goose step as they went about their long hunt for royalist fugitives. Any suspect who would not say his prayers was thrown into prison, or as one of the rhymes went, "Taken by the left leg and thrown down the stairs."

She recited the rhyme in rhythm to the hoofbeats. "Goosey, goosey gander, where dost thou wander, up stairs and down stairs, and in my lady's chamber; There I met an old man that would not say his prayers, I took him by his hind legs and threw him down the stairs."

"There must be hundreds of churches up and down the country whose windows once glowed with stained glass and whose niches were filled with treasured relics. But they, like the people, have been destroyed, then re-created according to Cromwell's whims."

To Quentin's mortification, he remembered the time he himself had been on patrol and had stabled his men's horses in a church. According to Cromwell's orders, the church had been vandalized and all evidences of "idolatry" smashed.

"And now he seeks to ruin me."

"It doesn't matter." Devondra silenced him by putting her fingers to his lips. "Somehow we will find a place to hide."

They rode on in silence, each deep in his own thoughts. At last, when they were tired and thirsty, when the horse's actions betrayed the need for a rest, they sought a place of refuge in earnest.

"There's a small cottage up ahead."

"Hmmm, it seems to be far enough away from London to be relatively safe, but I can not make any promises."

"We'll have to take a chance. We must stop somewhere. At least we may be able to warm ourselves by their fire and beg a drink of water," Devondra said.

Guiding his horse off the road and toward the tiny stone dwelling, Quentin agreed. Scanning the horizon for any sign that they were being followed, he hid the horse in a grove of trees, then helped Devondra down. His hands lingered on the soft curves of her body and she tingled at his touch. She remembered the exciting things he could do to her with those hands.

"Oh, how I wish . . ." she whispered.

He smiled. "When this is all over we'll spend a whole month doing nothing but making love."

"And I, sir," she said, standing on tiptoe to kiss him softly on the lips, "will hold you to that promise."

Keeping to the shadows, he sought out water from a well nearby. "Drink slowly," he cautioned, holding forth the dipper.

Though she promised she would, it was difficult not to gulp. Water rations in Newgate had been paltry, and what water there had been was so vile that Devondra had gone without as much as possible.

"Easy . . ."

Only after her thirst was assuaged did he drink himself. Taking her by the hand, he led her toward the cottage. Standing in front of her to offer protection in case there was any kind of trouble, he knocked boldly.

There was no answer. Pushing on the door, he found that it opened easily. He pushed his way inside to make a quick exploration, finding that the cottage was indeed abandoned; then he gestured for Devondra to come inside.

"So, God has smiled upon us once more," she whispered.

She made herself useful, gathering up wood to throw on the blackened ashes. Quentin worked with two sticks to start a fire and soon had one smoldering. He nourished the small flames until they caught and burned steadily filling the windowless room with light. It was a plain, square cottage with rough, unpainted walls. The only furniture was two stools and a table.

"It looks as if they took everything of value with them."

Quentin tried his best to keep up his spirits as he looked around the room. He had wanted to give Devondra the world but had fallen far short of his goal. Instead here they were in a tiny cottage roofed with thatch, hiding away from the world.

In truth, Quentin had forgotten just what keeping body and soul together entailed. He had not given much thought to the routine of the common man. He had been much too busy with matters of state, the Lord Protector's policies, and searching for and punishing all those who had committed crimes. His every need had been taken care of. Now all that had changed, and he wondered what was going to happen to them. Would they find someplace where they would be safe? And if they did, would there be enough firewood to keep them warm, enough food to keep them fed?

"I have no money. What are we going to do?"

Despite all that had happened, Devondra couldn't help smiling. "Well, if worse comes to worst I can always go back to the roads."

He laughed, hoping she was just jesting. "Oh, no! I'm afraid one rescue is all I can manage. The next time you will be on your own."

She laughed also, then quickly sobered. In truth, she had no skills, no way to make a living at all. All her life there had been someone to take care of her, and then there had been her days as the Notorious Lady . . .

"Oh, Devondra, where is all this going to lead?"

"It doesn't matter, as long as we have each other."

The love he felt for her was mirrored in his eyes. Just the feel of her in his arms seemed to melt away all his worries. He held her quietly in his arms, contenting himself with her nearness. His hands stroked her body gently, soothingly, his breath warm against her face. He could withstand even the worst barbs to his pride as long as he could be with Devondra.

When at last their embrace ended Quentin picked her up in his arms and, skillfully maintaining his balance, climbed the ladder to the loft. He tugged at her garments playfully. "We'll have to get rid of this red velvet. I fear it is like a cape to wild bulls, announcing your whereabouts. You had best go about in your chemise or better yet—" Slowly, appreciatively, he undressed her; then, when she was naked, he explored the soft contours of her body sensuously. "Mmmmm, I think I like you this way."

"Oh? Then shall I ride this way like Lady Godiva as we make our way to the coast?"

He ran his lips from the tip of her earlobe to the soft curve of her shoulder. "As long as you are covered by a cloak, so as not to attract too much attention."

"A cloak? And what of you?" Boldly, she pulled off his black boots, his breeches, hat and doublet. "Surely Cromwell's soldiers would be interested in capturing a man clothed head to toe in black."

"Perhaps we will spend the rest of our lives here." Holding her face in his hands, he kissed her eyelids, the curve of her cheek, her mouth. His tongue traced the outline of her mouth while his hand moved over her body, from shoulder to thigh, caressing the flat plain of her belly. He moved to cup her breasts, squeezing it very gently. Lowering his head, he buried his face between the soft mounds.

Oh, how he loved her perfect breasts, loved touching

them, touching all of her. Her legs were long and shapely, her hips just wide enough. He stroked her silken flesh, feeling desire arise in him as potently as it had the very first time he had made love to her. "And to think the hangman nearly took you from me forever. How could anything else really matter?"

"You suggested we lie by the fire," Devondra's voice was low. "Shall we?"

Quentin grabbed up his thick black cloak. Taking her hand, he led her back down the ladder. Spreading out the cloak by the fire, he pulled her down to lie beside him. They clung together, their bodies embracing, caressing as they kissed. Her breasts brushed his chest as she reached up to twine her fingers in his auburn hair.

"I love you so, Devondra!" he whispered, touching her neck so gently that she almost cried.

"And I, you," she answered, reaching down to feel the strength, the power of him.

He supported himself on his forearms as he caressed her, gently spreading her legs with his knee. Only by blending together could they appease the hunger they had for each other. Slowly, he filled her with the sweet length of his manhood. She wrapped her arms and legs tightly about him as if to hold him to her forever.

There were no sounds, no further words between them. The rhythm of their passion, the meeting of their eyes as they gazed at each other, said all that needed to be said. It was as if they blended their hearts, their souls, their flesh into one being as they made love, mingling themselves in the ultimate expression of emotion. Two halves of a whole came together to form one being. It was heaven in his arms, and as she was filled with him the explosion of their love brought forth a cry of joy from her mouth. She tightened her arms and her body, holding him inside her warmth.

When their passion was spent and they were lying face to face, they held each other. Quentin's hand moved down to where they were still joined. "I will never let you go. You were made to be loved and cherished. I pledge my love, my very life to you."

"And I pledge my heart." She smiled at him. "Perhaps we can stay just as we are."

"It would be nice, though I fear we cannot stay here that long. Someone might have glimpsed us as we rode along the path. Cromwell is a menace we cannot take lightly."

"I know." She wondered, lying with Quentin's strong body entwined with hers, if it was possible to feel any more contentment than she did at this very moment. Reaching out, Devondra touched his face, wishing they could always be together like this, wrapped in each other's warmth. He was her pillar of strength, a friend as well as a lover. Though the time they had spent together had been much too brief, it had strengthened the bond she and Quentin shared.

"Come, let us dress." Regretfully, he tugged at her hand.

They donned their garments, though they threw their hats and masks into the fire. "If we are lucky we can find some clothing at one of the farms along the way." Bending down, he reached for his cloak. "What's this?" Spying a crumpled piece of parchment that had escaped his notice earlier, he retrieved that as well.

"Quentin?" His face was etched with concern.

"Now I know why the occupants of this cottage have gone." Though the parchment had been torn, there was just enough left to divulge a horrendous plot. "It's Cromwell!"

"Cromwell?" Panicking, Devondra ran toward the door.

"No, I mean this paper. There's a plot to assassinate Cromwell while he sits in Parliament." The Royalists had not been squelched complety. A former Royalist soldier who gave the rebellion his name—Colonel John Penruddock—

was planning to kill Cromwell and put Prince Charles, upon the throne.

"What?" Though she had no fond feelings for Oliver Cromwell, Devondra knew well what such a plot could bring. Not only the evil would suffer, but many innocents as well.

Quentin fought a battle with his heart and his honor. "I'm going to take you somewhere safe."

"Somewhere safe?" She knew just where he was going. "You're going to London to save the very man who turned against you."

"I have to!"

"No!" She feared he might not come back, but she knew he was the kind of man who had to be given the freedom to do what he felt was right. "At least let me go with you."

"And find yourself standing before the crowd at Tyburn again? No, Devondra, my putting myself in danger is one thing; your peril is another." He was stubborn.

"Then take me back to Brentford. There are secret cellars and a passageway at the Devil's Thumb Inn that my father often used. I can hide away there."

"What of Scar?"

"Let's hope that he stays in Teddington where he belongs." Her glance was reflective. "But if by chance our paths cross, there is an important bit of old business I have to settle with him. Only then can I have any peace of mind."

Quickly, they set out again, knowing deep in their hearts that there were matters to be settled before they could be truly free. "We will need clothes."

Despite his abhorrence of stealing, Quentin took several garments where they had been set out to dry the branch of an old tree near a small farm house. Devondra soon wore a white linen cap, a brown dress with a laced bodice and a white apron. Quentin donned knee-length breeches and a gray jacket and wide-brimmed black felt hat under his black cloak, making him look like the staunchest Puritan.

"I doubt that even Tobias would recognize us now," she declared.

Nevertheless they were both more than a bit jittery as they neared Brentford and the inn.

"I'll come back for you sooner than you know, my love." Quentin promised. "Wait for me here."

Tears brimmed in her eyes, but she forced a smile to her lips. "I'll be here when you come back. But if I'm not here, I think you know where you must look."

"Devondra." Impulsively, he swept her into his arms, exclaiming, "Don't do anything foolish."

She pulled away from him regretfully, sliding down from her perch in front of him. Fearful of making a scene, she ran to the door of the Devil's Thumb as fast as she could. Turning around, she stood staring as his horse rode away, sad yet resigned to their parting. He would come back. Everything would be all right. She felt it in her heart. Still, as the horse vanished from sight she found herself crying.

Chapter Thirty-Six

If his horse had wings, Quentin couldn't have traveled faster. Despite the fact that there was no love lost between himself and Cromwell, he knew what the Penruddock Plot could do to the country—split it in two, creating another civil war. There would be renewed bloodshed at a time when England needed to be healed.

As he rode back toward London he reflected on the discarded missive he had found, which must surely have been targeted for the fire. According to his calculations, the assassination was to be carried out this very day, when the Parliament was reassembled after a short adjournment.

Quentin had been so agitated over Devondra's comings and goings on the Heath that he had been distracted from what had been happening elsewhere. Now he reflected on it, recalling bits and pieces of Edwin's conversation. Cromwell was still battling the Cavaliers, accusing them of putting the nation asunder again. He had talked of Parliament's imprudent activities, hinting that those who dissented would

not be allowed to return to the House. Cromwell had declared
Parliament dismissed, after appealing to both God and his
duty to the people. Now it appeared his ferocity could well
mean his defeat.

"Colonel John Penruddock!" He was a man Quentin had
never considered a worthy adversary; still any plot must be
taken seriously. And yet Quentin thought how foolish it had
been to put any plan in writing. Could it be that Penruddock
was conspiring with fools and country bumpkins? Or was
there someone far more important involved? And what
would be the consequences of Quentin's interference? He
decided it didn't matter; Cromwell had his faults, but at the
moment he was the only ruler England had.

It was a long, hard ride. Arriving at the heart of the city,
Quentin was relieved that his journey was at an end. Even
so, he had second thoughts. Would his sense of honor bring
him nothing more than a trip back to the Tower?

Whatever his fate was to be, he knew he couldn't turn
back now. He edged his way through the seething mass of
noise and motion that was London. Dismounting in front of
Edwin's townhouse, he assessed his appearance, deciding
at once that with his farmer's garments covered by the dust
of the road and his face smeared with grime, he hardly need
fear being recognized.

Taking the steps of the small townhouse two at a time
and finding his way blocked by two of Edwin's servants,
he soon found that anonymity had its problems as well.

"Let me pass," he ordered, ignoring their appraising looks.
"I must speak with Edwin at once."

"He is unavailable to the likes of you," was the answer.
"He is preparing himself for a meeting."

"Parliament." Quentin was relieved that he had not gone
already. "He has to hear what I have to say before he goes."

"No!" One of the servants sought to detain Quentin, but

he was no match for his strength. Pushing himself inside, he went in search of his friend.

Quentin found Edwin combing his thinning hair before the mirror. "Quentin! You look terrible." Having seen his reflection, Edwin turned around. "I, like all of London, have heard much about the daring rescue made at Tyburn. Congratulations. You give new meaning to the word 'chivalry.' It seems to me, however, that you have gotten your directions mixed up. You should have been riding away from London and not toward her."

"Someone's going to kill Cromwell!" Quentin blurted out.

"Kill Oliver?" Nervously, Edwin tugged at his sleeve. "Where on earth did you hear something like that?"

"I read it with my own eyes."

Edwin shook his head. "Ah, those foolish journalists. They go too far. It is one thing to call Cromwell 'King copper nose' or 'Beezlebub's chief ale-brewer' and another to perpetrate this."

"It wasn't something I read in a news sheet, but this." Quentin handed the scrap of paper to Edwin, astonished as he watched him tear it up. "Bigod, what are you doing?"

"Destroying something that is pure foolishness." Edwin threw the pieces on the floor. "I hope you did not come all the way to London because of this. If so, then I suggest you turn back around and ride posthaste to that lovely little highwayman of yours."

"Edwin!" Something in his friend's manner bothered him. "I found that piece of parchment in an old abandoned cottage. It was all that had survived the flames of a fire. I think somehow that it was fate that I found it."

"Fate?"

"If someone is sincere about murdering the Lord Protector, then mayhap God intervened with Devondra's execution. I must repay Him."

"God?" Edwin's laugh was scoffing. "God has no time in his busy schedule to care about what might happen to a devil like Cromwell. And neither should you bother with him."

"What?" Leaning against the door, Quentin stared at Edwin with a puzzled frown.

"Don't poke your nose where it does not belong."

The inflection in Edwin's voice as much as his words alerted Quentin to the truth. "There is a plot, and God's blood, you are in on it. Why, Edwin? Why?" He and Edwin had fought side by side during the war. He had thought that in all ways they felt the same. But not in this! Not in this!

"Cromwell has betrayed us all and made promises . . ."

Grabbing Edwin by the arm, Quentin stared into his eyes. "Of money, Edwin. Is that why you do this, because of greed?" Like himself, Edwin came from humble origins. He had never even entertained a thought that could be termed "Royalist."

Shrugging out of Quentin's grasp Edwin returned the stare. "In part. I—we all—were promised that our efforts would be repaid, but they were not. All that has happened is that Cromwell has steadily gained more and more power until he thinks himself invincible." Putting his hands behind his back, he paced up and down. "We were angry at Charles because he thumbed his nose at Parliament. We lamented the loss of any say in the government. Cromwell has done exactly the same thing. He is no longer one of us but has set himself up as a King. He who is no better than we."

"And so you want to kill him and replace him with who?"

"After his rule Parliament itself will rule." Edwin's eyes sparkled. "Just think! England ruled by a group of intelligent men for the good of all." Now it was he who grasped at Quentin. "Join with us!"

"And lose my honor?" Quentin shook his head. "No, not even if you promised me the moon."

Edwin took a step forward. "What then?"

The answer seemed obvious. "I have to stop you."

"In spite of our friendship?"

"Because of it!"

"Never!" To emphasize his reply, Edwin hastily plucked up his sword. "Move one inch and you are dead!" With grace he moved upon Quentin unmercifully. Though they had often sparred just for the fun of it, there was no jest intended now.

Not one to cower, however, Quentin threw himself into the fight with equal vigor. Swords clashed, tempers rose to a fury. The two fought a furious battle, a test of strength and of skill.

Again and again Edwin Trevor lunged, his anger at having been thwarted making him careless. Reacting to the warning of his senses, his sword arm swinging forward, Quentin blocked each thrust. At last he knocked his enemy's sword to the ground. The tables had turned quickly. Now it was he who held a sword at Edwin's breast.

"Go ahead and kill me."

"Kill you? Turn you over my knee is what I ought to do. John Penruddock is a simpleton. Any allegiance you may have to him will bring you down, Edwin. But I won't let that happen. You helped me get out of the Tower and now I'll help you."

"Help me?" For a moment Edwin dared hope.

"By saving you from yourself!" He bowed mockingly. "Thus, forgive me, I have to do this. . . ." Raising his sword, he aimed a blow not with the point but with the side of the blade and rendered Edwin unconscious. Then he flew out of the room and down the stairs.

* * *

The air was chilly and damp inside the hidden passageway beneath the Devil's Thumb as Devondra fumbled her way along. Though she had made a show of being brave, she had to admit to herself that she was jittery. Having been in Newgate had taken its toll.

"Quentin, God go with you and . . . and hurry back," she whispered, hoping with all her heart that everything would turn out well.

Besides Quentin's sense of duty to Cromwell, Devondra realized that there was another side to his courageous act. Surely if he saved the Lord Protector's life he would be rewarded for his deed. His manor and his prestige might be restored to him. And yet, were that to be, where would she fit into his life?

Life held no promises that dreams would be fulfilled. Was it any wonder that she was deeply troubled as she moved through the tunnel?

Suddenly she felt a prick at the back of her neck, a little stab that she at first feared had been caused by a rat. She reached up, her fingers encountering cold steel.

"Do not move on peril of your life," a voice said.

The cold chill of fear inching up her spine gave way to the greatest relief. "Tobias!" Except for the moment of Quentin's rescue at the gallows, she had never been so glad to encounter anyone in her life. "What are you doing here?"

"Little miss?" It was hard to say if he was more surprised by their meeting than she. He was certainly just as relieved. "I heard of your escape, but I thought you would be on the way to Scotland or Ireland by now."

"Quentin had other plans, but he will come back for me." When Tobias didn't answer she said, "He will!"

"I do not doubt it. The man loves you, and somehow such

emotions seem to be able to move mountains, or so I have heard." As if feeling more secure in the darkness now that she was here, his voice grew louder. "Thus, your dear love was able to at least nullify the evil that Scar perpetrated."

"Ah, yes. Scar."

"The evil bastard. May God forgive him for what he did, for I most certainly can not. The only question I have is why? Why did he hate you so?"

"Because of Anne."

"Anne? What on earth could she have to do with anything?"

Though there was a part of her that wanted to forget all about Scar's terrible accusations, Devondra knew that to be impossible. Either Scar's suspicions had to be proven true or her father had to be vindicated. "Tobias?"

"Aye?"

The dampness, or perhaps her emotions, made her hoarse, but she somehow got out the words. "Scar came to Newgate to see me. He said that he . . . that he did what he did because of Anne and—and my father."

"Anne and your father?"

"Anne died because . . . because she was with child. Scar said that my father was the baby's sire. He said that . . ." She paused, then croaked. "Was it true?"

"No!" With a gasp so loud that it startled her, Tobias made the denial that Devondra had hoped for.

"Then Scar is a liar!"

"Or the world's greatest fool." Putting his arm around her to give her comfort, Tobias tried to imagine what might have happened to so poison Scar's mind. "There was no liaison between Anne and Jamie; merely a friendship that the girl greatly needed." His tone was angry. "Had Scar been any kind of father at all, she would not have had to go to Jamie for advice."

"Advice?" Devondra was confused. "What do you mean?"

Tobias sighed. "Poor, dear Annie. She was so desirous of love that I fear she was not wise. She was swept away by soft words and moonlight. A baby was the consequence."

"Then you knew?"

"Aye. Poor Annie. She paid the price, but 'twas not because of your father, but the innkeeper's son."

"Tad?" An oafish rogue if ever there was one.

"He refused to marry her, you see and . . ."

"And so she went to my father for advice!" Though she had longed for just such an explanation, the truth proved to be far more than she could bear. "No! No!"

"Scar must have been witness to her meetings with Jamie and jumped to the wrong conclusion. His envy of your father fueled an evil fire."

"A fire that consumed us all." Devondra leaned her head on Tobias's shoulder, fighting against the bitterness that threatened to overwhelm her. Her dear father had been most ruthlessly betrayed, and all for what? For an act of kindness to a young woman. "Oh no."

"Scar has much to answer for! Why, when I get my hands on him, I'll . . . I'll . . ."

"Do nothing," she answered softly. The anger and hatred had to be ended. "'Tis up to me."

"Devondra . . ." Tobias knew her well enough to worry about what was on her mind. "What are you going to do?"

She pulled away. "I have to talk to Scar. I have to make him see." If nothing else, at least her father's good name had to be redeemed.

Chapter Thirty-Seven

It was dark and cloudy even though it was an hour before noon. In truth, it was the kind of day that might have made a superstitious man think twice about any heroics. Quentin, however, was not such a man. With his hat pulled down low on his forehead, he made his way toward the chamber of the House of Commons, where Cromwell was going to address his opponents.

The narrow cobbled streets were filled with Londoners curious about what was going to happen. "Privilege of Parliament!" he heard them cry out along the way. "Privilege of Parliament."

A cry against Cromwell, it was nevertheless a reminder of days gone by, when Charles had attempted a coup against *his* Parliament. Attempting to arrest five of his biggest opponents, he had stirred up a nest of hornets. Now Cromwell was doing much the same thing. Perhaps that was why he had chosen to enter the building before the crowd had a chance to gather.

Seeking the shadows, Quentin slowly walked up the stairs, watching as some of his old colleagues gathered together. He recognized the unsmiling profile of Thomas Hunley, a wise old man who had taken him under his wing; the arrogant swagger of Robert Marsden, whose manner often bordered on rudeness. And, of course, there was John Thurloe, the Secretary of State.

It was difficult for Quentin to concentrate on the proceedings. In truth, he didn't even hear most of what was being said. All he could think of was how important it was to second guess Penruddock's co-conspirators. Somewhere in that crowd there could be someone with a pistol aimed at Cromwell's heart. But who? What did he look like?

". . . The army pay has been allowed to become badly in arrears," Cromwell was scolding, "which is hardly the best way to maintain the security of the country." Cromwell was indignant about what he termed the foolhardy, even criminal decisions made by Parliament. He cajoled and threatened. In the end, his meaning was clear: He *did* intend to rid himself of Parliament.

There was a sudden movement outside in the hall. If the others were too preoccupied to notice it, Quentin was not. Looking out of the corner of his eye, he glimpsed a tall, well-muscled man. Like Quentin, he was seeking anonymity. Perhaps that was the thing that struck a chord inside Quentin's head.

David Grenville, the youngest member of Parliament and an ambitious man, stood before him. *His father had been a Royalist.* Still, with no clues to follow, Quentin could hardly accost the man on suspicion alone. Frustrated, he turned his head for just a moment, but long enough for him to nearly miss seeing the plot beginning to unfold. "What the . . ."

"Privilege of Parliament," he heard a voice cry out, just as a flash of steel foretold the pistol being drawn.

"No!" Instinctively, he flung himself toward Grenville, but Grenville moved first. Cocking his weapon, he fired.

There was a roar. Grenville staggered backward as Quentin flung himself upon the gunman and total havoc broke out.

"A shot, bigod!"

"Someone fired . . ."

"Who . . ."

"Wakefield!"

Having wrestled with the pistol and gained possession of it, things did indeed look bad for Quentin as all eyes looked his way, but Grenville's fear and his desperate bid to escape was soon apparent.

"That's Quentin Wakefield. He escaped from the tower. Arrest him!" Unmindful of his close brush with death, Cromwell gave his orders.

"Arrest me?" Coldly, Quentin froze, his eyes fixed on Cromwell's stony face. "A fine way to reward the man who kept you from an appointment with death's angel," he replied. "But then, I suppose, it is in keeping with your character, Oliver."

"Indeed?"

"You forgot to be grateful to all those who gave you help along the way. How then could I expect you to say thank you when I saved your life?"

Raising his brows, Cromwell seemed surprised. "That shot was aimed at me?" He didn't want to believe it, not until Grenville's questioning revealed the plot and the plotters.

Led by the frail but gallant Penruddock, the rising might have ended very differently had Quentin not intervened. As it was, the whole enterprise was marked by defeat. Made up of six regional conspiracies organized by local associations under the general command of Lord Rochester, the plot was certain to fall apart now that Cromwell, the principal target, had gotten away. As it was, the Royalist rendezvous that was scheduled for Marston Moor at the same time as Cromwell's attempted assassination, caused hardly a ripple of interest.

"We'll ward them off; have no worry." Cromwell froze; then, realizing what he had just said, he patted Quentin roughly on the arm. "Did you hear that, Quentin? I said *we.*" He made a rare confession. "Despite our quarrel, I missed you. It will be good to have you back." Hastily, he started giving orders. "We'll strengthen the Tower garrison. We'll bring back the troops from Ireland."

"And stiffen the guard 'round Whitehall."

"And hang any of the bastards who seek to turn against me." Cromwell was suddenly contrite. "You said that I was ungrateful a moment ago. How then would you suggest that I repay a man for saving my life?"

Quentin was in the mood to play it sly. "You could give that man back his properties and his titles. And . . ."

"And?" Cromwell reached for his purse.

"And allow him the blessed chance to be with the woman he loves for the rest of his life."

"Forever?" Cromwell's incredulous look seemed to hint that his marriage would be anything but a bed of roses. Still, he nodded. "A simple wish to grant. 'Tis yours."

"Even if my future bride has succeeded in getting away from the hangman? Even then?"

Cromwell's expression was sour. "Even then."

"Then ready yourself to grant my bride a pardon! And congratulate me, Oliver. I soon will enter the ranks of married men."

The bells of Saint Sepulchre's tolled, but for a happy event today. This very morn there was to be a wedding that had the Londoners gawking, hoping for a glimpse of the bride as she had arrived at the church in her sedan chair.

"The Notorious Lady is marrying our magistrate, you know," buzzed the gossip.

"And why not? First she stole his purse. Then she stole his heart. And now she steals his name."

"Steals?" As the onlookers took note of the smile upon his face, it was obvious to see how gladly it was given.

"Why, just see the way he looks at her . . ."

And why not? Clothed in a full-skirted dress made of white velvet, a wide-brimmed silver hat with a white plume and white boots, she was a most fetching sight.

"You are beautiful," he breathed, bending to take her hand as they met at the door. "The most beautiful woman I've ever seen. I thank God that soon you will be mine."

"And I thank God that if you believe hard enough, there can be a happy ending," she whispered, for truly everything had been resolved in the end. Everything, that is, except her quarrel with Scar.

Though Devondra had insisted on her father's innocence and Tobias had revealed the true reason for Anne's meetings with Jamie Stafford, Scar would not believe the story. Perhaps, Tobias had said, it was more comfortable for him to live with his hatred and anger than to accept reality. Nonetheless, Devondra felt peace and love in her own heart as the wedding ceremony progressed.

"Does Tobias have the ring?"

"Yes." Looking over his shoulder, Quentin smiled as he took note of the little man's determined grin.

She whispered, "God hope that it isn't stolen."

Devondra felt the gold ring touch first one finger, then another, to rest on the third finger of her left hand, an unending symbol of love. She would belong to Quentin

Wakefield forever. And she would make him happy, she vowed.

"Oh, Father, if only you could see me now." She knew he would be proud and that he would approve.

The ceremony was brief. Devondra slid her arms around her husband's broad shoulders, relishing the ritual kiss, thrilling with passion to know that this handsome, daring man at last belonged to her.

"Come, my love," he whispered, caressing her in such a heated embrace that Tobias blushed. "It is time we tasted each other as man and wife." Then he kissed her hungrily, enthusiastically, again and again.

The wedding feast was a lively affair, with the King's Head Inn's ale served by the barrel. Afterward there was dancing as a whirling, high-stepping, jubilant Tobias tried to prove that he could jig as well as any man. Then, amid jovial laughter and shouted congratulations, the newly wedded couple were escorted up the stairs to their nuptial bed, a custom that had been observed since the Middle Ages.

Though several pairs of eyes watched as they took their places in the large feather bed, Quentin and Devondra barely noticed, nor did they hear the drone of the minister as he gave the blessing. They had eyes only for each other. And then, at last, they were alone.

"My lovely, lovely wife. I love you so very much," Quentin whispered.

"Show me!" Devondra's eyes were boldly challenging, in the manner he had come to love.

Quentin's intense gaze clung to her as he beheld her naked beauty. He ran his hand lovingly over the softness of her shoulder, down to the peaks of her full breasts. This was his bride, his mate forever and ever. She was worth any sacrifice he had made.

With a quick, indrawn breath, he drew her to his chest,

molding his mouth to hers in a sweetly scorching kiss. His hands stroked her body, gently igniting the searing flame she always felt at his touch.

A blazing fire consumed them both as their bodies met. With hands and lips and words, they gave full vent to their love. Quentin caught her in his arms and pulled her down, rolling with her until her slender form was beneath his. They were entwined in love, in flesh, in heart, and with their very souls.

Epilogue

Devondra stood at the window of the manor, looking at the snow. It was so clean, so white, like the promise of a new beginning. Perhaps, she thought, that was what the future promised for Quentin, for herself, and for their four-year-old son, Jamie.

Had it really been five years ago since she had thought her life was over? It hardly seemed possible, and yet it was. Five years. And oh, what changes those five years had wrung. Oliver Cromwell had laid aside both sword and scepter. The loss of a favorite daughter had preyed upon his already failing health. He was seized with an ague and died quickly, leaving the way open for a Stuart to regain the throne.

"The Lord Protector," she whispered. His had been a short reign that had brought about peace for a brief time after the civil war, but his failure to work with Parliament and his use of military force had steadily worked to make his government unpopular. He had been the victim of "cruel necessity," words he had intoned himself over the dead body of King Charles.

Her husband had had the devil of a time of it as the people of London had become more and more disillusioned. Cromwell's religious policy pleased only a few moderates like himself. On the whole, the people had grown tired of Puritan discipline, which attempted to make men good by force.

Oliver Cromwell's successor had been his eldest son. Richard, a most unwise choice. Although he was an amiable man whom Quentin had soon grown to like, he was more suited for quiet country life. The task of ruling a turbulent nation had been too heavy for him.

"I will give you a shilling if I can be the one in your thoughts," Quentin declared, coming up behind her. He brushed a lock of her dark brown hair from her eyes in a gesture that always stirred her heart.

"I was just thinking about how happy I am." She leaned against his shoulder. "I like being married to you."

"Stand and deliver. Bang. Bang."

"What?" The high-pitched voice of their son interrupted both Quentin's and Devondra's musing.

"Your money or your life."

"Gads!" Picking up the small boy in his arms, Quentin shook his head. "He's been listening to Tobias again. We must make it a point to explain a few things to him, lest I have my hands full in a few years."

"Jamie . . ." Perplexed, Devondra shook her head.

Nestling his son in his arms, Quentin smiled. "Oh, let him be. In time he'll understand the way things were. I want to have you tell him about his grandfather. I want him to realize the way of things, and why some of us did what we did."

The bells of a nearby church pealed. "God save the King."

King Charles II, already in communication with members of Parliament, had signed the Declaration of Breda, by which he agreed to return to England and assume the throne. He had landed at Dover amid scenes of tremendous enthusiasm. On his thirtieth birthday, he rode from Rochester to London, through miles of cheering multitudes. The old times had come back.

"Oh, how I wish Father were here to see this day."

Quentin put one arm around his son and the other around his wife. "Perhaps he is, at least in spirit."

"Perhaps . . ."

The bells rang again, and Devondra knew in her heart that Gentleman James was with them. And she knew something else as well—that as long as love lived within men's hearts, all would be well.